Reader love The Sci-Regency series by J.L. Langley

My Fair Captain

"I simply adore this book and I can't recommend it highly enough…. If you love highly romantic tales that will live with you long after you finish the book, then *My Fair Captain* is the book for you."

—Top 2 Bottom Reviews

"I highly, very highly recommend to all of you!"

—OptimuMM

"In the end, I adored this re-release more the second time around."

—The Blogger Girls

The Englor Affair

"Political intrigue, murder, misunderstandings, sex… this book has it all. And I LOVED IT!"

—Love Bytes

"…a great addition to series and I'm hoping we see the next one soon."

—Gay Book Reviews

By J.L. Langley

THE SCI-REGENCY SERIES
My Fair Captain
The Englor Affair
My Regelence Rake
Diplomatic Relations

Published by Dreamspinner Press
www.dreamspinnerpress.com

DIPLOMATIC RELATIONS

J.L. Langley

DREAMSPINNER PRESS

Published by
DREAMSPINNER PRESS

5032 Capital Circle SW, Suite 2, PMB# 279, Tallahassee, FL 32305-7886 USA
www.dreamspinnerpress.com

Trade Paperback ISBN: 978-1-64080-693-1
Digital ISBN: 978-1-64080-692-4
Library of Congress Control Number: 2018960690
Trade Paperback published February 2019
v. 1.0

Printed in the United States of America

This paper meets the requirements of
ANSI/NISO Z39.48-1992 (Permanence of Paper).

Prologue

March 4, 4829: Planet Regelence
Pruluce Prison, in Downtown Classige, Pruluce

HE DID not want to die, but alas it might be too late for such thoughts. Dalton sat up on the cold stone bench that doubled as a cot, and stared through the menacing black bars of his jail cell. Someone was coming. He hadn't mistaken the sound of the steel-barred door leading into the cellblock. The metal clang was like nothing he'd ever heard before. He'd only been here for a few hours at the most, but already he was certain he'd hear that sound in his nightmares for as long as he lived. Which might not be long. He might hang. Did they still hang people for murder?

The sharp clap of footsteps echoed off the rock walls and came closer. In the next cell, someone's stomach rumbled, farther down a prisoner sneezed, and the inmate near the end of the row had a flatulence problem.

A shiver of revulsion snaked up Dalton's back, and he wanted to cover his ears. He'd never thought himself spoiled, but galaxy, he needed out of here.

The footsteps were right on top of him now, followed by a jangle of keys.

He'd gotten himself into this situation, and he had no choice but to own up to it and face the consequences. Forcing himself to unwind his arms from around his legs, he dropped his bare feet onto the cold floor and stood.

The guard stopped at his cell and another man drew up behind him.

Dalton gulped so hard it felt like glass going down his throat.

The dim lighting in the corridor cast the other man's face in shadow, but there was no mistaking that tall athletic form. Uncle Raleigh's poise spoke of discipline and grace all at once. Uncle always seemed ready for anything; he had a coiled energy even at rest. Right now, those shoulders were squared and a little rigid, like salvation and annihilation all wrapped into one.

Dalton took a deep breath and made himself hold his ground even though he wanted to crawl beneath the bench and hide.

He'd known his uncle would come. There had been no contest as to who he'd wanted the authorities to contact when they'd asked before stripping him of his cravat, stockings, and shoes. But now that his uncle was here, Dalton wished he wasn't. The very idea of telling Raleigh what happened made his stomach cramp and his tongue feel as though it were three sizes too big for his mouth. Perhaps it would have been better to ask for his father? He didn't care what his father thought of him or his actions, but Ravensburg probably would've ignored his call.

The guard opened the gate and stepped aside.

Raleigh walked into the light. His gaze swept over Dalton in one cursory glance, and a muscle in his jaw twitched. "Leave us."

The guard bowed even though Raleigh's back was to him. "Yes, Your Majesty." With keys clinking, he turned and retreated, leaving the metal bars wide-open and Dalton to face his judgment.

Dalton eyed the open door. Perhaps he could disappear? Catch a ship off Regelence and—

"You'll never make it."

Dust! He raised his head, afraid of what he'd find.

No expression at all graced Raleigh's gray eyes, and that somehow seemed worse.

The door at the end of the hall slammed shut as the guard exited the corridor, and Dalton jumped.

Raleigh didn't even blink. He stood there, staring at Dalton with his face as impassive as ever. Was he mad? Ashamed? Disappointed?

After a few moments, Raleigh took a breath and his whole body seemed to relax. He reached out a hand toward Dalton, then the other, leaving his arms open.

All the bravado Dalton had held on to for the last hour left him in a gasp of air. He wasn't even sure how he ended up in his uncle's arms—whether he moved or Raleigh had—but a sob exploded from him as Raleigh pulled him close, engulfing him in heat and comfort.

Those arms tightened like a band, and Dalton's tears would not be stymied. He rested his head on his uncle's shoulder and held on. "I'm sorry, Uncle. I didn't mean for it to happen."

"I know, but you have got to stop with this self-destructive behavior." Raleigh pulled back, holding him at arm's length. "You could've been killed, Dalton." The tight lines of his forehead emphasized more than his words how much the thought worried him.

"I never meant for things to get so out of hand."

"I know." After touching his cheek, Raleigh walked farther into the cell and took a seat on the bench. "But it's got to stop. In the last month, you've fought a duel over a married man, rode a horse naked around the Fallen Warriors Monument in Primrose Square, been seen coming out of Madam Roux's, and now you've wrecked a curricle. One that didn't belong to you, I might add."

Put like that, it sounded bad. Dalton supposed he'd deluded himself into thinking his uncles and cousins hadn't heard of his exploits. "Technically, I had my shirt on as a blindfold when I raced around the monument, so I wasn't naked."

One dark brow arched as Raleigh leaned back against the wall and stretched his long legs out in front of him.

Dalton sighed. Normally he prided himself of being featured in the gossip columns, but that was one exploit he wished had gone unnoticed.

Raleigh crossed his hands over his stomach like he didn't plan on moving for a while. It appeared this was an inquisition.

"It was at one o'clock in the morning; there weren't many people out at that time."

The other eyebrow joined the first one.

"Fine. It was stupid." It had been great fun, though, and…. "I did win two hundred pounds."

"Well, thank galaxy for that." Raleigh grinned but quickly masked it. "And the duel?"

"If Viscount-Consort Lawson would keep his husband satisfied, then the viscount wouldn't have to go elsewhere?"

Raleigh leveled the dad stare at him.

Don't squirm, Dalton chided himself. He couldn't help it, he squirmed. *Damn it.*

"And what about the curricle?"

Tonight's events, which he'd tried hard to forget for the past hour, came back to him in a rush. He started pacing to give himself something to do, because he didn't think he could retell the story if he had to look at his uncle. "William begged me to meet him at the races." He hadn't thought twice about it. He'd met the debutant the night before at the Yardley musical, and the shy man had blushed at everything. All Dalton's previous lovers had been experienced, so the idea of deflowering an innocent had excited him. "I agreed. Everything was fine until his father showed up. The, uh, earl didn't take it well."

"I wonder why?"

Ignoring the sarcasm, Dalton continued, "William pleaded with me to get him out of there."

"So you stole one of the curricles."

"Borrowed." William had mentioned being compromised, and Dalton had panicked. He'd wanted to fuck the cute little baron, not marry him. "I was going to take it back after I dropped William off at his house, but the earl caught up to us before we could even leave the park. He jumped in front of the horses, and…." Dalton stopped pacing, with his back to his uncle, and closed his eyes. His breath caught in his chest, burning like someone squeezed him. People talked about how everything seemed to slow down in a crisis, but it wasn't true. Things didn't slow down. They sped up. "I didn't mean to kill him." Tears blurred Dalton's vision. It hadn't seemed real until he said it out loud.

"What? Who?" Raleigh grabbed his shoulder and spun Dalton around so fast he wobbled before catching his balance again.

He looked at the bench, then at Raleigh. *When had he moved?*

Narrowing his eyes, Raleigh joggled Dalton. "Who?"

"The Earl of Wesley, William's father."

Sliding his hands down to Dalton's forearms, Raleigh dropped his head and his chest heaved in and out. When he raised his head again, a soft smile graced his lips. "You didn't kill him. He got knocked unconscious."

Air exploded into Dalton's lungs and his knees went rubbery. "He's alive?"

"Yes. He also has a much fatter purse now, thanks to you. I had to pay him a fortune to tell everyone he and his son had been walking when you nearly ran them down. He wanted you to do the right thing and marry his son."

At this point, marriage was the least of Dalton's concerns. With his heart hammering against his chest, he raked a shaky hand through his hair and came away with sweat.

"I also had to pay for Lord Henderson's curricle and a new matched pair. He's convinced you maimed one of the horses, though Brooks doesn't agree. However, if it will keep him from pressing charges, it's worth it. Now, if I can keep this out of the gossip columns, it will be a miracle. The scandal sheets adore you."

Brooks, the stable master at Townsend Castle, excelled at her job. If she thought the horse was all right, then it was. "So, I can go… home?" The smile slipped from his face, and his stomach dropped again. Home was the castle—not Fairfax House—and he couldn't go there. *Damned laws.*

"No."

"I know I can't go back to the castle, but—"

Raleigh began shaking his head.

A chill swept over Dalton at the expression of regret on his uncle's face. "What? You said he wasn't dead and that I could go."

Raleigh drew in a deep breath, then huffed it out, making the black hair on his forehead flutter. Those steel gray eyes, which were identical to Dalton's, stared at him steady and sure as he reached into his left coat pocket and pulled out folded white papers. "You will be released on one condition."

Dalton shook his head, not understanding.

"You know that I love you, Dalton. Don't you?"

He did know because his uncle—both his uncles—had told him often growing up. More importantly they'd showered him with attention and lots of hugs. Dalton nodded, but the hair on his arms stood up.

"I don't trust you to behave yourself. Not as long as you have to live with my brother." Raleigh touched his cheek. "If I could legally bring you home with me, I would, but you are heading in a direction that you might never return from, and I can't let that happen."

Dalton deflated a little. He'd done things in the last year that he would never have dared while living with his uncle, but when his father had sent for him and made him move back in with his parents after ten years, Dalton had gone a little crazy. He'd acted more like the eight-year-old his father had sent away than the nineteen-year-old he was now. He'd caused scandal after scandal. At first he'd hoped his parents would send him back to his uncle, but they hadn't, and Dalton had lost control. Being bad had become… fun. He'd done things that no young lord of his age was allowed to do, and he'd stopped caring what his parents or society thought of him.

"And we need to let this latest scandal blow over…. Therefore, I've purchased you a commission in the IN." Raleigh held out the papers.

With a shaky hand, Dalton took them. He was being sent away? Again? He glanced down at the commission, then up at his uncle.

Raleigh's stern expression never wavered.

"But…."

"You have only two choices. You can stay in here charged with theft, or go into the Intergalactic Navy. Do your two years there, come home, and do your two years in the Regelence Navy. We will tell everyone that you always wanted to join the Regelence Navy, like my father. I seem to remember you wanting to do just that as a child."

"Yes." Dalton studied the papers. When he was young, he had wanted to follow in his grandfather's footsteps, but he'd long since outgrown that notion. Now, though, he didn't want to leave his family. He wanted to move back home to the castle with them, even though he knew he couldn't. "My father doesn't know, does he?"

Raleigh shook his head. "I'll deal with my brother."

By law, even though Dalton was not of age by Regelence standards, he could join the IN without parental consent. The IN's legal age was only eighteen, and in five months, Dalton would be twenty.

Glancing around the cell, at its harsh stone walls, he shivered. He could not remain imprisoned. Maybe that meant he was the spoiled aristocrat the guards had accused him of being, but he knew he'd never last in here, and he didn't want to go back to live with his parents.

He peered up at his uncle's face. *Would he really leave me here?* If Raleigh thought it best, he would, and that firm jaw said so, loud and clear.

Nauseous and with no other choice, Dalton agreed. "I'll do it."

CHAPTER ONE

Rumor has it, a certain demon lord has come home for good. One wonders how many duels we will see this season?

—From *The Classige Morning News*, On-Dit column

March 1, 4831: Planet Regelence
Lawson Street Market in Downtown Classige, Pruluce (the ruling country of Regelence)

THE PLACE was madness, complete and utter madness. Standing just inside the main gate of the street market, Blaise watched wide-eyed, a sense of disgust and wonder all rolled into one, as a hawker strolled by with some sort of meat on a stick.

The sun was barely up, yet dozens of rows of whitewashed stalls filled with food and all manner of goods dominated every inch of free space; people filled the rest. Peddlers competed for attention by shouting over one another, and the smells.... They all meshed together in a collage of sweet, sour, sautéed onions, and sweat. *As if the scent of onions by itself wasn't bad enough.* He'd come here to find someone, but he'd had no idea the place would be so large and... busy.

"Are you sure this is a good idea?" With his hands stuffed down in the pockets of his greatcoat, Bannon sidled up next to him, staring slack-jawed at the hustle and bustle in front of them.

Bannon's valet, Louisa—who acted as their chaperone—stood next to him with a similar expression on her face.

Shrugging, Blaise breathed into his gloved hands, trying to warm his nose and mute the smells around him. He'd been wondering the same thing. It wasn't his best idea, but he didn't have any other options. His father was Regelence's IN councilman and in charge of protecting Regelence's interests within the IN. At the top of the list of concerns, he wanted Admiral Jenkins and his wife found. As an intern in the council office, Blaise's suggestions had fallen on deaf ears, so he'd taken matters into his own hands. If you wanted something done right…. "The runner said he trailed Betty Jenkins's former lady's maid here. She sells melons."

"Then why not have the runner contact the maid?" Bannon huffed out a breath and fogged the air around him. "We're wasting our time here. We could be at the haberdashery instead, shopping for a new hat."

Rolling his eyes, Blaise grabbed his younger brother by the arm and pulled them into the tidal wave of people. "Because I can't continue to pay a runner out of my allowance or Father will get suspicious and realize I'm investigating this on my own." He stopped for a woman pushing a trolley full of pottery.

"Why *are* you investigating this on your own?" Louisa leaned past Bannon to meet Blaise's gaze.

"Because the others won't listen to me. They think there's nothing to be gained by talking to the Jenkinses' servants." It was rather shortsighted on their part. The group had runners—paid for by the IN Councilman's Committee, of course—investigating neighbors and family members. Which was a good idea, but Blaise hadn't lived as heir to a dukedom for the past twenty-two years without learning a thing or two. If you wanted gossip, you went downstairs to the servants' quarters to get it.

The pottery cart passed, and he pulled Bannon forward again, only to have him shrug out of his hold.

"I can walk, ya know."

"Then come along." Shaking his head, Blaise strode down the aisle, leaving Bannon and Louisa to follow. Why of all days did Larkinson, his valet and preferred chaperone, have to get sick? He should have snuck out and come by himself. The risk would have been worth it.

The market was a lot bigger than he'd anticipated and definitely not for the faint of heart. It wasn't dirty exactly, but it wasn't pristine either. The streets were… well, they were streets. There was something that smelled suspiciously like horse manure, even though no animals were allowed. The place bustled with footmen in livery, upper servants and underbutlers mixed with even a few middle-class citizens, but there didn't appear to be *any* lords or ladies of the ton.

With a grimace, he pulled the lapels of his greatcoat higher on his neck and hoped it and his hat concealed his identity. He'd come too far to turn back now.

He walked another minute or so before he spotted the melon stand situated right between some orange fruit and grapes. "Let me do the talking."

No reply.

Blaise whirled around and came face-to-face with a woman holding a little boy by the hand. "Ack!" He jumped back.

She gasped and clutched her purse to her chest.

Bloody hell! "I'm so sorry, madam. I thought my brother was behind me."

The woman glared, raised her chin, and marched off, dragging the boy behind her as he looked over his shoulder at Blaise.

Sighing, Blaise shook his head and turned his attention back to the booth. He was going to box Bannon's ears when he found him.

Behind the rows of cantaloupes, a sweet-faced girl in her late teens waited on a woman in a gray wool coat and straw-rimmed bonnet. The girl wore a simple tan-colored pelisse, but on further inspection, it had fine tan embroidery on the lapels and the wrists done in a darker, shinier tan. Probably silk. It was much more fitting to a middle-class woman of some status rather than someone who earned low wages hawking fruit. Her cheeks were red from the chill, and she kept darting glances at the crowd, never making eye contact with her customers. This had to be the lady's maid.

The patron didn't seem to notice the maid's odd behavior. She picked up a fruit, but instead of putting it in the basket looped over her arm, she brought it to her nose.

Blaise frowned at the odd gesture. *Who smelled cantaloupes?*

But no, she wasn't sniffing it. She turned her head slightly, then scanned back the other direction as she too searched the crowd.

The hair on Blaise's arms stood on end under his layers of clothes, and it wasn't from the cold air. Something wasn't right. Making his way to the next stand over, he decided to watch a little longer. He picked up an orange—or was it a tangerine? He never could tell the two apart—and mimicked the customer, bringing the fruit to his face. He peered over the top of it toward the two women.

They chatted, but their gazes never actually met. When a man came over and picked up a melon, the female consumer turned away.

The man tossed the cash for his cantaloupe onto the stand and left. Only then did the woman turn her attention back to the purveyor. She put the melon in her basket without paying, and the girl never made a move to stop her.

Blaise stepped closer, trying to get a better view of the patron past her wide-brimmed bonnet and….

Oh, my galaxy! He pressed the tangerine to his lips to cover a gasp. *Betty Jenkins!*

A tickle of delight ran through him. It was like playing a new piece of music with no mistakes on the first try. No way could he be this lucky.

She appeared thinner than the pictures of Mrs. Jenkins tacked up around the councilman's office, and her hair was brown, not graying blond. Truth be told, she looked more like a kitchen maid than a baron's daughter, but there was a resemblance around the eyes. She even had the same beauty mark high up on her cheek at the corner of her right eye. He was certain this *was* the admiral's wife.

It was all he could do not to dance a little jig right then and there, but where was the admiral? Blaise searched the vicinity, but no one near remotely resembled the robust man.

Dipping her head at the girl, Betty left.

Blaise started after her, but the man behind the orange booth caught his sleeve. "Are ye going to be paying for dat, or am I to call the law on ye?"

Dust! He'd forgotten about the tangerine or orange or whatever. "Sorry!" He pitched the fruit to the vendor and hurried through the aisles, staying just far enough away to not look like he was following. But it wasn't easy.

Betty went in and out of his view as people crossed between them.

Her basket swung back and forth, and her wool coat swayed. If she went any faster, she'd be running. Even with his longer stride, Blaise had a hard time keeping up.

A blast of wind liberated Betty's bonnet from her head and slowed her pace.

Making a grab for his own hat, Blaise hurried to close the gap between them, but a man pushing a cart full of sweets cut him off. He rocked up on his toes to avoid a collision and darted to the left.

A herd of children following the candy man nearly trampled him.

Blaise jogged to the right to pass the cart, and someone slammed into his shoulder, spinning him sideways. *Star dust and imploding planets!* Couldn't people see he was in a hurry? Rubbing his shoulder, Blaise regained his senses, and…. *Oh no.* Betty had vanished, and up ahead a man in a bottle-green coat and a maroon hat ran as if trying to catch someone. That had to be the rude cod who'd smashed into him.

A chill washed over Blaise and down through his body. Was that man after Betty too? What if the IN found the Jenkinses before he and his group did? A swirling dread churned in the pit of his stomach, and he followed the billowing green coat. He had to get to her first.

Weaving his way through the throng of people, Blaise half skipped, half ran, trying to locate her.

In front of the man, a swath of gray disappeared behind the baker's stand, and Blaise picked up his pace.

Or rather he tried to.

A hand clamped down on his shoulder, bringing him to a standstill.

He shrugged, but the hand held tight, sliding down his arm and squeezing his wrist.

His heart beat so fast, the rushing blood in his ears drowned out the cacophony of the crowd. He hadn't even considered that he might be in danger himself if he found her. Tensing up, he prepared to fight, but a whiney voice stalled him.

"Blaise, can we go now?"

Bannon. Blaise sighed but didn't stop to enjoy the relief. He gripped his brother's hand and hauled him into the chase with him. "Come on."

Unfortunately they didn't get far; they turned right and ran into a waist-high rock wall. Beyond the wall, traffic concealed the other side of the street.

Where did they go? Breathing heavy, Blaise dropped his hands to his knees and tried to get his bearings. He'd run out of market, and there were no crosswalks or traffic signals nearby. Neither Betty nor the man in green was anywhere in sight. He leaned past the blockade to get a better view, but only a small boy huddled behind the baker's stand, eating a meat pie. "Blast and damnation." He'd been so close.

The boy stopped eating and held the food at his mouth. His hazel eyes seemed vibrant against his dirty face. A nervous energy filled him, as though he were about to jump up and run.

Bannon jerked Blaise back around. "Why are you running?"

Blaise jerked his arm back and gave one last look toward the street.

The child had used the distraction and taken off down the row between the stalls and the barrier. So much for asking him if he'd seen Betty or the man in green.

With a sigh, Blaise glared at his brother. "I found her."

"Who? The lady's maid?" Bannon's red brows pulled together as he lifted a peach to his mouth and bit into it.

Where had he gotten that? Blaise frowned at the fruit, and Bannon held it out to him. Shaking his head, he rolled his eyes. "No, Betty Jenkins."

Bannon's green eyes flared above the peach. "You did?" he asked with his mouth full.

"If you'd stayed with me like you were supposed to…," Blaise growled. What was the use? Bannon was never where he was supposed to be, but…. "You made me lose her." He used his most superior voice and gave his sibling a piercing stare.

Bannon, of course, was unfazed. "Since you lost her, can we leave? This is dull."

Blaise closed his eyes and counted to ten, trying to keep from throttling his brother. When he finished, he had to count to ten again, but finally he managed, "Where is Louisa?"

Bannon shrugged. "I left her at the apple place while I was talking to the nice man at the peach stand." The twinkle in his eye told a different story. He'd been flirting with the man selling peaches, which explained his valet's absence. Louisa failed miserably as chaperone. Not that Blaise really wanted or needed a chaperone, but if anyone had seen him….

As one of his father's interns—not to mention his father's possible successor—he had to mind his reputation, but seeing someone he knew here wasn't likely. A young lord in a market, except one of the livestock markets, was… well… it was bad form and just wasn't done.

"Come along. We have to find Louisa." He caught Bannon's arm and tugged him through the mazelike market.

They walked back the way they came, but Blaise did not catch sight of Betty again, nor did he see the man he thought had been following her. Which worried him. Blast it all, that man had spooked Betty, and now she knew the market wasn't safe. She would be even harder to find next time, and he couldn't keep looking. He had to be at the House of Lords in an hour.

The important thing was that he'd spotted her and could vouch she was alive… for now. Perhaps he could mention seeing her and get his colleagues to step up the search for her. He hoped that the other man hunting for her had not caught her.

"Redding? Bannon?"

Blaise turned to find Louisa hurrying toward them with a huge smile on her face. Her dark hair remained tucked up under her bonnet in its neat and elegant coiffure, but she had the skirt of her morning dress in her hands ruched up and showing her ankles as if she carried something in the folds of her skirt. The action completely dispelled the elegance of her attire and the importance she held in their household. She might as well have been wearing a plain drab dress like Betty rather than pale blue with flowers and a sapphire velvet pelisse.

"I got four apples to your one peach," she said in a singsongy voice and wagged her head sideways as she drew close. Holding out her skirt, she showed them the red apples.

"Blast and damnation." With a scowl, Bannon stomped his foot and crossed his arms, the peach still in his hand. "You swear you didn't buy them?"

Louisa smiled even brighter and pressed her free hand against her chest. "On my honor." Extending the hand against her chest she wiggled her fingers. "Pay up."

Bannon pulled a shilling out of his pocket and gave it to her.

Blaise could only imagine what that was about. Like he and Larkinson, Bannon and Louisa had been raised together and were dear friends. The daughters of their housekeeper, Larkinson and Louisa had been educated with them and groomed to be their valets since practically birth. But unlike he and his own valet, these two were always competing. Anything Bannon did, Louisa had to do and vice versa. It was like having two Bannons.

As if one wasn't enough.

"Come on." Blaise shooed them both forward.

The two of them started moving, but Bannon continued to glare at Louisa. She grinned at him in return, then strolled up next to Blaise. "Would you like an apple, my lord?"

"They probably have worms in them." Bannon took one last bite of his peach and deposited it in a trash can next to one of the stands.

"No, thank you, Louisa." He decided not to mention that she should walk behind them for the sake of propriety, and scanned the area around them. "How did you get the apples and the peach?"

"Louie cheated, I'm certain." Bannon stuffed his gloved hands into his greatcoat pockets, appearing quite petulant.

"Did not. We made a bet to see which of us was more charming." Now she gloated. "I won." Freezing in her tracks, she touched Blaise's arm. "You could probably get a bushel of apples. Men are always noticing you."

Blaise fought back a blush. "I doubt that." Besides, he'd rather have one Betty Jenkins right now than a bushel of anything.

Bannon snorted. "I doubt it too. Blaise is so oblivious to flirting. All he cares about is work."

"That's not true." *Was that...?* No, it was a milkmaid, not Betty. *Wait! What did Bannon say?* "Men do not flirt with me."

"See?" Bannon raised his hand toward Blaise and looked past him at Louisa. "Oblivious."

Blaise ignored his brother. Men did *not* flirt with him. Quite frankly, he'd yet to meet a man whose attention he wanted to gain either.

Up ahead at the entrance to the market, between two women, a bottle-green coat fluttered in the wind and disappeared into the crowd once again.

"Bloody hell!" He didn't wait to see if Bannon and Louisa followed, which was probably stupidity on his part.

At the sidewalk, the throng cleared a bit and revealed the man in the green coat disappearing inside a shop up the street. Had the man followed Betty there? The tightness in Blaise's chest eased a little. One thing was for certain—if the man was still running, he hadn't caught her. Blaise still had time; he might be able to get to Betty first!

"What was that about? Where are you going?" Bannon asked, short of breath as he stumbled up next to Blaise.

"To the haberdashery."

GROANING, DALTON Fairfax huddled farther down into his peacoat as he ran. Damn the luck, letting Ravensburg spot him leaving the IN base on the very day he returned to Regelence. His father, the Marquess of Ravensburg, was a pain in his arse. His parents had been making a fuss for weeks now about him moving back home and selling out his commission. Not bloody likely.

The wind whipped his cheeks so hard he'd lost sensation in them two blocks ago. He glanced back at the mass of people on the sidewalk from which he'd just escaped, but kept going. It was a little like trying to swim up the Bordo River on Lerdra. Shouldn't these people be sleeping off last night's excess? Most aristocrats didn't rise till ten or so, and it was barely six thirty. Dodging a nanny pushing a pram, he almost plowed into a young lord.

"Watch out!"

Dalton leaped over a frozen puddle before glancing back again.

Ravensburg had his arm in the air as if hailing Dalton, as he shoved through a mass of people on the sidewalk. If his face got any redder, he'd look like a tomato. When had Father gotten that out of shape? Or perhaps he was a victim of wind chill as well?

A stab of pity, mixed with something that felt suspiciously like guilt, niggled at Dalton, but not enough to make him stop. Eventually he'd have to talk to his father, but not now.

Skirting a trolley filled with oranges, he peeked over his shoulder again, and bam! He splatted up against a rather squishy body. *Oomph.* "Meteor dust!"

"Whoa!" The squishy body flew backward in a flurry of puce and flapping arms. A hat sailed forward off the man's head.

Dalton shot out a hand to grab the man, but the man's walking stick came flying toward him. He snagged the stick out of midair, but missed the owner's arm.

The man landed on his arse with his legs spread and his gray beaver hat between his knees. He brought to mind a toppled bowling pin as he floundered around.

Several fellow pedestrians stopped to gawk.

Dalton seriously considered resuming his escape, but how callous would that be? He wasn't a complete scoundrel, even if it meant his father caught up with him. Sighing, he planted the walking stick on the sidewalk and offered his free hand. "Terribly sorry, ol' chap."

"Oh, I say, Ashbourne. Is that you?" The bowling pin, er… man, blinked bright blue eyes up at Dalton. His lips flowed into a grin, making his jowls more prominent. Lifting his hat from between his legs, he plopped it on his head, turned his face upward, and took Dalton's hand in a warm clammy grip.

Oh stars. It was Viscount Tyndel. Of all times to run into a former paramour. Dalton pulled and failed to help the viscount rise. Galaxy, the man had packed on some pounds. He'd never had the toned physique Dalton preferred in his lovers, but the man had a talented mouth, so Dalton hadn't cared overly. Now? There were practically two of Tyndel.

Putting his back into it and using the walking stick for leverage, Dalton tried again to help Tyndel up.

Slowly, Tyndel rose to his feet, staggering a bit. He dusted off his chocolate-colored trousers and rearranged his waistcoat, jacket, and puce greatcoat. “When did you get back in town? Last I heard, you were serving in the IN on Lerdra.”

“Right. Um….” Dalton chanced a glance behind him. Was that Ravensburg? The man certainly seemed in a hurry and the hat appeared the right shade of brown, but Dalton couldn’t get a good look at him otherwise. An IN soldier kept pace in front of him and a much smaller blond man directly beside…. “Damnation!” The blond was his sire. Where had he come from?

Arthur Fairfax’s body lurched back in recognition. He said something to—yes, that was definitely Ravensburg—and pointed in Dalton’s direction. Great, now both his parents were on his tail. He’d managed to avoid them while on leave last year because they’d been in the country at Windswept Abbey, but evading them while they were in town was already proving more difficult.

Dalton sprang into a jog. Bloody hell. He’d forgotten all about Tyndel. He turned over his shoulder toward the now slack-jawed viscount and walked backward. “My apologies, Tyndel. We’ll catch up later.” His gaze strayed a few yards back. *Eep*. His sire was quick for such a small man. “Family emergency.” Which wasn’t a lie—it was an emergency that he get away from his family. He fled without another word.

“Oh, I say, how undignified,” someone called out behind him.

Dalton grinned at the absurdity of the situation and kept going. How very undignified, indeed. Both Lords Ravensburg running down a crowded sidewalk in the middle of downtown Classige. Dalton chuckled. He couldn’t wait to tell Uncle Raleigh.

After bolting into an alley, he came out on Green Street and looked both ways. There was a jeweler, a tailor…. There. The haberdashery. Maybe he could hide out and do some shopping.

He sprinted across the road, narrowly avoiding a lift. Glancing behind him, he made sure his parents hadn’t made it out of the alley yet, and then he flung open the door and hurried inside.

The bell tinkled, and…. *Ah, warmth!* His frozen face and burning lungs approved. Dropping his hands to his knees, he took a deep breath and then another. He really needed to get reaccustomed to the higher altitude in Pruluce. Having been stationed for the past year on a planet with nothing but plains had not done him any favors today. Thank goodness for the last six weeks of special training to go into the Regelence Special Regiment, or he'd be in worse shape.

"Ahem."

Dalton raised his head as a tall thin man in a dove gray morning coat and charcoal trousers came around the corner toward him. The pinched expression on his face clearly declared Dalton beneath him. The establishment did cater to the haute ton, but still… a soldier wasn't exactly riffraff. Besides, how could the salesman even see with his nose that high in the air?

Straightening to his full height, Dalton lifted his own chin; he could do haughty when necessary.

"How can I help you, lieutenant…?" The man looked as though he'd bitten into something quite sour, and the way he made Dalton's rank sound like the equivalent of horse droppings was very impressive.

Dalton barely suppressed a twitch at the corner of his lips. Staring down his nose at the man, he lifted a brow. "Lieutenant Lord Ashbourne." He wasn't above playing the lord card to keep from getting tossed out of the shop.

Normally that was all it took, and this proprietor was no different.

Mr. Lemon Sucker's entire demeanor changed, and the poker up his arse seemed to have disappeared. "Welcome, my lord. I'm Humphreys. How may I serve you? Please allow me to take your coat and…." He looked at Dalton's head.

Bloody black hole, he'd lost his cover in the mad dash to get away.

Humphreys quickly divested Dalton of his peacoat. "What can I help you with today, my lord?"

"I'll let you know. I'm going to browse around." Dalton stepped past Poker Arse, completely dismissing him, then felt guilty for it. But the man was rude to him first, he reasoned—not to mention he needed out of the doorway. Even though the bottom part of the door was wood, the top had panes of glass and a clear view to the street.

"Very well, my lord. Please let me know if I can be of service. I'll check back with you in a moment?"

Waving his hand behind him, Dalton continued walking. He did need a new civilian wardrobe more fitting to Regelence for when he was off duty. Though he was loath to give up the shorts and sandals he'd worn at the base on Lerdra during his down time.

Studying the shelves of cravats to his right, he decided to browse while he let his esteemed parents get farther away.

"Bannon, get down from there right this instant. What if someone sees you?"

Dalton froze.

The furious whisper had come from somewhere to his left. Whoever the speaker was, he whispered louder than Dalton's cousin Tarren, which was quite impressive.

"I mean it, Bannon."

Wait. A flutter racked Dalton's stomach. It couldn't be. Bannon was the name of his cousin Aiden's friend. And Bannon's brother.... Could that be Dalton's Adonis calling his younger sibling?

Before he'd gone into special training, Dalton had been home on leave and spotted the most angelic, gorgeous creature he'd ever laid eyes on. The man had starred in every one of Dalton's fantasies since then. That lovely face had even gotten him through those long nights in the surf while he'd suffered from hypothermia and starvation. He could still picture the man clearly. A real diamond of the first water. Lord Redding, Blaise Thompson, heir to the Duke of Eversleigh, had brown hair and the most brilliant green eyes Dalton had ever seen—like emeralds in the sunlight. He had kissable lips and a grace of movement that made him appear ethereal. He was beautiful, elegant, and very, very beddable.

Only Dalton hadn't been able to arrange an introduction. Somehow their paths had not crossed again, which wasn't surprising, considering that Dalton was a rakehell and Blaise was... well, respectable. None of Dalton's cousins had taken him seriously when he'd asked to meet the viscount.

Footsteps came from behind him. "My lord, can I—"

"Not now!" He waved his hand without looking at the man.

"Hrmph. Very well, my lord."

Bloody hell. Dalton swiveled around. "Pardon me, Humphreys. My apologies. I was deep in thought, and I'm still deciding, but I'll let you know."

"Very well, my lord." Humphreys dipped his pointy chin, turned on his heels, and left.

Dalton hurried to the very end of the aisle and glanced down the next one. Empty. Standing perfectly still, he closed his eyes and listened. *Where are you, lovely?*

"Eep." The shelving unit cattycorner on his left rattled. A black beaver hat fell from the shelf, bounced onto the navy blue carpet, and rolled in a circle before landing crown up in the middle of the floor. "Oh star dust! Blaise, let go of my feet and stop pulling…." A pair of dazzling green eyes peered down from the top shelf, under a shock of bright red hair. "Oh, hallo."

"'Ello." Dalton grinned. Not only was it Aiden's friend, Bannon, but Bannon's grousing confirmed that his gorgeous brother was indeed on the other side of that wall of hats as well. "Can you get that for me?" Bannon asked.

"Certainly." Dalton snagged the hat from the ground, and warmth spread through him as though he'd drank a shot of whiskey. At last, he was about to meet the breathtaking Viscount Redding. Finally.

"Bannon…," Blaise hissed from the other side.

"I have him," a female hissed back. "Bannon, get down."

The shelving teetered.

"Oh!" Bannon's eyes widened, and his head began to sink below the shelf.

Three more hats dropped from the top ledge, and one from the middle—right about where Bannon's foot would be—and hit the ground. Unlike the first hat, these didn't roll but instead pelted the ground like darts.

Dalton had a vision of the shelf falling and knocking over the rest like dominoes. He raced around the corner with his arms outstretched, intent on catching the hellion, and plowed right over the man of his dreams.

It was nothing like running into Tyndel, because Blaise was not at all squishy, and he never saw Dalton coming. He fell like a chopped tree—straight down.

Dalton reached out, but the impact had sent him reeling backward as well. The cuff of Blaise's soft wool morning coat flitted through his fingers, followed by a small current of air that sealed the deal. All he could do was watch with his mouth ajar as Blaise hit the blue carpet. The breath knocked from him was little more than a hiss.

Clutching his chest, Blaise gasped for air. The agony and surprise on his face hit Dalton so hard, he might as well have fallen himself. Those beautiful green eyes went wide and unfocused. His chestnut hair fell in an attractive tousle over his forehead, and those smooth alabaster cheeks grew botchy with spots of color, but for all that, he was still the most beautiful man on Regelence. Like an elven prince from one of the storybooks Grandfather used to read at bedtime.

Before Dalton could move forward to check on his hapless victim, Bannon screeched.

Hanging from his fingertips, the redhead dangled four feet off the ground. The shelving unit swayed back and forth as if hit by a gale force wind.

A woman tried to steady the shelves but had no success whatsoever. It was only a matter of seconds before the whole thing toppled, and who knew which way it would actually fall.

Dalton rushed forward through the rain of hats peppering the ground around him like tiny missiles and caught Bannon with one arm. After setting the young man on his feet, he used both hands to steady the shelf. The girl helped, and it stopped swaying, but most of its contents had crash-landed onto the carpet.

Dalton's lips twitched up into a big smile as he studied the turbulent sea of hats. Some on their sides, some upside down, others right side up, one or two still rolling. In their stuffy society, a little harmless folly was a godsend. Well, almost harmless. He supposed Blaise might disagree at the moment, but still it tickled Dalton.

Somehow all but one hat missed Blaise, who was now trying to sit while gasping for air and clawing at his cravat.

Dalton rushed to him, tossed the green hat from his abdomen, and helped him sit. Sinking down behind Blaise, he propped the viscount's back against his chest and couldn't help but feel tenderness. "Easy, sweetheart."

Galaxy, he smelled divine. Like cold nights around a campfire and the inside of a sweet shop all rolled into one.

Blaise leaned back into Dalton's arms, so warm and trusting, and despite the situation, Dalton's cock stirred. Gritting his teeth, he willed his body to behave and intercepted Blaise's hands. Pale, elegant hands that would look splendid on Dalton's slightly darker skin. And thoughts like that were definitely not a good way to get control of his body. Geez, the man couldn't breathe, and here Dalton was lost in a fantasy.

Unknotting the cravat, he pulled it free. "That's it, sweetheart, easy now. Try to slowly let the air back in."

Little by little Blaise began to relax and inhale. Soon he was breathing easier, and so did Dalton.

"There now. Much better, yes?"

Blaise nodded and snuggled, moving his back side to side, against Dalton's chest. He leaned his head back on Dalton's shoulder and closed his eyes with his face only inches away.

A charming sprinkle of freckles dotted his cheeks, and his slim neck begged to be bitten. The strong pulse throbbing there taunted Dalton's tongue. Would he taste salty or sweet? Or a combination of both?

"Oh bother." Bannon stood a few feet away with the black hat he'd risked life and limb to get, wringing it in his hands. His pale skin blanched nearly white. "Father is going to throttle me."

Humphreys appeared behind him with his mouth ajar. *Wonderful!* There was no telling what the very uptight man would say about this. Frankly, Dalton couldn't believe he wasn't already shrieking and calling the law on them.

The girl bit her bottom lip and shook her head at the damage before turning on Bannon. "I told you it was a bad idea."

"You did not!" Bannon shouted at her. "You said the hat would be dashing on me."

"I didn't mean for you to climb up and get…." She trailed off, looking over at Humphreys.

With a sigh and a prayer to anyone who'd listen that Humphreys didn't have an apoplexy right on the spot, Dalton met the older man's gaze. "I'll pay for everything, but allow me to revive Lord Redding first."

Surprisingly the proprietor did not explode. Standing up straighter, he closed his lips and dipped his chin. "Very well, my lord." With a glare at Bannon, he lifted his chin, sniffed, and walked away.

Like a bolt of lightning had struck him, Blaise jerked forward and scrambled to his feet. He spun around and locked gazes with Dalton, his mouth gaping open. For several seconds, they stared at each other.

Dalton couldn't have moved if he'd wanted to. He sat there transfixed by those grass-green eyes and the most profound feeling that his life had just irrevocably changed. He shook his head, trying to clear the insane thought, and hopped to his feet. It wasn't like he was a lad with his first infatuation. He didn't even believe in love at first sight, but there was… something… some strange pull he couldn't deny. The shock in Blaise's eyes made Dalton wonder if he felt it too.

Blaise swallowed hard enough to make his Adam's apple bob. A small, shy smile teased his lips, and those gorgeous eyes peeked out from under fluttering lashes. Pink tinged his neck and face as he bit his bottom lip. He took a step forward, and the color drained from his face.

Maybe it was the widening of his eyes or the jerky way he moved, but Dalton read his intent to flee and said, "Blaise, wait."

But he didn't wait; he took off at a brisk pace, kicking hats out of his way as he went.

Bollocks! Dalton reached out as if he could somehow stall the retreat, but Blaise increased his pace.

Bannon and the girl stumbled along behind him. After a few seconds, Bannon peered back over his shoulder with a sheepish expression. "Sorry. And thank you."

Dalton nodded. *Bloody hell!* What had he done? Well, other than knocking the man on his arse, of course. Rolling his eyes at himself, Dalton groaned. He watched Blaise disappear around the corner with his coattails flapping behind him.

Ugh. That had not gone at all like Dalton envisioned their first meeting. So much for a first impression. He'd just have to make a better second one. Glancing around at the hats littering the floor, he chuckled.

That shouldn't be too hard.

Chapter Two

A prominent member of the IN Councilman's Committee and his petite consort were seen sprinting down Platt Street this morning. Has the marquess lost his mind? Perhaps it's the long hours he puts in at the House of Lords. Rumor has it, he and Councilman Eversleigh have butted heads yet again over politics.

—From *Regelence Post*, the Happenings at the House of Lords column

THERE WERE moments in his life when he looked back and wondered if he'd taken leave of his senses. This was one of those moments. Actually, Blaise didn't wonder; he knew for a certainty.

Leaning back against the brick wall in the alley beside Hart and Sons Haberdashery, he stared down at his feet as if they had the answers. In all his twenty-two years, he'd never experienced the intense heat that had consumed him when he'd locked gazes with that man. He wasn't sure he liked the feeling. No, he was certain he didn't care for it at all. It made him hot despite the nip in the air and the absence of his greatcoat, and his pulse galloped out of control.

"I'm sorry." Bannon ducked down into his line of vision with his bottom lip caught between his teeth. "Are you okay? Can you breathe all right?"

Now he's concerned? Blaise ran his hand down his face and nodded. If Bannon thought him still suffering from being knocked down, Blaise wasn't about to tell him otherwise. It wasn't as if he could admit that he'd wanted to step forward and go right back into the man's arms. It was better to have run out and be thought a complete ninny.

"I saw that hat and had to have it. I didn't mean for all of them to fall. I should've listened to you, but I was certain I could reach it." Bannon plopped Blaise's hat on his head and proceeded to put his coat around his shoulders like Bannon was dressing a child.

Oh, for the love of.... Blaise stuffed his arms into his coat. As the big brother, he was supposed to take charge. He should give his sibling a severe dressing down. Bannon really deserved it this time. He'd not only put himself in danger, but he might have put others in danger as well. "You made me lose the man in green."

Louisa, who stood behind Bannon, winced. "Do you think the man in the green coat caught the admiral's wife?"

"I hope not, but I'm going to have to mention this to Father and the committee." And he didn't look forward to that. Their parents were not going to like that he'd gone to the market, but he couldn't very well stay silent to save his own hide now. "Betty might be in danger, and we need to find her fast." If anything happened to her because he'd drawn attention to her.... Well, he didn't want to consider that. Putting his hat on, he glanced around the dingy alley, and a shudder racked through him. He really had been out of his mind when he'd fled. There were cardboard boxes, wooden crates, and garbage strewn all over the place. "Come on."

A skitter—or was it a shuffle?—echoed off the walls of the buildings and one of the crates inched over. Probably rats or some other critter. *Egads*, he hated rodents. That was all he needed to top off this misadventure.

Louisa jumped at the sound and turned toward it. "Couldn't you have picked a better spot to run to?"

"I... panicked," he admitted reluctantly.

Louisa's lips quirked up, and as if she read his mind, she asked, "He was rather gorgeous, wasn't he?"

Very, but Blaise refused to admit it out loud. "You're missing the point entirely. Bannon has caused yet another scene, and this time he's embroiled me in it as well."

Bannon at least had the decency to give him a sheepish wince. "What exactly are you going to tell Father and Sire?"

Blaise raised both eyebrows.

"Oh no! You aren't going to tell them about the hat incident, are you?" Bannon bit his bottom lip again and peered over at Blaise from under his red bangs. "You remember what Father threatened last time, don't you?"

Bloody black hole! He'd forgotten about that. Last month when Bannon tossed his dance card across the ballroom floor at the Earl of Baxter's ball and made several of the dancers fall, Father had threatened to send Bannon to rusticate in the country. Blaise might want to strangle his brother at the moment, but he *did* love him. He tapped his fingers on his arm, trying to come up with a plan—and fast.

"I've got it!" Louisa stopped and turned toward them, putting herself between them and the mouth of the alley. "We'll say that something fell on Blaise and knocked him unconscious."

"What? A hat?" Blaise's lips twitched. "A hat fell on my head and knocked me senseless? And just how did the hat fall?"

Louisa deflated and turned back to the alley entrance.

Bannon giggled. "It was a very heavy hat teetering on the edge, and gravity is a bitch."

Blaise elbowed him in the ribs.

"How about we don't mention the haberdashery at all." He didn't want his brother to be sent away, and he certainly didn't relish telling his parents that he'd practically sat in someone's lap. A shiver snaked through him at the memory of the solid strength behind him and the warm breath that caressed his ear. "Did anyone else see us? Someone other than the proprietor and the… man?" Forget that he hadn't been able to breathe at the time; the ton would flay him alive for leaning against the other man.

Louisa shook her head. "I don't believe so."

Bannon, who'd gone back to studying their surroundings, jerked his head back toward Blaise, and his eyes widened. A slow smile oozed onto his face.

That did not bode well. He must have seen someone else or….

"And I was beginning to wonder if you were heterosexual."

What? Blaise had expected something, but not *that*. He stopped walking. After living with Bannon his entire life, he should be used to the way his brain bounced from one subject to the next, but apparently not. "What does that have to do with—"

"You just glowed, and your voice got all wistful when you said *the man*."

How in the world did one *glow*? "Don't be ridiculous. I did not. And how do you know what wistful sounds like?"

"You definitely glowed," Louisa chimed in.

Blaise glared at her. That was the trouble with consorting with a couple of artists; they were extremely observant. *Blast it all.* He motioned for them to get moving.

"If someone saw you, you can say that something fell on you—"

A person could get whiplash from all the subject changes around these two. "Like a hat?" Blaise interrupted.

Louisa continued as if he hadn't spoken, but at least she was walking, "—and the man rushed around to rescue you. It sounds more romantic than him crashing into you."

"That is not romantic." Unless one accounted for the breathlessly whispered "sweetheart," in his— *Blast and damnation.* Blaise's stomach got all fluttery again. "And I am not heterosexual. Even if I were, there is nothing wrong with that." He bobbed his head once for emphasis. *Great, now I'm the one bouncing to a different topic.*

"He's right. And there's nothing wrong with being heterosexual either." Louisa stuck her tongue out at Bannon.

"Okay, blind, then." Bannon snorted and gave an exaggerated mock shudder. "Have you seen the men you dance with?"

That was another thing about artists; they usually excelled in all the arts, including drama.

"Of course I've seen the men I dance with. I'm the one who dances with them. Whatever is the matter with my choice of partners? At least I dance."

"Maybe you should try dancing with Ashbourne."

"Ashbourne?" Grabbing Bannon's elbow, Blaise urged him forward. Why was he even having this—*these* conversations with them?

"The Earl of Ashbourne. You know, the man who so gallantly rescued you… er… us."

Oh my stars! He stumbled over his own feet. *An earl?* That meant their paths would cross again. Blaise's spine tingled at the thought just as much as his stomach churned. "Ashbourne? Where have I heard that title before?"

"He's King-Consort Raleigh's nephew."

"The Marquess of Ravensburg's heir?"

"Yup."

Damn. Ravensburg was a member of Regelence's IN Councilman's Committee, and his only son was rumored to be a prolific rakehell. An underage rakehell, which was even worse than the regular variety. The Earl of Ashbourne gambled, drank, flirted, and even consorted with light-trousers. He was a loose man, and for some reason that thought made Blaise's stomach clench. Stupid really, because he had no time for a suitor anyway.

The sounds of lifts on the street and the soft echo of wind in the alley seemed deafening. Blaise glanced over at his companions and realized why.

Neither Bannon nor Louisa said a word. Instead, they both stared at him without watching where they were going. Bannon nearly ran into a man walking his dog as they exited the alley.

Catching his brother's arm, Blaise steered him around the startled poodle. "Why are you both staring at me like that?"

"Trying to figure out how long you're going to pretend to be unaffected by Ashbourne." This from Bannon.

"I *am* unaffected by Ashbourne." *Liar.* That little shiver thing happened again, putting an exclamation point on his fib.

"Uh-huh, I see."

Don't ask. That's what he wants. Sighing, Blaise ignored the much smarter voice in his head. "What does *that* mean?"

Bannon giggled and walked past him toward their lift, which had just pulled to the curb, opened the door, and let down the steps. When he climbed in without another word, Blaise looked to Louisa.

She smiled and asked, "Where's your cravat, Redding?"

What? Glancing down, Blaise touched his neck, and sure enough there was only skin. *Blast!* No wonder his neck was cold.

Townsend Castle, Classige, Pruluce (home of the Regelence Royal Family)

"BLOODY HELL!" The cold liquid gushed down his front and poured over his polished boots onto the green marble floor. Being in the military on active duty, Dalton had seen and done his fair share of reprehensible things, but there were some things even too dastardly for him. Like say… bombarding a guy with water balloons as soon as he walked in the door.

As he stood there dripping, the castle foyer erupted in a chorus of laughter.

Dalton glared up at his cousins, who stood on the balcony. Apparently they didn't have the same compunction. Running his hand over his forehead, he wiped it—he brought his fingers to his mouth and touched it with his tongue; yes, thankfully, it *was* water—off. Talk about a welcome home. Now he had an answer to why Jeffers had not greeted him.

As if on cue, the butler said, "Good morning, Lord Ashbourne."

"Mornin', Jeffers. Thanks for the heads-up."

"I did not give you a heads-up, my lord. I was instructed not to open the door." Good ol' Jeffers. Sarcasm was completely lost on him.

"So I assumed." With a smile twitching at his lips, Dalton retrieved the busted red balloon from the top of his boot where it had landed after the brief meeting with his face.

"We were expecting someone else." Aiden pounded down the stairs with a blue water balloon clutched in one hand and a yellow in the other.

"And I thought this was my welcome home. I don't know whether to be insulted you forgot or glad I wasn't the intended target."

Aiden's stepson, Jeremy—who preferred the nickname Trouble over his title, the Marquess of Winstol—strolled out from behind the suit of armor next to the breakfast room, also carrying two balloons.

From the balcony, Tarren chortled, and Muffin peeked around the staircase on Dalton's right.

Colton sidled up next to Aiden, wiping tears of mirth from his eyes and holding his stomach with one hand. "Sorry about that, Demon." He was the only one with only one balloon.

"We thought you were Wentworth," Muffin said.

Ah, so Wentworth was the unfortunate target. Which explained Colton going first—he was trying to assault his consort.

"Think nothing of it. Might I borrow this, cousin?" Without waiting for an answer, Dalton snatched the yellow water-filled latex from Aiden and lobbed it at Colton's face.

Colton sputtered quite spectacularly for a full two seconds and launched his remaining balloon at Dalton's chest.

"Aaah…." This one was even colder than the last. "Colton, you are so dead."

After that, it was every man for himself. Balloons flew and water splashed. Everyone ran for cover, laughing and sliding on the marble floor. Galaxy, he'd missed this. It was the most fun he'd had in at least a fortnight.

Dashing to the study, he threw open the door with Muffin hot on his heels and pressed his back to the wall beside the door, feeling rather like a kid playing hide-and-seek.

The door closed with a *snick* as Muffin took up the spot next to him, only slightly less drenched than he felt. Her pretty red hair stuck to her face, and water dribbled down her chin as she smiled up at him, showing off two missing front teeth. "I'm on your team, Dalton," she said and handed him a purple water balloon.

"Thank you, my lady." After taking it, he gave her a bow and reached to pat her shoulder, but before he made contact, a bellow interrupted.

"What in the…?"

Dalton jumped, and Muffin squeaked. She might have jumped too, but Dalton wasn't sure. He'd already started searching for the source of the yelling.

Behind the big mahogany desk, Uncle Raleigh stood with hands in the air at shoulder level in a sign of disbelief. Next to him in the office chair sat Uncle Steven, who appeared a little dazed and a lot rumpled. On closer inspection Uncle Raleigh's cravat was partially undone and his ebony hair mussed. It seemed Dalton and Muffin had interrupted something. Which would account for why Raleigh hadn't stopped the water fight already. He obviously hadn't heard it.

Mirth bubbled up inside Dalton and spilled over into outright laughter. "Galaxy, it's good to be home."

With wide blue eyes, Muffin gawked at him, then at the king and king-consort before she flung the door open and fled.

A loud male grunt, a splash, and a small feminine squeal followed her departure.

Dalton laughed so hard his stomach hurt.

Uncle Raleigh, however, did not look nearly as amused. Shaking his head, he ran his fingers through his hair and said, "Welcome home, Ashbourne." Finally a smile emerged. "I suppose since you've just arrived I can't blame you for this?"

Dalton shook his head and gestured to his soggy uniform. "I'm an innocent victim."

Uncle Steven pressed his lips together in a thin line, but there was no disguising the shake of his shoulders or the sparkle in his eyes. Glancing up at Raleigh, he cleared his throat. "And you can't blame me either, because I was in here with you."

Groaning, Raleigh thumped Steven's ear.

"Ow." Steven slapped a hand over his mistreated appendage. "That's spousal abuse, Cony."

Ignoring his *abused* spouse, Raleigh strolled around the desk and held out his arms.

Dalton went into them. This was the welcome he'd been waiting for, though the water fight had been nice as well.

Raleigh leaned back to study him. "You've filled out."

"RSR training will do that to you." Dalton stood up a little straighter and puffed his chest out a bit. He'd never been what anyone would call overweight, but now he was in the best shape of his life, having gone up a full shirt size due to the new muscles in his shoulders and chest.

"You decided to do it, then?"

"That was the original ruse, right? That I wanted to follow in Grandfather's footsteps." His grandfather—Raleigh's father, the fifth Marquess of Ravensburg—had been a commander in charge of Regelence's Special Regiment. "So…." He held his arms out to his side. "I'm now a trained special forces soldier and set to go into the RSR two weeks from tomorrow under Commander Tippin." He'd never intended to turn it into a career when he'd agreed to the plan two years ago, but now he wouldn't consider anything else. The hard work had been fulfilling in a way that not much else had been.

"I'm proud of you, Dalton." Raleigh slapped his arm and stared at him for the longest time.

The love shining in Raleigh's eyes unsettled Dalton a little, so he cleared his throat.

"You've done well, Demon. Have you told your parents yet? They've been leaving messages for you," Steven said.

Happy feeling gone. Dalton couldn't control the groan, and he didn't try, but damned if he could stop the hurt niggling in his gut. He somehow doubted even if he told his parents, that they'd be proud of him. Part of him wanted to tell them to prove himself right, but the other part didn't want to tell them for that very reason. No, it was best he avoid them for now, because damned if he wasn't getting irritable thinking about them.

To deflect the attention off him, he shook the water balloon in his hand and said, "I interrupted something?"

"Yes, you did. We were celebrating." Steven glared at him.

"Indeed we were." Beaming from ear to ear, Raleigh held out his hand and made a give-me motion.

Dalton handed over the purple balloon. "What were you celebrating?"

"The fact that I finally deciphered the encryption on the hard drive that Robert Jenkins brought me. Payton, Jeremy, Jeffers, and I have all been working on it." Robert Jenkins was the son of the IN's former admiral who had disappeared shortly after he'd turned over his position to Nate, Aiden's husband. Six months ago, while Dalton was on leave, Robert had gone AWOL from the IN in order to try to find his parents, but instead he'd found the hard drive and brought it to Dalton's uncles. The last thing Dalton had heard was that everyone suspected the admiral was dead.

"Is Robert still hiding out here at the castle?"

"He is. He is now a Royal Guard, but because he is AWOL from the IN, he doesn't leave the castle." Striding past Dalton, Raleigh went to the office door. "And speaking of guards… just a moment." He peeked out. "Jeremy, if you throw that at me, I will beat you senseless." With that he lobbed the balloon.

Someone yelled. It sounded like Aiden.

Turning back to Dalton and Steven, Raleigh smiled with pure devilment.

Dalton bit his lip, but Steven didn't even try to hide his chuckle.

Sticking his head back out the door, Raleigh intoned very calmly, "Clean up the mess, boys, and no more water fights in the castle." He closed the door on a somber chorus of "Yes, Cony."

"If I had stuck my head out the door, they would have pelted me," Steven grumbled.

"They almost did. Trouble had me in his sights." Clapping his hands and rubbing them together, Raleigh perched himself on the edge of the desk next to Steven again. "Where were we?"

"Somewhere we can't continue to go with Dalton present."

"Something about guards…?" Dalton prompted.

"Ah, yes." Raleigh motioned toward the chair. "Now that you are home, I expect you to clear your outings with Wentworth and take a guard with you."

"You can't be serious." No way was he getting saddled with a guard. *How humiliating would that be?* "You do realize I now have the same training as Wentworth and his elite guards, don't you?"

"You sound like Nate," Raleigh accused.

"I have more specialized skills than Nate." Dalton did a quick check to make sure Nate wasn't standing there, because training or not, his cousin-in-law was a badarse with about five inches and two stone on him. "And it's not like I'm going to have a guard once I ship out in a fortnight."

"He's got a point," Steven said.

Raleigh growled at his spouse. "You aren't helping."

Steven shrugged as if to say *I tried.*

Dalton could practically visualize the headstone on the grave that was his social life. He bolted to his feet, prepared to fight for his freedom if need be. "Did you find something on the hard drive that makes you think I'm in danger?"

"No. But now I'm more convinced that Admiral Jenkins was murdered. Sit down." Raleigh waved toward a chair. "You're right. You do have the same training as Wentworth and his team, but—" He held up one finger and leveled the dad stare at Dalton. "—you do not have their experience."

"But—"

Raleigh waved him off again. "You can go without a guard. Galaxy knows I don't have enough to go around anyway, but if I even suspect someone is watching you or following you…."

"Then I'll have a guard."

"Correct."

Whew. Dalton knew when to leave well enough alone. He stood to make his escape.

"Where are you going?" Raleigh gave him *The Look.* The one complete with the raised brow that his uncle did so well. His cousin Rexley was pretty good at it, and Dalton wasn't half-bad, if he said so himself, but Raleigh was the master.

The Look worked just as it always had, and Dalton found himself squirming on the inside even though he'd outgrown the fidgeting on the outside. "Um…." He hitched his thumb over his shoulder. "To drink your best brandy and beat my cousins at billiards?"

The Look didn't falter.

"To help clean up the water balloon mess that I didn't make?"

"Run, Dalton! Get out while you're ahead." Steven chuckled. "And no brandy at this time of morning."

Raleigh smacked Steven's shoulder, then shooed Dalton away. "No brandy, period."

"Okay, bye, then." Dalton hurried for the door.

"Well, that's one problem solved, I suppose," Raleigh said under his breath. "I've got to figure out how to come up with guards for Eversleigh and his family."

Dalton froze with his hand on the doorknob. *No way... I cannot be this lucky.* He turned slowly to find Raleigh in Steven's lap, only seconds away from a kiss. "The Duke of Eversleigh?"

Both his uncles focused on him with twin expressions of confusion, and then Raleigh nodded. "Yes. Why?"

Dalton leaned against the door. "You mean Redding and Lord Bannon?"

Again, Raleigh nodded.

Oh boy, oh boy, oh boy. If he played this right…. "Maybe I can help."

"How so?" Raleigh frowned.

"Perhaps I can…."

Raleigh started shaking his head. "I'm not entirely comfortable with you guarding yourself, Dalton. Why would I have you guard someone else?"

"Because you said yourself that you're short guards."

Looking at Dalton, then up at Raleigh, Steven asked, "Why not?"

"Are you jesting?" Raleigh stood, put his hands on his hips, and glared down at Steven. "Demon and Bannon together? Why not let—"

"I meant Redding." No sooner than the words were out Dalton's mouth, he wished he could call them back, because once again he had both his uncles' undivided attention. And he wasn't sure that was a good thing.

Steven grinned.

Raleigh's eyebrow went straight up and hung there effortlessly.

"Well, you know, because like you said, me and Bannon…." Dalton rushed on, "He's a little on the mischievous side, and you know how I get. He could probably talk me into…." When their expressions didn't change, Dalton trailed off. They weren't buying it. He'd really stuck his foot in it, but damn it all, he wasn't ready to give up yet. "Let me do it, Uncle Raleigh, please. I promise I can do it. It will help you out and keep me from being bored before I report to the RSR in Devonshire."

"There would have to be a chaperone because you are both from the same class and of marriageable age," Raleigh mumbled and shook his head.

Damn it! He was going to say no.

"Let him do it, Cony." Steven grabbed Raleigh's hands in his. His thumbs rubbed along Raleigh's knuckles before he pulled Raleigh back into his lap. "Like he said, he does have RSR training, and for crying out loud, you taught the boy yourself when he was young. He was good then, but think of what he's like now with the additional skills." He nuzzled Raleigh's ear, then looked over his shoulder at Dalton and winked.

Dalton could have kissed him! *Please let it work.* If anyone could talk Uncle Raleigh into something, it was the king.

Raleigh leaned his forehead against Steven's. "You've lost your mind." He closed his eyes and after a few tense moments, whispered, "I've lost *my* mind."

"Yes!" With a fist pump, Dalton smiled so big it hurt his blasted face. Not only was he going to get a chance to make a better impression on Blaise, he now had the perfect excuse to be around him.

"I'm going to regret this, aren't I?" Raleigh asked.

"Of course not," Dalton and Steven answered at the same time. Dalton tried like hell to suppress his smile but failed miserably.

Raleigh shook his head, peered up at the ceiling, and mumbled something that sounded suspiciously like "Galaxy, help me." Finally he addressed Dalton with his face a mask of seriousness and pointed at him. "It's only for two weeks. Until I find a replacement *or* you have to report for duty. And… Redding has to agree." To Steven he said, "If this backfires, you are in as much trouble as he is."

Once again Dalton and Steven answered together, "Yes, sir," but Dalton added a smart salute.

Two weeks was just enough time for a seduction.

Chapter Three

After rumors of a row, a certain viscount was seen in Summerset Square with hay in his hair. Apparently he's out of the dog house and in the stables with his consort now.

—From *Pruluce Weekly*, the Beau Monde Happenings column

BLAISE LIFTED his hand to knock, but before his fist made contact, the castle door opened and Thomas, the underbutler, smiled at him.

It wasn't a big smile. Actually, it wasn't a smile at all—Thomas had never been demonstrative, but if he were the sort to show emotion, he would've smiled in greeting. Blaise was certain of it. He'd always gotten the impression the underbutler liked him.

Thomas inclined his head. "Good morning, Lord Redding."

"Good morning to you, Thomas."

"You're late, my lord." From any other underbutler in Classige, it would've been an admonishment, but Thomas was not the reprimanding type any more than he was the smiling type.

Still, Blaise couldn't help the heat that snaked up his cheeks. He'd arrived at the House of Lords at nine o'clock on the dot, only ten minutes late, to be told about an emergency meeting at the castle. If he hadn't had to buy a new cravat, he'd have been early getting to work and therefore he'd have made it to the castle on time. If he ever saw Ashbourne again, he would take him to task over his thievery. *Assuming you can actually get over this cow-eyed infatuation long enough to force syllables out of your mouth.*

"The meeting has started, but I'll take you there posthaste." Thomas took his coat, hat, and gloves, then handed them over to a footman. Leaning in close, he whispered, "Shall we go through the servants' entrance so that we might sneak in?"

Proof positive Thomas liked him. Blaise nodded and let the older man lead him through a door to the right of the entrance. With any luck, Thomas's plan would work. Father would know he was late, of course, but perhaps no one else would. Regardless, hopefully after he told Father that he'd found Betty Jenkins, all would be forgiven… *if* he could keep Bannon's latest incident quiet.

"Here it is, my lord, the conference room," Thomas whispered. "You should be able to slip in. When I took Lord Foxglove up, there were still several seats available in the back."

As Thomas stopped at a green baize door, Blaise gave his new cravat one last adjustment and tried not to blanch at the muffled voices leaking in from the other side. The meeting was in full swing, but that was probably a good thing if it meant no one would pay attention to him, right? Only one way to find out.

Cracking the door open, Blaise peeked inside.

Perhaps Thomas didn't like him as well as he thought. The crowd was not big, nor was the space. It was essentially a drawing room complete with a conversational furniture grouping with the castle's typical dark wood and jewel-toned colors, which made it cozy and intimate. No way could he sneak in. *Blast it all*, he did not want his father to be disappointed in him. He hated that feeling of despair when his father regarded him with a blank face and said nothing. It reminded him of the stuttering five-year-old he'd been, and he never wanted to go back to that feeling of isolation and worthlessness.

Maybe he should leave and pretend ignorance? He waited a few moments, trying that resolution on for size, but his sense of responsibility wanted nothing to do with it. *Deuced conscience.*

Blaise searched the room and found an empty chair at the back, right next to the Viscount Grantham. *Thank galaxy.* Griffin Wildsmith was one of his dearest friends. *This might just work out.*

The man speaking was Lord Pendleton, which could also work to Blaise's advantage. Pendleton was loud and obnoxious on his worst days, and loud and boisterous on his good ones. Apparently it was a good day, because he seemed especially animated, if his quick pace gave any indication. Now, if Blaise could only get Griff's attention….

"Psst…." He flapped his free hand to make himself more visible.

Griff's brow creased, and he cocked his head, but he didn't turn.

Gesticulating faster, Blaise bounced up and down as if that would somehow help, and apparently it did, because Griff finally turned and his lips curled up into a grin.

Guh, I probably look like a wet goose. Returning his friend's smile, Blaise waved and pointed to the chair.

Nodding, Griff grabbed it and pulled it closer to him. Thankfully the room was carpeted and the sliding made no sound. Once the chair rested about a foot away, Griff inched his way into the other seat and mouthed, "Where have you been?"

"Long story," Blaise mouthed back.

Turning his attention to the front, Griff motioned with his hand down by his leg for Blaise to come on.

He started forward, but Griff jerked his palm up in the universal stop sign.

Blaise rocked forward a little, making the door squeak, but he managed to halt. When his father didn't announce that he should come out, like he half feared, he relaxed.

Pendleton stopped talking, and someone laughed.

After a few moments, Griff nodded at him. *Coast is clear.*

Thanks. He squeezed through the barely opened door and closed it behind him without a sound. He slipped into the seat as Pendleton finished his discourse and Foxglove took up where Pendleton had left off. He was another long-winded… well, windbag.

Leaning toward him, Griff put his hand to the side of his mouth and whispered, "Prissy is up to something. He keeps glancing back here, and he asked about you before the meeting."

"Me?" Prissy was Blaise's fellow intern, but they were *not* friends. Sir Percy Edmonstone was the biggest coxcomb in the ton.

Following Griff's gaze to Prissy, Blaise was startled to see the blond man staring back at him; or did he stare at Griff? Prissy despised Griff and took every opportunity to comment on Griff's weight. Since Griff was only a stone overweight, Blaise prophesied the real reason to be jealousy because at twenty-five, Griff was new to the House of Lords and the youngest committee member.

Not knowing what else to do, Blaise inclined his head to Prissy in greeting and… caught the gaze of a pair of familiar green eyes. *Star dust!* His father sat beside Prissy.

Blaise's insides roiled. He felt rather like a bug on a microscanner. He rolled around an excuse in his head, but the words got all jumbled just as they always did when he was called on the carpet. Taking a deep breath, he let it out in increments to stave off his initial panic. It was a trick his governess had taught him, and it had been a lifesaver over the years. He had not meant to tell his good news now, but so be it. He opened his mouth to speak, but Father waved his hand about and shook his head. The heat in his eyes dissipated, and the easygoing man Blaise knew so well returned.

Eversleigh turned back to the front and stood, looking around the room. "I called this meeting because Sir Percy has some remarkable news." The duke beamed at Prissy.

Prissy met Blaise's gaze, and the left side of his lip curled into a snarl. Lifting his chin ever so slightly, he finally reciprocated Blaise's greeting, but it wasn't at all friendly.

Griff was right, Prissy was definitely up to something.

"On my way to the haberdashery today, I saw Betty Jenkins."

Blaise could not have heard that correctly. *Bollocks!* How was he going to explain his tardiness to his father now? It had taken him weeks to locate just the lady's maid. *He* was the one who had stumbled upon Betty.

Prissy finding her couldn't be happenstance. He was too much of a dandy to shop at Hart and Sons. He'd once commented at a soiree that he had his cravats designed special for him. Who had their cravats custom-made? It was a long piece of cloth.

"That arsehat." His legs buckled under him, and if not for Griff pushing him backward into his chair, he'd have planted his bottom on the carpeted floor.

"Er, are you all right?" Griff whispered.

"I… yes. I'm fine. Just stunned by Prissy's news." Blaise wanted to tell his friend, but the fear of censure held him back. If he said anything now, he'd seem as though he were trying to one-up Prissy.

"Here. Take this. You look like you need it." Griff nudged his arm.

Shaking his head to clear it, Blaise peered down and noticed the glass of water. "Thank you." He gulped down the entire glass and wished it had been something stronger. He'd imbibed once when he was fourteen and hadn't cared for the out-of-control feeling that came with being foxed, but now? He would welcome it. At least then everything would be topsy-turvy for a reason.

Griff took the empty glass back and set it on the table next to him.

The group quieted down and got to business trying to formulate a plan to relocate Betty.

"Perhaps we should question the Jenkinses' former servants," Prissy said.

That son of a.... Blaise stopped. He was too much of a gentleman to finish the thought.

Lords Tetterson and Cromley, who'd thought the suggestion silly a couple of weeks ago, pronounced it to be a "capital idea."

An image of bottle-green wool and a merlot-colored hat flitted across Blaise's mind, along with the knowledge that Prissy adored bright colors.

That son of a whoremonger. Nope, he wasn't too much of a gentleman after all.

THE RIDE back to the parliament building had gone a long way in restoring Blaise's mood, and stepping into the councilman's corridor gave him solace. The scent of old books, cigar smoke, and dust was like coming home. It was even more satisfying than the daydream he'd had in the lift about getting even with Prissy. He'd loved this place and wanted to be a part of it since the first time his father brought him here when Blaise was six years old. It had always stood for integrity and tradition to him, and even now it reminded him of what was important. He'd wanted a career in politics for as long as he remembered, and he did not want to be the sort of politician who ruined everyone who crossed him. The sort Prissy was well on his way to being.

"Good afternoon, Lord Redding." Hobbs, his father's secretary, dipped his head in greeting, but did not glance up from whatever he sorted behind the tall mahogany counter that acted as a reception desk. How the man seemed to know who was who without looking at them was one of life's greatest mysteries, or at least the Councilman's Committee's.

"Good afternoon to you too, Hobbs." Blaise tried to keep his head down as he made his way to his office. Hobbs always had some sort of busywork to be done, and more often than not he enlisted Blaise's help to do it. Normally, Blaise didn't mind, but today he just wanted the quiet confines of his dark office with its walls of books. He still had plenty of work to do on his father's speech for the council meeting.

"My lord, His Grace asked me to give you these."

Oh blast. He'd been inches from a clean getaway. Blaise gazed longingly at the red patterned carpet in front of him and considered playing deaf. Why was the door open?

Hobbs hefted a stack of journals from his desk and dumped them at Blaise, giving him no choice but to take them.

Blaise dipped under the weight. There must be ten four-inch-thick spiral-bound journals on the stack. How had Hobbs even lifted these with his bony arms? He'd started as secretary when Blaise's grandfather was councilman and must be close to eighty now. "Hobbs, what is all of this?"

The old man raised his bushy gray brows and looked at him as though the answer should be obvious. "The IN treaties, of course."

Right. His father had asked him to research the new pacts the IN had signed since the last council meeting. It was a formality, really, to make sure the councilman was up-to-date on the goings on and to ensure no new contracts interfered with the Regelence accord. Normally it was an easy job that didn't take more than a day to complete. "These are the treaties?" The last council meeting had only been last year.

"Yes, my lord. I also included unsigned treaties."

"Unsigned?" The top notebook started to slide, and Blaise leaned to the left to center it again.

"Pacts the IN proposed but planets have turned down." Hobbs nodded, then frowned.

"Ah." The journals started teetering the other way, but before Blaise could shift his weight, Hobbs righted them.

"Come to think of it, my lord, that is odd. In all my time as a councilman's secretary, I've never known the IN to be the one proposing alliances. Planets usually come to the IN, not the other way around."

"Rest assured, Hobbs, I will check into it." He dipped his head at the older man and headed toward his office again, lest the man find more work for him.

Hobbs rushed past him and stopped in front of Blaise's door. "I forgot to tell you that you have company." The way he said *company* sounded more like a question, as if he weren't sure of the caliber of the person involved. "Your, uh, guard is here."

His guard? Oh, yes. King-Consort Raleigh had mentioned that new security measures were being implemented for Father and some of the committee. That explained why his office was open, but.... "Hobbs, I'm merely an intern."

"But you are your father's son and our future councilman." The old man beamed at him, and Blaise smiled despite the strain on his arms. Galaxy, he hoped Hobbs was correct. The council member's job had gone to the Dukes of Eversleigh and their heirs for the last four generations, and Blaise refused to be the one to break that record. Hopefully one day, when Father retired, he'd be appointed councilman, but first he had to be appointed to the committee. Right now there was only one spot open and two interns. Unfortunately, Prissy was popular among some of the committee, and after today….

Hobbs stepped out of the way, and all thoughts of Prissy fled.

Ashbourne sat in Blaise's chair with his feet propped on the desk, his head tipped back, and his eyes closed. *What is he doing here?* He had changed out of the IN uniform and now sported a more genteel ensemble of buckskin breeches, brown-topped black riding boots, and a midnight-blue morning coat that simply must have padding in it, because no one that narrow of hip had such masculine, wide shoulders. His windblown blond hair had been tamed, but his lazy slouch kept him from seeming completely civilized. Honestly, it was rather ridiculous how handsome he was, even in repose. He looked like the start to one of those messy dreams that proper gentlemen pretended didn't happen.

Blaise gave a mental groan at the improper thought, and once again the urge to run away struck him. His stomach did that swirling thing again. *Please don't let me be glowing. Lud!* Now Bannon and Louisa had him self-conscious about *glowing*. He opened his mouth to call out a greeting, but the top book decided to make a break for it again.

The whole pile slipped from Blaise's fingers and hit the carpet with a muted thud.

Ashbourne blinked his eyelids open and sat up like a cat awakened from basking in the sunshine. He glanced at Blaise and then the pile on the floor, and a slow smile curved his lips as if he realized the effect he had on Blaise.

Ugh! Was he to be forever embarrassing himself in front of this man? Heat rushed to his face, and his rather large office seemed to close in on him.

"I'm so sorry, my lord." Hobbs bent to pick up the books, but his knees protested rather loudly.

Blaise came to his senses in time to catch the old man under the arm before he made it all the way to the ground. "Nonsense, Hobbs. It was my fault. I'll pick them up."

The old man hesitated, but Blaise did not let go of his arm. He might have made a laughingstock of himself, and he certainly wasn't anticipating being left alone with Ashbourne, but his conscience would not allow him to let an elderly man pick up his mess.

With great reluctance, Hobbs nodded his agreement and went back to his desk. He looked at the door but didn't even try to close it. Which was a good thing, since Blaise was on the threshold. "No one has thought to send for Larkinson, so I'll act as chaperone, my lord."

"Er, thank you, Hobbs." At least one of them was thinking straight.

Blaise squatted down and began stacking manuals to buy himself some time because he had no idea what to say to Ashbourne. *Hello* didn't seem quite right, but neither did *you stole my cravat*, and *kiss me* was completely out of the question. Sadly, it was not out of his mind. And speaking of minds… he was surely losing his.

"Hello, sweetheart."

Ack! A rather unmasculine squeak erupted from Blaise, and he fell flat on his bottom. He glanced up and found Ashbourne kneeling a foot from him. Damnation, the man moved silently. It must be the military training. *Thank galaxy*, he was on Regelence's side.

A deep masculine chuckle rumbled from Ashbourne's chest, sealing the deal on Blaise's mortification.

Hobbs frowned at him from his chair. "Everything all right, my lord?"

"Everything's fine. Just lost my balance."

As he turned away from Hobbs, a gloveless hand appeared in front of him. Not a gentleman's hand; it was tanned and bold, like the man. And blast Ashbourne, he was still smirking.

Blaise considered not taking the offered hand for a moment, and Ashbourne must have realized as much, because he wiggled his fingers.

With a sigh, Blaise allowed Ashbourne to pull him up, because how callous would it be if he didn't? Sometimes society and its rules of polite etiquette were a real pain in the arse. They stood nose to nose, and for several moments stared into each other's eyes. Blaise's legs refused to work, and every sense he owned went on high alert as Ashbourne's gaze roamed over his features.

The smell of musk and vanilla flirted with Blaise's nose, and the grandfather clock kept time with his pulse with its loud and deep tick. It was like being outside of time for a moment, and Blaise could not tear his attention from the heated gray stare.

He decided right then and there that Ashbourne was hazardous to his health as well as his sanity. He felt out of control and light-headed, and he didn't like it at all.

He moved back, but Ashbourne tugged him forward.

Gasping, he caught himself on the earl's shoulder, and.... *Oh my galaxy.* Hard muscle bunched beneath his hands, proving there was no padding hidden there. He squeezed just to make certain. No, definitely no padding.

A deep chuckle rumbled through the chest so close to his fingertips.

Blaise lifted his head and peered right at full pink lips. Lips so close and coming even closer. He shook his head and stepped back, this time shoving a little as he went. This man was not going to be his downfall.

Ashbourne let him go, but those lips were still turned up into a smirk.

"Don't laugh at me." Wonderful, he'd all but hissed. He was definitely out of control.

"I wouldn't dream of it, love."

Blaise gasped. "You can't say that." What could the man possibly be thinking? He was outrageous. If anyone heard him.... Blaise tilted his head backward just a bit to peek around the doorframe.

Hobbs looked up at him with his brows raised, but if he heard Ashbourne he gave no indication. "Yes, my lord?"

"Is there tea?" Blaise congratulated himself on his quick thinking.

The secretary nodded. "There is, my lord. Two cups?"

"Yes, please." To Blaise's utter mortification, his voice squeaked again. He stepped out of the threshold and into the room, but Ashbourne did not move back. Only Blaise's anger helped him hold his ground with the reprehensible man. "Are you daft? Hobbs could have heard you. My name is Redding, and you will address me as such, not...." *Meteor dust*, he couldn't even say it without blushing. "Ehrm.... Sweetheart or love."

"How about darling?"

Aurgh. "No. Not darling, sweetheart, love, or any other endearment, you scoundrel. If you are going to stay on as my guard, you will mind your manners. Or do you have any?" *Oh drat!* He snapped his mouth shut, horrified over his behavior. What had come over him? He'd never talked to anyone that way, even if they did deserve it. It was all Ashbourne's fault; the man brought out the worst in him. "I'm sorry, but—"

Ashbourne laughed. He just threw his head back and guffawed. It was not a polite discreet chuckle, but one full of mirth and from the belly.

Blaise groaned, but then something inside him snapped, and damn it all, he wanted to join in. He was tied into knots and strangely relieved by speaking his mind for once. "Perhaps we should start again." He held out his hand. "I'm Redding."

"Dalton." It was a nice name, and it fit him better than his title, though it was not at all proper for Blaise to use it, and *of course* Dalton knew that. The man was exasperating.

The earl took his hand in his much rougher one, but instead of shaking it, he bent over and pressed his lips to the back of it. "Please do not dismiss me. If you do, I'll be forced to search for a new position. Just think how horrible it would be to thrust me on some poor unsuspecting soul. They might even put me with your brother. Can you imagine how much trouble Lord Bannon and I could get into together?"

A tingle that had nothing to do with the idea of Ashbourne and his brother cavorting, streaked through Blaise, raced up his arm, down his body, and pooled in his abdomen. He jerked his hand loose. "Galaxy help us all." Something told him he would rue the day he agreed to this but…. "You can stay, but you have to behave."

"Of course."

Blaise didn't believe him for a moment.

Chapter Four

Today marks the Earl of Stratford's fifth annual preseason ball. One wonders what antics a certain troublesome young marquess and his artist friend, who happens to be the son of a duke, have in store for us this evening. They are usually more entertaining than the dancing.

—From *The Classige Examiner*

"WOULD YOU quit fidgeting?"

"My arse is asleep." Dalton stood and rubbed his backside, trying to get circulation into it. He'd been sitting on one of the firm, overstuffed red-and-gold brocade couches in front of Blaise's desk for the last hour, trying to be good, and galaxy help him, it wasn't easy. Dalton had always liked playing with fire, and Blaise was no exception. He might not be a redhead like his brother, but he had the fiery temper and passion redheads were known for in abundance.

"You should not say that word," Blaise intoned without even looking up from his book. He'd been behind his desk for as long as Dalton had been on the couch.

Didn't Blaise's arse hurt? Dalton would be more than willing to massage it for him. He started to suggest just that, but then Blaise started flipping pages back and forth. Tapping his lips with his pen, he hummed, then stuck the end in his mouth.

It was all Dalton could do not to groan and make a lewd suggestion, but he was not going to give Blaise another reason to try and get rid of him… at least not yet. He couldn't vouch for later on, though. There was something about riling the man that was damned near intoxicating.

To keep from losing his mind and to wake up his backside, Dalton walked over to the rolling ladder used to access the books on the top shelves. He put his foot on the bottom rung, gripped the sides, and shoved with his other foot. The room was octagon in shape, with high ceilings, but the rails that guided the ladder made a circle around the room, so the momentum carried him all the way to the next section of bookshelves.

"That's not a toy."

"Maybe not, but you've done this too, haven't you?" Dipping his head back, Dalton gave another push off of the carpet, expecting a firm "no," but what he got was a chuckle.

The sound was so delightful and unexpected, he reached out and stopped the ladder's progress. He'd begun to wonder if Blaise was capable of mirth; he was much too serious. Turning, Dalton leaned back on the tilted rungs, unable to help his smile. "You have." For some reason, he could not picture Blaise playing on the ladder or anything for that matter, but he wanted to. He wanted to watch this man come alive with pure joy. He wanted to share it with him.

Blaise shrugged. "Maybe."

"When?"

"When I was a child." Those green eyes appeared from under a shock of brown hair, his head cocked to the side, and a furrow appeared on his brow as though he thought the answer should be obvious.

It was the first time since their tea that Blaise made eye contact with him, and Dalton's body seemed to like the attention, because his cock twitched even as his heart melted a little in wonder. "What do you do for fun now?" He stepped off the ladder and strode forward.

"I…." Blaise shook his head and watched Dalton's every stride as though he expected him to attack. "I don't have time for recreation." The answer wasn't at all surprising.

"That is just sad. Everyone has time for fun."

"What do you do for amusement?"

"Well, I… I engaged in a water balloon fight this morning."

Clearly not expecting that answer, Blaise gaped at him. "You did?"

"Yes. It wasn't intentional, but yes, I did. Now tell me, what do you do for entertainment?"

Blaise blinked at him and didn't answer for several moments. Dalton thought he was going to ignore the question, but then he said, "I, uh… read?"

"You're reading now, and it doesn't look at all entertaining." Though Dalton did like the studious side almost as well as the passionate little dictator. There was something very appealing about a smart man. "What are you reading?"

"Treaties."

"Ugh, it's worse than I expected," he teased. "How can you contain yourself? You must be ready to jump out of your chair with the sheer joy of it."

Another chuckle. "I find it extremely interesting."

"Well, there is no hope for you, then."

Blaise growled, but not before his lips twitched. "It's really not all that hard to sit still when you can read."

Dalton laughed and leaned forward, planting his hands on Blaise's desk. "Touché." This verbal sparring was even more fun than rousing Blaise's temper. He glanced down at the documents. It looked like a lot of legalese to him. "Why is this interesting?"

"Well, it's not so much the treaties as the fact that—"

A voice in the hall caught Dalton's attention. Though Blaise kept talking, explaining, Dalton didn't hear him. His chest suddenly felt hollow. He used the reflection of the display case to the right of the door behind Blaise to see the office door—it was open due to Hobbs's insistence that Blaise needed someone to protect his virtue. Having a chaperone and a guard was a little redundant, but their society was paranoid. Probably rightly so, in Blaise's case, because who wouldn't want to seduce him?

There was no movement in the reflection, but someone spoke again. This time closer. *Fuck!* He knew that voice. So much for avoiding his parents until he shipped out.

Dalton didn't bother running to the closet or the powder room; there was no time. Instead he hurried around Blaise's desk, dropped to the ground, and patted the trouser-encased thigh next to him. "Move aside."

Blaise gasped. "Ashbourne, what are you doing?" He could not possibly sound more offended or repressed. It was actually cute in a way.

"It's Dalton," he corrected automatically. "Shh… not so loud. I need to hide, so please scoot aside."

Blaise's brow creased in a furrow, but he shoved backward. "From whom?"

"M' father." Dalton crawled in and leaned back. This would work. The front façade of the desk went all the way to the floor, and he only had to tilt his head a little to the side to fit. It certainly wasn't the worst place he'd ever hidden. At least there wasn't a jealous husband with a sword searching for him this time.

Blaise sputtered for a full ten seconds. "Are you daft? I can't possibly sit here with you under my desk." His cheeks lit up like a campfire. He was such an innocent that he practically begged to be debauched.

Dalton's heart was already galloping, but he was certain if it wasn't, that blush would have done it. "Why ever n—"

"My lord? Lord Ravensburg is here to see you," Hobbs announced.

Blaise dropped down into his chair and scooted forward so quickly, Dalton had to grab his booted foot to keep from being hit in the groin. "Show him in."

After a few tense moments of silence, Ravensburg spoke first. "Redding. How are you this fine day?"

Popping right back up out of the chair, Blaise said, "Ravensburg," sounding more than a little breathless.

There was a long pause as if Ravensburg were assessing Blaise. And he probably was because Blaise acted more than a little suspicious. "Do you have the information I asked for on the IN dog tags?"

"I do. Let me just get it for you." Blaise turned toward the back wall and grabbed a drive off the shelf by the display cabinet. When he turned back, he frowned down at Dalton.

Dalton frowned back and mouthed, "*Stop it.*"

Ravensburg was a lot of things, but foolish was not one of them. In fact, the man was a tad bit paranoid, in Dalton's opinion. It would be just like him to search the room if given cause.

Stepping up close to the desk, Blaise gave Dalton a perfect view of his knees.

A rustle came from above, and Ravensburg said, "Thank you."

"You are welcome."

Muffled footsteps grew distant, then stopped altogether.

Blaise sat back down in his chair and rolled back—presumably to peer down at Dalton—but Ravensburg interrupted.

"Redding?"

Go away, Dalton urged silently. He was starting to get a crick in his neck.

Blaise stopped rolling and stood again. "Yes?"

"Good job."

There was no sound for a few seconds, but Dalton imagined Blaise shrugging and blushing at the praise, though his knees gave no indication of such. "To what do you refer?"

"I know you found her."

Who?

"What?" Blaise gasped. "I—"

"*Mr.* Edmonstone is not smart enough to locate his own boots whilst wearing them." Ravensburg's tone was biting, and he'd purposely called Percy *mister* instead of *sir*.

Dalton hated agreeing with Ravensburg on anything, but he'd had problems with Percy before. Namely because of the jackanapes's big mouth. He was certain it was Percy who'd gone to Lawson's consort the night Dalton had had to sneak out the viscount's window.

"I know you found Betty Jenkins," Ravensburg said. "You shouldn't let him take credit for your achievements. I know he's done so before as well."

Betty Jenkins had been found? That must be what the meeting at the castle had been about. Dalton had not waited around on the off chance his father attended, and it seemed his assumption had been correct. He'd borrowed his cousin Rexley's clothes after cleaning up the last of the balloon massacre and made his way here to wait for Blaise.

"I… I…." Blaise cleared his throat.

"Make certain no one else has anything on you. I talked to Sir Percy after the meeting, and he mentioned seeing you at the haberdashery, and…. How well do you know my son?" Ravensburg asked, voice louder.

Damnation! Was his own father warning Blaise away from him? Dalton's hands tightened into fists, and damned if his temperature didn't spike up.

"I don't. I…." Blaise's voice wavered, illustrating his lie.

Again there was a brief silence. "Redding, take this for what it's worth, but stay away from him. It pains me to say, but being associated with him could ruin your reputation."

Dalton fumed. He didn't even realize he'd started to crawl out from under the desk until Blaise's boot landed on his calf and pressed down. Hard.

"I assure you, my reputation is always foremost in my mind."

"Good, good. It would never do for a certain intern to cast doubts on our future councilman."

Pulling his leg back under the desk, Dalton marveled at the soft encouraging sound of his father's voice. Had he ever heard that particular tone? His father obviously respected Blaise. Then something else occurred to Dalton. Percy Edmonstone had seen them at the haberdashery, and damn it all, that was a second thing he agreed with his father on. He could not let anyone use his reputation against Blaise, because, galaxy help them, if Percy got the empty committee job instead of Blaise…. Percy would likely sell the entire planet out to the IN, and that was something Dalton could never allow.

"I HAVE a surprise for you."

That sounded ominous. Blaise pushed back from his desk and rubbed his eyes. He had been studying treaties for the last hour and a half and wasn't sure he wanted any more surprises. Especially Ashbourne surprises. The earl was maddening, confusing, and entirely too charming for Blaise's peace of mind. It was just his luck the first intense physical attraction he'd ever had involved a man completely unsuitable. "It is not at all proper for you to be bringing me gifts."

Ashbourne, who had left to run an "errand"—with strict directions that Blaise not leave the office—now lounged in the doorway with a smile on his face so brilliant it should be a crime. It was quite easy to see why he had the reputation he did, and Blaise was even more leery of that reputation after talking to Ravensburg. Galaxy, the thought of Ashbourne hiding under his desk with his face so close to Blaise's… er, unmentionable anatomy still had the power to make him blush. And who hid from their own parents? Blaise should have told Ravensburg and wasn't certain why he hadn't. He'd like to think it was because having a man under his desk while he sat at it would look suspect, but that wasn't the only reason.

Ignoring Blaise's reprimand, Ashbourne held up a thumbnail-sized drive.

"What is that?"

The smile got even wider as he pushed away from the doorframe and closed the door behind him.

It swung back open so quickly, Ashbourne had to jump aside to keep from being hit in the bottom.

Sticking his head inside the room, Hobbs glowered. His gaze landed on Blaise, and he asked, "Is everything all right, my lord?"

Blaise tried to stop his grin but couldn't. Just like his secretary duties, Hobbs took his job as chaperone quite seriously. "Everything is fine."

The old man bobbed his head, but instead of leaving right away, he eyed Ashbourne some more.

Grinning, Ashbourne rolled his eyes and held up his hands. "Sorry, Hobbs. I forgot."

When Hobbs finally left, pushing the door wide-open, Ashbourne came all the way to the opposite side of Blaise's desk and glanced back over his shoulder.

Something told Blaise he wasn't going to like this. Whatever *this* was.

Setting the small black square on the open pages of the book featuring IN treaties with planets in the Calluna system, Ashbourne put both hands on the desk across from Blaise and whispered, "This is a way to put a certain Mr. Edmonstone in his place."

Star dust. "What exactly is on the disk?"

Ashbourne's grin grew downright devilish. "Blackmail material. Sir Percy in flagrante delicto. Or more precisely, Sir Percy with his lips wrapped around—"

"Stop!" Heat flared up Blaise's cheeks so quickly he grew light-headed. He pushed farther from his desk and away from the disk. Good galaxy, what could Ashbourne be thinking? Percy was underage and would be ruined. Which, on second thought.... *No!* He wanted nothing to do with it. He waved his hand toward the desk. "Take it away."

That lovely blond brow arched. "By telling my father he saw both of us at the haberdashery, Edmonstone sent you a veiled threat."

He had, hadn't he? Blaise sighed. Maybe he should keep it and let Prissy know that he had it? He didn't have to give it to anyone. *Dust*, he couldn't believe he was even considering it. If he were somehow caught with it, he would be just as ruined as Prissy. He'd have no career, and any hopes for a future marriage would be over. The scandal would be so big he'd even kill *Bannon's* hopes for a future.

Blaise sat back down in his chair and pressed a hand to his forehead and spun his chair around backward to collect himself. He caught Ashbourne's reflection in the glass of the display case behind his desk, which did nothing to help him "collect" himself. "How did you even get this?"

"I got it from a friend of mine who recorded it in secret. The man has a whole collection of such vids." Staring at the back of Blaise's head,

Ashbourne shrugged, then met Blaise's gaze in the reflection. "In case he should ever need the leverage."

Unnerved at having been caught staring, Blaise turned back around. "Friend?"

"Not like you're thinking, though not that the fellow hasn't offered. But I know about his little insurance policies and have no desire to add my name to his list."

Strangely, Blaise was glad. Which made no sense at all, because Ashbourne was nothing to him. Well, nothing except a guard and not a very good one at that. He'd left Blaise alone for two whole hours. *But he left you alone to get this... to help you. Even if it's wrong, it is kind of sweet. Lud! Listen to yourself....*

Blaise shook his head to clear it. He couldn't even believe he participated in this conversation. He would never consider engaging in such talk with any of his friends.

But then again, none of his friends were like Ashbourne.

"Let's just say, I helped him out once and he owed me. It's free and clear with no strings attached." Ashbourne propped his hip on Blaise's desk. It was a nice hip, and goodness weren't his trousers tight? And his legs were very muscled, that must—

Guh! Ashbourne had turned him into a wanton. Blaise jerked his attention upward. This job was important to him. So important that he couldn't do anything to jeopardize it, including getting rid of the competition. Ravensburg's warning rang in his head like a death knell. He couldn't afford to let Ashbourne get to him. The man had brought him pornography, for crying out loud. How disastrous did one's reputation have to be to even know where to get a sex tape?

Pushing the disk forward with his fingertips, he girded his loins and said, "Take it back. I can't possibly use it. And please don't bring me anything else. We are *not* friends. You are my guard. That is all." There, he'd said it.

The expression on Ashbourne's face almost had Blaise recanting his words. His face froze, like his emotions closed up. He showed no hurt, no surprise, no nothing. He could have been a statue. A beautiful statue.

Finally he pushed the disk back at Blaise, ending his stillness. "Keep it."

"Are you ready? Oh, 'ello there, Ashbourne."

Ashbourne and Blaise both jumped at the sound of Bannon's voice.

Devil take it, he'd forgotten about the late lunch with his brother. They were supposed to meet their parents in the Parliament cafeteria downstairs after his father got out of his current meeting. He peeked up at the clock on the wall. *2:20 p.m.* "It's not quite time."

He returned his attention to the innocuous black square on his desk and something akin to horror clogged his throat. *Bloody hell!* If his brother found out about this.... Well, Bannon would encourage him to use it; he hated Percy about as much as Blaise did. Blaise brushed the disk under the edge of the book on his desk.

Ashbourne caught his gaze, still looking as though he was made of stone. Then he glanced up and a smile returned. Only it wasn't directed at Blaise. "'Ello, Bannon. Did you get the hat?"

"Hat?" Blaise asked.

"Oh yes! Thank you!" Bannon sounded odd, and his cheeks flushed. Was he flirting? Surely not.

"What hat?" Blaise asked again.

Both Bannon and Ashbourne stared at him as though he were daft, and then Ashbourne answered. "*The* hat. You know. The hat he risked life and limb for."

Blaise groaned. "And destroyed the haberdashery for. You mean *that* hat?"

Bannon rolled his eyes. "Thanks for reminding him, Ashbourne."

Ashbourne chuckled. "Call me Dalton."

It was on the tip of Blaise's tongue to inform them both that that would not be proper, but then Bannon beamed and said, "Okay, Dalton."

Again Blaise groaned. Why did he even try?

While Bannon and Ashbourne talked about Bannon's friend and Ashbourne's cousin, Aiden, it occurred to Blaise that they had an easy camaraderie like they'd been friends forever. It irritated Blaise, which irritated him even more because he refused to be jealous of his own brother.

Ignoring them both, Blaise picked up the book, making sure to get the disk as well. He discreetly pocketed it and flipped back through the book on his desk, searching for the name of the planet he'd found earlier.

Ah, there it is. Planet Skye. The planet not only refused the IN's invitation to join, they were the planet the IN asked again after the first refusal. That had to be significant somehow.

There was a rattling sound.

"Blast. It's locked," Bannon said.

More rattling.

"Bloody hell! Blaise, do you know the combination to this?"

Sighing, Blaise stopped reading and peeked over his shoulder at his brother.

Bannon stood in front of the display case that housed their father's knickknacks and assorted things of interest he'd gotten in his duties as Regelence's top diplomat. "You do not need to open the display case."

"I need to see something. I have a brilliant idea." Bannon tugged on the case's door again.

"No." Blaise attempted to return to his book.

Ashbourne, who now lounged on one of the sofas, caught his attention. "Why can't he look at something in the case? You heard him. He has a great idea."

Bannon nodded. "It's a really great idea. You know how I am when my muse is bothering me. You might as well give in…." He put his hand up to his ear. "What's that, Timothy? You want me to sing a song for Blaise?" With that he proceeded to sing. "Oh, Redding is the bestest brother in the whole wide world, whole wide world, whole wide world. He wants us to paint paint paint, paint paint paint…."

Ashbourne burst into laughter so boisterous it made Blaise's stomach flutter, but when he glanced up and caught Blaise watching him, the sound froze in his throat.

Ugh! Blaise dragged his attention away from the earl and back to his brother. "This is emotional blackmail."

"More like psychological warfare… fare fare fare," Bannon sang. "Fare fare fare…."

"Okay, okay. Stop already." What could it hurt? It wasn't as if Bannon would steal their father's things. Besides, Bannon would continue to sing until he got what he wanted, and singing did *not* qualify as one of his many artistic abilities. He gave Bannon the code and said, "Make sure you lock it after you are done."

"Thank you."

"Welcome."

Bannon picked up their father's prized possession: a nineteenth century Terran snuffbox that once belonged to the King of England. Their sire had given it to their father on the day they were married. Bannon studied the pastoral scene on the outside of the lid. It had faded, and the paint was chipped off in places, but the flaws made the pretty little box all the more unique.

"It's time to go downstairs," Ashbourne said.

Bannon replaced the box in the case, then turned toward the door, leaving the case wide-open. "It's a great idea, isn't it?"

What idea? Blaise glanced at his brother and realized Bannon wasn't talking to him. He sighed, and got up from his desk, and went to the case Bannon had, of course, forgotten to lock. He closed it as Bannon's and Ashbourne's voices filtered back to him from the corridor. Something about the pastoral scene on the top of the lid.

Blaise snorted. At least Bannon hadn't shown Ashbourne the inside of the lid. The box had a hidden compartment with an erotic painting of a man and a woman engaged in sexual congress. Blaise had always found the erotic art both fascinating and a little disturbing. Staring at the small artifact, he started to press the lock on the case but stopped.

The secret compartment was so well hidden that it was indeed undetectable. And speaking of erotic… things.

Blaise opened the case back up and pulled out the box. He unlatched the concealed section. Only a thin space rested between the lid and the hidden chamber…. Would it even fit? He pulled the disk from his pocket, put it inside, and closed the lid. It snapped closed, and Blaise gave a sigh of relief. At least that would keep the disk safe until he figured out how to get rid of it. He couldn't just throw it away. Anyone could stumble across it. *Uh-huh, sure*, his conscience mocked.

"Blaise, are you coming?" Bannon yelled from the outer office.

"Yes." He shut the case and hurried out of the office. He would throw that thing away as soon as he got the chance.

Chapter Five

While the ton is dancing around 'nother booorrring ball, come enjoy y'self at the Frost Fair. Enjoy a hot drink, munch on some roasted chestnuts, and take a gander at the artistic accomplishments in ice.

—From *The Regelence Times*, the advertisements section

"Heee-yaaaah!"

What in the bloody hell? Raleigh spun around.

A flash of rainbows splashed about the foyer as light from the stained-glass window above the front door hit metal. It was colorful and bright enough to momentarily blind him. After a split second, he realized it was a sword slashing toward his side.

The breath caught in his throat, and everything seemed to slow. There was no time to draw his own sword, which was tucked away in the scabbard at his hip. Instinct and training took over. He made a calculated risk and rushed forward into the swinging blade and into his attacker to remove the leverage and the advantage. The closer in he was, the less likely he was to get cut, especially if he was in his attacker's face. He gripped the hilt with one hand and wrapped the other around the smooth pale throat with just enough clarity left to realize who he held and not to squeeze the windpipe. With a sigh, Raleigh stepped back and snatched the sword away.

"Whoa." Jeremy's aquamarine eyes widened. His mouth dropped open, then curled into a grin. "Oh my God! That was awesome!" He flipped his head and blew upward, trying to dislodge the platinum curls off his forehead. "You have got to teach me that."

Raleigh frowned. The kid was going to be the death of him. All these years, he'd thought it would be his boys, but now he was certain it'd be Jeremy. He definitely lived up to the nickname Trouble; Nate had hit that nail on the head. Taking a deep breath and trying to get his adrenaline somewhere back in the normal range, Raleigh turned and headed toward the ballroom, where they were supposed to meet. "Why aren't you in the ballroom already?"

"Why aren't you?" Jeremy skipped along beside him, looking like an angelic sprite rather than someone who'd just tried to eviscerate him. "You know I thought I had you that time."

"I thought you did too." Raleigh's lip quirked up on the side. It had become a game between them since Raleigh had started training him. It was fun, and it kept him on his toes, as long as the kid didn't pull a fragger on him. Truth was, Jeremy was easy to be around. A lot like his sire had been. Oh, he wasn't anything like Patrick in temperament, or looks, for that matter. He was so much a combination of his parents that it was hard to see the similarities sometimes, but Raleigh enjoyed the kid's company just as he'd always enjoyed Patrick's. Patrick had been more like a brother to him than his own, and Raleigh missed him.

That little cherub face turned up toward him as Jeremy matched Raleigh's steps. "So what were you thinking about? You were slower than usual."

Raleigh raised a brow at that. He'd reacted pretty damned fast, if he said so himself. "Dalton."

Wrinkling his nose up, Jeremy shook his head, making his curls bounce around. "I'm impressed. He's only been here a few hours, and he's already in trouble?"

"What? No, he's not in trouble. I just don't like the idea of him shipping out again. I was looking forward to having him home." They reached the ballroom, and Raleigh extended his arm, indicating Jeremy should go before him.

Turning to face him, Jeremy started walking backward through the door and held his hand out for his weapon. "You're commander in chief over the Regelence Navy, right? So, couldn't you just have him stationed here in Classige?"

"No, it doesn't work that way." Raleigh handed him his rapier.

"Why not?"

"Well, because it just doesn't. I suppose I could suggest that he stay here in Pruluce, but he's RSR, and RSR is now stationed in Devonshire."

"Since when?"

"Since two years ago."

"Oh." Jeremy seemed to think about it for a moment, then said, "So just have the Navy move the RSRs back to Classige."

Sighing, Raleigh removed his own sword from the scabbard and took a couple of steps forward. If only it were that easy. Why did everyone think since he was king-consort he could just ignore the rules? This wasn't a dictatorship. "Again, it doesn't work that way. Now get your sword up."

"Okay, so what if you make his being Redding's guard a permanent thing? You can give him a new duty instead of doing whatever it is the RSR does. You can give him a new job description to be a guard. Wentworth and Knighton were RSR, and they're now guards."

"His being Redding's guard is a temporary thing. His specialty is recon, and there won't be a lot of call for that as a guard." With a shake of his head, Raleigh gave up trying to solve the issue for now and gave Jeremy's sword a pointed look.

Jeremy finally raised his weapon. They parried back and forth twice, and then Jeremy stopped. "You could train Dalton to be an assassin like you're training me. He even has the perfect nickname. Lord Demon is a great assassin name."

"I am *not* training you to be an assassin. I'm giving you the training your parents would give you if they were alive. The training and education you should've had from the beginning." Where did the kid come up with these ideas?

"Of course you are. I'm like your squire or something." Jeremy dropped his sword, resting the tip on the wood floor. He twirled it around as if he had lost interest in sparring.

"I am not, and no, you aren't. Don't scratch the floor."

Jeremy scoffed and lifted his blade, then immediately dropped it again. "I wish I had a cool name like Demon. Maybe Tarren and I can change nicknames. Terror sounds more like an assassin name than Trouble."

Raleigh's lips twitched at the sudden change of subject. "Focus, Jeremy."

"Whaaat? I'm just saying…."

"You don't need a new nickname because you are not going to be an assassin." Because galaxy help Regelence if that ever happened. "Can we get on with today's lesson?"

"Yeah, I guess." He didn't immediately move, though. Instead he scrunched up his face a little. "Nate still didn't take a guard with him to the base today. Maybe if you train me to be an assassin, I can join the IN and protect Nate?"

"What? Nate didn't take his guard?" Raleigh had been after his son-in-law for months now to take a guard with him. Nate, being the stubborn arse that he was, refused, saying it made him look weak. *Galaxy save me from stubborn men.* And yes, he knew that was ironic since he was more stubborn than any of them.

"He says he can't take a guard because the IN will know he's onto them." Jeremy shrugged, then snorted. "You know, he has a point."

"He does not have a point. He is now part of the royal family. The IN will attribute a guard to that." Raleigh hoped, but honestly he didn't care. The IN had already killed one of their admirals. If they found out Nate knew what they were doing and was working to stop them, they'd have no qualms about murdering him too.

"Tell him that."

"I have," Raleigh growled. Repeatedly. Perhaps he could have Sebastian follow Nate to the base every morning unnoticed?

They fenced back and forth for several moments while Raleigh pondered his problems. He was going to have to have another talk with Nate. *Or.... What if...?* Maybe Dalton would consider staying in the IN? It wasn't recon or special forces, but—

"Okay, you can't blame *me* for stopping this time."

Raleigh frowned and realized it was he who had stopped.

Jeremy stood opposite him, twirling his sword like a baton this time. "You're gonna do it, aren't you?"

"Do what?"

"Train me to be an assassin." His smile was a thing of beauty, lighting up his entire face.

Today's lesson was going to be a really long one.

Pryor House, the Earl of Stratford's residence in Classige, Pruluce

BLAISE STARED at his list of dance partners for the night and frowned. *The things one must do for a career in politics.* He'd spent most of the day going over treaties, but he wasn't done with work yet. He had two open sets, and he needed to play nice with Councilman's Committee members and mingle. Lord Oglesby was one of the members who seemed partial to Prissy. Playing nice with him could help Blaise's campaign to win the committee position, but was it worth an entire dance? The man had two left feet.

"I say, Redding, move aside. You've been staring at your dance list for long enough. Let someone else in." Someone shoved Blaise from behind, making his finger slide on the screen, and his partner list disappeared.

Heat infused the back of his neck, and he clenched his teeth together. He knew that voice. Whirling around with a quip on the tip of his tongue about manners and waiting one's turn, he swallowed it back when he saw the queue behind him.

Several of his peers stood with their dance cards in hand, waiting to use the card reader.

Perhaps he'd been standing here longer than he'd thought, but he did not deserve to be manhandled. He directed his glare at the instigator—Percy Edmonstone.

Prissy had his arms crossed and his lips pursed in annoyance. The pompous little cad even tapped his bejeweled foot. Who wore gemstone-encrusted buckles on their shoes? And ruffles. Lots of ruffles. The dandy's scalloped cuffs hung out a good three inches beneath his evening jacket. Galaxy help them all if it caught on and became a trend.

"What? Nothing to say as usual, Redding?"

Blaise gnashed his teeth together and heat raced farther up the back of his neck. He yearned to give the man the set-down he deserved. He should get in the family lift and go right to his office and retrieve the disk. Galaxy, he was tempted.

"Ah, Redding, there you are." Griff hooked his arm under Blaise's elbow.

Where had he come from? Not that Blaise particularly cared; he was just glad Griff was here.

"Sod off, Edmonstone." Griff lifted his nose in the air and marched right past the dandy as though he hadn't a care in the world.

Prissy puffed up like a peacock and sniffed, but his eyes narrowed on Blaise rather than Griff.

When they were out of earshot, Blaise smiled at Griff. "I should thank you for the rescue and tell you that it was not polite to tell him to sod off. There is sure to be talk tomorrow."

Griff shrugged. "Unlike you, I am not trying to become the next IN councilman. Therefore, I do not have to mind my reputation as closely."

"Well, there is a thought." Blaise rolled his eyes. "Every time someone angers me, I shall just have you put them in their place."

"And it was a spectacular way to put him in his place, eh wot?" Griff's brown eyes practically disappeared with his sunny smile. "Though I have to say, that wasn't at all rude." Griff tapped his bottom lip with a finger. "Rude would have been saying 'Sod off, *Prissy*.'"

Blaise groaned but ended up chuckling. Eventually the nickname they'd given Percy was going to come back to haunt them. Slapping a hand over his mouth, he muffled his laughter as they made their way around the edge of the dance floor. "Thank you, Griff. I needed that. You are a knight in shining armor, to be sure."

"You are very welcome. But I have a confession; I have an ulterior motive. Two, actually. What is between you and Ashbourne?"

The mention of Ashbourne had his spine stiffening, blast it all. He'd felt like a real heel today after telling Ashbourne they couldn't be friends. The man had delivered him to his parents for a late lunch and then met him afterward, taking his duty seriously. He'd sat in the room while Blaise poured over treaties without a single word, and then Father had dismissed him, and they'd ridden home together with Father's guard. "Nothing. We only just met. Why?"

Griff shrugged again but glanced sideways at Blaise. "I heard that he was in the haberdashery with you and Bannon this morning. He has a horrible reputation, and I'd be remiss as a friend if I didn't tell you so."

Blaise sighed. It was the second warning he'd gotten about Ashbourne today.

Griff's head swiveled around, and he stopped walking. "You like him?"

"What?" Blaise shook his head. "No. Yes, he's nice enough, but we just happened to be at the shop at the same time. We were not there together." Though when people found out Ashbourne was in charge of Blaise's security, that excuse would no longer hold water, but he'd cross that bridge later. "He's my guard. That is all."

"Your guard?" Griff clutched a hand to his chest. "When did this happen?"

"Today."

As they walked by the statue of Ares at the end of the ballroom, Lord Thistlebottom, one of his sire's cronies, raised his sherry glass and dipped his head in greeting.

Blaise inclined his chin.

"You should ask for another guard. He's the very reason Lord William Downing got banished to the country all those years ago. Don't be foolish."

That rankled. He was no fool, and he *was* keeping his distance from Ashbourne. "I am not my brother."

"Speaking of your brother…." Griff stiffened again, then hurried his pace. "Come on." He dragged Blaise in his wake, and they were starting to gain the attention of a few peers they passed.

Blaise quickened his steps and pasted a smile on his face. *Nothing to see here. Everything is normal.* "Where are we going?"

"To earn my spurs."

"What?"

"You know, a knight in shining armor? That was the other reason I came to find you. Your brother and Winstol have gone outside alone. I was about to go after them myself, but I spotted you on my way. Thought you'd want to know." He tipped his head toward the doors, now to their left.

Blaise *had* warned his brother before they'd left Thompson House this evening to stay out of trouble. "I'm going to throttle them both this time."

"I'll gladly help you," Griff said, though no heat laced his words, just assurance that he had Blaise's back.

"It appears I owe you for the second time tonight, Griff." Blaise let go of his friend's arm and glanced around at the ballroom. A group of lords had stopped in front of them, shielding them from view. No one seemed to be paying them any attention now, so Blaise used the cover to slide behind the heavy violet curtains and open the door. Thanks to his brother, he excelled at slipping out of ballrooms in the middle of soirees.

Griff followed him out and eased the door shut behind them. "Nonsense. What are friends for?" If ever a friendship had been tested, it was theirs. The times Griff risked his own reputation to help Blaise with Bannon were too numerous to count, and the man never complained. He seemed to view it as a grand adventure.

Blaise started to step off the porch, but Griff caught his arm. It wasn't at all proper for them to be outside alone, but since Bannon and Winstol were outside, they wouldn't be by themselves.

Smiling, Griff glanced out at the garden, then back at Blaise. "For the record, I didn't mean to upset you about Ashbourne, but I thought you should know." Griff shrugged and a blush rose up his cheeks. He acted nonchalantly, but his actions said otherwise.

"It's okay. It's just that I've already been cautioned, and really there is nothing to warn against. Ashbourne and I are merely acquaintances."

Nodding, Griff returned his smile and lifted his arm to indicate that Blaise should go first. "Come on. Let's find your brother."

Let's go find my brother, indeed. Then Blaise would throttle him. He headed down the stairs at a fast clip.

Now away from the shelter of the veranda, Blaise noticed it was bloody freezing. He rubbed his arms and studied their surroundings. It was a typical Regelence town house, with a compact garden in the back and a gate leading to the street behind them that ran all the way around a small park. Leaks Park, if Blaise wasn't mistaken. It consisted of a few trees, a swing set, and a picnic area. In the yard itself were several rose bushes, some topiaries, and a bench. In other words, not a lot of places to hide. A brick wall bordered the garden, but Bannon and Winstol were nowhere in sight. "Do you—"

"Shh…." Griff closed his eyes and leaned forward as if that would somehow make him hear better.

Blaise stood still too but drew the line at closing his eyes. Over the traffic and the music from inside, he could make out voices coming from their right, toward the back of the garden. Hugging his arms to his body, Blaise headed in that direction, and it didn't take long to find the missing duo.

Bannon and Winstol—currently living up to his nickname Trouble—stood behind a hideous topiary in the shape of a….

"I say, Blaise, what are your brother and Winstol doing to that duck?"

"I think that's a swan." Its neck was much too short for a swan, though. Blaise hurried toward his brother, Winstol, and the bird.

Winstol had his arm shoved into the branches up to his shoulder. That in itself was odd, but when one considered that he did this at the posterior end of the duck or swan or whatever it was, it looked… well, it didn't look very nice at all. His blond hair had tangled in the tail feathers or tail leaves or whatever they were.

Bannon was attempting to disengage Winstol's curls from the plant without much success. He finally gave up and tried to pull Winstol away by wrapping his arms around his waist and tugging.

The duck swayed back and forth, still impaled on Winstol's arm, in a rather obscene display.

"Bannon, cease and desist right this instant."

Bannon peered up at him with wide green eyes. "He's stuck."

"So I see." Blaise stopped beside them. "What are the two of you doing?"

Griff snickered.

Blaise had to admit, if it hadn't been his brother involved, it would have been amusing, but since it was his brother involved.... He narrowed his gaze.

Griff's mirth increased. "Sorry, Blaise."

Ignoring him, Blaise said, "Winstol, get your hand out of that duck's bottom."

Griff's snickers morphed into giggles. Honest to goodness giggles. It was a little on the disturbing side to realize a man of his stature could titter.

"I'd love to, if someone would help me get unstuck." Winstol sounded more than a little put out.

Blaise bent toward the topiary to get a better view of the situation, and Bannon started tugging again, making the leaves sway and swish.

"Stop it," Blaise hissed, swatting at his brother.

Somehow, one of Winstol's platinum curls had entwined itself around a tiny branch.

Grabbing the wood between his fingers, Blaise snapped it in half.

Winstol lifted his head, now adorned with a twig and two leaves, but not his arm. He yanked some more, setting off another round of swaying. "I've almost got it."

Griff began making snorting sounds, and his face now resembled a ripe apple. "Never seen a man fist a duck." Spittle flew out the corner of his lips.

He really overdid it, in Blaise's opinion. *Wait. Fist a duck?* He rolled his eyes. Fist was not a verb. "You mean punch a duck." Bending down, he peered into the bush to no avail. Whoever carved it, or whatever they did to trees to make them resemble animals, was very good at leaving leaves intact. "You've got what? Isn't this a little extreme for discarding a dance card?" Winstol and Bannon were infamous for destroying their dance cards.

When no one answered, Blaise leveled a stare on his brother.

Bannon bit his bottom lip. "I'm going to restore it."

Oh dear. A sinking feeling settled into Blaise's stomach, and a chill that had nothing to do with the weather trickled down his spine. "Restore what?"

"I brought it to show Aiden and get his opinion. He's supposed to meet us out here, but I got excited about it and decided to show Winstol first, and, well, he tripped over a rock after I handed it to him, and—"

"I have it," Winstol crowed and backed away from the bird. He stood next to the white picket gate and turned his outstretched hand to reveal a small box resting on his palm. A snuffbox to be exact. A very familiar snuffbox.

Dread slithered through Blaise at the speed of a magnetic hover train, and he swore his heart stopped. "You took it out of the case? When?"

"After lunch when you were in the powder room." Bannon strode forward and snatched the box from Winstol. "Relax. I'm going to repair it. See the top?" He pointed to the lid where the paint had chipped away from the spot the couple's hands should have been. "That was my brilliant idea. Weren't you paying attention?"

Blaise's insides quivered, and his heart beat in his throat. When he managed to speak, it came out as a breathy whisper. "Was there anything in it?"

"No."

"You're certain? You didn't take something out of the hidden compartment?"

"It has a hidden compartment?" The complete surprise on Bannon's face could not possibly be feigned. "Where?" He opened the box and shook it.

Blaise's whole body flushed and his knees threatened to buckle. It was still there. *Thank galaxy.*

Bannon continued to shake the box. It didn't make a sound, but then Blaise wouldn't expect it to. The disk had fit snugly against the false top.

"Where is it?" Bannon turned the trinket over in his hand, studying the bottom.

"What is…? Oh dear!" Having finally gotten a good look at the antique, Griff slapped a hand over his mouth. "Is that what I think it is?"

Griff didn't know the half of it. He only knew that it was the Duke of Eversleigh's prized possession. He had no idea that it contained a sex tape of Prissy.

"We are going home right this instant." Blaise glared at his brother. "I'm going to plead a headache, and you are going to offer to accompany me home. Then tomorrow afternoon when I go to work, I will put it back." He'd throw out the disk tonight. As soon as they were away. He'd crush it under his heel and leave it on the sidewalk....

"You're overreacting. I'm going to restore it for Father's birthday next month. He'll love it." Bannon flipped the box over again.

Winstol came closer, also inspecting it.

Bannon shook it again.

Blaise reached out a hand toward his brother. "Give me the box."

A snowflake landed in the very center of his gloved palm. Then he noticed the flurries floating down all around them.

"You're going to ruin my surprise." With a dramatic sigh, Bannon placed the delicate box on top of the now-melted snowflake.

CHAPTER SIX

Rumors have always abounded regarding a certain betting book in a certain gentleman's club. Now if this book were real… this author wonders if it contains any bets on a certain earl. Will the demon earl find a new conquest making his debut this season or return to a former paramour?

—From *The Classige Examiner*

HE HADN'T missed this. Not one bit. Dalton stared out in apathy at the crowd of people gathered around the dance floor. As typical for a ton ball, there were way too many people for the small space. They reminded him of a flock of pigeons fighting over bread crumbs in the park. Not that Pryor House's ballroom was particularly small. It was actually one of the bigger ballrooms, if memory served, but the peerage tended to… well… flock together. They also cooed like pigeons, or at least that was what the continual drum of voices sounded like to him. He grinned at the image, wondering what the ton would think of being likened to a bunch of birds.

A footman in crimson livery walked past with a silver tray full of glasses headed for a group of men in the corner. No doubt the drinks were ordered specifically, because the tray contained tumblers rather than fluted glasses, which was the norm at a ton gathering. The ton did like their ratafia and sherry. In addition to the punch bowl, there were nearly always servants walking around with the two drinks at soirees.

Using the cover of shadows on the edge of the room, Dalton snagged a tumbler as the servant passed, none the wiser. For all the modern conveniences, some lords still preferred the traditional lighting of candles rather than modern electricity. Lord Stratford was one such lord. It certainly made the setting cozier, and it had definite advantages, like say pilfering a glass of…. Dalton took a sip. *Ah, brandy*—a very old brandy, if his taste buds could be believed. The dimly lit soiree also made it much easier to engage in an assignation, but tonight romantic entanglements held very little appeal. *Damn, Blaise.*

"Why are you brooding?"

Dalton glanced to his left as his cousin Aiden slid deftly beside him. Did the man read minds now? Aiden was dressed impeccably in navy trousers and evening coat with a beige waistcoat. He was quite dashing, though his evening coat didn't quite sit flat against his chest. A sketch pad no doubt. He never went anywhere without one. "I'm not brooding. I'm… bored."

"I see." A smile flitted across Aiden's handsome face, but he made no effort to look away from the dance floor. The grin was both knowing and sarcastic all in one.

"What does that mean?"

Aiden shrugged.

Dalton elbowed him in the ribs. "Give over."

The smile increased. "Just that normally when you are bored, you seek entertainment, whether it be gambling, chasing light-trousers, playing billiards, or getting foxed."

Dalton held up his glass. "I'm working on the *getting foxed* part."

"No, you aren't."

Fine, he wasn't. Why wasn't he? Dalton frowned down at his drink. "I'm savoring it. This brandy is quite the thing. Mid-4600s vintage, I believe."

Aiden snorted and finally looked at him. The smile was still in place. "Redding isn't falling at your feet, is he?"

Dalton sighed. "No. He wants nothing to do with me."

"It can't possibly be that bad?"

Dalton raised a brow.

"Zooks."

"Exactly. He basically told me that I was his guard and that was it, and that I was a mannerless oaf with no sense of propriety."

"Not that. There…." He pointed toward the group of men and the footman. All of them were turned around, looking at him. Or rather, glaring at him. They did not appear happy. Was that Stratford?

Dalton raised his tumbler to them.

Their host—it was definitely Stratford—frowned and started forward. His face took on a mottled red shade.

Chuckling, Aiden shook his head. "You swiped that from them? You're incorrigible." He tugged Dalton back a few steps behind a group of gentleman watching the minuet out on the dance floor and out of the line of sight of the angry minimob of pompousness. "Blaise said that?"

"No, but he might as well have." The whole thing was rather disheartening. It should make Dalton want to give up his suit, and it did… sort of. But damn Blaise, the more Dalton learned about him, the more Dalton liked him. Unfortunately he seemed to have the opposite effect on Blaise. Blaise had more integrity than most anyone Dalton knew. It was puzzling and vastly appealing. Dalton wanted to know what made the man tick.

"Well… I'd tell you to just forget about him, but I can see by the look on your face that you aren't going to, so we'll just have to work on your manners. You should start with not pilfering other men's drinks. But in the meantime…." He tilted his head toward the side of the ballroom. "Come on. I can at least relieve your boredom." He didn't wait for an answer before he headed toward the veranda door.

Dalton smiled and followed his cousin. The irony of being taught manners from a man intent on sneaking out of a ballroom tickled him, but an adventure was much better than brooding. "Ah, so that is why you came and found me. You needed an ally."

"Nonsense. You looked…." He waved his hand about. "Distracted and lonely." Aiden slipped behind the curtain in front of him. Dalton waited, not wanting to draw too much attention. One lump in the curtain was suspicious enough, but Aiden's hand came out of the curtain, beckoning him forward.

With a shake of his head, Dalton joined his cousin. "Really, you aren't even trying."

"Okay fine, I'll get yelled at a lot less if you are with me." Aiden unlatched the door and slipped out onto the veranda. "Brr… it's fucking freezing out here."

The breeze from outside caught the curtain, blowing it into the ballroom. Aiden, however, was oblivious. He continued out the door. Dalton grabbed the fabric with his free hand, trying to make it billow less, and with the other hand, tried to keep from spilling his drink. It wasn't easy, since the curtain decided to wrap around him in its tug-of-war with the wind. He shut the door as quickly as he could, letting go of the velvet curtain at the last minute. "No, I meant that you aren't even trying to sneak."

"Why bother? Everyone knows I'm going to go outside at some point during the ball anyway." He had a point. He was rather infamous for leaving balls in the middle of them. "Bloody hell! Would you look at this?" Aiden threw his arms out toward the garden and the curtain of snow—or perhaps it was a show of disgust rather than pointing out the weather?

The snow was magical. It always was when it first started falling. The way it swirled around in the night air illuminated only by street lamps was beautiful. It was home. Dalton stepped to the edge of the veranda and stuck his hand out, watching the snowflakes dance around his arm and dust his sleeve. It was one of the things he'd missed about home when he was away, especially around this time of year. It was supposed to snow during winter. He'd spent this past holiday season, from St. Nicholas Day to Twelfth Night, on a desert planet, and it had felt so wrong.

Aiden huffed out a disgusted breath, and a plume of condensation fogged the air around him. His bottom lip came out in a petulant pout, and he wrapped his arms around his waist and gave a mock shiver. "Damnation."

Grinning, Dalton took a drink of his brandy. He had the sudden urge to have a snowball fight. "Isn't it wonderful?"

"No," Aiden grumbled, snatched the tumbler out of Dalton's hand, and swigged the rest of it back before handing it to Dalton and stalking out into the snow. "It's cold."

Dalton frowned at the now-empty glass he'd been nursing and set it on the railing with a clunk before he followed. "That is not how you drink two-hundred-year-old brandy, and if you hate the snow so much, what are we doing out here?"

"I didn't realize it was snowing. And to answer your question, we're meeting Bannon. He wants to restore a snuffbox for the duke's birthday as a surprise."

Uh-oh. Dalton stopped with one foot on the bottom step and one on the ground. The image of the antique snuffbox out of the duke's curio cabinet popped into his brain along with the thought that Blaise was going to have an apoplexy. Dalton had told Bannon this afternoon that he should get permission to restore the box first. "Please tell me his father knows about this."

Aiden's steps faltered, and he raised his brows. "It's a little hard to surprise someone if they know about the surprise."

Damn. "Aiden, that isn't the kind of thing you restore without the owner's permission, and I don't think you should have any part in it."

His cousin nodded and patted his arm as if to placate him. "And now I know you aren't feeling all right."

Dalton shrugged the hand off of him. "Cut it out, smartarse. That snuffbox is worth several million pounds."

"Bannon is a very good—" Aiden shook his head. "No, actually he's an *exceptional* artist. One of the best." It was high praise coming from an artist as talented as Aiden, but still….

"That is not the point."

Rolling his eyes upward, Aiden turned and started back out toward the garden. "You sound… parental." The word parental was said with the same inflection one would use to tell a person they had a terminal disease.

"I'm not parental; I'm just using my head. What if something happens to it? What if it falls out of his pocket and gets trampled on? It should not be bandied about in public." *Ugh.* Dalton frowned; he did sound a little on the parental side, didn't he? Still… someone needed to be the voice of reason, and since Blaise was not here….

"We're not bandying it about. You've seen the box?"

"This afternoon." Dalton hurried his pace. Perhaps he could persuade Bannon to take the box to the duke immediately for safekeeping. Only maybe that wasn't such a good idea because then Blaise would find out, and he'd still blame Dalton. And why did it really matter if Blaise was mad at him? The man didn't like him anyway. Maybe he should give up this featherbrained idea to seduce him?

Following his cousin around the corner, Dalton froze in his tracks.

As if his thoughts conjured him, there stood Blaise. There was no mistaking that regal profile. He was in front of the gate, with snow fluttering down around him like some sort of fairy king before his subjects. He was turned sideways, with something resting on his palm. His pale cheek practically glowed in the moonlight as white speckled the exquisitely tailored brown evening coat. His gloved hand rested on the top of the gate like a knight bestowing favors. Even the wind seemed in harmony with him as it fluttered the rich brown waves of his hair in an attractive way. He looked untouchable and beddable all at once.

He stared at the trinket—the snuffbox no doubt—in his hand with a look somewhere between reverence and relief. Apparently, Dalton wasn't the only one who thought bringing it to a ball was a bad idea. Blaise took a deep breath and closed his eyes. His fingers began to close around the box, but before they could, a grubby hand shot over the gate and snatched it.

Dalton hadn't even seen the kid standing there. But then, he had been completely enamored by the vision in front of him. The urchin took off, and his shoes clacked against the cement.

Blaise's eyes shot open. He stared at his empty hand for several seconds, and then his pretty mouth opened on a strangled cry. He turned slowly toward Dalton, no not to Dalton, to the people around him. His gaze settled on his younger brother, and his face blanched, going almost expressionless. His vibrant green eyes dulled.

It pinged every one of Dalton's protective instincts. He hadn't even realized he had protective instincts until now, but he couldn't deny the urge to make things better. He strode past Aiden, determined to erase that look from Blaise's face. Determined to catch the thief. But before Dalton even made it to the fence, Blaise jerked the gate open and took off.

BLAISE RAN as fast as his legs would carry him, with the wind slapping him in the face. A person would have to be a complete dolt to miss the irony of the situation. He—who never stepped a foot out of line—had jumped over the line and gotten a running start, and damned if he'd been lecturing Ashbourne about propriety all afternoon. But what choice did he have? It would be a miracle if he actually made it out of this bumblebroth with his reputation intact.

The boy disappeared among the trees, but rustling and the movement of branches marked his path. It wasn't a large park, but the trees in the middle of it were more closely packed than most.

Following the boy, Blaise squinted, but it took another few yards until he caught sight of him again. When he did, it was just as the kid cleared the park. The tails of the boy's battered coat flapped out behind him. In the street again, Blaise's heavy footfalls joined the kid's in the otherwise quiet night. On the other side of the park, the buildings seemed to grow denser and darker. No cheery awnings here or brightly painted shop doors. The structures were redbrick, covered with a layer of grime, and industrial-looking. Even the scent was different, harsher.

The sound of voices and a crowd pierced the quiet. Behind the building at the end of the alley, the dark sky grew lighter. How had he failed to notice that before now? Gads, where was the thief leading him? Could it be some sort of trap?

He might be able to defend himself against the skinny boy in front of him, but he wasn't sure he could triumph over more people. The only self-defense he knew was fencing, and he wasn't very good at it. Not that it mattered, since he didn't have a rapier.

The glow lengthened the crook's shadow, making it stretch out behind him like it reached for Blaise as the sounds of people talking became a dull roar. *What in the galaxy?* He turned a corner and ran right into the middle of a party. Apprehension sliced through him.

There were tents, wagons, and bonfires scattered about. And people, lots and lots of people. Steam rose into the air, surrounding the crowd like a bubble. It was like a whole other world.

The kid disappeared into the throng, and the horde seemed to close in around him, concealing him from sight.

Panic hit Blaise so hard it nearly brought him to his knees. He pushed his way through the sea of people but couldn't see the thief anywhere. Huffing and puffing, he stumbled to a stop with a sinking feeling in his abdomen. *Now what?*

Trying to catch his breath, he decided to find higher ground. If he could get above everyone, he could find the boy. Turning in a circle, looking for a bench or anything, he noticed everyone was staring at him. People were mostly still walking and milling about, but heads were craned in his direction. Some folks had even stopped to stare.

A lump formed in his throat that had nothing to do with his accelerated breathing and everything to do with his sense of self-preservation. These were not his people. These were not even servant class, who he was comfortable with. These were working-class people. Rough people and they were looking at him like he was an unwanted intruder. Butterflies fluttered to life in his stomach like a wildfire in the country.

A pretty woman about Blaise's age with lots of cosmetics winked at him. She wore a brown dress at least two seasons out of style, but compared to the rest of the crowd, she was attired nicely. She stepped closer, way into his personal space, so her smoky voice breathed across his ear. "You lookin' fer comp'ny, lovely?"

Goose bumps sprouted on his arms, and the hair on the back of his neck rose. He shook his head and knew it came across as frantic but couldn't seem to help it. He was in way over his head.

Everyone closed in, or so it seemed. They weren't surrounding him precisely, only going about their business, but bodies brushed against him. Jostling him around as if he were of no consequence. It was as if these people didn't like him. But why? They didn't even know him.

A sharp pinch nipped his bottom.

"Eek." Blaise whirled around to see who was taking such liberties and to put them in their place, but there was no one there. Just the retreating backs of several men.

A voice rose above the cacophony, offering roasted nuts for two shillings. A man shouted, "Rent your skates here." Some woman crowed about having the best scones in town for only six pence.

An unseen hand groped the front of his jacket, looking for his purse no doubt, and Blaise slapped it away in a panic.

A boy, several years younger than Blaise, stopped in front of him. "Two crowns fer a blow job, guv?"

"Wh-what?" Every last bit of heat Blaise had worked up running evaporated, and cold, gripping fear took its place. He didn't even know what the boy was asking. It was like being dropped into a foreign country where he didn't speak the language.

"Hands off, kid. He's with me," a smooth, strong voice said as someone grabbed Blaise's arm.

Blood pounded through his ears, and his heart took off in a race of its own as panic rose up inside Blaise. He wheeled around toward his captor.

Ashbourne stood there, looking flawless and confident. His gray eyes were calm and stormy all at once.

Oh, thank galaxy! Blaise had never been so happy to see someone in his life.

Dressed in all black from head to toe, Ashbourne personified dangerous and rakish. "Come along, angel. We have things to do. No time to tarry."

The relief of rescue was so intense, Blaise didn't even mind Ashbourne calling him angel.

"Begging ye pardon, milord." The boy jumped back from Blaise like he'd been burned and swallowed hard as he peered up at Ashbourne, then took off.

With a nod, Blaise let Ashbourne pull him through the crowd, feeling a little more in control. At least he wasn't alone. The earl was like him. Sort of....

Blaise did his best to match Ashbourne's stride, to blend in, but wasn't sure he was successful. No matter. Even though the people still stared at him, they kept their distance now, thanks to Ashbourne's appearance. "Wh-wh-whe…." *Bloody hell.* Stopping, Blaise slapped a hand over his mouth. He'd been so disturbed by his surroundings, it had never occurred to him to keep his mouth shut. He should have known better. He didn't stutter often nowadays, but stressful situations still brought it back.

One blond brow hiked up, and Ashbourne pulled Blaise's hand away from his mouth, but he didn't comment. Instead, he wound their fingers together and squeezed, offering support.

Just like that, the tension between them vanished, and Blaise took a deep breath, trying again. "Wh-where are we? Wh-what is this place?"

"We are in the middle of a Frost Fair, it would seem. They sprout up every couple of years. As sort of a tribute to the Frost Fairs in ancient England, only without the river. My grandfather used to take me when I was a kid. They are quite fun." Looking at something over Blaise's shoulder, he frowned. "But we should get out of here. We're not exactly dressed to mingle." Ashbourne tugged his arm and started walking.

Before Blaise could protest, a man pushing a cart with a steaming beverage dispenser on top walked past. The scent of hot chocolate followed. Behind the man and his cart were a couple of kids in ratty clothes, trying to get the man to stop.

The thief. The box! Reality crashed back into Blaise with a renewed sense of panic. He pulled back against Ashbourne, stopping them, then looked around to find a bench. Spotting one, he tugged Ashbourne toward it. "W-w-w…." Blaise reworded his question to take out the *w*. "Do you k-k…." Nope, the *n* sound was no good either. "That box must be found." He stepped up on the bench, next to a woman sitting down, and heard Ashbourne mutter an apology.

Blaise searched the crowd in the direction the boy had run. There was nothing but a sea of people. He looked for a space in the crowd. For people turning back or parting. Anything to indicate someone running in their midst, but there were no angry shouts or a single space in the crowd. He was beginning to despair, but then to his left on the edge of the crowd, he spotted a tattered brown coat moving fast toward the alley.

"Um, Blaise?"

Something jostled his arm, and he realized he still held Ashbourne's hand.

"Come on." Blaise jumped down, tightening his hold on Ashbourne, and took off running once again. "We need to get to that alley over there."

"Great idea!" Running with him, Ashbourne glanced back over his shoulder.

What in the…? Blaise chanced a peek behind them. At first he didn't see anything except people going about their business, but it was hard to see with Ashbourne pulling him. The people behind them gawked as they passed, but their expressions mostly contained surprise. There might have been disgust on a few faces, but Blaise couldn't be sure, as quickly as he was passing them.

Ashbourne pulled on his arm, running even faster. "Come on. We have to get out of here."

Blaise didn't argue since Ashbourne was going in the direction the thief had disappeared, but he did peer back again. This time a brisk movement caught his attention.

A tall, skinny man in a brown derby whirled around and started talking to a shorter man with a big nose and wearing a dark peacoat and a knit cap. Big Nose shoved the skinny man and started striding forward as though he were looking for something or someone. His gaze connected with Blaise's and slid past him.

He called out something to a man beside him. This man had on a black many-caped greatcoat. They both seemed like a rough lot with their broad shoulders and thick necks, but they were dressed nicely.

The man in the black coat studied something in his hand and then pointed right toward them.

Shock made Blaise gasp as he turned back to the front. "Are they following us?"

"Yes." Ashbourne tugged his hand harder.

They stepped into the alley, and immediately the buildings muffled the sounds. There was a darkness up ahead where the lights of the Frost Fair didn't reach.

"Wh-why? Wh-who are they?"

"No clue." As they stepped into that darkness, Ashbourne hissed, "Run," and took off, giving Blaise no choice but to come with him. *Dust!* He'd started out as the chaser and ended up as the chased.

Chapter Seven

The new fashion accessory for gentlemen this year…. Hay. A certain captain of the Royal Guards was seen sporting hay in his cravat knot and hair. This author wonders what will be next? Paint splatters?

—From *Pruluce Weekly*, the Beau Monde Happenings column

DALTON WAS tired of running already. It was like being back in basic training, only with worse shoes. Two-hundred-pound highly polished Hessians might be all the crack, but frankly, they sucked for running.

Still holding Blaise's hand, he darted around a metal trash can and crowded Blaise toward the wall. If they could get around the corner without being seen, they might be able to lose the ruffians chasing them. Too bad he hadn't put his knife in his boot this evening while getting ready for the ball. Not that it mattered; he wouldn't dare fight with Blaise in tow unless he absolutely had to. But he'd feel much better knowing he had a weapon if those men caught up to them.

At the end of the alley, Blaise stopped abruptly and jerked his head left, then right. "Where did he go? Oh, my galaxy! Where is he?" With his bottom lip caught between his teeth, he furrowed his brow and studied the lane in front of them, then clutched a hand to his chest.

Dalton nearly groaned. There were really big, really rough-looking men following them, and Blaise was still worried about the snuffbox? *Unbelievable.* "Blaise, we have to—*oof*!"

Jerking on his arm, Blaise started running again, only he wasn't watching where he was going. He was squinting at the ground.

In the snow were partial footprints. The tread was flat in some places and rough in others. And was that a toe print at the tip? They turned the corner, and Dalton glanced back to see if the men were still following. Fortunately there were only buildings, snow, and litter. A piece of paper floated in the wind about a foot from the ground like some sort of apparition, but no ruffians. Though their shouts echoed off the brick walls along with the whistling wind.

Up ahead, the alley grew darker as they ran out of the lights of the Frost Fair. The buildings blocked most of the weather from the narrow alley, but at the cross street ahead of them, it was like a curtain of white. The violent breeze whipped the flakes nearly horizontal at times with its gusts.

As they rounded the corner and into the cross street, Blaise's hand pulled on his, his gloved hand nearly slipping out of Dalton's as he slowed again. His cheeks had turned bright and rosy. Dalton was beginning to think it was impossible for Blaise to be anything but gorgeous. But Blaise's breath had a distinct whistle to it that sounded suspiciously like wheezing as he looked left and right again.

The men's shouts behind them grew louder, and Dalton made the decision for them. He led them up the next alley.

A big dinted metal container sat at a slight angle to the brick wall, leaving a perfect slim triangle in which to hide and catch their breath.

Blaise tugged on his arm, trying to go the opposite direction. "But the box…."

"Where the 'ell are they?" a shout echoed through the alley.

Blaise's eyes widened.

Now he remembers the men following us? Dalton squeezed his hand and led them behind a paint-peeling green dumpster.

On the same page now, Blaise smashed himself up against gray bricks, wedging his shoulder into the dumpster as close as he could get and trying to get his breathing under control.

"Stay put. I'll be right back."

Thankfully instead of asking questions, Blaise only nodded.

Dalton ran up the alley to try and mask their footprints. It wasn't perfect, since it was only one set of prints, but hopefully the men wouldn't look too closely. They seemed in a hurry and not really paying attention to tracking clues such as footprints.

After Dalton left prints leading out of the alley he tiptoed his way back through them to return to the dumpster. Picking up handfuls of snow, he threw it over the track leading to their hiding place.

Blaise was right where he'd left him. He looked adorable with his eyes closed and his head tipped back. A line formed down the middle of his forehead.

If concentration alone could make him disappear into the wall, Dalton would have been staring at bricks. The urge to kiss those flattened lips was like a hot poker in the side. What was it about this man? He'd railed at Dalton this afternoon about his reputation, but it didn't seem to matter. There was some sort of strange attraction, and not just physical. Dalton definitely wanted to get to know Blaise better, and to do that he had to prove to Blaise that he wasn't a total scapegrace. Which meant he had to get them back to the ball without anyone finding out they were gone.

The thought had Dalton's teeth gnashing together. They were flirting with disaster, and his neck in a parson's noose might be the result, but he was certain he'd done the right thing. No way could Blaise have faced this on his own. Dalton just hoped that doing the right thing didn't come back to bite him in the arse. He was certain Aiden would come up with some story if asked where they were.

Grabbing two of the cardboard boxes from in front of the dumpster, Dalton quickly stacked them so the dumpster covered them on one side and the boxes on the other.

There were also trash cans and some crates on the opposite end of the alley as well as more boxes. The place was a mess and smelled moldy, but that was to their advantage. This did not look like a place two lords would take shelter, or so Dalton hoped. Though truth be told, he'd been in a lot worse places while in the IN.

Leaning up against the rough brick wall, he became very aware of Blaise's wonderful heat beside him. They stood shoulder to shoulder, arm to arm. Connected. It felt like the most natural thing in the world for Dalton to grab the hand next to his and lace their fingers together.

Blaise jolted as if startled but didn't pull away.

The scent of sweat and that same smoky sweetness that he realized was unique to Blaise drifted up to him as snow fell around them.

Dalton's abdomen heated and his cock took notice, filling just a bit. Not enough to make him hard, but there was a spark. If not for the men following them, it would have been almost magical, or maybe it was because of the men following them. Adrenaline had always been a turn-on to him. Whatever the reason, Dalton wanted to work them both up into a frenzy. Gads, how long had it been since he'd gotten laid? Months? Not since he'd come home on leave and spotted the temptation beside him across a crowded ballroom, taking away a drink from his brother.

The sound of feet pounding by echoed off the walls, drawing Dalton back to the here and now. Dust, he'd lost his mind. Half an hour in Blaise's presence and all his military training had flown out the window.

"Where did they go? He just disappeared. I got nothing," a man shouted.

Blaise sucked in a quiet breath beside him.

"This way," another answered.

The footsteps started again, going away and growing more distant.

Through the small space between the wall and the dumpster, Dalton could just make out the men racing down the next alley, away from them.

Blaise, too, had turned his head to peek out the crack, but he didn't let go of Dalton's hand. If anything, his grip tightened as if he were holding his breath.

The men disappeared from sight, their footfalls swallowed up by the howling wind.

Blaise's stiff shoulders sank about an inch, leaving his hair stuck against the rough bricks as he did so. When he turned his head, the tip of his nose bumped the tip of Dalton's.

It was like a shot to the nervous system. More of that delicious awareness swirled around them. The widening of his eyes said Blaise felt it too, and for several moments they just stayed there, staring at each other. Those beautiful green eyes not even blinking when a snowflake caught on his long lashes. The air fogged around them, and that spark of arousal inside Dalton grew into a flame. He couldn't look away even if his life depended on it.

In Blaise's gaze was the acknowledgment of shared danger and some shyness too. His attention drifted down to Dalton's lips, and his lashes lowered. Blast, he was beautiful. The nickname *angel* was perfect, whether Blaise liked it or not. His pale cheeks had a rosy glow, but it only added to his flawless complexion.

He swallowed hard, making his cravat move, and Dalton wished he could see that slim neck and Adam's apple. Wanted to taste it. If he didn't, he would surely lose his mind. The compulsion gnawed at him. His hands actually shook with it. He had to taste, to feel. Maybe then the hunger would go away. God, he needed it to go away, because there was no way he could keep this up. The tension between them all afternoon had built to a crescendo. Maybe one small kiss….

Dalton leaned forward, pressing his lips to Blaise's. They were cold but oh, so soft. He tasted sweet, just as his looks promised. Like honey and butterscotch. *Delicious.*

A warm puff of breath caressed Dalton's mouth as Blaise gasped. His eyes fluttered closed, and he kissed back, his lips puckering so innocently. One gentle caress, then another and another.

With his free hand, Dalton touched Blaise's cheek and pulled him closer with the other hand, the one woven with Blaise's.

Blaise followed, turning his body to face Dalton and leaned into Dalton's gloved hand. A soft sigh feathered across Dalton's lips as Blaise's free hand came to rest on Dalton's waist. Another peck, and another.

Lust coiled in Dalton's lower abdomen, and his prick strained at the placket of his trousers. In the back of his mind, he knew he should pull back. He knew it was getting out of hand and not at all what he'd planned to do.... He licked the seam of Blaise's lips, and when Blaise opened, he pushed in, taking complete advantage. He couldn't help the moan that escaped as his tongue touched the velvety recesses of Blaise's mouth.

Blaise stiffened, then jerked back as though he'd been clocked. Touching his lips, he stepped back even farther, taking the lovely heat of his body with him. His eyes widened, then narrowed accusingly. "Did you j-j-just stick your tongue in m-my mouth?"

Dalton blinked. He'd known Blaise was innocent, but he was even more so than Dalton thought. That should have killed any remaining desire, but it didn't. Galaxy help him, it didn't. He should be relieved Blaise had just saved him from himself, but he was shaken to the core. He'd known he felt something for Blaise when he'd first seen him, but this went beyond anything he'd ever felt. Dalton suddenly found himself in foreign territory where men were concerned, and not just because Blaise was not wooed by his charm like all Dalton's other conquests.

"Wh-why w-w-would you do that?" The glare gave way to curiosity, complete with a slight head tilt with the tuft of deep brown hair standing up in the back waving like a flag. But something about the way he ran his fingers over his lips and how his gaze kept drifting to Dalton's mouth said he wasn't as appalled as he pretended to be.

Dalton, for his part, felt something akin to being underwater too long without coming up for air. In a moment of panic, he pasted a cocky grin on his face. Trying to save face after losing himself so thoroughly in that kiss, he drawled, "It's called a kiss, darling. Shall we try it again?"

OAF, CAD, bounder.... Rakehell, that was a good one. The most apt, anyway. Blaise kicked a half-crushed disposable cup and continued walking, searching for small footprints in the snow. *Degenerate.* That was another good one. He felt like a complete muttonhead. And to think he'd anticipated that kiss. He'd actually felt a kinship with Ashbourne.

Snorting, Blaise wiped away a snowflake caught on his lashes. That wasn't a kiss. If that was a kiss.... Well, it certainly wasn't a respectable one. No decent man would allow such a thing. So why did his lips and the inside of his mouth still tingle? Why did he want to try it again and see what would happen next? Good grief, he'd become a wanton *and* a buffoon. He didn't need or want Ashbourne's help.

Blaise continued walking, looking for any clue to where the thief went, but he wasn't finding anything, and he was beginning to worry they'd lost the boy. If he failed.... His stomach churned, threatening to cast up its accounts. He didn't want to think about that. He simply could not fail to find that box. The snow was really coming down now. He had to hurry and catch the kid's trail. In no time, all prints would be covered.

"Blaise, wait up." Ashbourne jogged up next to him, and his heat was immediately apparent, like a buffer from the wind on the right side. He was still smiling, though it appeared a little strained, and his hair was tousled by the wind, giving him a carefree, almost boyish appearance.

How dare he look so dashing when Blaise's life was falling down around his ears. "I have not given you leave to call me by my given name." Was that a footprint?

Undaunted, Ashbourne chuckled and glanced behind them. "Very well, I'll just call you angel."

Blaise snarled at him.

"How about darling?" His voice was low and seductive, like hot chocolate on a cold night in front of a fire.

It sent a shiver down Blaise's spine, or maybe that was the frigid air. No, it was definitely in response to the nickname Ashbourne had apparently given him. Not only was he ruined, he'd become a wanton. Blaise nearly groaned. "Fine, you may call me Blaise."

Another rusty chuckle and he wasn't even looking at Blaise, he was scanning the alley, only half paying attention. And why was that appealing?

Call me doomed.

"You know, if you don't like calling me Dalton, you could always call me Demon."

What? Stopping midstep, Blaise turned. He opened his mouth, then closed it. Much to his surprised chagrin, a chuckle escaped. "Oh yes, that's perfect. Better than cad, bounder, or oaf. Demon is even better than scoundrel."

Dalton turned too. One blond brow rose, but the perpetual smile did not lessen.

Oh stars! He'd said that out loud. Blaise slapped a hand over his mouth. "I'm so sorry. I didn't mean… I…."

Dalton's other eyebrow joined the first one, and then he threw his head back and laughed. Deep and hearty. Laugh lines tugged at the corners of his eyes and splotches of color covered his cheeks. It was not at all the thing. It was way too boisterous to be proper, but Blaise found his own lips turning up.

In no time, Blaise was chuckling as well. He couldn't believe it, especially in a situation like this. He was only a hairsbreadth away from scandal, and that thought was enough to wipe the smile off his face. But still… Ashbourne had obviously not taken offense. Thank goodness. Rake, bounder, or demon, it did not excuse Blaise's bad manners. Dalton seemed to bring out the worst in him. "I didn't mean to call you names. I should be thanking you for rescuing me back there."

Shaking his head, Dalton waved it away as his laughter died down. "I'm your guard. It's my duty." He held out his arm, indicating Blaise should start walking again. "Besides, I've been called all of those things before and a lot worse." He held out his hand. "Truce?"

Blaise shook it. It was cold even through their gloves. "Truce. And I really am sorry. That was badly done of me. If not for you, I w-would have been in big trouble back there." Actually, he wasn't out of trouble yet.

"Relax. We're going to get you back, and no one will be the wiser. Aiden will cover for us."

Wrapping his arms around himself, trying to control his shivering, Blaise resumed his search for clues. "I can't go back yet. I have to find that box."

Dalton groaned and grabbed Blaise's arm, pulling him to a stop. "We are never going to find that boy now. The box is gone, Blaise. We have to get back to the ball before anyone realizes we're missing."

Anger swept through Blaise right along with panic at the thought that Dalton might be right. He jerked his arm free. "Fine. Go back. I'm not giving up." He couldn't give up.

"Blaise, look around you." Gesturing toward the end of the alley, Dalton continued, "It's practically a blizzard. We'll be lucky to find our way back to the ball." He pointed at the ground behind them. "We can't even see our own footprints anymore."

Oh galaxy, he was right. Their footprints were gone. There was nothing but a blanket of white behind them. A curtain of white surrounded them. A gasp escaped Blaise, sounding loud in the snow-induced silence. Oh galaxy, he couldn't breathe. What was he going to do? He turned to Dalton and grabbed a handful of his evening jacket, shaking him a little. He had to get through to him. With gritted-out words, Blaise enunciated slowly, "The. Disk. Is. In. That. Bloody. Box."

Dalton's eyes flared wider, and he glanced down at Blaise's hands tangled in his coat, then looked back up the alley.

"Are you paying attention to me? I hid the disk in the snuffbox."

Dalton gave him his attention again, but when he spoke, his voice was irritatingly soft and calm. "It doesn't matter." He covered Blaise's hands with his own. When he finally glanced up, his expression was as gentle as his voice. "How is that street urchin going to do anything about it? Even if he has the means to see what's on the disk, he won't know who it came from. He won't connect you to the disk."

Was he right? Some of Blaise's steam evaporated, but his mind whirled. "But how am I going to tell my father the box is missing?" The thought was nearly as bad as being ruined. The result was the same. His father would be disappointed in him. The thought niggled in his gut like he'd eaten a bad meat pie. "You don't understand," he whispered and tightened his hands in Dalton's coat.

Dalton unhooked Blaise's fingers from his lapels and held on to them. His thumbs rubbed back and forth over the tops of Blaise's numb hands. "Then help me understand."

Blaise's attention wandered to his hands, but he didn't take his gaze from Dalton's. It was like every sense in Blaise's body focused in on his hands and the man before him. Dalton's lips appeared impossibly red on his pale face and his eyes a darker gray. The look was full of empathy and… caring? His eyes seemed to see right through Blaise. In that moment, there was something there. Something that made Blaise believe he could trust Dalton. "When I was young, I stuttered. It was an embarrassment to my father. He was… ashamed."

He expected Dalton to protest and tell him it was his imagination. That's what everyone else did, but Dalton didn't. His eyes softened, and he continued to rub his thumbs over Blaise's hands.

"I was at Rust Creek, the village closest to Eversleigh, with my sire. We'd gone there to get a pair of boots, and there were some children outside playing." He'd asked to go play too, and his sire had agreed, telling Blaise to stay close because Father was meeting up with them for lunch. Blaise had been so excited to play with new kids. He'd only ever had Bannon, Larkinson, and Louisa for playmates, and the boys looked to be his age. "I tried to say hello, and I stuttered."

"They made fun of you?"

Blaise nodded. "They laughed and said I was a disgrace to Eversleigh and I'd never be a good duke. I got so upset that I started running. I ran right into my father. He'd seen and heard everything. He had to have. He was so close, but he didn't say a word. He just stared at me. I'll never forget the blank look on his face." Blaise shook his head, remembering the pain. He wished so hard his father would say something to the boys, anything. He'd expected it, but his father hadn't said anything except to tell Blaise to come along.

Dalton just stared at him. He gave Blaise a sad smile, a knowing one. Dalton understood. He knew what it was like to feel like a disappointment. Even if Dalton still suffered the disappointment, this was something they shared. He didn't tell Blaise he was imagining it or that he was making it a bigger deal than it was, because he understood. He knew what it felt like to not measure up.

The snow enclosed them, and Dalton was the only thing he could see clearly. The flakes darting to the ground around them blurred their surroundings. It was like being alone in the world, and yet there was this strange connection. This shared experience. It was magical and.... Blaise found himself leaning forward.

One of Dalton's hands dropped his and came to rest on his shoulder, barely touching his cheek. By some magnetic pull, they came closer, their breaths mixing in a cloud of vapor. Their lips touched in an icy warmth that was both exciting and disconcerting and—

A screech broke through the soft staticky sound of the snow hitting the ground. Some sort of animal raced past, into the street ahead of them, and disappeared into the wall of flurries.

Blaise jumped, and his heart tried to beat right out of his chest.

A soft voice to their left hissed, "Get back 'ere."

The animal, a rat, must have made a wide U-turn, because it came running back into view. Straight for them. *Eeeee.... Great!* Now on top of everything else, he was going to get rabies.

Blaise jumped out of the way, but just as the rat was about to reach them, it veered off to the left into a pile of boxes behind a beaten-up, rusty dumpster.

Dalton stepped in front of him and turned toward the trash. He wrapped one arm around Blaise's waist, snugging them up together, but sadly Blaise was so cold, he barely registered the heat given off by Dalton's body. "Come out."

Blaise started to protest about the embrace, until it dawned on him what Dalton had said. "You're talking to a rat?"

"It's not a rat. It's a weasel or maybe a ferret." Dalton probably rolled his eyes. It certainly sounded like an eye roll was in progress when he spoke. "And I'm not talking to—"

Some rustling came from behind the dumpster.

Both their attentions snapped back to the trash.

"I know you're there. Come out now, or I'm coming in after you." Dalton sounded stern and confident, leaving no doubt he'd do just as he said.

"We're going to get rabies. We should just go," Blaise whispered through chattering teeth and rubbed his hands together. The longer they stood here, the colder he became.

Dalton ignored him. "I'm going to count to three. One. Two...."

A grimy face appeared from behind the dumpster, followed by a small body dressed in tattered clothes. The boy couldn't have been more than ten summers. He had long stringy brown hair that hadn't seen a brush or a good washing in months. His eyes seemed overly bright against the backdrop of dirt. His pants were two sizes too small, his gloves only covered three fingers and the dark coat was threadbare. His big toe stuck out the end of his shoe. He had a piece of cloth around his neck, tied like a scarf, but it was more like an old frayed tablecloth. In his arms was the rat. It turned its beady eyes to stare at Blaise and Dalton.

Two more children stepped out. One from behind the trash can a few feet down the alley and another one, a girl, from behind some boxes. They, too, looked as if they hadn't seen a bath in ages.

"We weren't doin' nuffin' wrong," the first boy said.

"You've been following us for two blocks," Dalton accused.

They had? A chill traveled up Blaise's spine that had nothing to do with the near-blizzard conditions. How had he not noticed? He could have been robbed... again.

"Blimey! We was just lookin' fer some food an' thought yew gents might 'ave some. At's all," the boy said, petting the rat and somehow managing to appear smaller than he had only a few moments ago.

The other two kids nodded their agreement. The one next to the trash can nodded, her lip trembling a little. At least, Blaise thought it was a girl.

His stomach sank to somewhere near the vicinity of his ankles. They were all on the scrawny side and out in the elements. Even though they had on more than Blaise, they had to be freezing. He certainly was, and he was pretty sure that even his waistcoat and evening coat offered better protection against the elements than their frayed and worn coats.

Dalton put his hands on his hips. "Then you didn't mean to rob us?" His voice said he didn't believe that for one moment.

All the kids shook their heads, their eyes wide. Even the rat turned to look at Dalton.

Scoffing, Blaise tapped Dalton in the back with his fist. Not enough to hurt but enough to let him know he was wrong. How could he not feel pity for these children? Knot in his throat, he stepped out from behind Dalton and dug into his coat pocket for his purse.

Dalton's arm shot out and hit Blaise's hand, slapping it up against his chest and trapping it inside his coat. He gave Blaise a sidelong look that was easy enough to interpret. It said—no, it demanded—that Blaise let him handle this.

Indignation tightened Blaise's jaw. *Of all the high-handed....* Before he could say anything, Dalton turned back to the kids.

"We're looking for a boy about this"—he held his hand up to his chin—"tall. He wears a long brown coat and hangs out on Hannan Street. He took something that doesn't belong to him, and I want it back."

Brilliant. He was going to kiss Dalton when this was all over. Hope flared in Blaise's chest, lessening the despair put there by the children's plight. They could help these kids and get the box back.

The girl shrugged. "We 'aven't seen 'im, guv."

Hope diminished.

With the hand that had been plastered against Blaise's chest, Dalton made a give-me motion.

Blaise abided, pulled his purse out, and dropped it into Dalton's hand.

"Well, now that's too bad. It's worth a reward." Dalton tossed the purse up into the air and caught it, making the coins inside clink together.

The children watched the brown pouch the entire way. Their eyes were glued to it.

Blaise thought he could hear their stomachs grumble in protest, and his clenched in sympathy.

For several seconds, no one said anything, and then the boy with the rat sighed and shook his head. "We don't know who 'e is, but if 'e's stolen somethin', 'e'll take i' ter Killer. That's where everyone goes ter get rid ov their goods. Da Killer pays da best. Know what I mean?"

They knew a murderer? Blaise swallowed hard. "The Killer?"

The boy by the boxes, who'd remained silent until now, nodded. "Yee know. The Killer." The look he gave Dalton was somewhere between disbelief and mistrust. "He's da champ. He takes da stolen goods an' sells 'em fer money so we don't 'ave ter be involved. His pub is down on da wharf."

"Like a fencing ring?"

Dalton held a hand up as if to shush him. "What's the pub called?"

"Southpaws."

With a nod, Dalton opened the purse and pulled out three crowns, tossing each of them one.

Instead of blending into the background like expected, they all chattered among themselves for a few seconds in an accent so thick it was hard to understand. There were even a few giggles. They looked more like healthy, active children than they had only moments ago, and something told Blaise they'd just been played.

His purse appeared in front of his nose—or where his nose would be if it hadn't been buried in his cravat. Gads, he couldn't even feel his nose anymore. Blaise followed the arm up to Dalton's tightly pinched face and rosy cheeks, but before he could take the purse, a small dirty hand snatched it.

The children took off running up the alley as fast as their little legs could carry them in a flurry of giggles and snow.

"Bloody hell." Dalton started after them.

Blaise grabbed his arm. "They need it more than I do." The most important thing was that he now had an idea where to look for the box. He might just be able to salvage this situation. If he wasn't so bloody cold, Blaise would have smiled. He just hoped those children had some shelter inside by a fire somewhere.

"We have got to get inside."

"But the box…."

"Tomorrow." Dalton, who had sounded so strong and stern moments ago, now sounded as miserable as Blaise felt. His teeth chattered, and his face was practically white with a touch of windburn pink at his cheeks. Even his lips were pale, but there was a look of understanding. Dalton grabbed his arm, pulling him closer to the wall of the building, and began to walk up the alley. "It will wait until the morning. No one in their right mind will be out in this. I promise, I will help you find it tomorrow."

Dalton made a very good point, and Blaise found he just didn't have the strength to argue. "All right."

ONE OF these days, Ravensburg was going to push him too far. Raleigh took a deep breath and calmed himself, then shut the front door and dipped his head at the guard on duty. Raleigh had run into his blasted sibling just as he was leaving Stratford's ball, and instead of saying hello or asking how things were going, the first thing out of Barclay's mouth was "Send Dalton home." It had been on the tip of Raleigh's tongue to say Dalton was at home, and it had taken every ounce of his restraint not to throttle Barclay right then and there. Truthfully the only thing that had stopped him was the fact that killing his brother would only cause more problems. There'd be a mess to clean, and a body to hide. His brother-in-law would end up being the marquess, and Arthur was a bigger pain in the arse than Barclay. So then he'd have another mess and another body to deal with after he killed Arthur. And unfortunately they had friends who would realize they were missing. The bodies could really start piling up, blast it all.

What a fine mess. Raleigh turned toward the office without even handing his coat and hat to the footman. He needed a good stiff brandy and to figure out how in the devil he was going to keep Dalton here at the castle now that he was back on Regelence.

"Cony, your jaw is twitching."

Raleigh stopped short of the office doorway.

Tarren was coming down the stairs toward him. He was missing his cravat, evening coat, and waistcoat. No doubt because he, and everyone else, had gotten home hours before Raleigh. He'd been stuck at the ball playing referee between his brother and Eversleigh. Tarren had obviously been waiting for him to get home.

Taking a deep breath and trying to stop the tick in his jaw, Raleigh smiled at his youngest son as he reached the foyer. The boy was nearly as tall as he was. He was easily Steven's height. Raleigh hadn't seen Tarren all evening. Unlike his brothers, Tarren tended to be more social, so their paths had not crossed during the ball. "How was your evening, son?"

"Better than yours apparently." Tarren eyed Raleigh's outerwear and darted a glance at the footman behind them. "Do you have a moment? I wanted to talk to you about something."

"Of course." Raleigh gestured for Tarren to precede him into the study as he pulled off his hat and coat and tossed them to the footman, who caught them easily.

Without a word, Tarren strolled toward the window. The pensive look on his face was both sweet and a little alarming. The staff hadn't named him Lord Terror for no reason. When he reached the window, he pulled the curtain open and peered out at the falling snow. Tarren furrowed his brow.

A pang hit Raleigh in the gut as he sat down in the chair opposite the desk and began to peel off his gloves. Whatever Tarren wanted to talk about must be serious. This was so unlike him. Out of all the boys, Tarren was most happy-go-lucky and, well… energetic. Raleigh had always joked that Tarren had two speeds: full blast and sound asleep. As a young child, they would find him passed out all over the castle, as if he'd just run out of steam and collapsed where he stood, usually with a toy still in hand, or more likely a pile of puppies near. Dogs had always been his preferred "toy."

Before Raleigh could ask what the matter was, Tarren turned back to him. "Cony, can I ask you something?"

"You can ask me anything, son."

Wringing the burgundy curtain in his slim, pale hands, Tarren bobbed his head once as if steeling himself. "How did you know Father was the right man for you?"

Raleigh blinked back his surprise and tossed his gloves on the desk. He wasn't sure what he'd expected, but that wasn't it. He thought back to what Steven had told him this evening and couldn't remember him mentioning anyone offering for Tarren. There had been a few betrothal requests last season, but no one serious. This sounded serious. "Is there someone you're interested in?"

Tarren shrugged.

Again, not the response Raleigh expected. "If you're no more enthusiastic about him than that…."

Dropping the curtain, Tarren turned back to the window. "I'm not sure. I like him just fine. I admire him. He's smart. He's fun. He's friendly and quite dashing. He's positively beautiful, and everyone likes him." His voice started to warm a bit.

"But do you love him?" Raleigh racked his brain, trying to remember who Tarren had been hanging around recently, but came up with no one new.

Again a shrug, then a shake of the head. Tarren came forward and gripped the back of the love seat. "No. But I think I could. That's why I wanted to know how you knew Father was the one."

Raleigh got up and headed to the sideboard. He needed a drink, and damn it all, he'd love to have Steven in on this conversation. "I knew because he fought for me. No matter how much I tried to dissuade him, he wouldn't give up." Of course, Raleigh hadn't been positive even then, but he wasn't going to tell Tarren that. He hadn't been positive until their wedding night, when Steven had come and found him after he'd run off. After the plug tradition. The thought of how Steven had come charging after him, forbidding everyone from following him, made Raleigh smile. Then the man had befuddled him even more by encouraging him to join the Navy if that was what he truly wanted. That's when Raleigh knew. "So does this mystery man of yours have a name? And should I tell your father to expect a visit from him soon?"

"Percy Edmonstone. And I don't know. He hasn't stated his intentions yet, but…." Tarren shrugged.

A snort came from the doorway. "That little popinjay is a buffoon."

Raleigh agreed, though he didn't say so. He turned toward the voice.

The Duke of Knighton stood in the doorway, looking as though he'd combed his hair with a headboard. He probably had, knowing Rourke. He leaned against the doorjamb and crossed his arms over his chest, making his shirt gap open a little and showing off a bit of dark curly chest hair. He, too, was without a cravat and waistcoat. Though his evening coat was on, it was unbuttoned.

"What are you doing here? I thought tonight was your night off?" Raleigh handed over his freshly poured glass of brandy to Rourke and reached for another glass.

Tarren glared at Rourke and mumbled, "Dust for brains."

"It was, but duty called." Rourke smiled and raised the glass. "Thanks, Raleigh." He tipped his head at Tarren. "Your Highness."

Making a disgusted little sound, Tarren shook his head and walked over to Raleigh. He kissed his cheek and said quietly, "Good night, Cony."

Raleigh started to call him back but decided against it. If Percy hadn't declared himself yet, then there was still time. Time to hopefully talk Tarren out of betrothing himself to the man, because Rourke had it right—Edmonstone was a buffoon. Raleigh poured himself a glass of brandy. He'd talk to Tarren on the morrow. "Good night, son."

Tarren lifted his hand in acknowledgment and brushed by the duke, hitting Rourke with his shoulder and making the older man grunt and step out of his slouch to keep his balance.

What in the devil was that about?

"Good night, Your Highness." Rourke's voice was sugary sweet as he turned to watch Tarren leave. Somehow the sarcasm didn't quite match the lengthy gaze.

Hmmm.... He'd never known Tarren to be so rude. Blinking in surprise, Raleigh took another drink and raised his brow at Rourke.

After closing the door, Rourke came inside. "I told him to take his dogs outside the other day because they were being too loud. He took exception and called me a dog hater. Of course, that was after I refused to let him go to the bookstore on his outings." He shrugged. "It wasn't on the agenda, and there were way too many people in there. One of them being Edmonstone."

Nodding, Raleigh crossed the room to his desk and sat on top of it.

"He called me an impossible arsehead."

Raleigh didn't know whether to gasp in horror or laugh. "How long has this thing with Edmonstone been going on? This is the first I've heard of it."

Again, Rourke shrugged. "About a week." Taking a swig of the brandy, Rourke walked over to the chair Raleigh had vacated earlier and sat down. The man somehow managed to look decadent and bored all at once. He was a handsome devil. It was no wonder most men twittered and lost their minds in his presence. "Edmonstone is not good enough for him." The opinion was offered in a nonchalant manner, but those nearly black eyes bore into Raleigh.

No, Percy wasn't good enough, but Raleigh was beginning to wonder if Rourke might just be perfect. Not that he'd let Rourke know that. And galaxy help him if Steven came to the same conclusion.... It was way too soon to tell if the two were suited, but Raleigh would definitely watch them together. Maybe give a nudge if it appeared his assumption was correct. "Agreed. Let me know if you see Edmonstone sniffing around. Now, what brings you here? Isn't this your night off? You look like you just crawled out of someone's bed." They said rakes made the best husbands. It certainly seemed true in Wentworth's case.

With a scoff of mock effrontery, Rourke swallowed down the last of his drink. "I'll have you know I left my own bed. Of course, the lovely Baron Hamsburg was in it, but that is completely irrelevant."

Raleigh chuckled. "Of course."

Rourke sat forward, all traces of playfulness gone. It was remarkable how different the rakish duke looked from the dangerous ex-special forces soldier turned Royal Guard. He'd aged five years in a matter of seconds. "Jeffers called me." The man took his work seriously. Which was why he had become Wentworth's right-hand man and why Raleigh trusted him implicitly. "Someone activated Ashbourne's dog tag."

Raleigh nearly dropped the tumbler in his hand. A plethora of obscenities wanted to spill from his mouth, but he held them back. When they'd found out the IN could use the tags as tracking devices, they'd come up with a way to erase the data on the dog tags and reformat them so only the Regelence Navy could access them. It beat taking the implants out of all former IN soldiers. They'd already reformatted Wentworth's, Rourke's, and all of their elite team of guards' tags. Until they found out why the IN wanted their procreation technology and why they'd gone to such great lengths to get it, they had to consider the IN their enemy. And it wouldn't do for their enemy to be able to track their movement since all Regelence Navy soldiers were once in the IN. The only problem was that they could not deactivate dog tags for Regelens who were still in the IN. Which was why Dalton's tag had not been done yet. Instead Raleigh had just had Jeffers turn Dalton's and Nate's off. He'd planned to reformat Dalton's once he got home and out of the IN. But sadly, he'd been so busy with the upcoming IN council meeting and dealing with his pain-in-the-arse brother, he had only seen Dalton briefly in the lift on the way to the ball. “Was Nate’s tag activated?”

“No. Only Dalton’s. I had Jeffers turn it back off, and I had him trace where the activation came from.” Rourke frowned.

Raleigh knew why. He nodded. “He can’t trace who turned it on.”

“That isn’t exactly true, Your Majesty,” Jeffers, who’d been silent to this point, replied.

“What?” Raleigh looked up and then back at Rourke.

Rourke leaned forward, holding the empty glass between his spread knees, but it was Jeffers who answered.

“I usually cannot tell who activates a dog tag. My assumption is that when it comes from the IN, they have a program to keep me from seeing this. However, it seems I can trace the signal when it comes from outside sources. I tested this theory by having Dunston activate the admiral’s dog tag. I then turned off the admiral’s tag, but the source was clearly from Englor and from Hollister Palace.”

Interesting. This meant the IN didn’t want to be tracked back to the dog tags and their GPS tracking capability. “So where did the signal come from to activate Dalton’s tag?”

It was Rourke who answered this time. “Throckmartin Avenue.”

“Bloody hell!”

Chapter Eight

Ruffles are all the crack this season! A most *fashionable* gentleman was seen sporting ruffles from head to toe at the Stratford ball last night.
—From *The Classige Morning News*, the On-Dit column

Townsend Castle

THERE WAS nothing quite like a mysterious summons to make a man feel like a child again. Dalton stepped into his uncle's office, wondering why he was there. Old habit had his mind whirling with his current misdeeds. Had someone seen him and Blaise at the Frost Fair?

"Ah good, you're here." Uncle Raleigh looked up from the monitor on his desk and motioned toward the chairs in front of it.

Blast, no escape now. "You asked to see me?" *More like demanded.*

Raleigh nodded. "I did." He gave Dalton an assessing look, but there was no hint about what he wanted to discuss.

Dalton fought not to squirm, because he knew this game. Raleigh was the only person Dalton knew who could interrogate a man without actually asking questions. He'd wrung more than one confession out of Dalton and his cousins this way. Well, except for Rexley. Rexley had always been impervious to the silent torture.

Raleigh must have realized the inner war he waged, because one brow went up. He might as well have raised the heat in the room by fifty degrees; it was a decidedly uncomfortable assessment, as though he could see right through Dalton.

Countering the brow with his own, Dalton crossed his arms over his chest, determined not to break. He didn't feel remorseful about any of the things he'd done in the past couple of days. He'd followed Blaise to the Frost Fair to protect him.

"Are you going to sit?" Raleigh's voice was mildly curious. With still no hint of a smile, Raleigh leaned back in his chair and crossed his hands over his abdomen like he had all the time in the world.

"Oh bloody hell!" Dalton planted his hands on his hips and glowered at his uncle. "I know what you are doing, and it's not going to work because I haven't done anything wrong."

A hint of a smile flitted over Raleigh's mouth. "Are you certain?"

"Yes." Dalton glowered some more and flopped down in the chair.

Raleigh started chuckling.

Dalton picked up a pen off the desk and threw it at him.

Raleigh laughed even harder. *The fiend.*

"You are evil." Dalton grinned but did his best to sound grumpy. "What do you want?"

"Is that any way to talk to your beloved uncle?" After setting the pen back down, Raleigh grabbed what looked like a necklace off the desk and tossed it at him.

Catching it easily, Dalton said, "I think you mean bedeviled not beloved." He turned the necklace over in his hands, more than a little confused. It was a gold Celtic cross. It was plain yet elegant all the same, with a ruby right in the middle where the bars intersected. "What's this?"

"It will be your dog tag once we take it out of you."

"I don't understand." He was leaving the IN. Dalton flipped the cross over, studying it. There were no openings on the cross, no seams. He ran his thumbnail along the edge.

"Your dog tag was activated last night."

Dalton jerked his attention away from the cross to his uncle, more than a little startled. Who would want to track him? Could that be why those men had followed him and Blaise last night? Dalton shook his head. No, that didn't make sense. "Are you certain?"

Raleigh nodded. "It was your father. The activation came from Fairfax House. I had it deactivated again, but we need to get it out of you."

Dalton relaxed marginally. "Bloody hell." So, the men last night had just been after his and Blaise's purses as he'd suspected. "He's spying on me."

"Have you gone to see him?"

He shook his head. He knew he needed to, but he was dreading it.

"You need to go see what he wants, but in the meantime, I'll get the dog tag out of you."

Dalton nodded. Good idea. He didn't want his father or anyone else following his movements. He glanced down at the necklace again and held it up to Raleigh. "But why do I need it back? I'm leaving the IN, remember?"

"I know, but I have a proposition for you." Raleigh glanced past Dalton and nodded. "*We* have a proposition for you."

Dalton turned to look over his shoulder as his cousin-in-law, Nate, who was also the IN Aries Fleet admiral, came strolling into the office with a big smile on his face. He was rugged, handsome, and aloof. Wide-shouldered and heavily muscled, the admiral had a commanding power about him that men envied and respected. That power also made him very appealing. Tonight he was dressed as a gentleman rather than a soldier, in a black evening coat and trousers, with a royal blue waistcoat and a snowy white cravat. The man was the very epitome of sex. When Dalton had first heard of his cousin's marriage, he'd envied Aiden. Oh, not the marriage, Dalton didn't want to be leg shackled, but a night with Nate? Before Dalton had really met the man, he'd have jumped at the chance, but now? Nate was utterly and truly devoted to Aiden. Dalton would never be disloyal to his cousin, and his tastes tended toward tall, lean muscle, and captivating green eyes nowadays. Shaking his head, Dalton glanced behind Nate, expecting to see Aiden, but Nate was alone.

The confusion must have shown on Dalton's face because Nate closed the door and asked, "What?"

"You're smiling."

The smile twisted sideways a bit. "So? I smile."

"Yes, but usually it's when Aiden is with you." Nate seemed in a perpetual good mood in the presence of his consort.

Grin still in place, Nate shrugged and went to the sideboard. He pulled out three glasses and started pouring scotch. "I'm celebrating."

"What are you celebrating?" Raleigh asked.

Nate's grin grew wider as he stoppered the decanter. He carried the three tumblers over, then gave one to Dalton and one to Raleigh before sitting in the chair next to Dalton. "My father is getting remarried."

It wasn't like Dalton needed an excuse to drink, but what the hell? He raised his glass. "To your father and his prospective duchess."

No one said anything, nor did they move to drink. They both stared at Dalton. Raleigh with his brow furrowed. Nate with the same silly grin—or perhaps it was a different grin, it was hard to say, but he looked amused.

"Umm.... Okay. What did I say?" Dalton had never met Nate's father, but the man was an Englorian duke, the Duke of Hawthorne. He knew from his cousins that Englor was a Regency society like theirs, only without artificial procreation.

"I presume that Hawthorne is marrying Oxley." Raleigh raised a brow in question.

For the first time Nate's smile slipped. "How did you know?"

"Oxley?" Dalton asked.

"The Marquess of Oxley." Raleigh looked rather smugly back to Nate. "How did you not? Anyone with a set of eyes could clearly see the two of them are a couple and have been for some time."

Nate shook his head and asked Dalton, "Has he always been like this?"

"A know-it-all?"

"Yes."

"Oh yeah."

Glaring at both of them, Raleigh raised his glass and said, "To Hawthorne and Oxley."

"To Hawthorne and Oxley," Dalton and Nate parroted and drank.

"Now back to our discussion." Raleigh set his glass on the desk and leaned back in his chair again.

Dalton sat forward, anxious to hear about this proposition.

"I'd like you to stay in the IN."

"But—"

Raleigh held up a hand, stalling his protest. "You will be working for Nate directly and helping him spy on the IN. It's a dangerous job, and honestly, I'm not sure how long it will last, because I'm pulling you both out of there at the first hint of trouble, but it would help us."

Not knowing how to feel about it, Dalton frowned. He'd wanted out of the IN because of the danger it posed to his planet. Anyone who stood against Regelence stood against Dalton, as far as he was concerned. In the past year, the IN had been behind various secret plots against Regelence. The latest, during Dalton's leave last September, when Admiral Jenkins, the former Aries Fleet admiral who Nate had replaced, was discovered to be missing and was suspected dead. Like all the other plots, they could not prove that the IN was responsible, but all the evidence led back to the IN or at least to IN intelligence. The thing was, they weren't certain who all was involved and to what extent. They weren't even positive what the IN's end game was, but the IN wanted Regelence's procreation technology. If Dalton could help his planet….

"What about my special forces training?"

"It will be an asset." Nate set his now-empty glass on the desk and leaned forward in his chair. "You will be able to get in and out of places that I can't. Everyone recognizes me, but you aren't as easily recognizable…." Nate shrugged. "And I need someone at the base and IN functions who I can trust. My staff is made up of Regelens and Englorians, but they aren't privy to the stuff we are."

"Have you learned more?" When Dalton was home on leave six months ago, Raleigh had gotten a hold of a hard drive that belonged to the former admiral.

"A little. I've got a lot to go through." Raleigh sighed. "I can't find proof that they killed Jenkins, but he says himself on the hard drive that if he turns up dead, the IN is behind it. And he confirmed that the IN wants our procreation technology because they want to implement it and create their own soldiers. I've found out about the weapons that were stolen by mercenaries hired by the IN. They were set to be used against a planet in the Calluna system, where Nate confiscated them, but I have no idea why."

"The Calluna system? Is it near Lerdra?" He'd been stationed on Lerdra when he was in the IN.

Raleigh shook his head. "No, it's a small system near Englor, but that isn't all of it. According to Jenkins, there is something on one of their planets, a planet called Skye, that belongs to us. Something he thinks I need and something that will be able to give me more information."

"Do we know who in the IN is behind all of this?" Dalton asked out of curiosity. Obviously not everyone in power in the IN was privy to the plan, whatever the plan was, because Nate as a fleet admiral knew nothing about it from the IN.

"No, though we suspect IN intelligence." It was Nate who answered. "Simon has an intelligence agent in custody, but they have not been able to get information from him." Simon was the King of Englor and another of Dalton's cousin-in-laws. He was married to Dalton's cousin Payton, though Dalton had never met Simon or Simon and Payton's infant son, Garrett.

The idea of playing spy and working so directly against the threat to his planet was an intriguing one, but it would also mean a lot of paperwork and he had always hated paperwork. He was a soldier and good at fighting. This job would not include fighting, well, not unless things went wrong.

The grandfather clock in the corner chimed the hour. He had to meet Blaise in fifteen minutes, and he didn't dare be late because Blaise would go without him. Dalton glanced down at the cross in his hand, then set it on the desk. That was one positive about working with Nate—he'd be able to stay here with Blaise. "Can I think about it?"

Raleigh smiled. "Of course."

"Then I'll take my leave." Dalton stood.

"Wait. We need to get your dog tag out."

Dalton groaned. He'd been so caught off guard with the proposition, he'd forgotten all about the dog tag. "I can't do it right now."

Raleigh's brow went up.

Oh bloody hell, he didn't have time for this. "I have to save Blaise from himself."

The other brow joined the first, but a smile crept onto Raleigh's face. "Then by all means."

Thompson House, town house of the Duke and Duke-Consort of Eversleigh, in Classige, Pruluce

AFTER A fitful night of sleep, Blaise had come up with a plan in the wee hours of the morning and sent a note off to Dalton to inform him of the plan. Now standing in front of the mirror, he wondered if he were dicked in the nob. He sure seemed to be pondering that thought a lot lately. He had gone from being scandalized by Dalton and slightly horrified the man had been assigned as his guard, to first-name basis. Even though his common sense yelled at him not to get any more involved with a known rake, his gut said otherwise. He actually liked Dalton, blast it all. He buttoned the brown houndstooth waistcoat, giving the simply tied cream cravat a tug, and sent up a prayer that his gut wasn't wrong. Galaxy knew, he was already tempting fate where his reputation was concerned.

"You look good."

Dusting the sleeves of the cocoa morning coat, he smiled at his valet's voice. "Why, thank you, miss." He was the very image of a simple hardworking man. A shopkeeper, perhaps. Thankfully, he most definitely did not resemble a lord of the realm. He'd learned his lesson last night at the Frost Fair. He would get a better reception from the people on the wharf dressed as one of them. "Whose clothes am I wearing?" His cravat was still askew. Turning back to face the mirror, he tugged on the right side.

The silly thing drooped to the left.

Before he could adjust it, two dainty well-manicured hands came around him in the mirror, untied the cravat he'd just tied, and proceeded to rework it into a slightly more elegant knot. "Henry, the footman's."

"Hey! I just tied that." Blaise gave his valet a friendly hip bump. "Can Henry be trusted to be discreet?"

Without letting go of his cravat, Larkinson grunted and kneed him in the bottom. "Yes, he can be trusted. He's sweet on my sister. Behave. You looked like a butcher or a delivery boy. And speaking of fashion…. Have you read the scandal sheet this morning?" Her voice held a hint of laughter. Only Larkinson knew of his guilty pleasure—reading the gossip columns—and she loved to tease him about it.

"I did." He'd been scouring them for mention of Dalton, and if he were truly honest with himself, it wasn't only because he feared both of their absences might have been noticed last night. "If you try to dress me in ruffles, I shall have you tarred, feathered, dragged out in the street, and shot, and perhaps even run through with a rapier." He bumped her hip again.

She responded by pulling his cravat tight and choking him with it.

After a few reciprocated shoves and a lot of laughter, he asked, "Henry is sweet on Louie? Whatever is the matter with him?"

"Nothing. He just doesn't know her well." Larkinson giggled. "Boy, is he in for a bit of a surprise."

Wasn't that the truth. Henry seemed a responsible sort, and Louie was… well… Louie.

Flattening the ends of his neckcloth, she tucked them into the folds. "Now you look more like a banker."

"I was going for shopkeeper. I'm supposed to look like I don't have a valet."

"Well, you do have a valet, and no self-respecting valet would allow you out of the house with a cravat tied so poorly." With one final pat, she let go of his neckcloth and brushed off the shoulders of his coat. "There. I've upgraded you to shop owner." She leaned to the side of him, and her pretty oval face and neck appeared in the mirror beside his shoulder. She nodded once. "Perfect."

Blaise's attention narrowed down to her neck, which sported a cravat tied like his. *What in the…?* Whirling around, he gawked at her.

She wore men's attire. Her color scheme leaned more to the green side of the spectrum, but it was definitely men's clothing. A hunter-green morning coat, a beige-and-emerald waistcoat, and a snowy white cravat. Not only were her clothes masculine, but her dark chestnut hair was slicked back into a tight bun, making her neck appear longer than usual and her cheekbones seem sharper. The clothes were at least a size too large for her, but even still, she made an elegant, if effeminate-looking man. Women in breeches weren't an unusual sight, but for a woman to try and look manly? It was, however, out of the ordinary and not exactly professional for a valet of her status.

"What in the galaxy are you wearing?"

"Some of Henry's clothes." She preened a little in front of the mirror.

"But why?"

Larkinson scrunched up her nose and scoffed at him as if to say *isn't that obvious?*

It wasn't obvious at all.

"Same as you. It's a disguise."

"I'm wearing it to blend in. You would blend in just fine with a nice but serviceable dress." Of course, her dresses were suited to high-ranking women, so she'd have to borrow one from one of the maids.

She snorted and rolled her eyes. "And I'd look like a valet. What's the fun in that?"

"Indeed." Groaning, he crossed his arms over his chest. "And just how do you expect to get out of the house without being noticed?"

"Same as you. With a greatcoat covering me up." She bobbed her head in that particular so-there way she had.

"Only you don't usually wear a greatcoat."

She sighed. "We're going out the service entrance, so no one will pay me any mind."

"We're going to get caught, then…." He hadn't told her or Bannon about the disk, and he had no intention of doing so. The fewer people who knew, the better. For now, it was his and Dalton's secret.

"Then?"

Then my life will end in scandal and everything I've worked for will be for naught. Guh, just the thought made his palms sweat and a lump form in his throat. And he most definitely couldn't say that without telling her about the disk, so he said, "Then Bannon will get sent to the country or worse. Hell, *I* might actually get sent to the country too."

At first, Larkinson cocked her head at him like a confused puppy, but her grin wasn't long in following.

"What?"

"I think you have Bannon's flair for dramatics."

If ever there was a time for dramatics.... "Galaxy, help me." He threw his hands in the air before he even realized what he was doing, which only made Larkinson laugh harder. "Though I might actually need his acting talent to get the box back." Turning to his bed, he grabbed the greatcoat and the hat that Larkinson had set on the end of it.

"How exactly *are* we going to get *the box* back? I know you have a plan, because you were up until the early hours of the morning. So when are you going to share it?"

"I was up researching how to fence stolen goods." And about orphanages, but he kept that to himself. He wasn't even sure they'd encounter any orphans today. With any luck those children hadn't been orphans at all, just scam artists.

Larkinson giggled again.

When Blaise looked at her, she covered her mouth with her hand.

"What?"

She shrugged, but the twinkle in her eyes didn't disappear.

"Tamsin...," he said, using her first name.

"Only you would research something like that."

Now it was his turn to sigh. "I like to be prepared." Besides, he was good at research. "How else am I going to learn about that sort of thing? It's not like I've ever disposed of stolen property before."

"And you aren't doing that now either."

"No, I'm doing the reverse. If I want to find the box, I have to think like a criminal."

She crossed her arms over her chest and tucked her lips tight together as though she were trying not to laugh.

Blaise rolled his eyes and proceeded to put on his borrowed coat and hat, ignoring her amusement. He was very open-minded; he could think like a criminal if need be.

"Knock, knock." Bannon's words preceded his disheveled red hair poking through the crack in the door leading from Larkinson's bedroom and a knock after he'd already opened said door. Then his smiling face appeared, followed by the rest of him. The rest of him was dressed similarly to Blaise and Larkinson, only in shades of violet.

"Faith!" Blaise slapped a hand to his forehead. Between the three of them, they looked like a giant bruise. "Are the two of you trying to get us caught?"

"What?" Bannon came on into the room, after closing the door behind him. At least he'd had the presence of mind to go through the servants' door instead of the hallway.

"You are not going," Blaise said.

"But…."

"No buts."

"I'm going to help," Bannon continued.

"You are helping. You're staying here to run interference and cover our tracks with Father and Sire." Speaking of which… they needed to hurry.

Blaise grabbed the printout he'd made last night and stuffed it in the inside pocket of the brown greatcoat. Time to enact the stealthy part of his plan. He opened the door and peeked out cautiously. No servants in the hall. Looking back inside he pointed at Bannon, who appeared on the verge of following. "No!" Galaxy help him, he was still perturbed at his brother for getting them both into this mess in the first place. To Larkinson, he said, "Meet me around back."

Out back was deserted, thank goodness. The morning was chilly and snow-covered, but there were no servants or delivery people about.

Larkinson came out the servants' entry, wearing a black derby and a black frock coat. It was a rather nice frock coat.

His brother was on her heels.

Bloody hell! Blaise pointed at the house.

Kicking the doorjamb, Bannon hung his shoulders and stomped back inside as Larkinson joined Blaise at the curb.

"We should let him go."

"No, we should not. He's the reason I'm in this mess in the first place." He grumbled and started walking down the sidewalk.

She strolled beside him, her coat flapping in the wind and hitting Blaise's legs as well as hers. "Don't pretend you aren't enjoying this. At least a little."

He was, actually, which was a bit worrisome. He'd never thought himself a clunch. "I most certainly am *not*." After pulling the paper out of his coat, he looked at the map. "Southpaws is on the west side of the docks. It's not too far from where I was last night, but first we must meet Dalton. Then we will hire a lift."

"Dalton?" Her voice rose an octave with her interest, and Blaise cursed himself for a fool.

"Er… Ashbourne. He is supposed to meet us at the corner of Halston Street and Lummex Lane. Didn't I mention that?"

"You did, but you know that is not what I meant." With a raised brow, she pushed back the cuffs on her coat where they were too long for her. The coat had a silk lining, so it would look odd if she rolled the cuffs.

Wait a moment. They paid their servants well, but even still, a footman would probably not have a coat with silk lining. "Is that my coat?"

She bit her bottom lip, darted her gaze to the side, and nodded. "Yes. Henry only had one coat. Now stop changing the subject. You call Ashbourne *Dalton*?"

With a sigh, Blaise gave in because he knew her well enough to know she wasn't going to drop it. "Yes. We agreed to dispense with the formalities. After last night, it just seems silly not to."

"You like him." Her brow wrinkled.

"I do. I know I shouldn't, and he can be very exasperating, but I do like him." Never in a million years would he have thought to count a rake as a friend, but he could see him and Dalton becoming friends. There had been a real connection between them last night, and that kiss…. He fancied he still felt the tingle. It had been shocking and exciting all at once.

"Why are you blushing?"

"What? I'm not blushing." *Oh, stars! Please don't let me be blushing or…. Galaxy forbid, glowing.*

She wasn't fooled. She was quiet for several tense seconds and continued to watch him.

Blaise didn't look at her. He should probably tell her all, but somehow it just didn't seem right to do so. Though it was his first kiss, it had meant nothing to Dalton. There was no future in it, and admitting it out loud would make it sound more than it was. It would be admitting it had meant something to him. And he just couldn't make himself do that. This flirtation Dalton seemed intent on engaging in with him would end eventually.

Finally, she looked away and very quietly asked, "Do you trust him?"

The question gave him pause. It wasn't at all what he expected. Did he trust Dalton with his feelings? No, absolutely not. Did he trust him to not try and seduce him? Unequivocally no. But did he trust him to keep his secret? To make sure Blaise was not ruined by scandal? "Yes. I do. He has his own sense of honor."

She nodded as if satisfied.

They walked for several blocks without saying anything else. This part of town was not nearly as nice as Regelence Park Square where they lived, nor was it the fashionable part of town around Platt Street, but it still catered to the gentry. There were banks, law offices, and assorted professional services rather than actual shops. It was quiet at this time of morning. The gentry were sleeping off last night's excess.

A smile eased onto her lips, but before Blaise turned to see what she was staring at, she said, "Now I see why you were blushing. Is that him?"

Striding toward them, about twenty yards away, Dalton looked just as perfect as he had last night. Today he wore a burgundy morning coat, a white cravat, tight buckskin trousers, and gleaming black knee-high top boots. His outerwear consisted of a very expensive black wool many-caped frock coat and a beaver hat. He even carried a walking stick. Everything about him screamed aristocrat. And everything about him sent Blaise's senses reeling. He was somehow even more gorgeous than he had been last night.

"He's very handsome. It's quite easy to see how he got his reputation."

"Yes, he is." Breathtaking was more like it. "But he is illiterate." As they drew closer, Blaise said, "I said dress in civilian clothes."

Dalton graced them with a smile worthy of the libertine he was known to be. "These are my civilian clothes."

"I meant, to dress like a civilian, not in—"

A hackney pulled to the curb behind Dalton, and two rough-looking men jumped out. They seemed rather out of place for this part of town.

The confusion must have shown on his face, because Dalton turned to peek over his shoulder, but not quickly enough.

The men grabbed him, one on each arm, and began to drag him toward the lift.

Chapter Nine

Either this author needs spectacles or there is a new fad going around. A future duke and his valet were seen walking about Classige this morning dressed as commoners. What is the world coming to?

—From *The Pruluce Prattler*

DALTON ONLY had a brief moment to take in his captors before the danger of the situation hit him. "Run!" he yelled at Blaise, but his hopes that Blaise would get to safety were quickly dashed when Blaise finally did run.

The. Wrong. Fucking. Way.

Bloody hell! Dalton had meant for him to run away from him and the assailants, not toward them.

Blaise charged forward, leaving the girl dressed as a boy who had accompanied him standing there gaping. The fierce expression on his face could only be described as malicious, like a Greek god angling for revenge. He was almost frightening. *If* he hadn't opened his mouth. "Unhand him, you, you rapscallions!"

The girl looked like someone had slapped her. Whether from the situation or from Blaise's demand was anyone's guess.

Dalton suspected his expression matched hers. Why he was surprised by Blaise running into the fray, he didn't know. The one thing he'd learned about Blaise so far was that the man never did what you wanted or expected him to do. And who the hell used the word *rapscallion*?

The men, for their part, didn't look the least bit concerned about Blaise. The larger of the two, a bald man with a black mustache, jerked on Dalton's arm. "Come along, milord." The *milord* was said with so much venom it was a wonder the man didn't have fangs.

Damn it! He should have let his uncle remove the dog tag. *Please let this be because of my parents.* His own parents wouldn't have him killed, would they? But what if this had nothing to do with his parents and his dog tag? One thing was for certain—he wasn't going to wait and find out, and he wasn't going to endanger Blaise in the process.

The other man, this one a bit shorter and a tad more muscled, followed suit and tugged Dalton's arm so hard his shoulder popped. Neither of them were watching Blaise. They weren't even looking at Dalton. They were focused on the plain black lift idling at the curb.

Not giving Blaise time to make a heroic rescue and put himself in more danger, Dalton took matters into his own hands. Going limp, he lifted his legs up and sank all his weight toward the ground.

His knees hit the cement, and fire blazed into Dalton's bones and radiated up his thighs. He bit his lip too, but it had the desired result… mostly.

The man on his right let go with a curse.

The other captor held firm but went down with Dalton. Well, not down so much as over. He bent at the waist and huffed out a breath in surprise. His eyes widened, and his grip tightened to the point of pain. "You li'le…."

Taking advantage of the nearness of the man's face, Dalton hauled back and planted his fist in the man's nose.

"Crikey!" Blood sprayed, dotting the man's cravat and the ground as he yelped and slapped both hands over his nose, freeing Dalton. "You damned bloody arse!"

Blaise finally got to him, but before Dalton could tell him to get back, the mustached goon snagged Blaise's wrists. He struggled to free himself, but there was no way he was going to win. The man outweighed him by at least three stones. Blaise, however, didn't stop kicking the guy's shins.

Dalton hopped to his feet quicker than even he thought possible, and he'd always been quick, but before he took even a step, a hand snagged his ankle.

The girl, presumably Blaise's valet, pounded Blaise's attacker in the back with her fists. She wasn't very effective, but she certainly tried, and it was enough to distract the brute because Blaise freed one wrist.

Together they faced the kidnapper. It was like a couple of ants trying to take down a horse.

"Would you stop?" Still holding Blaise, the bigger man put his entire hand over the valet's petite face and shoved.

She landed on her arse with a grunt.

Finally breaking the grip on his ankle, Dalton swung his walking stick and walloped the mustached man across the head, breaking the stick in two, but he didn't stop there—he also kicked the man in the knee.

The man went down like a chopped tree, barely missing falling on the girl, but it had the desired effect. He let go of Blaise.

Dalton didn't have time to feel relief or anything else. He grabbed the girl's arm. They had to get out of here before the men recovered, because no one seemed interested in helping them. The streets were oddly deserted this morning. Probably because of the early hour, or perhaps last night's snowfall, but the few people on the streets seemed to have tunnel vision. They hurried past, not wanting to get involved.

"Eeek!" a small squeak came from behind them just as Dalton hauled the girl to her feet. Something in the soft sound sent the hair on the back of his neck standing on end. A sense of dread washed over him. This was not going to be good, because he was pretty sure the squeak had come from Blaise.

He whirled around, and it was worse than he'd thought.

The man he'd punched in the nose had a blade to Blaise's long, delicate neck. The silver seemed to gleam against the white cravat. How had the man gotten past him?

A shaft of fear lanced through Dalton as he met Blaise's wide grass-green eyes. He'd come here today to avoid this sort of thing. He'd come to keep Blaise safe, and he'd failed.

Blaise closed his eyes and took a deep breath before opening them and looking back at Dalton. The expression was calm and steady now, as if he were waiting for direction from Dalton.

It hit Dalton in the chest like a kick from a mule. That trust and the sense of camaraderie he'd felt last night came rushing back.

Centering himself, he looked up at the man holding the knife to Blaise's neck. He had no choice because there was something familiar in that hard gaze. Something Dalton had seen time and again in battle. The knowledge of death. Those eyes had seen and done despicable things.

Raising his hands, Dalton said, "Let him go, and I'll do whatever you want." He'd get himself out of this later, once Blaise was safe.

The man smiled. "Good ta 'ave yer cooperation. Get in the lift."

Damnation! With no other choice, Dalton got into the hackney.

Fairfax House, town house of the Marquess and Marquess-Consort of Ravensburg, on Throckmartin Avenue in Classige, Pruluce

Fairfax House reminded Dalton of a dollhouse. A sinister dollhouse. He'd always felt rather like a doll being moved around and discarded on the whim of the house's owners: his parents. *Damn them to the devil!* As he stared up at his family's town house, a shiver snaked down his back. It felt… sad, and he could not shake the feeling of pain, like something bad happened here, which was silly. Violence was not in his parents' natures, even if they were obviously not above having their only son kidnapped. A part of him was relieved they had been behind the kidnapping, but the other part of him fumed.

As Dalton tried to make himself relax—because planting Ravensburg a facer would get him nowhere—Mustache barged past him, opened the iron gate, and went right up to the front door, like he owned the place. Or at least like he was a frequent visitor, which was highly unlikely. His parents were too self-important to deal with someone they'd see as lowly. No doubt they'd had a servant deal with the man.

As if to confirm his suspicion, the front door opened, and Rutherford, the underbutler of Fairfax House, stood in the doorway with a frosty glare on his face. Upon spotting the large man standing there, he shook his head and pointed to the side, the servants' entrance.

The man ignored him and barged right in.

"Ge' moving, milawd." The other half of the dastardly duo shoved Dalton's shoulder.

Rutherford's steely composure slipped a little with a slight uplift at the right side of his lip. If Dalton hadn't been looking, he'd have missed it. The hint of a smile settled back into its usual stoic line, but there seemed a little bit of worry in his old brown eyes as well. He darted a glance past Dalton's shoulder at the other kidnapper and snarled like he'd smelled something bad.

Faced with the reality of his situation again, Dalton had to muster up a smile for his old ally. "Mornin', Rutherford." Because what else could he do?

Closing the wrought-iron gate, Dalton made his way up the short walk to the steps. Tipping his head right and left, he relieved some of the tension through sheer willpower alone. Calm, cool, and collected. One of the many things he'd learned in the military. Keeping his wits served him well. His parents were too proper to get into a shouting match, and blast it all, dueling was illegal.

"Welcome home, my lord," Rutherford said, and Dalton had no doubt the greeting was sincere. The man had to be pushing seventy. He had a few more gray hairs, and his bald spot was definitely bigger, but his demeanor was exactly the same. A little foreboding, but kind.

"How are you, Rutherford?"

"Good, my lord. Thank you for asking." He glanced down at Dalton's empty hands and raised a brow. "Hat and coat, my lord?"

Dalton reached for his hat, and realized it wasn't there. Damn it all, he'd lost another hat. "Thank you, Rutherford, but I'll keep my coat. I won't be staying long."

With a nod, the old man swept out his arm toward the entrance.

With another shiver, and trepidation weighing on him, Dalton walked in.

The entryway hadn't changed in the last two years either. It was still bright white, airy, pretentious as hell, and cold. The contrast to Townsend Castle was almost overwhelming. A stark reminder why he did not like to be here. The place always made Dalton feel dingy in comparison, because no matter how hard he'd tried as a child, he could not keep from tracking dirt on the floor. He'd eventually given up trying.

With no indication of shock whatsoever, Rutherford glared at the remaining kidnapper. He snapped his fingers, and a footman came forward. "Show this man to the kitchen."

"I'll jus' wai' 'ere faw John an' make sure 'is lawdship doesn' run off." The kidnapper gave Dalton a nasty grin.

Rutherford looked at Dalton.

Dalton shrugged. He was saving his energy for the true villains—his parents.

With a haughty sniff, Rutherford turned his attention back to the footman. "Stay with him. He's not to leave the foyer."

Dalton couldn't help but grin at the old man's cheek. The kidnappers had met their match in Rutherford.

Rutherford looked around, then gave Dalton's shoulder a quick pat in affection. He leaned in close and whispered, "They're awaiting you in the parlor. Been plotting something all morning." Then he straightened and darted a glance behind him again.

Dalton squeezed his shoulder in a show of thanks.

Stuart, the computer butler, was already announcing him.

He went in as Mustache left. The man hit his shoulder in a hurry to leave. *Arsehead.* Dalton shook his head and walked the rest of the way into the parlor, not bothering to shut the door.

His father sat on one of the two light green brocade sofas, and his sire stood peering out the window. They complemented each other very well. His sire with his smaller frame and his boyish good looks had been referred to as pretty by the gossip columns, and it certainly fit. Ravensburg was the exact opposite, with dark hair, a tall athletic build, and his classically handsome face. Dalton supposed he should be glad, because he certainly benefited from it. He had his father's height, the Fairfax gray eyes, and his sire's blond hair, though not nearly as light. His was a darker blond. Still, he wasn't a bad-looking man, if he did say so himself.

Both his parents turned as he entered. For a brief moment, a pleasant expression, not quite a smile, tugged at the marquess's lips as he looked Dalton up and down. Why did he almost appear pleased?

Both marquess and marquess-consort were perfectly turned out, without a hair out of place and with their cravats perfectly starched. His father was sans his morning coat, but somehow still managed to look fashionable in a light purple waistcoat and his charcoal trousers.

Ravensburg got up from the sofa as Dalton entered, and one dark brow rose, no doubt expecting Dalton to start hurling obscenities.

As much as Dalton wanted to do just that, he resisted. "Father." He turned and dipped his head at his sire. "Sire."

"Ashbourne." As if he were inviting Dalton to tea, Ravensburg motioned to the sofa across from him as he took his own seat again. "Please, won't you have a seat. We've been expecting you." Apparently, they were going to pretend they hadn't had Dalton dragged here.

Fine, whatever. "I'll stand, thank you. I think we all know why I'm here."

With a dramatic sigh, Arthur Fairfax strode over to his spouse in a show of solidarity. *Typical.* He sat a respectable foot away, as was proper, with no part of their bodies touching. Dalton couldn't ever remember them so much as looking at each other improperly. Yet, they seemed to genuinely care for each other. It was odd. Especially in comparison to his uncles' open display of affection.

Arthur crossed his leg over his knee and stretched his arms out on the sofa back. He looked relaxed, like he hadn't a care in the world, like he'd had no part in having his own son kidnapped. "You gave us no choice, son. You ran from us and were conveniently not at the castle yesterday evening when we paid a visit. After the report from our investigators about you traipsing around the wharf with some light-trouser at an ungodly hour last night, we deemed the situation dire."

Un-fucking-believable. Heat exploded up Dalton's neck, and his jaw tightened to the point of pain. He should have had the dog tag removed last September when his uncle had warned him it could be used as a tracking device, but he'd been waiting till he was out of the IN.

"I told you on our last televid call we wanted you to live here," Arthur continued.

"And I informed *you* in that last televid call, I had no intentions of living here," Dalton spat out. "You want what I can't give you, so in the name of family harmony, I've decided to live at the castle."

His parents shared a glance, and then Ravensburg turned back to him and said, "That is unacceptable, Ashbourne." He looked down his nose at Dalton, and those gray eyes dared him to argue.

Dalton had been on his own too long for it to work now. "I'm sorry, Father, but we've been over this."

"No, Ashbourne, we have not been over this to *my* satisfaction." The way he said "my" made it crystal clear that his satisfaction was all that mattered. A sentiment that was typical of him. "You will retire from the armed services. I did not approve of you joining, but I allowed it. Now, you will come home and settle down."

Not bloody likely. His father had not been happy about him joining, but by law, a man could join the armed forces at eighteen without parental permission, even though a man did not technically reach his majority on Regelence until he was twenty-five. So really the idea that his father was now trying to dictate that Dalton get out of the Navy was preposterous. They could not legally make him. Dalton raised a brow, trying on one of his father's superior looks for size. "I've only done two years of my term."

"And you are a lord of the realm. The Regelence Navy will exempt you from doing the required two-year term."

Sadly, if Ravensburg forced the matter, that was probably true, but.... "I'm not retiring. I plan on going career and staying with the Regelence Navy."

"You will retire, or you will not have your inheritance." Arthur had darted a glance at his consort. "It's well past time for you to marry and produce an heir."

A sinking feeling settled into Dalton's stomach.

"If left up to you, you will have no reputation at all," Ravensburg said.

His sire nodded his agreement. "It's bad enough the ton refers to you as Lord Demon. It's an embarrassment." He pursed his lips in a moue of distaste.

"So you expect me to just retire and do your bidding? I suppose you have a husband all picked out." Dalton couldn't help but smirk at the idea. They couldn't honestly think he'd agree to this.

"We have a couple of eligible men in mind who we'd like you to consider, but you will have to clean up your reputation first. Then you can pick your own consort." His sire seemed to forget about looking elegant and leaned forward, dropping his hands off the back of the couch. "No one will have you as is."

It was like having a heavy object thrown at you with very little warning. Surprise and fear all rolled into one. Only he didn't catch the object and feel relief. Gads, he wanted to knock that smug look right off his sire's pretty face. "I have no interest in getting leg shackled."

"I will not sit by and watch Ravensburg go to a bounder like my father. You *will* retire, and you *will* repair your reputation, or I'll do my best to see you beggared." Ravensburg stood and walked over to the mantel. "Then who will pay for your light-trousers, your gambling and drinking? As much as my brother adores you, even he will not give you an allowance to blow on your rakish pursuits." When he turned back, his face was blank. He clearly thought he'd won.

"Don't bring Grandfather into this. This has nothing to do with him. My grandfather actually gave a shit about me. That's what bothers you, isn't it? He loved me more than you."

His father recoiled as though he'd been slapped, and then he narrowed his eyes, and there was something more. Hurt? Anger? Before Dalton could decide, his father's normally placid mask fell in place.

Part of Dalton swelled with pride for scoring a direct hit, but another part of him regretted doing so. He'd never seen that many emotions play across his father's face before. It was a low blow. Even for him. He of all people knew what it was like to be found lacking by one's parents. "You can take my allowance and the revenues I get from Ashbourne, but you forget, I do get a salary from the Navy." And if he had to live at the castle until he was twenty-five, then so be it.

"No, son, I'm afraid it's you who has forgotten something." Ravensburg rested his elbow against the mantel in a casual pose. "In Regelence, you are under age, and even the Regelence Navy takes that into account. By law, I can have your pay deposited into your inheritance where you can't touch it until you are of age."

All the blood drained from Dalton's upper extremities. He knew this because his face and hands suddenly felt ice-cold. He grabbed the back of the chair in front of him to keep his legs from buckling.

His sire pointed his bony finger at Dalton. "So, you—"

Father grabbed Sire's hand and pulled it down, effectively cutting Arthur off and earning himself a frown.

Ravensburg, however, was not deterred. He patted the hand affectionately and said in a much calmer voice than his spouse, "I'll make you a deal. If you prove to us you are not the bounder you were when you left, I'll release your money, but I still want you out of the Regelence Navy."

He'd take what little reprieve he could get until he could come up with a better plan. "How long do I have to prove it to you?"

Ravensburg didn't even take time to think before he said, "A week, and you *will* eat dinner and sleep here. I expect you here this evening."

Chapter Ten

The ton's most *fashionable* beau was seen paying an awful lot of attention to a member of the royal family at the Earl of Stratford's ball last night. Could there be another royal wedding on the horizon? Or were they merely sharing fashion tips?

—From *The Classige Morning News*, the On-Dit column

WITH DALTON'S hat still in his hand, Blaise got out of the hackney and frowned up at the Marquess of Ravensburg's town house. "This can't be right."

Larkinson stepped up beside him, also staring at the mansion. "The hackneys are controlled by a central computer. I can't imagine it would be wrong. Are you certain we got the number correct?" The lifts for hire had white numbering on the top left side of each end of the black vehicles, and after Dalton had been taken, they'd quickly hailed another passing hackney with instructions to follow the one that had taken Dalton.

"Four hundred and fifty-three?"

She nodded. "That's what I saw too."

At least he wasn't losing his mind. "If the coach is right…." Unable to stop gawking at Fairfax House, Blaise shook his head, having a hard time fathoming the reality of the situation. "Why would his parents kidnap him?"

"I have no idea." She sounded just as in awe and puzzled as he did.

Ravensburg was a bit odd, but he'd never seemed demented, and this…? This seemed… well, it definitely didn't seem like something a sane person would do. "Makes me thankful for my parents."

Again, Larkinson nodded.

"Redding? Is that you?" a familiar voice asked from behind them.

Startled out of the revelation that one of the IN Councilman's Committee might be dicked in the nob, Blaise turned at the voice and nearly bumped heads with Larkinson. They steadied each other and glanced back toward the voice.

Idling at the curb where their transportation had been moments ago—yikes, he hadn't realized it had driven off—sat a very expensive, very shiny black coach that was definitely a private conveyance rather than one for hire. In addition to the sleek design, the silence of it attested to that. There were no identifying marks on the lift, but the door was up, so it was hard to tell if it were adorned with a family crest. A tall man darkened the open door, with his face shadowed by a black D'Orsay-style hat.

"Er, yes."

Prince Rexley Townsend leaned out of the lift, and the butterflies in Blaise's stomach immediately ceased.

With a slight upturn of his lips and a furrowed brow, Rexley beckoned them with his hand. "I thought that was you. Quickly. Get inside here, both of you." He stepped back out of the doorway so they could enter.

Blaise looked at Larkinson. Why was Rexley acting so discreet, as though he didn't want to be seen? This *was* his uncle's house.

As if reading his mind, Larkinson shrugged at Blaise and grabbed his arm to usher him inside.

The silent door closed behind them, casting the inside in brief darkness before his eyes registered the dim lighting made to mimic candlelight. The interior was as spectacular as the outside, with plush burgundy velvet seats and curtains with gold brocade. The walls and ceiling were paneled in ebony wood. It was opulence and simplicity all rolled into one. It fit Rexley's personality, and it was also new, or at least Blaise had never seen it. He tossed Dalton's hat on the bench closest to him and sat across from Rexley.

Rexley peered out the tinted window. The curtains were pulled back on each side by a gold braid, but the windows were so dark no one could see in. He looked at Blaise and Larkinson. "What are you doing here?"

"I was about to ask you the same thing," Blaise countered by way of avoidance. Though he really was curious why Rexley was here. How would Rexley have known his cousin had been kidnapped? "And how did you get out without a guard? Even Bannon and I have guards now."

Rexley raised an enigmatic brow, which usually meant he wasn't going to answer, but he surprised Blaise by saying, "My father and sire are both in meetings, Rourke is off today, and Wentworth is with Tarren and Colton on an outing."

"So you snuck out without whatever guard was on duty."

Only a small smirk gave any indication that Rexley had heard him. "Jeffers alerted me that Dalton's dog tag had been activated to give his GPS coordinates." Rexley motioned to the seat beside him, where a small com-pad sat. Next to the com-pad was a fragger. "It happened last night as well, but Rourke had the signal turned off, and it wasn't activated again until this morning. I followed Dalton's signal here." His nose wrinkled, and he shook his head lightly. "I have to say, I'm surprised he came here."

"Blast!" Blaise leaned back in the seat a little harder than he'd intended and knocked his hat askew. Two things occurred to him simultaneously. The men following them last night was not by happenstance and…. "This is my fault! I gave Ravensburg a disk with the codes to dog tags of Regelen IN soldiers yesterday afternoon." Guilt niggled in his stomach. "I didn't think he'd use it against his own son. The dog tags are a hot topic right now among the IN Councilman's Committee because we are looking into options to get them removed and keep the IN from installing them in our soldiers. Ravensburg is heading up the subcommittee, so I never thought it was strange that he wanted the info. He seemed genuinely concerned that the IN is able to track Regelens who served in the IN. We all are. So why would he risk activating the tag to kidnap his own son?"

One elegant dark brow rose, but otherwise Rexley gave no indication of surprise. "You're saying that Ravensburg abducted him?"

"No." Blaise shook his head. His hat swiveled, so he took it off and handed it to Larkinson, who sat next to him. "He had two thugs grab Dalton off the street. Why would he do that? I know their relationship is a bit problematic, but…. Is Dalton in any danger?"

Rexley stared at him like he'd said something completely mutton-headed, and then the corner of his lips lifted slightly.

Blaise blinked and wondered if it was a trick of the dim lighting. Because Rexley now wore the blank mellow expression he excelled at. That stony face made a man want to confess their deepest darkest secrets to him. It made Blaise replay everything he'd said, and he realized his faux pas in calling Dalton by his first name just as Rexley spoke.

"You like him. And there is no use denying it, because you would not have followed him here if you did not. I will refrain from asking what the two of you were doing together this early in the morning, however, as it is none of my business."

"I…." He swallowed and nodded, deciding not to fib. Rexley would likely see through it anyway. "I do. There is more to him than meets the eye. And as to why we are out so early, I'm running errands, and he is my guard."

This time the smile was definitely there and very genuine. It lit Rexley's handsome face up and made him seem younger, almost boyish. Something about the twinkle in his eyes made Blaise think he wasn't believing the guard bit. "Good. I'm glad you like him. He's a good man, but unfortunately not everyone looks past his reputation. Do me a favor…." He got quiet again, as if measuring his words. "Don't hurt him. I suspect you really could."

It took everything in Blaise not to scoff at the notion that he could harm a hardened rake, but Rexley seemed serious, so instead he shook his head. "I don't really see how. As I said, we are only friends."

Rexley just smiled. "Promise me."

"I promise." Again the snort wanted to come out, but Blaise held it back. However, in the back of his mind, a small niggling delight tried to take hold. Did Dalton really care about him? Now he was being ridiculous. They'd just met, and it really did not matter because they were all wrong for each other. Weren't they?

"Now, to answer your question, I don't believe he is in any danger. I think this is more of a case of Ravensburg getting tired of being ignored. Dalton is rather good at trying one's patience when he wants to."

Blaise snorted. "No kidding."

Rexley continued as though Blaise hadn't spoken. "But we do have to get that dog tag out of him. If Ravensburg can use it to spy on him, anyone can."

"But why would his father spy on him?" This was from Larkinson, who'd been quiet up until now.

"My uncle has never been pleased with the company Dalton keeps." Rexley shrugged. He glanced at Larkinson, then back at Blaise. For several moments he didn't say anything, and then he nodded as if coming to a decision. "Dalton's parents sent him to live at the castle when he was eight, and since then he and my uncles have not gotten along. Dalton has done everything in his power to irk them. His infamous reputation is because of my uncles."

“Then he’s not a rake?”

Rexley chuckled, but it wasn’t a nice sound. “Oh, his reputation is real, but he started drinking, gambling, and whoring to get even with his parents. My point is, Dalton is not a bad man. He’s… misguided. He started acting out as a sort of revenge, but it got away from him. Once he had a taste of that freedom, he couldn’t stop himself. My sire sent him into the IN to save him, and it did. Dalton loves the Navy. He loves being a soldier, and he’s good at it.” He looked at Larkinson again. “That is not common knowledge.”

“And it will remain that way, Your Highness.”

Satisfied, Rexley bobbed his head and met Blaise’s gaze again. “I’m telling you this because you need to know why he is like he is.”

Blaise nodded, but inside his heart ached for the lonely eight-year-old who felt abandoned by his parents. Blaise could not imagine. His own parents were interfering, but it was done out of love. They were overly attentive. Anger at Ravensburg filled Blaise, making him tighten his fist. This explained a lot. It explained the kindness he’d seen in Dalton. It explained his flirting too. He was trying to get attention the only way he could, but underneath, Blaise had also seen the sincerity. “Thank you for telling me.”

“You’re welcome.”

A pounding knock on the outside of the coach startled them both, effectively ending their conversation.

“OPEN THE bloody door, Rexley. I know it’s you.”

Bloody hell, what was taking Rexley so long to open the blasted door? Dalton had stepped off the porch of his parents’ evil lair and was buffeted with a gust of wind that cut right through him. He’d been about to hail a ride, but then he’d noticed the shiny black conveyance Rexley had shown off to him yesterday morning, idling at the curb. He had no idea how his cousin had found him, but he was quite glad of it, because he really could not afford to hire a lift now.

Dalton thumped his fist against the door again. “I’m freezing my bollocks off, Rexley.” And other parts…. The only reason Dalton’s ears hadn’t frozen was because of the anger heating them. Never in his life had he wanted to draw someone’s cork as badly as he did Ravensburg’s.

Actually he wanted to bloody his sire's nose too. He should be canonized for not assaulting them both.

The door slid open, the steps descended, and a smug voice came from the interior. "Haven't you heard that patience is a virtue, dear cousin?"

Climbing the steps, Dalton entered the coach. It took his eyes a few moments to adjust, but when they did, he was going to give Rexley a good thump on the noggin. He actually fancied going a few rounds with someone, and Rexley would do. "Let me guess, my dog tag was…." The statement froze in his throat as he blinked and realized there was more than just his cousin in the coach. "Blaise?" The sight of his angel sitting there knocked the wind right out of his sails.

"Hi." Blaise smiled up at him, then picked up the hat off the seat next to him and offered it to Dalton.

Dalton stared at it for a few seconds before realizing it was his hat. He took it and glanced around. His cousin sat on the opposite bench, watching him with a self-satisfied expression on his handsome face that made Dalton want to flick his ear. Giving into the desire, he thumped his cousin, then sat next to him.

The smirk Rexley gave him promised retribution, but Dalton ignored it and looked back at Blaise.

"What are you doing here?"

"He likes you." Rexley grinned so big, it was comical and no doubt a taunt. Dalton had seen the same shit-eating grin millions of times over the years, usually when Rexley was teasing him. "Oof."

Blaise had kicked Rexley in the shin. He frowned and his brows drew downward in a glower.

"What…?" Rexley blinked innocently.

The scowl on Blaise's handsome face gave way to the worst surprised face Dalton had ever seen. "Very sorry. My foot slipped." For all his lovely qualities, Blaise was not much of an actor.

Dalton actually chuckled, which was no easy feat, considering his state of mind, but then he was beginning to realize Blaise had a way of lightening Dalton's mood. "How did you find me?"

With so much production it would have made Winstol proud, Blaise explained how he'd followed Dalton and met up with Rexley. He apologized for giving Ravensburg the disk with dog tag codes. Rexley chimed in with how he'd come to be outside Fairfax House, and Blaise admitted that while he wasn't glad Dalton had been kidnapped, it had all been a grand adventure. By the time they finished their explanation, Dalton felt less like throttling someone. There was something about having people care about your welfare that really spoke to a person. And Blaise must care, at least a bit, or he wouldn't have come to find him.

"Why did he have you abducted?" This from Rexley.

"Umm…." He glanced at the valet, unsure what he could safely say, knowing that servants liked to gossip. Then he decided what the hell, because Blaise obviously trusted her. Hesitating for only a second, Dalton told them about the conversation with his parents.

"That explains why I couldn't get into your accounts this morning," Rexley said.

"Damn. They've already frozen my accounts?" Dalton shook his head, aghast at how swiftly his parents did things. He noticed Blaise watching him and explained. "Rexley handles all my finances and oversees Ashbourne."

Blaise nodded. "Your father is diabolical. What are you going to do?" He scrunched up his nose as though he'd smelled something bad.

"I have no idea." Which was the truth. He'd been too busy fuming to come up with a plan. "Aside from drinking a bottle of my uncle's finest whiskey."

Blaise rolled his eyes and stuck out his tongue in the universal "Eeew" sign. Somehow it wasn't surprising that he didn't like spirits. He would probably be adorable in his cups.

"I'm also not quitting the Regelence Navy." What would he do if he wasn't a soldier? He'd be bored out of his mind. He was not a man for idleness.

"You could always take the offer my sire and Nate proposed to you this morning," Rexley suggested. It really wasn't a surprise that he knew of the offer. Dalton was convinced Rexley had spies everywhere. The man seemed to know everything. "They can't do anything about the IN paying you. By IN laws, you're an adult, and they can't touch that money."

That was another plus for staying in the IN, but…. "Then I'd be stuck here in Classige, and they'd never stop hounding me." Dalton looked at the other plus.

Blaise gave him an awkward smile full of sympathy.

"What about…." The valet, who'd been quiet until now, trailed off as if remembering whose company she was in. "Sorry," she mumbled and peered down, wringing her hands in her lap.

Rexley chuckled. "Honestly, Larkinson. Do you think we are buying the meek act? Speak your mind. My cousin is no different than Blaise and I. As far as we are all concerned, you are an equal."

She grinned. "Which is why I adore you, Your Highness." She peered up at Dalton with a questioning look but didn't say anything.

Dalton stuck his hand out to her. "I'm Ashbourne."

Grasping his hand in a firm grip, she shook it. "Larkinson. I'm Blai… er, Redding's valet."

"Nice to meet you, Larkinson. Please, finish what you were going to say." Dalton gave her a wink.

Blaise beamed at him, and Dalton found himself transfixed. Damn, but the man was just beautiful when he smiled. His entire face lit up, and his green eyes practically sparkled. It gave him a carefree look, rather than his normally stuffy countenance. It made something tickle way down deep in Dalton's stomach. Though there was something very sexy about the stuffiness, Dalton preferred the smile. It was a rarity with Blaise, or it had been so far. Maybe it wasn't so much a rarity but an act of caution with whom he shared that smile? Rexley had said that Blaise liked him. The thought made Dalton warm inside.

Rexley nudged him with his foot, and he realized Larkinson was speaking.

"—errand we had planned for this morning?" Larkinson glanced around the lift, looking a little uneasy.

"Damnation. I'd forgotten all about that." Honestly, he didn't feel much like going now, and he still thought it was going to be a wild goose chase, but he'd given his word. "We will go after the bo—oaf!" A booted foot connected with his shin. Dalton glared at Blaise.

Blaise only smiled. "Oops. My foot slipped again." He shrugged. "Unfortunately I need to run this *errand* within the next twenty hours."

Ah! He didn't want Rexley to know. Dalton nodded and rubbed his leg. Damn, but Blaise kicked hard. There was no way Rexley was not going to grill him about this later, but if it made Blaise feel better, he'd play along. "Why does this *errand* need to be done so soon?"

"I read… er… that is to say, I suspect the item I want to purchase will be sold by tomorrow." Blaise darted a quick glance at Rexley.

Dalton followed his gaze to find Rexley was peering out the window. "How about I go purchase the item for you tonight? I don't particularly care to go to the Blinkford ball."

If looks could kill, Dalton would be burned to cinders on the spot. Blaise glowered at him with his mouth pinched together. "This is my pro… um, that is to say, I am the one who wants to purchase the item, so I should do it rather than trust someone else to do it."

Dalton raised a brow, getting a little angry. Why didn't Blaise comprehend he didn't like putting him in danger? "What part of guard don't you understand?"

"Exactly! You are my guard, not my servant," Blaise shot back.

"Hey…." Larkinson put her hands on her hips, turning slightly toward Blaise. "I don't like the way you said that."

Blaise patted her leg, and his tone softened. "I meant no offense."

Larkinson nodded.

"But…." Blaise turned his attention back to Dalton. He even pointed one bony finger at him. A finger he was liable to lose if he….

"How about both of you go after the snuffbox this evening. I believe we've all been invited to the ball at Filmore House." Rexley had looked away from the window and positioned himself diagonally where he was able to watch Blaise and Dalton.

Blaise gasped.

Larkinson gawked.

But Dalton grinned. Somehow he wasn't the least bit surprised his cousin knew exactly what they were discussing. Rexley was nothing if not wily. Ever since they were kids, he'd always known what Dalton was about without Dalton having to tell him.

In way of explanation, Rexley gave them an almost smile that appeared rather superior. "Jeremy talks in his sleep."

Mirth trickled up from Dalton's gut. "Oh? And when and where exactly did you see Jeremy sleep?"

A sharp pain flared in his shin. The one opposite of the one that Blaise had just kicked.

"Whoops. Foot slipped," Rexley said without so much as a hint of amusement. He peered down at the floor, then up at Blaise. "Perhaps the floor was waxed a bit too thoroughly."

"Perhaps." Blaise took a deep breath and ran his hands down his thighs. "How are we going to do that? Dalton has a dog tag that can be tracked, and I can't very well leave a ball in the middle of it. If Ravensburg gets wind of me sneaking out…." He shook his head. "He's already warned me away from Dalton." He winced and met Dalton's gaze.

Dalton waved it off. "Ravensburg was never a fan of mine, and I find it refreshing that he actually thinks highly of you. It shows the man has some taste. But if you are so worried about my father, then we shall make certain you have a chaperone."

Rexley looked at Dalton, then back to Blaise, then dipped his head. He touched his index finger to his other index finger as though he were ticking off points on his hand. "I will take Dalton's dog tag out as soon as we get back to the castle." He touched his middle finger. "I will cover for you when you come down with a horrible migraine and choose to go back to Thompson House." Finally, he touched his ring finger, and this time he turned his attention to Larkinson. "And Larkinson will hire a hackney and meet you at the mews behind Sir William Blinkford's residence so that she may serve as a chaperone."

Blaise shook his head, appearing as though he were going to disagree, but then he chuckled. "Rexley, you are positively devious."

Rexley looked inordinately pleased with himself. "I do try."

"Well, now that that's settled…." Dalton chuckled and leaned his head back on the seat, placing his hat on his face. If only dealing with his parents were as easy….

Chapter Eleven

It has been remarked upon that a certain demon lord was seen at his parents' town house this afternoon. As he is rarely there, one wonders what the visit was about. Could there be a reconciliation in the works? Rumors abound. Stay tuned, readers.

—From *The Classige Morning News*, On-Dit column

Filmore House, Sir William Blinkford's residence in Classige, Pruluce

Only thirty minutes. Blaise took one look at the packed ballroom and had to remind himself he only had half an hour.

They'd just been announced, and beside him, Bannon went up on tiptoe, trying to peer over the crowd.

Their sire stepped up behind them both and rested his hands on their lower backs. "Whom are you searching for, dear?" At six foot seven, Pierce Thompson towered over most of the other men in the ballroom. He was thin, with hair even brighter red than Bannon's. He was not an easy man to overlook, and predictably, several arms went up across the room, motioning him over.

"Do you see Prince Rexley?" Blaise asked. Already the urge to peek at his pocket watch was niggling.

Bannon shook his head. "Nope, but there's Rupert." He came off his toes and bounded into the sea of bodies. *Brave man.*

Blaise would rather stab himself in the eye with a hot poker than mingle in this crush. Unfortunately there were no fireplace pokers to be had, or seats apparently. It was standing room only. Even the chairs and chaises, typically found at the edge of the ballroom for chaperones and wallflowers, had been removed to make space.

Sire waved at someone and departed as well, leaving Blaise standing inside the door.

"Have a nice time, son." Father, who'd been behind all of them, clapped him on the back, smiled at him, and then he, too, left.

Blaise watched with a sense of relief as his family deserted him. This whole clandestine business was easier than he'd thought. He'd been half afraid he'd have to make excuses to lose them, but in this crowd? His absence would go completely unnoticed, and he'd already made it clear he was trying to locate Rexley, so when they couldn't find him, they would look for Rexley. Assuming Rexley didn't find them first in.... He pulled his pocket watch from his waistcoat. Only six minutes had passed? *Guh!* This rained meteors. It had felt like at least fifteen minutes, but no, he still had twenty-four minutes and thirty-two seconds until he met Dalton in the music room and Rexley informed his father he'd left with a headache.

Someone cleared their throat behind Blaise.

Oh, please don't let that be someone I will have a hard time getting away from. He could not get caught up in conversation tonight. Biting his lip, he turned slowly, pasting a bored look on his face.

The reason for the current disastrous state of his life glowered at him from behind a bejeweled eyeglass. Once again, Percy was outfitted in ruffles; this time they were lilac, under a teal tailcoat. The ridiculous-looking eye accessory was new. No doubt it would be all the rage by tomorrow.

Blaise considered casting up his accounts all over Prissy, but sadly it wasn't something he could do on command. Too bad too, because it would have added to his story of being ill.

"Once again you are in the way, Redding."

With as much physical sarcasm as Blaise could muster, he stepped sideways and swept his arm down, then up. Anyone watching would assume he was only being polite and giving Prissy the "after you" gesture.

Prissy snorted and stomped past.

Taking a step back and then another, Blaise looked beyond Prissy and spotted his parents strolling farther into the chaos. As per usual, they were arm in arm, greeting people as they went. They were very popular and loved to socialize. Eventually they'd make their way all the way around the ballroom and back to where Blaise stood by the entrance, which meant he had to move. Unfortunately he did not see Dalton or Rexley anywhere, so he made a break for it.

To his left was a pair of double doors that had been left open to give access to the rest of the mansion, but his parents were way too close to that escape route, so Blaise decided to go out the "in" doors and did an about-face, slipping past the Marquess and Marquess-Consort

Timmer, who waited to be announced at the ballroom door. They gave him odd looks, but when Blaise lifted his hand in greeting, they returned the gesture without a word. *Thank galaxy.*

He was supposed to meet Dalton in the music room, which was at the end of the hall on the left side. So what if he was early? He'd just have to be careful not to be seen. He could do this…. He hoped.

Hurrying his steps, he reached the narrow corridor beside the main staircase. It was at the back of the house and well out of view of the revelers in the foyer, waiting to be announced.

There were only a few members of the ton in the hallway, but all of them were going into or coming out of the retiring rooms under the main staircase. No one paid Blaise the least bit of attention, so he continued down the hall. Just as he left the corridor into the gallery, a door to his right began to open.

Blaise didn't even think; he rushed forward to the music room door, flung it open, and darted inside. The room was dark. He pressed his back against the door and closed his eyes, listening. For the hundredth time since last night, he asked himself if he was losing his mind. This whole thing was so far from his normal. He did not sneak out and break rules. That was Bannon's specialty. Did Bannon get this nervous when he did things he wasn't supposed to do?

A door in the hall clicked shut. People started talking. The voices moved closer, and Blaise held his breath until they moved past.

Opening his eyes, he looked around. A window across from him had the curtains open, letting the full moon and the gleam of snow shine in. It only lit the center of the room and the back wall beside the door, but it was enough light to determine he was alone. He huffed out a breath. He'd half hoped Dalton would be waiting for him already. They had not seen each other since Blaise had been dropped off at Thompson House this morning. Dalton had gone on to the castle and then sent Mr. Julian Towers, one of the castle's elite guards, to escort Blaise to the office and act as his bodyguard. Mr. Towers was a nice man and very well educated; he was a part of their set, and Blaise should have been pleased with the substitution, but he'd found himself missing Dalton's outrageous conversation. Mr. Towers had remained quiet and watchful, reading a book while Blaise did research. It had been all rather normal and… boring.

Galaxy help him, it had only been a day that he'd known Dalton, and he already missed him. No, no, not missed him exactly, but.... Blaise sighed. Perhaps it was just his desire to help Dalton with his parents? He felt really bad for Dalton, but he had no idea how to help. Yes, that was it; it was his desire to help to make things better, to.... There was no use lying to himself. Though he did want to help, he missed the man. Shaking his head, he pushed off of the door, refusing to think on it anymore.

A pianoforte sat against the wall just to his right, with several comfortable-looking chairs in the center of the room and a harp on the other side of the door. He wished he could light a fire in the fireplace—it would light up the rest of the room and help with the chill in the air—but he didn't feel right about it since he wouldn't be here long.

To get his mind off Dalton while he waited, he went to the pianoforte and ran his fingers along the smooth white veneer top of the instrument. Not as nice as his Lizzy, but then, not many were. Lizzy was a special-order, glossy black baby grand piano made by the Hodge Brothers, the premier piano makers in all of the Regelence system for more than a hundred and sixty years. His parents had given him Lizzy—named after his favorite composer, Francisco Lizarrago—for his fifteenth birthday. She'd been custom-made and put together in his bedroom parlor by none other than Raymond Hodge, the great-grandson and current owner of Hodge Brothers.

Blaise sat down on the bench and ran his fingers over the keys, testing the sound. Not Lizzy, but not a bad sound. He played through the piece he was currently composing in his spare time, until he got to where he was stuck. Sadly, inspiration did not strike and help him finish the composition, so he decided to play a piece he loved but wouldn't dare perform in public. It had the tempo of Earth's fiftieth year of the twentieth century, known as their rock-and-roll genre, and was considered vulgar and uncouth by most of the ton. But what the hell? He was already breaking so many of society's rules, what was one more? Besides, it wasn't like anyone could hear him. These rooms were well insulated and soundproof. He couldn't even hear the orchestra in the ballroom.

Trying not to pound the keys as hard as he would at home, Blaise played through the bridge and even quietly, the notes seemed to reverberate through his chest. Using his imagination, he could almost hear an accompaniment of drums and strings. For all its vulgarity, it was moving. Blaise got into the music until something clicked. It sounded like a door closing, but that was impossible. He'd been in this room before, and the only door into the room was right next to him.

He froze with his fingers poised over the keys.

Footsteps clacked on the parquet flooring behind him, and the small hairs on his arms stood on end. He swiveled around. "Hello?"

The room was still. Only the dust motes floating in the light of the window dared to move.

After a moment in which Blaise watched his life flash before him—he'd always thought that saying was ridiculous until that very moment—there was movement in the far right corner.

His heart couldn't possibly beat any harder and faster. How was he going to explain not only the song but his presence? He was here alone, unchaperoned. It would look like he was waiting for a lover, because who left a ball to be by themselves? Oh galaxy, why hadn't he considered that before now?

The shadows undulated as a man stepped forward into the moonlight. A very handsome, very familiar man.

IT HAD been dusty and smaller than Dalton remembered, but worth the dirt on the knees of his trousers. He'd first learned of the tunnel during his misspent youth while spending nearly a month courting Anthony, Sir William Blinkford's oldest son. It was the perfect escape route for him and Blaise. Which was why he'd suggested they meet in this room, only he hadn't told Blaise the reason. That might have been a mistake, judging from the glare Blaise was currently giving him.

Blaise marched across the room and, before Dalton knew what he was about, swatted him on the side of his shoulder. The exact shoulder from which he'd had his dog tag removed earlier that day. *Ow.* Dalton winced at the sting of pain that traveled through his arm and to his upper right shoulder. He rubbed it gently, but it didn't do much to help the pain.

"You scared the life out of me. Are you trying to give me an apoplexy? What are you doing skulking around? And how did you get in here?"

"Good galaxy, you're violent. First you kick me, and now you're hitting me where Rexley dug that blasted tracker out of me."

"I, uh…." Blaise bit his bottom lip, and though it was dark in the room, his blush was obvious. "I'm sorry, I didn't think. Are you all right?" He walked around behind Dalton, unbuttoned his claw hammer coat, and began pulling it down Dalton's arms. What he thought he would accomplish by that, Dalton didn't know—he wore a waistcoat as well, so it wasn't like Blaise could see anything. But he wasn't about to tell Blaise not to undress him. Especially not with him so close. His warm, sweet-smelling breath caressed the back of Dalton's ear. His neck.

It sent tingles of awareness right down Dalton's spine to his core. He closed his eyes and dipped his head forward, the pain in his shoulder forgotten. The fact that they were alone together in the dark suddenly seemed paramount in his mind.

"Why is it whenever I'm around you, I end up doing crazy stuff?" Blaise whispered. He was quiet for several moments. His fingers trailed over the back of Dalton's neck to his shoulder.

Dalton felt it even through the cravat, shirt, and waistcoat.

"I think you are hazardous to my health." Again, Blaise's voice was soft, almost seductive in tone. His hand froze, then disappeared like he'd snatched it away, and Dalton felt rather than saw him shake his head. Gripping the armhole of Dalton's waistcoat, Blaise pulled it aside. His hand slid between it and his lawn shirt, brushing so softly, it could have been Dalton's imagination.

Galaxy, the shirt might as well not have been there, for all the good it did. Dalton's cock began to take notice. It realized all the things his mind had already picked up on—their seclusion, their closeness. How damned easy it would be to turn around and take Blaise's lips…. "I *know* you're hazardous to mine. I'm trying like hell to be good." Dalton's voice came out barely more than a whisper, and so lust-roughened, he didn't sound like himself. "But you make it difficult."

"It seems that I'm trying like hell to be bad, and you make it very easy." Raising his head slowly, Blaise peered up at him with those gorgeous green eyes. The look was both shy and full of… longing? He held Dalton's gaze. There was so much vulnerability there. His eyelids fluttered as his gaze shifted to Dalton's lips.

Dalton's cock, now fully hard, begged for attention. He wanted to kiss Blaise until neither of them knew their names. He couldn't remember ever wanting anything so badly, but he was not going to scare Blaise away again. He was not going to—*bugger that!* He leaned in and pressed his lips to Blaise's. Softly, just a soft press of warm lips against warm lips. It was heavenly and as addicting as hot chocolate laced with whiskey.

Blaise's hands slid out from under his waistcoat, but he didn't pull back. He didn't move either. He stayed perfectly still. Even his breathing seemed to stop.

When Dalton stepped away, he was prepared for the shock or the cold anger he'd received before, but he didn't get either of those things.

Blaise stared at him with eyes full of wonder. Somehow he'd ended up in front of Dalton, with his hands resting on Dalton's coat where it was pulled down over his arms. For several moments, he didn't say anything. His lashes lowered again, caressing those pale cheeks. "I shouldn't do this, but I really want to," he whispered as he leaned forward.

Dalton exhaled the breath he'd been holding and leaned in too, but before their mouths touched, Blaise pulled back and put his fingers against Dalton's lips.

"Teach me." He swallowed and glanced down again. "Teach me… how you kissed me before."

Lust shot through Dalton so fast his head spun. His cock throbbed, pinching where it was constricted in his pants. He'd never relished playing teacher before, but he did now. He wanted to teach Blaise everything he knew.

After shrugging his coat back onto his shoulders so he could use his arms, he hooked his finger under Blaise's chin, making him look up, and once again pressed his lips to Blaise's, the whole time staring into his eyes. The intimacy of it was both thrilling and… too much. Dalton closed his eyes. "Open your mouth," he instructed.

Blaise nodded, and their foreheads bumped. His lips opened against Dalton's. His breath sweet and warm against Dalton's mouth.

"Caress my tongue with yours." Bloody hell, this tutoring was turning him on even more. The simmering excitement coursed through him, demanding to be let out.

Again, Blaise nodded, and when Dalton covered his mouth with his own, Blaise did as he was instructed. He didn't even wait for Dalton to get things started. As per what Dalton was coming to know about Blaise, he jumped in with both feet. His tongue swept against Dalton's tentatively. It didn't take him long to get the hang of things. He followed Dalton's lead and matched him stroke for stroke. The innocent and testing caresses were more erotic than anything Dalton had done with seasoned courtesans or jaded consorts.

The pleasure sizzled through him; just who was doing the seducing? When Blaise moaned low in his throat and brought his own hands up to Dalton's shoulders, Dalton decided he better end things now before they got carried away. Getting caught with his pants down in a music room did not sound like his idea of fun, so he pulled back and stared into the beguiling face inches from his own.

Blaise still had his eyes closed, his fingers idly toying with Dalton's collar.

The mix of innocence and passion inspired a deep contentment like he'd never felt. He ran his knuckles over Blaise's cheek and watched as his eyes slowly blinked open.

For several seconds, Blaise just stared at Dalton, and then it was as if reality crashed down on him. He dropped his hands and cleared his throat. This time there was no mistaking his blush. The splotchy redness crept up his cheeks. He should have looked ridiculous not irresistible. "I, er…. Your shoulder, um… doesn't feel like it's bleeding. I can't see with your shirt being black, but it feels dry."

Tracing a thumb over Blaise's bottom lip, Dalton chuckled.

"I… ahem." Blaise's gaze trailed down Dalton's body. "We probably shouldn't do that a…." His gaze got to Dalton's very visible erection and darted away, looking at anything but Dalton, like he'd never seen an aroused man before, which was patently ridiculous since he was sporting a sizable bulge as well.

Blaise saw him looking and cleared his throat again and averted his gaze. The blush grew darker as he reached inside his evening coat and pulled out a pocket watch. He flipped it open, read the time, closed it, and put it back inside his evening coat. "We have to go. Larkinson is waiting for us."

A lesser man would start questioning his prowess, but Dalton knew this was all new to Blaise. He was simply trying to stave off embarrassment, so Dalton played along. He extended his hand toward the hidden passage. "Very well, lead the way."

"Where?"

"The secret tunnel."

"A secret tunnel? This is perfect. Why didn't you tell me about it?" Blaise's voice filled with excitement and he bounded past Dalton to the corner as though they hadn't just been about to rip each other's clothes off. "Where does it lead? Does it lead outside?"

He should have known Blaise would be intrigued by a hidden passage. "Yes, it leads outside and to three different rooms. Here, the dining room, and the breakfast room. I didn't tell you because it's a secret."

Blaise shot him a glare over his shoulder, then turned back and patted along the edge of the bookcase just behind the harp, tipping books forward and releasing them. When he failed to find the door, he turned around and glared at Dalton again. "If you don't show me where it is, I'm not going to help you with your parent problem." The annoyance in his tone was so obvious, it really should have been accompanied with a stamp of his foot.

With a smile, Dalton went to the life-sized portrait of Sir William Blinkford's great-great-grandfather, the Baron of Hilldale, and flipped the catch on the back of the gilded frame.

Smiling, Blaise rubbed his hands together in glee and stepped over the bottom of the frame.

Dalton caught his shoulder.

Blaise turned and stared at him.

"You have a solution to the problem with my parents?"

Blaise nodded. "I do. We are going to show them that you can be respectable. I'm going to dance with you at the upcoming balls, and you are going to hang out with me and my friends. Starting tomorrow night. My sire is hosting a ball at Thompson House." With that, he disappeared into the tunnel.

Could he have heard that right? Dalton blinked and shook his head. "Blaise, wait up." He hurried into the passage and closed the door behind him.

The little adventurer was already several yards in front of him, so Dalton hurried to catch up. "What about your reputation? What about my father warning you?"

One elegant shoulder rose in front of him. "Your father likes me, and I daresay respects me. What better way to get him to view you in a different light than to let him find out you are friends with me?"

What better way, indeed. Dalton grinned so big his face hurt. "We're friends?"

Blaise stopped and turned toward him, his brow furrowed. "Aren't we? Friends help one another and they… like one another."

"You like me?"

Blaise kicked him in the shin—it was more of a nudge really—then grumbled, "Didn't you hear Rexley this morning?" He turned back around and strode down the passage.

Dalton followed much more slowly. He'd never actually had friends. Oh, sure he had acquaintances and lovers, and his cousins were his friends, he supposed, but he wasn't positive he'd ever had a… friend. Not someone who wanted to be around in spite of his reputation. Most people hung around him because of it. They stayed because he was fun and unpredictable. They wanted to be seen with him to be scandalous or to make someone jealous. Blaise didn't want any of those things. In fact, those were fine reasons he shouldn't be seen with Dalton, but here he was. True, Dalton was helping him, but it was now a mutual thing. No one besides his family had ever offered to help him before. And Dalton definitely liked him.

Huh! Imagine that. We are friends.

Chapter Twelve

There is a smashing new unmarked black lift driving around Pruluce. One wonders to whom it belongs.

—From *The Pruluce Examiner*

BLAISE HAD always thought he preferred detached town houses, like Thompson House, but Sir William Blinkford's terrace town house was like a maze. A maze with a secret passageway, and Blaise adored puzzles. He could spend hours exploring here; unfortunately he didn't have hours.

After pushing open the door at the end of the darn tunnel, he stepped out into the area at basement level that tradesmen and servants used. He closed the door and looked around at the narrow passage. It was like a whole new secret tunnel, only not nearly as claustrophobic. The cement walls were stark, but there were planted troughs and the top was open to the night sky. Snow drifted down on him in dancing flurries. It must have started up again when he was inside. Just as Dalton had said, there was a set of stairs to his right. He took the steps two at a time to ground level until it opened up into the garden, which was really more of a square courtyard with potted plants and a fountain. Though the fountain was currently off and the plants were wrapped in burlap.

"Where is Ashbourne?"

"Bloody hell!" Jerking in surprise, Blaise slapped a hand to his chest and turned to glare at Larkinson.

She stood across the garden, outside the stable door, dressed as she had been this morning in Henry-the-footman's clothes.

He had the sudden urge to pack some snow and pelt her with it, just as they'd done as kids, only not for fun. Striding forward, he hissed at her, "You scared the life out of me. I thought you were supposed to wait behind the mews?"

"I was, but you're late, so I decided to investigate. Come on." She grabbed his arm and started tugging him toward the stables. As she opened the door, she held a finger to her lips and whispered, "The groomsmen are upstairs."

Inside the dimly lit stables, there were muted voices and laughter as though they were drinking and playing cards, but as she had said, no one was downstairs except two matching grays and a very fine-looking chestnut. The chestnut snorted and leaned over his stall as they passed.

Blaise petted his nose on the way by.

Once they reached the side door, which was next to the much larger barn-style doors for the livestock, she eased it open and ushered him out.

The alley was deserted except for a lift idling behind the mews. The snow was at least an inch deep here, with no tracks. No one had come in or out in quite a while. "How long have you been waiting?"

She sidled up next to him and shrugged. "I left Thompson House right after you."

"Whatever for?"

Again she shrugged, but this time her generous mouth quirked up to the side. "I was excited. You have to admit that it isn't often we go on adventures."

They *never* went on adventures, unless going to the music shop counted, but she had a point. He hadn't really considered it until now, probably because he was worried about getting caught, but this whole thing, while nerve-wracking, was rather… exciting.

"Where is Ashbourne? And good heavens…." Larkinson started brushing off his evening coat. "You look as though you've been dragged through a narrow tomb"—she patted down his hair—"backwards."

"I crawled through a secret passage." He couldn't help but smile. As strange as this whole ordeal was, it was indeed fun. He'd always wanted to go through a hidden passage. As a child, he'd investigated every inch of Eversleigh Manor, but much to his chagrin, for all its grandeur and history, his family's estate did not have any secret lairs or a dungeon. Though this experience wasn't quite what he'd expected. Instead of the tall narrow walls lined with torches, cobwebs, and mysterious suits of armor, it had been little more than a crawl space.

Larkinson stopped dusting his backside and leaned around to gawk at him. "You what?"

Blaise chuckled at the dumbstruck expression. "I crawled through a tunnel to get out of the ball."

She stared at him for a full two seconds, shook her head, then grabbed his arm and started towing him toward the waiting hackney. "I'm sorry I asked. Now, where is Ashbourne?"

As if on cue, the stable door snicked open, then shut behind them.

Dalton strode toward them with a frown on his face, a hat on his head, one in his hand, two coats over his arm, and a walking stick. "I had to retrieve our hats and coats." He pointed at Blaise with his walking stick. "And don't you dare laugh."

Too late, Blaise had already begun chuckling silently to himself, and Dalton's warning only made it come out louder. If he was in as much disarray as Dalton…. Well, no wonder Larkinson had been aghast.

Dalton's hair stuck up as though it had static in it. The normally sunny blond was grayish, giving a hint at what he might look like as an old man. Not bad, in Blaise's esteemed estimation. His all-black evening clothes showed every speck of dust. His knees were completely covered in dirt from crawling. But for all that, he was still ruggedly handsome. Perhaps even more so, because this seemed to fit his personality better. Blaise was coming to realize that Dalton was not at all stuffy. He had a very genial way about him that put everyone at ease, and the walking stick did not fit him.

"You have a walking stick?" Blaise asked as Dalton approached.

"I do." He plunked Blaise's hat on his head and handed him his coat. Their eyes met, and Dalton grinned. It felt intimate.

Blaise found his gaze drifting toward Dalton's lips, and his own tingled in response. He shook his head to clear it. He wasn't certain how to act with this newfound relationship they'd embarked upon. They weren't lovers, but they weren't only friends, were they? This was new territory for him.

Raising the end of his walking stick, Dalton gripped it between his hands and pulled. The end of the stick slid down to reveal a gleaming silver blade. "I thought it might come in handy."

It was a stark reminder of where they were headed. Butterflies swirled in Blaise's stomach, but it wasn't an entirely unpleasant feeling.

"Well, come along," Larkinson said from beside the lift. "We'll get you both cleaned up on the way. Though I suppose for where we're going, it really doesn't matter."

The hackney door opened, and the steps came down from the side with an electronic hum. They all climbed in. Blaise took the seat next to

Larkinson, and Dalton sat across from him. "Close doors and go to 805 Wharf Front Road," she barked out to the hackney.

The steps pulled back into the lift, and the door began closing.

Blaise met Dalton's gaze across the coach as it started moving, and heat climbed up his cheeks.

"You both seem different," Larkinson said as she picked something off of Blaise's cravat.

He didn't want to know what it was. "Because we're covered in dust."

"And cobwebs," Dalton added, swatting at a web on the arm of his evening coat. "No wonder the footman looked at me so oddly when I asked for our coats. I thought it was just because I came in through the front door and confused him."

Larkinson shook her head. "No, I can't put my finger on it, but it's not the despicable condition of your clothes." She studied him for a few more moments, then glanced at Dalton.

Dalton looked amused at her survey and raised his brows at Blaise.

Twirling his finger beside his head, Blaise smiled.

"I am not crazy." Her eyes narrowed, and then her eyes widened and her mouth dropped open. A slow smile eased onto her lips, and she started bouncing in her seat.

Blaise had just enough time for apprehension to race through him. He had no idea what she was about to say, but he'd bet just about anything that it wasn't good. He shook his head at her and frowned, but she didn't take the hint.

"Oh my galaxy, your lips are red. That's it. That's what's different. Your lips are red. You kissed. You both look well and thoroughly snogged. Just like Bannon and Louie that time we caught them practicing kissing."

Oh, the humiliation. Larkinson was so going to get it when they got home. Blaise did the only thing he could think of; he kicked her in the shin.

Dalton burst into laughter as Larkinson swatted Blaise and rubbed her leg. "I'm beginning to think you have a nervous twitch." Dalton looked pointedly at Blaise's foot. "You should get that checked."

Groaning, Blaise ignored him and glared at his bigmouth valet. "Our lips are red because it's cold outside. It's called wind chill. Your face is pale and your lips are red too."

Dalton nodded, though it wasn't very convincing with the smirk he wore. "Who is Louie?"

"Bannon's valet. She's Larkinson's sister."

When Dalton's eyes widened, Blaise explained, "They were six at the time."

Larkinson gave him a grin that promised this inquisition wasn't over. But then, he'd never thought it was. She knew all about his nonexistent love life. She'd even caught him touching himself a time or two.

"When I was six, I was much more interested in acting out my favorite stories," Dalton said and gave Blaise a wink. He was trying to change the subject, bless him. No doubt Larkinson would grill him when they returned home, but for now… maybe he could help distract her.

"You read?" Blaise asked, hiking his brows up.

Chuckling, Dalton nodded. "Yes. Regardless what you think, I *can* read, but my grandfather read to me back then." His smile faded a bit to a more whimsical expression. "He used to come home and set me on his lap and read me stories. My favorite was about the blacksmith who was in love with a fairy prince and went on many adventures to save his prince. He had to slay a dragon and cross a troll bridge. He fought an army of ogres." His voice took on a dreamy quality. "I used to study the pictures in the book and make a battleground in the middle of the parlor. Then Grandfather would read it to me again, and we'd act out the fight with the dragon and the trolls. Then my father and sire would come in, and we'd enact the big battle, complete with wooden swords and pillows as shields. My sire was always the fair prince and would sit and watch our battle from the settee until I rescued him." His voice faded and he blinked. "I'd forgotten about that."

Something in the way he said it, full of wonder and sadness, made Blaise want to reach out to him. He'd never really thought of Dalton as a boy, though he wasn't sure why, because Dalton was like a boy who'd never grown up.

Dalton shook his head. "I was much more interested in the fighting than the kissing at the end. Though my sire would kiss me on the cheek and hand me over to my father, and he'd take me to get biscuits before taking me to bed." His cheeks seemed to darken with a blush, though it was hard to see in the dim interior of the coach. "What about you, Blaise? You never did say what you did for fun. And don't say reading."

"Erhm…." Blaise bit his lip. "Does music count?"

"Sure it does. He composes music in his spare time," Larkinson said.

"Really?" Dalton looked from Larkinson to him. "Will you play something for me?" Something about the way he asked made it sound much more sensual than it should, and Blaise wondered if they were still talking about music.

He nodded. The idea of playing for Dalton was.... It made him shiver. His prick began to fill. Blaise crossed his legs and dragged his coat over his lap.

"The piece you were playing when I came in? Was that yours?"

Blaise shook his head. "It was an old Earth song."

For several moments they stared at each other, and Blaise wondered what Dalton would say if he told him about the song and how scandalous it had been back in its day. It was still scandalous, actually, at least for an unmarried man of his age to be playing. It was about sex. And why did that thought make him imagine kissing Dalton again and slowly stripping his evening coat off and…? Blaise squeezed his eyes closed. *Galaxy, was it getting hot in here?*

When he opened them, Dalton still watched him. He winked, and more heat coursed through Blaise, pooling in his abdomen and groin.

"What is that?" Larkinson's voice broke the silence.

"Huh?" Blaise blinked out of his daze more than a little startled. Only he wasn't sure if the start was from Larkinson's interruption of his own thoughts. He glanced over at his valet.

She sat motionless, staring out the window. "Blaise, what is that?"

Out the window, all the buildings had turned dingy. Not even the pretty floating snow could distract from the dirt and neglect. They passed by a street, followed by another and another. There were so many boxes in the alleys. Not just one but several. Boxes and crates. In one of the alleys, there were pallets stacked together with old rags draped over it. Something about them looked odd, but Blaise couldn't put his finger on why.

Glancing at Dalton, Blaise realized his attention was focused out the window too. His face was still, watchful.

Something about the way Larkinson gripped the windowsill seemed unnatural and tense. Her knuckles were white.

Dalton shook his head. "This is bad."

"I think I've heard of it, but I didn't think it was real," Larkinson said almost absently.

"You've heard about this?" Dalton asked with a voice void of emotion.

"What exactly is this?" Blaise asked.

"One of the maids at Thompson House mentioned it. They call it Foundling Town."

Blaise turned back to the window as the hackney slowed to turn again. That's when he saw the little face peeking out of a box, and it dawned on him what had looked so odd about all the boxes. They were makeshift houses.

DALTON STOOD beside the hackney, across the street from Southpaws, and decided it was like most seedy dockside bars he'd been to, and he'd been to quite a few while in the IN.

The building itself was small and unimpressive. An undistinguished wood structure once painted dark blue nestled among other buildings that looked much the same. A lot of gray weathered wood showed between slashes of faded paint. A quaint, iron and carved wood sign dangled from chains mounted on a perpendicular bracket above the door. The sign was shaped like a shield with elaborate scrollwork around the edges. In the middle, it featured a taped pugilist's fist and the word Southpaws spelled out in red. The numerous voices from inside produced a ruckus outside, and if the smell of fish wasn't testament to the fact that it was only a street away from one of the biggest ports in Regelence, the number of patrons would be.

People milled in and out in a constant stream. One here, two there. Mostly men, sailors and dockworkers, judging from the drab colors of their clothing and the lack of evening coats. Most wore heavy outer coats, shirtsleeves, and roughly tied cravats, but there were a few middle-class men as well. It seemed some things did not really change from planet to planet.

Blaise stepped down from the hackney and placed a hand on Dalton's arm, interrupting his survey. "There were so many of them."

Dalton didn't have to ask what he was referring to. Blaise had been very quiet and withdrawn since they'd spotted Foundling Town. They all had.

"Where did they all come from?"

"I don't know."

"Why aren't they in an orphanage where they'd be warm and safe?" The sadness in his voice was heart-wrenching and understandable. He'd probably never seen such poverty.

There was nothing quite like seeing someone suffering to point out how spoiled and pampered you were. Dalton had spent his entire military salary on the homeless the first time he'd come across them. It had been on Lerdra, and his fellow soldiers had thought him insane. It had taken a while, but he'd learned that his small contribution wasn't enough to make a dint. He'd gotten used to the sight of poverty, but here on Regelence… his home…. Maybe he could make a difference. He needed to mention this to his uncles because he was certain they didn't know about what appeared to be a huge orphan population. Back when Rexley had found Muffin five years ago, orphans had been a rarity.

Dalton shook his head. "I don't know that either." But there was no time now; they had a small window of operation before Blaise's family returned from the ball, and Blaise had to be there when they got back. He touched Blaise's arm. "We have to go."

"What if the boy didn't bring it here?" His voice was soft and unsure.

"Then we will find another lead and follow it until we find the snuffbox," Dalton said with more confidence than he felt. He was good at finding out things, like troop positions and army tactics. As a Cavalry scout, it was his job, but he'd never had to find a stolen object. He thought it was a lost cause, but until he could convince Blaise of that, he was going to try.

"Are you sure you don't want me to go?" Larkinson said behind them.

Dalton's lips twitched. As much as he liked Larkinson, and he did like her, he did not want her to accompany them. If he could make Blaise stay in the lift, he would, but after assessing the place, he suspected it was relatively safe. More to the point, he knew there was no way Blaise would consent to staying in the hackney. "No, hopefully we won't be gone that long. Stay and keep the hackney for us."

"All right, but Ashbourne…."

Something in her tone made him turn toward her.

She stood in the doorway, her gaze steady as she glanced at Blaise, then back to Dalton. "Take care of him."

Nodding, Dalton put his hand against his chest. "You have my word."

With that, she ordered the door shut.

Blaise scoffed and shook his head, but there was a hint of a smile on his face as well.

"What?"

"She mother hens me to death."

"Nothing wrong with that. She cares for you." Dalton rubbed his hands together, then clapped them once. "Well, let's go in, shall we?"

"Please proceed." Blaise held his arm out as if to indicate that Dalton should go first. And he looked every bit the pampered aristocrat. *Bloody hell.*

Lifting off Blaise's hat, Dalton ruffled his hair until the brown strands stood on end, much as they had after he'd crawled through the tunnel and before Larkinson had gotten ahold of him; she took her duty as valet very seriously. Putting the hat back on Blaise, he retied Blaise's cravat into a simpler knot while Blaise's protests of "hey" rang in his ears.

"What's that for?" Blaise glowered at him.

"To make you look less—" *How to put this without giving offense?* "—less pompous, and I mean that in the nicest possible way."

Blaise's nose wrinkled in an adorable little scrunch.

Without thinking, Dalton leaned forward, kissed that crinkled nose, and got blinking eyes and a gasp for his effort. He pulled Blaise's frock coat tighter, gave a nod, and said, "Follow me, and let me do the talking."

"Why didn't you mess up your hair and your cravat?"

"Because I don't look—"

"Pompous?"

Dalton chuckled at the amount of disgust put into a single word. "Exactly." He wouldn't be living that comment down anytime soon.

Blaise snorted. "Uh-huh… and that walking stick isn't the least bit pompous. Only thing you're missing is a quizzing glass," he mumbled.

With a smile on his face, Dalton walked inside, leaving Blaise to follow. No one seemed to pay them any attention. *Thank galaxy.* He'd been half afraid everyone would stop and stare at them as if they were interlopers.

He pulled off his hat but left his coat on, and with a remindful nudge, Blaise did the same.

The pub looked about like he expected.

Men sat at tables drinking and a few were playing cards. The place was loud but in a joyous way with laughter and slaps on the back. The fish smell had given way to ale and cigars. Smoke hung low on the ceiling like a rain cloud.

The place was surprisingly clean. No litter marred the floor and no dirty dishes or glasses lay in wait on the empty tables, and there weren't many of those. A two-seater in the corner caught his attention, and he gripped Blaise's hand and pulled him to it. For all the cleanliness, he *still had* to peel his soles from the floor with every step.

They stopped for a young man with a rag tucked into his belt, carrying a bin of dishes. There was another boy about Muffin's age with a broom bigger than he was, trying to sweep up the floor in the corner.

Blaise squeezed his hand and leaned into him. "Is it normal for kids to work in a pub?"

Shaking his head, Dalton frowned and gave the place another scan and quickly realized these were not the only two minors.

At least one of the people waiting on tables was definitely a girl with rust-colored curly hair piled atop her head. She wore an apron and a plain gray dress. The other—it was hard to tell—wore their black hair long and down the back. From the looks of them, they were both between ten and fifteen summers. The other two people serving tables were most definitely women, and the men were treating them as such with pats on the bottom and lots of flirtatious talk. No one bothered any of the children. Not only that, no one seemed to think it was strange for them to be in here.

Behind the bar on the back wall, a lanky teenage boy with stringy blond hair served drinks alongside a woman of middle age. She worked one end of the bar, and the teen worked the other. The children working in here outnumbered the adult employees two to one. Weren't there laws that prohibited child labor? He was certain there was.

"What if they're being taken advantage of? Aren't these places rife with prostitution?" The last word was garbled and barely audible, but the rest were said in a slightly higher voice than normal. A blush darkened Blaise's cheeks, and he couldn't look any more repressed if he'd tried.

Dalton held back a chuckle, knowing Blaise would not appreciate it. Where did Blaise think they were? A brothel? His innocence was refreshing. Had Dalton ever been so innocent? If so, he couldn't remember it. Dalton continued to scan the bar. "Not usually." Though it did happen on occasion. Prostitution was legal in Regelence, and most whores made way more money at a brothel. It also required a different license, a much more expensive one, so most pubs, bars, and gaming hells did not dabble in the sex trade. Dalton pulled out a chair for Blaise and handed him his hat and walking stick. "I'm going to go order some drinks and ask about the owner. Just sit still and don't say anything."

Nodding, Blaise sat and placed their hats on the table in front of him, then studied the room. Even with his dusty clothes, he looked a little out of place. He was every bit the pampered lord, but there was no help for it.

Making sure to keep Blaise and the majority of the room in his sights, Dalton squeezed in between a man staring into his cup and a group of revelers who talked among themselves. As he waited at the bar, Blaise engaged in conversation with the kid with the broom. Only he didn't have a broom now but a mop and there was another small boy with him holding a bucket. It looked to be a lively conversation; the kid smiled and used his hands to talk. At one point, he nearly dropped his mop, but Blaise reached out and snagged it before it hit the ground, then gave it back to the kid.

Dalton ordered ale for himself and Blaise and asked to see the owner. The lady behind the bar eyed him skeptically, but sent the teen to get the owner as she poured their drinks.

He paid her and with a nod of thanks took the drinks back to the table. He must have had a scowl on his face, because the boys took one look at him and stuttered out a goodbye to Blaise and went back to mopping.

Dalton set the mugs on the table and then took a seat. "What was that about?"

Blaise smiled so big, his eyes twinkled, and he picked up his mug. The smug expression was as attractive as it was disconcerting. He reminded Dalton of Muffin when she had a secret. He'd found out something and apparently it was good. "That was Billy and Howie." He sniffed the mug, wrinkled his nose, shrugged, and took a sip, then immediately made a face before taking another drink. "I did a little poking around and—"

"I'm Gabriel Kincaid, the owner. You asked to see me?" a voice so deep it rumbled asked.

Dalton looked up and up and up. The biggest man he'd ever seen stood at their table. This guy was even bigger than Nate and Rourke, but he was nowhere near as refined. The nickname Killer fit him to a T. His nose appeared as though it had been broken more than once, and his long brown hair, which was pulled back into a queue, showed off ears deformed from having been hit too many times. His jaw was on the square side, his chin had a dimple, and his shoulders were so wide, they blocked out the view of the wall behind him. His most striking feature was his sky-blue eyes. They were almost hypnotic and way older than his years—which Dalton placed in the midthirties—they probably didn't miss much and brought to mind a snake about to strike. He was not handsome, but he was appealing in a dangerous sort of way, like a grizzly bear or a shark.

No way could Dalton talk to this man in a submissive position, so he stood and offered his hand. Blaise did not follow suit, but it probably never occurred to him, being a higher rank than Kincaid, which was fine with Dalton. The less attention drawn to Blaise the better.

At first Kincaid just stared at Dalton's hand. After a few seconds in which Dalton considered lowering his arm, Kincaid wiped his hand on a towel he held in his other hand, slung it over his shoulder, and gripped Dalton's hand in a shake. The look he gave was assessing and suspicious rather than inviting.

"Dalton Fairfax."

"Uh-huh." The sardonic tone as he studied Dalton made it clear he was not fooled into believing Dalton was a mere mister.

"What can I do for ye, *Mr.* Fairfax?" Kincaid glanced down at Blaise with the same stony expression but didn't say anything.

"I understand you are the man to see if a guy has something to sell that he wants to get rid of quickly, and word has it you may have come across such an object recently. A small box. It would have been brought in last night."

Kincaid's face did not change. "Sorry. Ye heard wrong. Now if ye will excuse me." Dipping his chin, he turned on his heel and started to walk away.

Dalton sighed and opened his mouth to let the man know he'd make it worth his while, but before he got a word out, Blaise bounded up from his seat so fast, his chair screeched and wobbled.

"You lie!"

Kincaid's back stiffened, and he stopped walking.

Bloody hell. Dalton glared at Blaise. If they made it out of here, he was going to throttle him. Doing a quick mental inventory, he located his walking stick, which was leaning against the table between him and Blaise, and tried to push Blaise back into his seat with a hand to his shoulder.

Blaise shrugged his hand right off.

It was then that Dalton noticed that the room had gone quiet. *Damnation.*

Kincaid turned slowly. Instead of anger, his face was again devoid of emotion.

Dalton was beginning to think that was a very bad sign. Anyone who could control their anger so easily was fucking terrifying. It reminded him of his uncle Raleigh. Raleigh was cold and calculating when angered, not emotional.

"Howie said you have the box," Blaise blurted out.

Great! Now Dalton was going to have to save the kid right along with himself and Blaise.

Turning his head slowly, Kincaid looked at Howie.

Howie seemed to find the contents of his mop bucket extremely interesting, but mumbled, "The box Brandon brought in."

"A snuffbox," Kincaid said.

Blaise closed his eyes and took a deep breath. "Yes. We want to buy it from you."

One massive shoulder shrugged. "It ain't fer sale." With that, Kincaid turned back around, patted Howie on the shoulder, and started toward the door again. It could have easily been a "we'll talk later" signal, but Howie seemed relieved, and it suddenly occurred to Dalton that this man was probably the reason none of the patrons bothered these children. He cared for them.

Maybe he could use that to his advantage? With a sigh of resignation and a fervent hope that getting beaten to a bloody pulp didn't kill him, Dalton said, "Isn't there a law against child labor?"

Turning slowly, Kincaid's face finally changed into a sneer. Which was probably a very bad sign.

Dalton instinctively stepped in front of Blaise, but Blaise, stubborn arse that he was, moved to the side.

"If not for yer kind, maybe I wouldn't have to hire them," Kincaid said.

"My kind?"

"Yeah." Kincaid stepped closer. "Yer kind. Ye and yer fancy clothes and lazy lifestyle. Partying with yer friends and yer gambling fortunes back and forth to each other. Yer kind is the reason we 'ave such poverty. Sittin' on yer arses in yer plush chairs in the 'Ouse o' Lords. Ye make laws to line yer own pockets and to the devil wiff the rest of us as long as ye all look good to dem other lords."

Blaise flinched beside him.

The irony wasn't lost on Dalton. He'd always done his best to portray the very thing Kincaid just accused him of, but anger infused him anyway.

A man called out, "Yer a selfish lot," then spat loudly.

Billy and Howie shuffled past Kincaid.

"Quit making work for muh kids, Gregson," Kincaid said. "Everybody go back to what ye were doing."

With a bit of a fuss, the crowd started chatting among themselves again. Glasses clinked and thudded behind the bar again, but the noise was nowhere near as loud as before.

Kincaid stepped even closer, till he was back at the edge of the table. "Good day, gentlemen." Kincaid motioned to Howie to follow him, then left and went back in the door he came out of.

Blaise turned to Dalton, a frantic look on his face. "Do you think he'll hurt Howie? I shouldn't have said that Howie told me about the box, I—"

"Shhh…." Dalton grabbed his hands and sat down in the chair, urging Blaise into his as well. "He's not going to hurt the kid."

As if to prove his point, Howie came back out of the door and headed for their table. He stood there for a moment, then quietly said, "The boss said to give this to you and to tell you not to come back." He opened his hand, revealing the snuffbox. Setting it on the table, he gave Blaise a lopsided smile. "He's not a bad man. He helps us." With that, he walked away, going back to his mop bucket and leaving Dalton and Blaise staring at the box in shock.

CHAPTER THIRTEEN

A certain prince and his betrothed have been spending a lot more time together during ton events. Are those wedding bells we hear? Could it be that there will be a royal wedding sooner than expected?

—From *The Regelence Tattler*, the Royal Happenings column

HE'D DONE what he set out to do, so why didn't it feel like a victory? Blaise shuffled back to the hackney, feeling like he'd had his face smashed in the mud after going a few rounds with a prize fighter. He supposed that was actually true because he had gone a few rounds with "The Killer," only it'd been verbal sparring instead of physical… thank galaxy! He glanced down at the antique snuffbox in his hand, then over at Dalton.

Dalton hadn't said a word since Howie had laid the box on the table in front of them. He'd just calmly grabbed Blaise's hand and escorted him outside, appearing as dazed as Blaise felt. His mouth was pinched tighter than a miser's purse strings, and his shoulders were so stiff it was he who looked pompous now.

"You look like I feel."

Squeezing his hand, Dalton smirked. "You too?"

Blaise nodded, taking comfort in the strong hand holding his own. It was grounding, an assurance that they were in this together, and somehow that helped make it less… miserable. "I thought I'd be happy and relieved to get the box back."

"You're not?"

"No. Yes. I don't know. I'm happy to have it back because now I know Bannon won't be sent away because of it."

Dalton stopped walking. "That was in question?"

Blaise shrugged. "My father said if Bannon committed one more indiscretion, he'd send him to rusticate in the country at Eversleigh Manor. Though who knows if he'd have followed through. My father is a bit of a softy, truth be told, and my sire is practically a marshmallow. He probably would have talked Father out of it. But this whole thing feels insignificant now and not just because we got the box back."

For several seconds, Dalton didn't say anything, and the sounds of the dockside seemed so much louder and more depressing. Even the snow wasn't as happy and mystical as it had been on the way over here. Now it punctuated the starkness of this area. The poverty.

"Is the disk in the box?" Dalton asked.

"I don't know. I haven't looked. It… doesn't matter." It amazed Blaise to realize the truth of that statement. Was it really just a few hours ago that he'd feared losing his job if the disk were found?

Dalton turned to him, one brow arched up under his elegant snow-dotted black hat. "You cannot save the world, angel." He touched Blaise's cheek.

Heat speared through Blaise that had nothing to do with Dalton's touch, making him step back. Or maybe it did. Dalton knew exactly what he was thinking without them having to say anything, and that felt… intimate. "I'm a politician. That *is* my job."

"Hmmm…." Dalton tugged him toward the coach. As they approached, the hackney door opened, and Dalton let go of his hand and held his arm out, motioning for Blaise to go first.

He stepped inside, and Larkinson gave him a questioning look, but he wasn't ready to answer her questions. He felt… numb. Tossing his hat onto the seat beside him, he leaned back in the lift, closed his eyes, and put his hands over his face, only to realize they were shaking.

Dalton slid in next to him, his leg butting up against Blaise's. "What can you do as a politician? You're an intern for the IN councilman. This has nothing to do with the IN Council." He spoke very calmly and quietly as though he were making small talk about the weather.

A good thing, since the way Blaise felt, he wanted to snap back. "Nothing, damn it," he answered without removing his hands. Dalton was right, he was only an intern, not to mention his politics had more to do with intergalactic diplomacy, but those kids needed help. "Do you think Kincaid was right? Do you think it's our fault?"

"Not ours per se, but yes, probably. At least that has been my experience when I've seen poverty in my travel with the IN. And as such, nothing we do is going to help very much until policies are changed. If we want to help, we have to find out why there is a problem in the first place."

Blaise sat up and dropped his hands. Instead of angling for the top political position on the planet, he should be doing something now. He was a lord of the realm and had power and clout. As an intern, he had connections. This might not be an intergalactic matter, but it was a political one. As a lord, he was supposed to make things better for the lower classes, for those without a voice. That was what being a lawmaker was all about. The glory and prestige shouldn't matter as long as the job got done. Somehow he'd forgotten that, or had he ever truly known it? "I'm going to fix this. I'm going to help those children."

"What is going on? Did you get the box?" Larkinson asked.

"Blaise wants to fix the orphan problem single-handedly."

Ugh. Put that way.... "Maybe not single-handedly, but I'm going to fix this. It's the right thing to do."

Dalton calmly set his top hat in his lap and rested his hand on Blaise's thigh. "You're right, it is."

"It.... Wait, did you agree with me? Does that mean you'll help?"

The smirk Dalton gave him was breathtaking. "Of course I agree with you. This will ruin my reputation as a degenerate, but yes, I'll help."

Larkinson's head went back and forth, watching them both with a scowl on her face. "The two of you are maddening. I assume we're talking about Foundling Town, and I want to help as well, but right now I want to know if you got the blasted box."

In answer, Blaise handed her the box. To Dalton, he said, "You are far from a degenerate."

"Oh," Larkinson said, taking the box. "He's right. You are definitely not a reprobate, regardless what others think. They obviously don't know you well."

Groaning, Dalton shook his head. "I assure you both, I've earned my reputation. Now open the box and see if the disk is still there."

"Disk? What disk?" Larkinson looked at Dalton, then at Blaise. "What's he talking about?"

No use hiding it now. With a sigh, Blaise answered, "Dalton gave me a disk of Prissy engaged in a lewd act, and I hid it in the box."

Larkinson's eyes widened for a split second. "So you didn't go after it just to keep Bannon out of trouble?"

Blaise shook his head. "No, though I did hope to keep Bannon out of trouble as well." And didn't that put a fine spin on things? He really was a selfish dolt. The thought niggled at his psyche like a rock in the shoe. This was not who he wanted to be. How ironic was it that he'd gone after the disk because he didn't want to be like Prissy?

She scowled at him, but instead of the reprimand he expected, and deserved, she said, "You should have used the disk to blackmail that little weasel."

"That's what I told him," Dalton groused.

"What exactly was Prissy doing in the vid?" Larkinson leaned forward.

Blaise leveled a stare at her. This was serious. "It doesn't matter. You're missing the point."

She nodded and opened the box, but not the secret compartment. "Now tell me about the plan. How are we going to help the orphans?"

"I have no idea," Blaise answered honestly. After taking the box from Larkinson, he opened the secret compartment. The disk was still there. He took it out, handed the box back to Larkinson, then tossed the disk onto the floor of the lift and smashed it under his bootheel. "I thought I could use my influence to make some inquiries."

Dalton nodded, his hand tapped Blaise's leg, and when Blaise moved his foot, Dalton picked up the smashed disk and put it in his coat pocket. His other hand stayed on Blaise's knee. "I will throw this away when I get home, and I'll talk to Rexley and see what he knows. Muffin, his ward, is an orphan after all."

Glancing down at Dalton's hand, Blaise clutched it to keep it from moving. Dalton's hand moving on his thigh was not a way to get his mind to work. He was very aware of how close that hand was to his… er, nether regions, and blast it all, the thought sent heat right up his face and neck. Clearing his throat, he tried to shift his focus back to the task at hand. "I'd quite forgotten about that, but I doubt Rexley is aware of the problem. If he were, he'd already be doing something about it, so making him aware is a good idea. Rexley has a tremendous amount of influence."

"I'll talk to the servants." Larkinson glanced at their entwined hands and smiled.

Blaise nearly groaned aloud. He should let go of Dalton's hand, but he didn't want to. And how strange was that? He rather liked touching Dalton. So he decided to deal with the consequences later. If Larkinson wanted to tease him, then so be it.

Fortunately she didn't want to tease him. Instead they all planned, getting down their assignments. They were in this together, and somehow it felt… not right exactly, but better. He had his two close friends working on the problem with him. Larkinson he knew was a hard worker and adamant when she set her mind to something. And Dalton? Well, Dalton was just as stubborn and hardworking, but he also brought a craftiness to the table that made Blaise actually believe they could do this.

The next fifteen minutes passed so quickly, they were back to their side of Classige before they knew it.

"We are at your destination," the hackney computer announced as the lift began to slow.

Larkinson touched his arm. "I asked the lift to take us around back, but stay here until I give you the signal. I'll go make sure the coast is clear." She stopped in front of Dalton on her way to the door. "Ashbourne—"

"Dalton." He looked up at her with a grin.

The smile she gave him in return was radiant. "Dalton, thank you for watching after him." She held out her hand, but instead of shaking it, Dalton kissed her knuckles.

"It was my honor."

Larkinson shook her head and glanced back at Blaise with her grin still in place. She was completely and utterly charmed by Dalton, or perhaps not too much, because she lifted a brow at Blaise and gave him a pointed look. There was a lot of warning in that expression, her playing mother hen again. "Listen for my signal." Turning to the door, she said, "Door up, steps down."

When the lift complied, she poked her head out and looked side to side. Satisfied no one was there, she darted out of the lift and plastered her back against the fence of Thompson House. She slinked to the gate, stopping every so often. When she kneeled down to peek through the gate, Blaise grinned.

"She's taking this clandestine stuff seriously." Dalton's laughter joined his.

"She takes everything seriously."

Reaching up, she gripped the latch on the gate and inched it open. Blaise shook his head and turned back to Dalton.

Dalton was no longer watching Larkinson. His gaze roved over Blaise's face, and the look was tender and something else. He licked his lips then.

Blaise's attention was narrowed to that pink tip slowly caressing those full lips. An answering tug somewhere low in his abdomen had him shifting in his seat. His lips and the inside of his mouth began to tingle in remembrance of their earlier kiss. He was going to ignore Larkinson's warning. He should scoot back, clear his throat, and act as though he was uninterested, but it would be a lie. And he was tired of lying to himself.

"I'm going to kiss you." Dalton's voice was low, seductive. "If you don't want that, you'd better say so now." He brought his hand up and rubbed the backs of his knuckles across Blaise's jaw.

And there it was. His way to finally put distance between them, to regain the more acquaintance-like relationship they had. If he'd never seen the things he had tonight, he might have done just that. "I want you to kiss me."

Dalton captured his lips with such commanding force, Blaise could do nothing but relent. He might have even moaned a little as Dalton's tongue swept into his mouth. This time he knew what to do. It still felt awkward, but so sweet. Their tongues parried and thrust.

The hand against his cheek threaded into the back of his hair, gripping and turning his head to a sharper angle. His blood soared through his ears, and his cock lengthened. The tingling in his lips spread down his body, making him feel alive. It was too much and not enough, and it was over way too soon.

Dalton pulled back, leaving Blaise gasping. Somehow his hands had ended up gripping the lapels of Dalton's greatcoat, and there was something poking his hip. Good galaxy, how had he ended up in Dalton's lap?

Blaise scrambled back to the seat with heat in his cheeks and a pounding heart. Larkinson had been right to give him a warning look. "I'm sorry. I, uh…." His voice was rough, almost hoarse.

"I'm not." Dalton gripped his hand and pulled it into his lap against his erection.

Gasping, Blaise jerked his hand back. Tonight he'd realized that reputation wasn't everything, but some habits were hard to break. "Thank you."

Cocking his head, Dalton furrowed his brow as though the gratitude puzzled him. He stared at Blaise for the longest time, and then a slow smile oozed across his kiss-swollen lips.

Oh, why did Blaise have to notice that they were swollen? Larkinson was right. You could tell when someone had been kissed.

Dalton touched his cheek again. "You're welcome." He looked over his shoulder, then back at him. "Larkinson is calling you."

Blaise glanced around him and noticed Larkinson hiding behind the bush beside the back servants' entrance with a light. She was flashing it at the hackney. She needed better timing. Five minutes ago would have been good. Groaning, he stood, still holding Dalton's hand. Their hands were the same size. They fit well together. Blaise squeezed once, then got out of the lift. Galaxy help him, he was actually looking forward to dancing tomorrow night.

HOME SWEET hell. He'd finally found something better than a cold shower to cool his ardor. Dalton stepped into the dark foyer of Fairfax House and looked at the big grandfather clock next to the drawing room—*2:46 a.m.* Not a normal time for a household to sleep in Pruluce, but judging by the empty state of the foyer, his parents were abed. They'd never been big fans of ton events. No matter. They'd know he was here from Stuart, their butler, so he was living up to his end of the bargain, or rather blackmail, since he hadn't actually negotiated anything. Glancing at the main staircase, he decided he just couldn't bear to drag himself to his lonely room. A room he hadn't been in since he was a child. Sighing, he walked farther down the hall and pushed open the library door.

It had been a long night—overall a good one, since they'd gotten the box back and he'd really enjoyed Blaise's company, but a long one nevertheless. He needed a drink, and the one thing he could at least count on in Fairfax House was good brandy. His sire had a love of brandy and considered himself a connoisseur.

He closed the door behind him with a quiet click. "Stuart, light a fire."

"Yes, my lord."

A fire sprang to life in the fireplace, and Dalton tossed his hat on the chair beside the door. He laid his coat over the back and began working on his gloves, one finger at a time. The gesture made him think of Blaise and how he'd wanted to strip off their gloves tonight so he could feel Blaise's skin against his. Something had changed between them tonight. He wasn't sure what it was, but he liked it. Galaxy, that last kiss had made his blood boil. That lovely mouth and those nervously questing hands made him want so much more. It was charming as hell how Blaise didn't know where to put his hands. He'd place them on Dalton's arms, then move them to his shoulders, then to his back, then again to his forearms. For all the man's confidence in his job, he was shy when it came to men. Tonight it had been wildly apparent. Just thinking about that tongue cautiously caressing his made Dalton ache. His cock was half-hard like some randy schoolboy.

After adding his gloves to the pile of outerwear, he made a quick adjustment to his prick and strode toward the rolling cart in the corner, intent on pouring himself a brandy. He had to stop thinking about Blaise or he'd never get to sleep, even with the liquid sleep aid.

And speaking of liquid sleep aid.... Where was the bar? He went to where the bar was supposed to be, but in its place was a desk. A small oak writing desk with gray leather inlaid into the top. He hadn't thought that the place had changed much, but perhaps it had. He turned, taking in the room. The library had always been airy, with light oak shelves all around it and pastel colors. Nothing like the cozy jewel tones and dark mahogany wood at the castle that invited you to sit and stay. But now.... The light colors were gone, even the shelves had been stained a dark walnut color, and the furnishings were different. More... welcoming? Where were the high-backed pale green brocade chairs? The stiff, delicate-looking chairs had been replaced with ebony overstuffed leather ones. And ottomans! There were actually ottomans. It changed the whole feel of the room. This was no longer a stuffy, uncomfortable showplace, but a place he might actually feel comfortable in. Not enough to lounge around in his stockinged feet and read, of course, but to drink....

Dalton continued his perusal of the room.

The portrait of his great-grandsire was missing from the prominent place above the mantel, and in its place was a stormy landscape. Was that Windswept Abbey, Ravensburg's county seat, in the background? It had been even more years since he'd been to Windswept Abbey, but he was certain that was it. It was beautiful, with the stark and rugged moors surrounding it. The landscape was a much more aesthetic painting than the portrait. Why had it been changed? His parents liked the cold, prim decor, didn't they?

There was a small picture frame on the writing desk, but Dalton couldn't see it. There were also papers. He picked them up and studied them. His sire's handwriting. There looked to be a hologram display port on the desk for a monitor and keyboard as well. Was his sire using the library for an office? Why would he, when the marquess-consort's office was on the second floor, where it had been for, well... forever?

He picked up the photo, turned it around, and nearly dropped it. It was a picture of him. The photograph taken of him when he'd graduated basic training. He was in his dress whites. He'd sent this photo to Uncle Raleigh. So how had his sire gotten it? And why would he want it? Especially on his desk, where he could see it every day? Dalton frowned and set the photo down. Maybe it was for show? His parents had always been keen to appear a happy, normal family.

He stepped away from the desk and continued around the room, noticing other differences. With each change, his stomach got a bit more unsettled. The small portraits by the window of his grandfather and grandsire were gone, replaced with one large still life of a gentleman's gloves, hat, and discarded cravat. There was also no bar in this room. *How odd.*

Feeling more than a little uneasy—which was silly, because what did he care if the library had changed? He'd never liked it anyway—Dalton shrugged and left. He'd find brandy somewhere else and take it up to his room.

First he tried his father's study, but there wasn't any brandy in there either. *What the devil?* Every subsequent room he looked in had undergone a makeover, at least the portraits had. All the portraits of his grandfather and grandsire had been replaced, and he hadn't found a drop of alcohol. He peeked into two more rooms—the parlor and the morning room—but the situation was the same.

With confusion clouding his head, Dalton went across the foyer to the drawing room. There was a liquor cabinet in there, if memory served. Though to be honest, he no longer felt like having a brandy. He went more for curiosity's sake.

He found the cabinet, but instead of spirits, knickknacks now took the place of the assorted bottles and crystal decanters. What was going on? Surely they wouldn't discard all of his sire's vintage brandy and Father's preferred scotch just to keep it from him? The idea made his shoulders tense and his ears hot. He rarely drank to excess anymore. Turning to leave the room, he noticed the painting above the chaise. It was another still life. He was certain there had been a painting of his grandsire. A rather hideous painting at that. He remembered because it had never made sense to him. His grandsire had been wearing a bear skin, complete with the head, hanging off his right shoulder and a bear claw necklace around his neck. Bears had nothing to do with his family line. It wasn't like their family crest had a grizzly in it or anything, and according to Grandfather, he hadn't killed the beast himself.

Shaking his head, Dalton let himself out of the drawing room and started up the stairs toward the portrait gallery on the second floor. Something about this whole situation bothered him. Were all the portraits gone? He barely remembered his grandsire, but he remembered the portraits. He'd always felt as though there were eyes following him. According to the stories, Grandsire was a patron of the arts, which accounted for all the paintings. It was also said he was a surly, serious man who did not get along at all with his spouse, and thinking back, Dalton didn't remember seeing them together often. How anyone could not get along with Grandfather was beyond him.

Grandfather had been a congenial man who laughed easily. He'd been an intelligence commander in the Regelence Navy. According to rumor, he'd left the running of Ravensburg up to his spouse while he worked at the base, whoring in his spare time. Dalton didn't know much about the whoring, though. To the best of his recollection, Grandfather had always come home after work. He'd spent his evenings with Dalton. Riding in the park, reading stories, and even playing with soldiers. Galaxy, he missed his grandfather.

Halfway down the hall, Dalton noticed there was only one closed door. The room that was formerly the marquess-consort's study. He knew it, because as a child he'd never been allowed inside. And he didn't want to go in there now. A deep sense of foreboding swamped him, making his knees weak, and bile rose in his throat. He swallowed hard and shook his head to clear it. Dust, what was wrong with him? It was just a room. Grabbing the knob, he twisted. Nothing happened. The door was locked. *Thank galaxy.* For some reason an image of the room popped into his head. Pastel blue walls, massive white furniture, huge chairs with floral prints. It was as if he were seeing them through a tunnel; a heavy fog surrounded the perimeter of the room making it dark despite the light interior. The perspective was off—lower, like it would have been when he was a child. *A memory?* With a groan, he rapped his knuckles against the door lightly.

A maid came around the corner, her arms loaded down with a tray. There was a teapot, a cup, and a domed platter of some sort. She was pretty, with blonde hair and big blue eyes. He didn't know her, but then he doubted he would. She was young, probably his age. She cocked her head at him and asked, “My lord?”

“Yes?”

“There isn’t anyone in there.” Her eyes darted past him to the door.

“But the door is locked.”

She nodded. “That door is always closed. No one goes in that room.” Her voice lowered almost to a whisper by the time she was done speaking. She even seemed to shrink away from the door.

“And why is that?” Dalton half expected a ghost story to match his intuition.

Shaking her head, she stepped closer. “I have no idea. It’s all very bizarre. I saw the room open once, and there is nothing in it.”

“Nothing?”

She shook her head.

“Not even the furniture?”

“No, my lord. My understanding is that everything was thrown out.”

That strange itchy feeling in his brain that Dalton had upon not finding any alcohol and the missing portraits increased. He nodded and thanked the girl before trying the knob again. He was about to ask Stuart to open the door when he heard something behind him and realized the maid was still there. Turning, he arched a brow at her. “Is there anything else?”

A blush shot up her cheeks, and she looked away, not meeting his eye. “Sorry, my lord, it’s just this”—she dipped her head toward the tray—“is for you. I was on my way to your room with it.”

“I didn’t order anything.”

“No. Cook sent it up, thinking you might be hungry. Their lordships have retired early this evening.”

“Oh, well….” Smiling, Dalton hurried to her and tried to take the tray.

She shook her head. “I’ll carry it for you.”

“Don’t be silly. It’s too heavy for you.”

She gave him a breathless sigh that doubled as a smile. He’d caught her off guard. “It’s my job, my lord, but I would love it if you opened the door for me.”

Dalton nodded. “Very well, lead the way.” He glanced back at the door and decided he’d come back to that later. “Is Mrs. Jennings still the cook?”

"She is, my lord. She said she sent some of your favorites, and I was to tell you welcome home from her."

"I will give Mrs. Jennings my thanks at breakfast. Does she still make cinnamon buns for the staff every morning?"

The maid nodded.

"Excellent. Then I will probably see you for breakfast too."

She chuckled. "You aren't at all what I expected."

"I do hope that is good." They reached his door, and Dalton stepped in front of her and opened it.

"Very good, my lord." She walked past him into the room.

Dalton stood in the doorway, marveling at the change. This was not the same room he'd left before going into the IN. Everything was different, right down to the wallpaper. Instead of bright and airy like the rest of the town house used to be, it was dark and cozy. The walls were a deep burgundy above mahogany wainscoting. Gone were the toys and preadolescent trappings that had still been present when he was forced to return home. This was a room fit for a sophisticated man of leisure. Dalton had never considered himself sophisticated, but it was a very nice room. The furniture was big, taking up a lot of space, unlike the smaller pieces that had once been in there. There was even a cozy fire burning in the hearth. And two comfy-looking leather chairs and a table in front of the fire. The maid had set his evening snack on the table. Dalton marveled at the change. It reminded him of his room at Townsend Castle. It fit his current taste just as well as if he'd designed it himself. Right down to the large hedonistic canopy bed draped in dark red heavy brocade curtains. "Who did this?"

The maid turned to face him. "The marquess-consort mostly, but I believe the marquess picked out the wallpaper. The footmen, myself, and Mary—she's the other maid—we moved all the belongings in and out of here just last week."

The information nearly staggered him. Dalton felt as though someone had hit him in the gut. He even took a step back in his surprise. His parents did this? Why? And where was all the old stuff? Things sure had a way of coming up missing here. Not that he'd miss any of the things. Well, no, that wasn't true. He wanted the toy soldiers his grandfather had bought him.

The maid came toward him, stopped to curtsy, then began to walk past him.

Dalton caught her by the arm. “Where is the stuff that was in this room?”

“The children’s toys and clothes and things?”

“Yes.”

“In the attic, my lord.”

Dalton nodded and let her leave. With a sense of wonder and puzzlement, he closed the door and went to the table. What was going on? This was not at all what he’d expected from his parents. He liked it, but he was afraid to trust it.

Chapter Fourteen

Rumor has it that Lord Demon has been absent from his usual haunts since his return and was seen conversing with honorable gentlemen at a ton ball. Could he be turning over a new leaf and becoming respectable? Gads, this author certainly hopes not. Wherever will we get our entertainment? On second thought, there is always a certain mischievous marquess and his artist coconspirator.

—From *Pruluce Weekly*, the Beau Monde Happenings column

Thompson House

BLAISE STUDIED the crowd of people in the Thompson House ballroom and decided that the ball was a smashing success. A good thing too, since he'd missed an entire day at the House of Lords in which he could've been making inquiries about Operation: Orphans. All afternoon, he'd helped his sire prepare for the ball, and it was a good thing he had, because Bannon had spent all afternoon chalking the dance floor. It had been a long, tiring day, and Blaise hadn't gotten to see Dalton. Not that he missed him or anything, but he wanted to know if Dalton had any news on Operation: Orphans. *Really, Blaise? You are a lousy liar.* Those kisses had haunted his dreams all night.

With a sigh, he made his way to the punch bowl, keeping an eye out for Dalton as he went. He passed by the door to the parlor, which was doubling as a card room tonight, and.... Did he just see what he thought he saw? *Surely not.* Blaise glared at Lord Fitzhugh's retreating back and hurried to the flower arrangement he'd spent thirty minutes working on. The flowers sat upon a black half-column pedestal, and there were all sorts of tall spiky leaves and full flowers. It looked brilliant with all the gleaming white-and-black marble ballroom. The roses he'd used really stood out.

He stopped in front of the pedestal, and sure enough, there was a red rose missing right out of the front middle of the composition. Not a bud but a big full-opened bloom that he'd used as his main focal point. Now there was a gaping hole. *Ugh!* Going around behind the stand, he looked for a replacement flower.

"What are you doing?"

Blaise peered through the fronds of spiky things and found Griff standing just in front of the floral design. At least the person sounded like Griff and he had a Griff-shaped body; there was a lily where his head should have been. "Fixing this arrangement. Fitzhugh, the bloody old goat, stole my rose."

"At least he did not steal your cravat."

"What?" Blaise glanced down at his chest out of instinct as a prickling sensation skimmed over his scalp. He gave up on rose hunting and stepped around the flowers. "Whatever are you talking about?" He had not told Griff about his run-in with Dalton at the haberdashery…. Gads, it seemed like ages ago.

"Prissy. He's made a point to stop by my office at the Lords and tell me that…." Griff pressed a glass into his hand—he had two of them—and leaned close to whisper, "Ashbourne took your cravat off of you in public."

Blinking back his surprise, Blaise waited for the anger to hit him full-force, but it never did. Oh, he wasn't thrilled about Percy starting rumors, but he found he no longer cared. Perhaps he should, but after last night, it seemed trivial. Prissy seemed petty and pathetic. He had no idea what being a representative of the people was all about. Shrugging, Blaise lifted the glass toward Griff. "Thank you for this." He took a drink of the rich ratafia, relieved to see that no one had spiked it yet.

"Then it's not true?" Griff paused and gave him a strange look that made Blaise wonder if they were discussing the same thing. "Because if it is, you have to know that I'll offer for you and—"

Blaise shook his head and waved the suggestion away. "No need. I appreciate the sentiment, but…."

Griff's face fell.

Whoa. A lump formed in the back of Blaise's throat. Did Griff actually want to offer for him? Before Blaise could think of something to say, Griff smiled and chuckled, making Blaise wonder if he'd imagined the reaction.

"Of course. Marrying to deflect a scandal is not exactly the ideal situation, is it?"

"No."

Taking a drink of his ratafia, Griff gazed out at the crowd. He was quiet for several moments, then said, "I tried to find you last night at the Blinkford ball."

"I went home with a migraine last night." Blaise glanced out at the ballroom too. He still had to find Dalton. Was that Bannon? Where was he going?

Grabbing his forearm, Griff turned him slightly. "Are you all right?" The concern on his face stabbed Blaise with guilt.

"Yes. I got up this morning and my headache was gone."

"Good." Griff continued to look at him but didn't say anything else.

The silence was odd, and Blaise became very aware of a waltz playing. It was as if he felt the notes in his pulse. *Where are you, Dalton?* He'd never thought he needed a rescue from Griff, but tonight things seemed… awkward between them.

Finally, Griff turned back to the ballroom. After a few moments, he said, "I like the chalk drawing. Bannon?"

"Yes. Bannon drew it this afternoon. You should have seen him afterward. He was covered in chalk from head to toe." Blaise grinned at the memory as he gazed out at the dance floor and the drawing in question. Couples swirled around, destroying the lovely chalked floor. There were only smears of color left of the Thompson coat of arms in the center, but a few of the red and black arabesque scrolls Bannon had done on the edge of the floor were still partially in place. Speaking of Bannon…. Blaise scanned the area he'd thought he'd seen him. His gaze traveled along until…. *Yes! There!*

Just beyond the punch bowl in the far corner of the ballroom, there was a crate draped in black cloth and concealed behind three large potted parlor palms. On top, the crate had a huge fan-shaped flower arrangement with red and white roses and those long spiky leaves he'd used in all the floral presentations. The crate contained the new garden fountain that had arrived too late today to be installed, so they'd had to use it as a backdrop for the punch bowl. It actually looked rather good as decor. However, at present, Bannon was holding his linked hands down like he was giving someone a boost up on a horse. It didn't take a genius to guess the "horse" was actually the crate and the rider was actually Winstol.

A couple danced into his line of sight, blocking the view completely. "Blast." Blaise leaned to his left. "Griff, can you see Bannon? He's by the punch bowl."

"Oh dear. We'll never make it over there in time."

"What's going o—*oh no*!" The couple moved and gave Blaise a great view of his brother.

Winstol was on the crate, crouched down behind the flower arrangement. Bannon handed him something. Blaise would bet his right arm that something was a dance card. How could no one see them? The House of Lords needed a class on observation. They danced, they talked, they drank, but none of them seemed to notice the disastrous duo.

Blaise watched in horror as Winstol's head popped up above the flowers. He drew his arm back.

"We should do something," Griff said with way too much of a smile in his voice.

"What is there to do?"

Winstol threw the card into the orchestra stand on the balcony overlooking the ballroom. It went sailing over the pianist's head and hit the back wall.

Blaise swore he heard a thud, but common sense said he imagined it, because the music was too loud. "There. That's that. Now they will get down."

"I wouldn't want to bet on it," a new voice chimed in. This one way more sardonic than Griff's and practically engaged in outright laughter.

Dalton. Blaise knew the owner of the voice before he turned. Not only did he recognize it, but his stupid heart decided to dance a spry little jig in his chest.

Dalton looked dashing as usual in his evening clothes. Tonight instead of the black cravat and black shirt and waistcoat, he'd gone with white. And his hair was perfectly tamed. It gave him a more wholesome look, not so dangerous. It should seem wrong on him, but it didn't. He appeared respectable, but Blaise had the urge to ruffle his hair and get that dangerous air back.

But the rake wasn't completely disguised. When Dalton met Blaise's gaze, there was a devilish twinkle in those gray eyes, and the smile could only be called rascally. Thankfully it didn't last long, because Blaise wasn't sure he could take it. He swallowed the sudden lump in his throat as Dalton dipped his head in greeting to Griff and said rather curtly, "Grantham."

Griff returned the acknowledgment with an equally curt "Ashbourne."

Dalton turned his attention back to the spectacle that was Bannon and Winstol, though Blaise was very aware of the heat coming off the shoulder butted up against his as Dalton stood closer than was considered proper.

On the crate, Winstol had reached into his coat pocket and was once again standing with his arm cocked back.

"Wait for it," Dalton said, still sounding on the verge of laughter. Then he chuckled outright. "Ho there. Rexley has seen him."

Prince Rexley strode across the ballroom with a look on his face that could only be termed "amused but trying not to appear amused." His lips were tucked in together, his brow furrowed into a glare, but there were very obvious laugh lines peeking out of his cheeks, despite the pinched mouth.

Bannon, who'd been playing lookout, spotted Rexley and started tugging on Winstol's trouser leg.

"Ten quid says he throws it anyway." This from Dalton.

"You're on," Griff shot back.

Groaning, Blaise shook his head, but couldn't help but add, "Someone is going to see him. Any moment now."

"No, they aren't," Dalton said smugly.

Chuckling, Blaise elbowed him in the ribs. He turned back to the spectacle but glimpsed something in his peripheral vision. When he turned, Griff was staring at him with a puzzled frown. Heat sizzled up Blaise's neck and face, and he peered back at his brother to try and cover for his act of familiarity.

Winstol darted a glance at Rexley and cocked his arm back again. Rexley reached him, grabbing his ankle just as he let the dance card fly.

It hit the violinist right in the middle of his forehead. There was a loud screech as the musician's bow took an untimely pass over the strings. The other musicians kept playing. Fortunately for Bannon and Winstol, the ballroom seemed to stare as a whole up at the violinist.

"I shall gladly give you ten quid for that, Ashbourne," Griff said with a chuckle that didn't quite reach his eyes. He looked between Blaise and Dalton.

Blaise moved, trying to put some space between them, but Dalton grabbed his hand and placed it on his forearm.

"I believe this is my dance." Dalton tipped his head to Griff and led Blaise out onto the floor.

Blaise glanced over his shoulder and smiled at Griff. "I'll talk to you later."

Griff nodded but did not seem happy. In fact, if his eyes could shoot real daggers, Dalton would have a back full. Not, of course, that Dalton cared. *Smug man.*

"That was rather rude."

"What?" Dalton feigned innocence. "You did promise me a dance."

"That I did." And blast it all, he'd been looking forward to it all day. He meant to ask Dalton about Operation: Orphans, but Dalton smiled at him, and oh my, didn't he dance divinely. But then he would. Dalton did everything well. There was something so magical about floating, er, dancing, across the floor with this man. He almost imagined they were alone. How soon could he get Dalton out of here before they could kiss again?

Those perfectly shaped lips began to move and it took Blaise several seconds to realize that Dalton was speaking. Guh, what a ninny he was being. He shook his head to clear it.

Dalton raised a brow. "You don't like that idea?"

"I'm sorry, tell me again. I was thinking about Bannon." It seemed as good a lie as any.

"I was saying that last night I came up with an idea." And it was a good one, judging from the smirk on Dalton's face.

Blaise grinned back. "Tell me about this idea, O Wise One."

Dalton threw his head back and chuckled, exposing just the top part of his throat, and Blaise wondered what he'd look like without a cravat.

"We can give my old furniture and clothes to foundling homes. It will be a great way to gain access and ask questions." He leaned forward as if to impart a secret, and the whiff of sandalwood and bergamot teased Blaise's nose. "And I can appear as though I'm being charitable for my parents."

"You would be being charitable."

Dalton shrugged.

"Well, do you know which home we should start at?"

"I do." He pursed his lips. "I've only found one so far, so I thought we'd start there."

"Okay. Tomorrow morning. Then when we get there, we can ask about other orphanages."

Dalton gave him a smart nod. "My thoughts exactly."

They continued to dance, parents forgotten, and it occurred to Blaise how easily they danced together. He usually worried about having to talk to dance partners in fear that he'd stammer, but with Dalton, he wasn't worried. In fact, he couldn't remember having such a lengthy conversation with a dance partner before, and he was positive that was because they were friends.

Dalton stiffened, staring off to his right. "Bloody hell."

"What?" *Please don't let it be Bannon and Winstol again.*

"What's he doing here? He never comes to these things."

Blaise followed his gaze and found the source of his disapproval.

The Marquess of Ravensburg. He was arguing with someone near the door of the ballroom, and that someone was Blaise's father.

"You don't think that's about us, do you?" Dalton looked at him and swirled them closer to the action. "I thought us dancing together would help my reputation, but I don't want to get you in trouble." The concern in those gray eyes practically melted Blaise.

Blaise shook his head. "I doubt it. It's probably about Councilman's Committee business." Or so Blaise hoped.

King-Consort Raleigh was there now. He'd stepped between the two men and begun ushering them both from the room.

Blaise glanced around and noticed no one was watching them. They were all tuned in to the new spectacle. He stopped dancing and tugged on Dalton's hand. "Come on."

DALTON DIDN'T have a clue what Blaise was about, but he followed him to a door at the back of the ballroom and through the servants' hallway. They went up a flight of stairs and came out on the second-floor hallway overlooking the foyer.

Peering left, then right, Blaise made an exaggerated motion with his hand to follow and took off in a full sprint, leading them to the third door on the right. As soon as Dalton cleared the door, Blaise started to shut it but stopped short of slamming it. He gently pressed the door closed, turning the knob to keep it from making a sound. *The little sneak.*

Dalton bit his lip to keep from laughing, but couldn't keep the smile off his face. He started to point out that their pounding feet on the upper balcony probably negated the quiet door closing, but decided against it when he saw how serious Blaise looked. For some reason that made Dalton smile even bigger as he turned to see where they'd ended up.

It was a lovely drawing room. Unlike the drawing room in Fairfax House, which was cold and meant to impress and show off his parents' wealth, this drawing room was done in browns, beiges, and blues with plush wall-to-wall carpet the color of cinnamon that sank in several inches under his feet. The space was lit by two table lamps on either side of the overstuffed brown leather couch. There was a huge, dark blue granite fireplace in the center of the back wall that was only missing a cozy fire to make the room even more intimate. Which was a problem. It *was* very intimate. "Um, Blaise? What about the computer butler? And why are we in here?"

Waving off his concern, Blaise made a beeline toward the fireplace. "We won't be discovered because there is a glitch in the system. Our parents undoubtedly went into the study, which is directly beneath this room, and Coleman leaves not only the room he's asked to leave, but the one above it." He got down on his knees in front of the fireplace and looked back, giving Dalton the most beatific grin he'd ever seen. "Bannon and I found that out quite by accident years ago, and I've used the knowledge ever since." With that, Blaise stuck his head in the fireplace.

Here is hoping that the duke asked for privacy from the butler when they went into the study. "What are you doing?"

"Listening. The acoustics here are great. The two rooms share a chimney and the flues run side by side."

He had this all figured out. Would wonders never cease? This elegant, sophisticated man was adept at eavesdropping. Chuckling, Dalton shook his head and walked over to the fireplace. "You know it's not polite to listen in on others' conversations, don't you?"

"Shh…." Turning his head, Blaise put his finger to his lips. "If we are too loud, they can hear us too. You have to whisper." With that, he stuck his head back in the fireplace, and his delectable behind wiggled as he scooted closer.

Dalton groaned. He wanted to reach down and grip that rounded bottom in his hands and squeeze, but was fairly certain Blaise would screech and hit his head on the top of the firebox, and that would certainly get them caught. It just might be worth it, though.

Completely oblivious to the tempting picture he made, Blaise shushed him again. "Come down here and listen. I can hear Ravensburg."

With a shake of his head, Dalton gave that pretty arse one last longing look and went to his knees next to Blaise. He should be commended for not kneeling behind him. Whatever was the world coming to? He was secluded in a cozy room with a beautiful man, and he was eavesdropping on his father. Crawling forward onto the granite tile hearth, he settled in next to Blaise. It hurt his knees, but the proximity to Blaise overrode the discomfort. Funny how a lot of things with Blaise didn't seem as bad. The man always smelled so nicely of mint and musk. And damn, but Blaise was right, he could hear his father almost like he was in the same room with him.

Ravensburg was complaining about dog tags, of all things.

Dalton's shoulder protested by throbbing.

"We need to amend the treaty to keep the IN from tagging our soldiers." Ravensburg probably had his chin held high and his arms crossed over his chest. He always did that when he was angry. Dalton used to imagine it was to keep from throttling the person he was angry with, but now he suspected it was to appear superior, because it puffed his chest out and made him look bigger, more imposing.

"You are one to talk." This from Uncle Raleigh, and he did not sound happy. It wasn't so much the volume that clued a person in to Raleigh's anger, but the very nonchalant, almost bored and sarcastic tone. "You used your own son's dog tag to track him and have him kidnapped."

There was a gasp, then, "You did what?" the Duke of Eversleigh asked in his deep voice.

Turning his head, Blaise bumped his nose against Dalton's. For several seconds, he just stared and everything seemed to disappear aside from those lovely eyes, so full of wonder. Then he blinked and broke the spell. "I really am sorry for giving him the codes." Sweeping his lashes downward and back up, he bit his bottom lip and swallowed hard.

Had Dalton ever had a sincerer apology? He didn't think so. The utter sweetness in Blaise's tone made him feel warm and… happy. Blaise made him happy. Blaise made him want to be good and noble, but Dalton started to lean forward and capture those lush lips. Then his father spoke again.

"I had to get him to come home. He wouldn't even see me." Did he sound regretful?

"That's neither here nor there," Eversleigh said. "I've told you we cannot amend the treaty without letting the IN know we are onto them."

"Eversleigh's right," Raleigh agreed.

"So we're going to let them continue to track our soldiers?" Ravensburg's voice rose in outrage. "My son has a dog tag."

"Not anymore," Raleigh said with a little gruffness.

"Does it still hurt?" Blaise whispered against his lips.

"No." That wasn't entirely true, but Dalton couldn't seem to focus on anything but Blaise's lips long enough to elaborate.

Their lips were touching now even though neither had actually moved to kiss the other.

"Good." Blaise's eyes closed, and a soft sigh pushed into Dalton's mouth. His breath smelled like ratafia. Dalton wasn't a big fan of the drink, but he was certain he would learn to crave it if he tasted it from Blaise's lips.

"I'm not ready to show our hand yet. Not until I find out more. I've talked to the commander in charge of Regelence Navy's medical in-processing about either removing or reformatting the dog tags after our soldiers leave the IN, but until I find out what Admiral Jenkins thought was on Skye that belongs to Regelence…."

In the back of his mind, Dalton realized he should be paying closer attention to the conversation below, but damned if he cared at the moment. With Blaise's ragged breathing and the feel of his soft, warm lips against Dalton's, it was all he could do to concentrate on staying upright. His body thrummed with excitement and his eyes seemed to close of their own volition and he gently raised his hand and rested it across the back of Blaise's neck. Part of him didn't want to move; he just wanted to stay here, sharing a breath with Blaise. It was probably the strangest notion he'd ever had, because he could not remember ever not rushing into pleasure. But this was a pleasure of its own.

The ratafia on Blaise's breath called to him. Taunted him. He snaked his tongue out, sliding it across Blaise's bottom lip and the passion ignited. The conversation from below them was completely forgotten and only his sense of self-preservation made him urge Blaise out of the fireplace.

They slid off the hearth onto the soft carpet with their tongues and limbs tangling. Dalton ended up lying on top of Blaise, cradled between his thighs, his arms supporting most of his weight.

For once Blaise seemed to have no hesitation about putting his arms around Dalton. His hand snaked up the back of Dalton's neck as he lifted himself up until their bodies touched. A soft moan bled out of Blaise's sweet lips and the hard ridge of Blaise's cock pressed against Dalton's.

Galaxy help him, knowing Blaise was as excited as him fired Dalton's blood, but when Blaise began to writhe beneath him, it was nearly too much. He broke their kiss and positioned himself to Blaise's side. "Slow down, sweetheart."

"Yes." Blaise nodded, but his actions didn't match his words. He clutched at Dalton's shoulders, trying to drag him back on top of him.

"Shh… I know what you need." Very slowly, Dalton slid his hand down over the planes of Blaise's stomach to lightly rest against his erection.

Blaise bucked up into the touch and kissed Dalton's lips, then his jaw. He nuzzled, rocking his head back and forth against Dalton's neck with abandon that Dalton hadn't realized he was capable of.

His spine tingled with arousal and his balls felt impossibly tight, but rather than his own release, he wanted Blaise's. As Blaise continued to mouth his neck and jaw, he removed his hand long enough to unbutton the falls on Blaise's trousers. Dalton moaned at the spot of wetness on Blaise's undergarment, where the tip of his cock was. He simply had to touch.

As he pushed down Blaise's smallclothes, the cascade of breath across his skin stopped. Without looking away from the luscious cock he was revealing, Dalton felt Blaise raise his head and watch. *Please don't stop me, angel.*

His dick was a work of art. Perfect, really. Just like the rest of him. Dalton slipped his hand down, finally taking the heated flesh into his hand.

Blaise continued to watch as if he were transfixed, but he did not object. Instead he pressed up into Dalton's ministrations, and Dalton slowly stroked up and down as more moisture gathered on his hand.

Something tickled Dalton's cock and it took him a moment to realize Blaise's hand was there. He glanced at Blaise's face, only to be met with wide-eyed wonderment.

"I… I… I want to touch you too." A blush shot up his cheeks.

Bloody hell! Dalton caught his lips and thrust his tongue into Blaise's mouth, throwing himself into the euphoria. "Then by all means, touch me, angel."

The pressure of Blaise's hand increased, and he grabbed Dalton through his trousers. He squeezed, trying to rub in time with Dalton's strokes. It was heaven and pure torture rolled into one, but the returned attention didn't last long. Soon Blaise was gasping, his body tightening into a beautiful arch.

Dalton stroked faster; his own cock seemed impossibly hard and ready to explode. "Give it to me."

"Ah…."

Covering Blaise's mouth with his own, Dalton swallowed the sounds of release as the cock in his hand contracted. His own dick throbbed to the point of pain. Rolling himself against Blaise's hip, he thrust himself into completion only seconds behind Blaise.

Blaise broke their kiss, his hand coming up to touch Dalton's cheek tentatively.

Dalton stared down into the face below his, wondering who looked more surprised. He or Blaise? He'd never in all the time he'd been sexually active done something like this. Something so innocent yet so provocative. Good galaxy, they hadn't even gotten their clothes off. And the thing that truly bothered Dalton the most was that it was the best sex he'd had in… well, ever. For the first time, he wanted to lie there and bask. He wanted to hold Blaise and never let him go. It was frightening, but then he'd known from the start that things were different with Blaise. He found himself in the unique position of not knowing what to do, so he decided to let Blaise give him his cue.

Instead of the embarrassed retreat he expected, Blaise kissed him on the lips. Then he sighed and the lovely blush Dalton expected appeared.

He smiled and kissed Blaise back.

"Every time we kiss, I tell myself it can't happen again. I tell myself that you're leaving soon and you're all wrong for me."

"I am."

"I know, but I find that I do not care. Just tell me something and tell me the truth." He peered up at Dalton so unsure, so vulnerable.

"What is it?"

Tucking his bottom lip in, Blaise stared at him for several seconds. Then, as if he'd worked up the courage, he nodded, making his hair fall into his eyes. "Tell me this isn't some sort of game to you."

Joy and a sense of rightness overcame Dalton. He smiled in relief and brushed the hair off Blaise's forehead. "It's not a game."

"Where do we go from here?"

"I don't know. This is new territory for me too." He bent to kiss Blaise again, but the sound of a door shutting downstairs stopped him. "Is that—"

"The study door!" Blaise's eyes widened.

The next thing Dalton knew, he was on his back about two feet from where he lay, while Blaise scrambled to his feet and fastened the falls on his trousers. Who knew the man had that kind of strength?

The butler's voice intruded only a second later. "My lord, if you do not put distance between yourself and Lord Ashbourne, I'll be forced to notify their graces."

Blaise finally gained his feet and took three exaggerated steps backward. Then he looked down at himself. "Oh my galaxy." There was a blob of semen on his waistcoat. A blob Dalton was rather proud of putting there.

Dalton raised himself on his elbows and smiled at Blaise. "Yeah, I seem to have the same problem." And he wasn't the least bit ashamed. "What do you suggest?"

Groaning, Blaise picked up the pillow off the sofa and threw it at him.

Townsend Castle

STANDING WITH his arm resting on the mantel and his head against his arm, Raleigh stared into the fire in the billiards room. The green marble fireplace was usually calming—he liked to watch the flames dance and crackle—but not tonight. He was determined to talk this out and not lose his temper for Dalton's sake, but it wasn't easy. He still, several hours after his encounter with Ravensburg at Eversleigh's town house, wanted to throttle Ravensburg.

"Thank you for removing Dalton's dog tag," Ravensburg said in a soft, almost hesitant, voice. He obviously didn't know how to do this any better than Raleigh did.

Raleigh had asked him to this room because as children they'd always talked over a game of billiards, but neither of them had made any move to pick up a cue. It was sad, really. At one time they'd been close. They'd spent their summers together at Windswept Abbey playing, hunting, and swimming whenever Ravensburg hadn't been learning to be the marquess and Raleigh learning to be… well, arm decor as Aiden called it. Now they were nearly strangers. They'd rarely talked after Raleigh married Steven, but after Ravensburg had asked him to raise Dalton, they'd seen each other even less. Perhaps once a year in passing when Ravensburg and Arthur came to town to buy new wardrobes.

"I'd planned on doing it since the moment he got out of the IN. I'd never endanger him, you should know that," Raleigh said.

"I do know that, or else I'd never have left him with you."

And that was the crux of the situation, and why they were both here now with a strained relationship after all these years. Raleigh hated to admit it, but he was nearly as bitter about the situation as Dalton. He loved Dalton like his own and to see him hurt, to wonder why and how someone Raleigh had looked up to for so many years could abandon his only child…. Raleigh shook off the thought and turned from his slouch against the mantel.

Sitting on the sofa with his feet firmly on the floor, Ravensburg rested his elbows on his knees and stared at the floor as if it were overly interesting. It wasn't; it was mahogany hardwood, just like most of the other rooms in the castle. With only the fireplace and the low-hanging fixture over the billiards table providing light, the edges of the room were dark, giving it a cozy feel.

Ravensburg glanced up at him and suddenly looked exhausted and older than his fifty years. With a sigh, he ran his hands down his face and sat back. "I want him in my life, Raleigh. I need your help. How do I gain his trust? How do I rebuild our relationship?"

Had it not been for the genuine despair in Ravensburg's eyes, Raleigh might have given a flippant sarcastic answer, but the anguish was real. "It's not going to be easy, and you won't do it by bullying him and cutting off his access to money."

"I have no intention of sticking to that. I was just trying to get him back home. I need him to give me… us, Arthur and I, a chance." His words came out as a plea. "I want…." He shook his head and looked down at his feet again.

"What? What do you want, Barclay?"

He peered up, this time with tears gathered in his eyes. "I want my son back, and I want… my brother back too."

"Then why did you push us away?" Raleigh couldn't quite hold back the anger in his voice. He'd never forget Barclay leading Dalton into the castle and placing Dalton's little hand in one of Raleigh's and setting Dalton's portmanteau at Raleigh's feet. Together he and Dalton had watched Barclay walk out the door, not realizing that Barclay was shutting them both out.

"You know why." Ravensburg heaved himself up off the sofa and crossed to the bar. He poured himself three fingers of brandy and swallowed it all. "Ahhh… that is good. Burns… I haven't had anything alcoholic in years." He poured another drink, stoppered the decanter, and leaned against the bar.

Raleigh frowned. Why hadn't he had liquor in years? No matter; that was an entirely different discussion. "I know Sire beat Dalton. I saw the marks. It took everything I had to not go murder the bastard, but why didn't you come visit? You abandoned him. You abandoned me." Bloody hell, he hadn't meant to say that. This was about Dalton, but he couldn't seem to help the resentment. "You and Arthur retired to the country, and the only time we heard from you was when you'd send the occasional Christmas or birthday gift. How did you expect Dalton to react when you just showed back up all of a sudden after our sire died, to claim the title? How did you think I'd feel?"

Ravensburg's face paled, and he took another drink, looking anywhere but at Raleigh. Finally he nodded, as if fortifying himself, and met Raleigh's gaze. He swirled the liquid in his glass nervously. "I'm sorry. I never meant to abandon Dalton or you. Don't you see it was hard on me too? It's not what I wanted. I missed not only Dalton growing up, but all of your boys. I missed you, Raleigh, but I had no choice."

"Because of our sire? You could have taken Dalton with you to the country, Barclay."

"I had nothing. All the houses were legally his; I could not keep him away. There was no way to guarantee Dalton's safety."

"You could have stayed here. Don't you know I would have supported you until you took up the title? I would have provided anything you needed. You could have avoided him here just as well as you could have at Windswept Abbey. And he could not legally barge in here."

Barclay scoffed. "You don't understand!" he all but shouted before he tossed back his drink and slammed the glass down on the bar. "He was worse after Father died. You don't know the half of it. It wasn't just about Dalton. I had to protect… my family. I knew Dalton would be all right with you. I knew he'd never want for anything."

"Except his father's love," Raleigh said quietly and watched his brother retreat into himself. *Damn it.* "I'm sorry."

"No, it's true. You're right. I did what I thought was right at the time, but…." He shook his head and walked back over to the sofa, his bootheels clicking angrily on the wood floor. He sat and clutched his head in his hands.

Raleigh walked around the billiards table and stopped in front of him.

Finally, Barclay stared at him with his gray eyes haunted more than ever. "Just tell me I can fix this? Tell me it's not too late."

"It's not. Dalton will forgive you, but it will take time."

"And you? Will you forgive me?"

"Yes. Eventually. I love you, you big dolt. I just don't understand why you didn't ask for my help. I could have helped you with our sire."

Tears leaked out of Barclay's eyes, and he shook his head. "I wouldn't ask that of you. I wouldn't ask that of anyone. You just don't understand what he was like, Raleigh. He lost his mind after Father died. He did so much damage."

Their sire had never had much of a mind anyway. He was a frivolous, cruel man, and he hated their father even more than he hated both of them, but something in the way Barclay said the words, something in his expression…. He was keeping something from Raleigh. Something big. If they had any hope of rebuilding their relationship and if he was going to help make Dalton understand…. "I need the whole story. You have to tell me what happened, and don't just say I know how he was. This is more than that. Isn't it?"

Ravensburg swallowed so hard his cravat moved, and he sat back and ran his hands through his hair. With a sigh, he finally nodded, confirming Raleigh's suspicion that there was something specific that led to this paranoia and the feeling that he had to abandon Classige and his son. "Okay, but you better sit down."

Something told him this was going to be bad. Barclay had never been one to exaggerate things. Raleigh sat down next to him. "Tell me."

Chapter Fifteen

Battle dress uniforms may not be considered the height of fashion, but perhaps they should be. They show off a certain demon lord's assets rather nicely.

—From *The Pruluce Prattler*'s Fashion Weekly column

South Street Foundling Home, South Street in Downtown Classige, Pruluce

A LUMP formed in Blaise's stomach as he stepped out of the lift. He wasn't certain what he expected the orphanage to look like, but the place certainly needed their help. There was no playground equipment out back, no yard for the children to play in. There wasn't even a small fence around the front. With only three stories and being rather narrow, it didn't look like it would house many children. The only reason he knew it was the orphanage rather than one of the row houses next to it was because of the dark metal placard to the right of the door that read South Street Foundling Home.

"Why the long face, angel?" Dalton's warm breath fanned his ear as he sidled up next to Blaise.

Blaise grinned at the nickname that a day ago annoyed him and said without much heat, "Don't call me that."

A soft chuckle sounded beside him, slithered down his back, and pooled in his stomach in the form of warmth. Dalton had a wonderful laugh that was contagious. Being around him, Blaise had laughed more in the past couple of days than he had in years.

"It's very…." Blaise shrugged. "Depressing." Even the snow here was starting to look gray, whereas around Thompson House it was still pristine.

"That's why we're here. Operation: Orphans. Our assignment is to make orphanages less bleak."

Blaise elbowed him. Last night Dalton had thought it hilarious that Blaise named their undertaking and accused Blaise of being a thrill-seeker.

The accusation had seemed a little too close to the truth after Blaise had gone upstairs to change waistcoats and snuck back down to bring Dalton a pair of smallclothes and trousers. Trying to get up to his room and back unnoticed had certainly been breathtaking, and not in a pleasant way. "Stop making fun of me. Every mission deserves a name. It helps keep the goals clear. Didn't all your missions have names in the IN?"

"No." Dalton peered up at the façade and grinned. "Looks like we've been noticed."

A curtain swung closed in the window above the door, only to be thrown open again. A little round face peeked out, a big smile appeared, and the curtain closed again, then swooped back open and another joy-filled face replaced the first.

Blaise chuckled, feeling a bit better. At least the children were happy. It still made him feel like a privileged oaf, though. Perhaps he and Dalton should've gone to Foundling Town instead of sending Larkinson and Henry the footman? Blaise had considered it, but he needed to find out about the orphanages first if he were going to try and send children there. "I'll go get a box."

He went back to the hackney and grabbed a small open crate of toys off the seat. Dalton had packed several small crates full of toys and clothes. Blaise had contributed by stopping off at the bakery for biscuits. He set the biscuits on top of the toys and exited the lift, his foot crunching in the snow. "Do you think Larkinson and Henry will be all right?"

Dalton smirked at him. "And you accuse her of being a mother hen."

"I can't help it. She and I have been together since the cradle."

"I'd feel the same about Rexley, even if he weren't my cousin, but I think Larkinson is fine. Henry is a big lad, and he seemed like he could take care of her. Honestly? I suspect Larkinson can take care of herself. She's quite fierce."

"That she is."

Dalton's voice dropped an octave, and his gaze turned heated. "I suspect it's a good thing she was in the kitchen when you brought me those trousers last night. She'd have trounced me but good for compromising you."

Heat coursed through Blaise at the reminder, and only part of it was from embarrassment. He was saved from responding when the door to the foundling house opened, and three excited little boys rushed out.

Unlike the children the other night in the alley, these foundlings seemed well cared for. Their clothes weren't at the height of fashion—in fact they were several years old—but they were in good repair, and they all had sound shoes. Well, all but one of them. The smallest of the boys, a tyke about four, had only one shoe on, and the laces were untied. Best of all, the children looked as though they'd had a bath recently. Again, with the exception of the smallest, who had what appeared like the remnants of his breakfast on his chubby cheeks and chin.

At first, Blaise thought they were overjoyed about the toys, but it soon became apparent he'd misjudged when they all gathered around Dalton. Apparently, Blaise wasn't the only one awed by Dalton in battle dress uniform.

This morning when he'd arrived, explaining he had no other clothes that didn't make him look like an earl, Blaise had nearly swallowed his tongue. The sight was still breathtaking. With the exception of wider shoulders, Dalton was the same size as Blaise, but he looked much bigger in his uniform and much more rugged. Blaise had known he was a soldier, but for some reason he'd imagined Dalton in an office somewhere, issuing orders to underlings. This uniform said otherwise. The dark green camouflage made him seem dangerous and untouchable, yet his smiling face as the children gathered around him disabused one of the notion. He was a conundrum.

The boys looked up at Dalton in wonderment and began talking all at once. "Have you ever killed anyone?" "Do you ride a horse and lead charges?" "Where is your saber?" "Have you ever fired a cannon?" "Are cannon balls heavy?" "Do you have a fragger rifle?"

On and on the questions flew at Dalton, and he took them all in stride, smiling down at the children. He didn't even seem to mind the smallest one tugging on his trouser pocket.

Blaise joined them on the stoop, and Dalton winked at him. Sadly he was glad they'd taken an interest in Dalton instead of him. He never knew quite how to act with children. He liked them, but interacting with them was… awkward.

"Come along, boys. I'll answer all of your questions, but first I must speak to your headmaster."

"You mean Mrs. Clarkson?" one of the boys asked.

"Yes, he means me." A woman barely older than Blaise and Dalton stepped into the doorway, shooing the boys back into the house as she wiped her hands on her apron. She had a pleasant demeanor and a face that looked as though it smiled a lot, given the laugh lines at the corners of her eyes, but she wasn't smiling now. She appeared tired, or perhaps worried. Her brown hair escaped her bun, curling into tendrils along her neck, and her plain serviceable dress was covered by a stained apron. "Why don't you boys go back to your studies and let me talk to the gentlemen."

As the chorus of groaning boys filed past her, she caught the ragamuffin with one shoe, used her apron to wipe his face, then stood and offered a tentative smile to Dalton and Blaise. "Good morning, gentlemen. What can I help you…." Her voice trailed off as she noticed the boxes. Her face went from surprised to relieved in the span of a heartbeat. Then tears gathered in her eyes. "Oh bless you! Bless you both. Please come in."

This was not the greeting Blaise had anticipated. He looked at Dalton, and Dalton looked back. The shared trouble didn't have to be spoken. Somehow Blaise knew Dalton read his mind and his concern. Apparently the foundling house needed more help than they'd assumed.

They followed Mrs. Clarkson into the house.

The place was clean and smelled of lemon, but it was very sparse. There was only a coat rack in the foyer.

Several more children peeked over the balcony at them, all of them boys. The shoeless child peered out from behind the staircase. A woman, this one much older with her gray hair in a topknot, came out of a room upstairs and ordered all the children back inside. The children complied but not without a few grumbles. One of the smaller boys waved down at Blaise and Dalton before he left.

Blaise juggled the crate and waved back.

"Gentlemen, I'm Nancy Clarkson. Thank you. Please come inside my office. I'll ring for tea."

They eventually ended up settled in the modest but bright and airy office. It was really more of a morning room. So far, from everything they'd seen, the house was more like a private residence. Like someone had just decided to open their doors to foundlings in need of a home. Sadly it was as small as it appeared from the outside. It reminded Blaise of the stables behind Eversleigh Manor. Not that it seemed like horses belonged here, but it was of a comparable size. It was true that the stables at Eversleigh were large in comparison to most, but it was nowhere near big enough for more than six people. He knew because there were exactly five grooms and the stable master who lived above the stables.

In his hands Blaise had a teacup with tea and some of the biscuits he'd brought, while Dalton had Archie, the shoeless imp, in his lap.

The headmistress, Nancy, sat across from them with the box of clothing at her feet that Dalton had carried inside. "How did you hear about us? We don't get many donations anymore, and with our move coming up…." She stopped going through the clothes to blot her eyes. "I'm sorry. It's just that we haven't been able to afford clothes lately, and with the children outgrowing them so fast…." She shook her head. "We've been saving all our money for a new place." She trailed off and picked up the teacup beside her on the end table.

Archie smacked his hand against Dalton's chest to get his attention. The sleeve on his shirt rode up, revealing a birthmark on his forearm. "When we go, I go to big boy room."

"Do you?" Dalton asked. He glanced down with a puzzled expression at the reddish purple spot on the pale skin, then shook his head and grinned. "That must mean you are all grown up. How old are you?"

"Three." Archie held up four fingers.

Dalton chuckled and pushed one of his fingers down. He was really good with the boy. Way more at ease than Blaise would have been. Who would have thought a rake would be so good with children? Weren't they supposed to shun all things that symbolized commitment? It made Blaise wonder what Dalton would be like with his own kids.

Across from them, Nancy's face paled, and her smile turned brittle. She awkwardly took another sip from her cup before glancing back. Something wasn't right.

A swirl of unease bombarded Blaise's stomach. And even though he suspected the answer, he asked the question anyway. "Are you moving to a bigger place?"

Shaking her head ever so slightly, she set her cup down and glanced at the boy. She smiled at the child with genuine affection before her smile completely disappeared. Still watching the boy as he galloped a toy horse across the arm of the chair toward Dalton's toy cow, she said, "The landlord wants us out of here by the end of the month." She turned back to Blaise and lowered her voice. "He says we're too big of a disturbance to the other tenants."

Without stopping his playing with Archie, Dalton asked, "Won't the assistance from the government help buy a bigger place?"

Nancy scoffed. “Government assistance?” Shaking her head, she wrung her hands in her lap. “That was cut off two years ago.”

“Cut off? But why?” Blaise asked. The place seemed in order. It was clean, and the children were obviously cared for. Why would the government cut off assistance?

“They cut off funding to all the homes.” Tears filled her eyes again but did not spill over. “And it’s been tough ever since, but this….” She shook her head. “I don’t know what we will do. My parents have a farm in Marlowe. I guess we will all go there if we cannot find a place we can afford, but even at my parents’ farm there is only so much room. I hate turning away children now, but to have to turn away children who are already here….” The tears leaked down her face now. “I got all these boys as infants and toddlers.”

A pain started in Blaise’s chest right behind his sternum.

Dalton had stopped moving his cow to stare at her, and Archie protested, “Dollun!”

“Sorry.” Dalton made his cow run up Archie’s arm, eliciting a giggle, but his own face remained stony.

Blaise took a deep breath as Nancy wiped her eyes. “Can you send them to other foundling homes?”

The look she gave him was of complete and utter shock. “Other foundling homes?”

“Yes, we were hoping you could tell us where they are. We were hoping to take them some things as well, but we were only able to find this one.”

She shook her head and gave them a sad smile. “There are no other homes.”

The House of Lords, Classige, Pruluce

IF THERE was ever any doubt that Dalton didn’t want to take up his seat in the House of Lords, he could now put that doubt to rest. Researching laws… well, it sucked, as Winstol would say. Dalton’s back hurt, his eyes were going crossed, and his arse felt as though he were sitting on a bed of knitting needles. The patterned red carpet in Blaise’s office was fashionable, but it was not comfortable. Apparently the House of Lords designers had gone cheap when it came to the carpet; there was hardly any padding under it.

Closing the book he was currently searching through, Dalton leaned back on his hands and stretched his neck. He was surrounded by books. The space in front of Blaise's desk resembled a mini maze with all the books littering the floor, and so far not a one of them had the information he was searching for. "Are you having any luck?"

Blaise grunted. It sounded like a *no* grunt, or perhaps it was a *hold on a moment* grunt. It was hard to tell, but Blaise's last few grunts had sounded the same and they'd all been *no*.

Since the moment they'd walked into the office—some four hours ago, according to the grandfather clock out in the lobby—they'd been researching laws, trying to find out why the government assistance was taken away. Dalton had started looking through the books while Blaise scoured the electronic records. It would be so much easier if the House of Lords had a computer butler like the private homes.

"Why doesn't the House of Lords have a computer butler?" Dalton lay the rest of the way down on the floor to try and work the kink out of his back and landed on a book. Good galaxy, he was sure to have nightmares about law books attacking him tonight.

Blaise grunted again and mumbled something about privacy and lords spying on each other. Which made sense, Dalton supposed. He could see how lords would use a butler to snoop on one another, but it sure would have made researching a lot easier.

Pushing the book out from beneath his shoulder, Dalton turned his head toward his co-researcher.

Blaise sat at his desk with nearly as many books stacked on its surface as Dalton had on the floor. Though his books had something to do with the IN council meeting. His fingers flew over the holo keyboard as his eyes were narrowed at the screen. The look of sheer concentration was arousing. Or perhaps it was just Blaise who was inspirational. Dalton had planned to use the coach ride today to his advantage, but on the way to the orphanage there hadn't been a lot of room, and on the way back they'd both had a sour disposition over their visit. But now.... They needed a break.

Hauling himself up, Dalton made his way around the six-foot radius of dusty old law tomes, only stepping on one of them. He walked up behind Blaise and began kneading his shoulders. "I can't get that birthmark out of my mind. One of the other boys had one similar on the back of his hand. Do you think there is anything to that?"

"Ahh…." Blaise ceased typing and dropped his head. "That feels wooonderful."

Hobbs, the watchdog, poked his head around the doorjamb with raised brows. Dalton much preferred Larkinson as a chaperone. Hobbs was thorough, though. The man had ears like a… well, Dalton didn't know what, but suffice it to say, his hearing was excellent for a man his age. He'd been at that door every time so much as a moan leaked from either of them.

Hobbs narrowed his eyes on Dalton and opened his mouth to say something.

Caught between amusement and annoyance, Dalton lifted his hands off Blaise's shoulders and held them up in surrender. "I was only coming over to look at what he was doing."

Hobbs bobbed his head once, and it disappeared back around the doorjamb.

Dalton didn't put his hands back right away, but bent over as if he were reading over Blaise's shoulder, because he knew Hobbs's routine.

Sure enough, the old man's head came bouncing right back with those bushy gray brows struggling to touch each other.

Biting his lip to keep from chuckling, Dalton glanced at the computer screen.

The screen read, *not found*.

Blaise tilted his head side to side. "I doubt it. You said the marks weren't roses."

"No, but they were similar shaped blobs."

"Perhaps Archie and the other boy were brothers?"

Dalton shrugged. "Maybe." He hadn't thought to inquire, but Blaise was probably right. Those born of artificial procreation had very definite rose-shaped birthmarks. Dalton had one; Blaise had one. All children born of Regelence's artificial procreation method had that same birthmark located in the exact same spot: under the right arm. Archie's mark and the other boy's had been in different locations and definitely not rose-shaped. "What have you found?"

"Nothing. You'd think that there'd be some record of foundling homes. I've checked for planet-run homes, county, and town-run homes, but I can't find any mention of them." He glanced over his shoulder up at Dalton. The disillusion made his eyes heavy-lidded and his lips press tightly together.

Dalton had the urge to kiss his pinched lips. Checking to make certain Hobbs had stopped giving him the evil eye, he spun Blaise around in his chair, rested his hands on the arms of his chair, and leaned close.

Blaise seemed to anticipate the move because he lifted up as Dalton bent down. Their lips touched in a sweet caress, and then Blaise tentatively swept his tongue against Dalton's lips. It was a far cry from their first kiss in the alley, and it was all Dalton could do not to moan and bring the watchdog down on them. The kiss was just so sweet, and the fact that Blaise had been the one to deepen the kiss was quite the aphrodisiac.

Placing one knee on the chair seat next to Blaise's hip, Dalton leaned them back as Blaise's hands entwined behind Dalton's neck. Dalton's cock stood up and paid attention, urging him to put his other knee on the chair and press against Blaise for some relief. It sounded like such a good idea, he complied, straddling Blaise. Oh, yeah! Blaise was as hard as he was. Dalton started to reach between them, but someone cleared their throat. *Bloody hell!*

Sitting up abruptly, Blaise planted both hands on Dalton's chest and shoved.

Dalton landed on his arse and couldn't help but chuckle. They were going to have to talk about Blaise and his habit of pushing away.

A familiar feminine chuckle joined in, and Dalton raised himself up on his elbows.

Blaise mouthed, "*Sorry*," and turned to glare at the door.

It clicked shut.

"I see you are both hard at work." Larkinson came closer. "Good grief, it looks as though this office has been ransacked." She came around the desk, appearing quite elegant in a maroon gown. It was not the drab gray dress she'd worn when they'd dropped her and the footman at the hackney stand this morning, so she must have gone home to re-dress. Blaise had had to change out his waistcoat, cravat, and morning coat in the lift on the way back. Dalton had just left his BDU on.

Dropping his head back, Dalton smiled up at Larkinson. "We have been hard at work. We were just taking a break."

"You were supposed to be here over four hours ago," Blaise groused. The plan had been for her to have met them a few streets away so they all arrived together. Instead, Dalton had gotten out around the corner and let Blaise arrive by himself in the coach while Dalton had walked the rest of the way so as not to raise suspicion by arriving together unchaperoned.

She winked down at Dalton, then leaned against Blaise's desk, looking quite smug. "I would have, but I was busy learning something very interesting."

"What?" Blaise asked.

Dalton made himself comfortable, crossing his hands behind his head and resting his feet on Blaise's thighs. He received a sharp look, but then Blaise rested his hands on Dalton's ankles.

Larkinson took a deep breath and leaned back on her hands, taking her time, but she had a big grin on her face. Whatever information she'd gotten must be good.

Unfortunately for her, Blaise was not as patient as Dalton in letting her revel in her discovery. He kicked her ankle. "Give over."

"Ow. Remind me to tie your cravat too tight tomorrow morning." She frowned at him, then sighed. "I talked to several people in Foundling Town, and it just so happens they aren't all foundlings. Most are children, but there are also entire families there. It seems that the reason there are so many homeless is because of the increase in grain and textile prices. No one can afford to feed and clothe their families. Several of the children we talked to were told to fend for themselves." Her face took on a stormy expression, letting on just how she felt about that, and Dalton had to agree with her. It was despicable to turn a child out in favor of making things easier on one's self.

Blaise gasped. "There should be a law against abandoning your children."

"Isn't there?" Dalton asked.

"I don't think so, but then my specialty is intergalactic diplomacy, not planetary." Blaise wrinkled up his nose and didn't say anything for several seconds, and then he said, "How odd. At the orphanage, there were only boys. Boys Mrs. Clarkson found or had brought to her as infants and toddlers."

Frowning, Dalton nodded. "She did mention having to turn children away. I guess they ended up in Foundling Town."

The door clicked open.

"Blaise, do you have.... What in the galaxy?"

Who was that? Dalton removed his feet from Blaise's lap and sat up to peer over the desk. In hindsight, he probably shouldn't have, given the surprise on Viscount Grantham's face. His position on the floor in front of Blaise did look suspicious, but they were properly chaperoned.

Grantham frowned at him, then at Larkinson. With a slight shake, he refocused his attention, and his face softened when his gaze landed on Blaise.

Irritation swept over Dalton in a wave, and he barely kept from snarling at the viscount.

"Blaise, what is all this?" Grantham indicated the floor as he practically danced around, trying to miss the mess in front of the desk.

Dalton took the opportunity to get to his feet.

Larkinson turned and curtsied.

Grantham ignored her like most lords would. It said a lot, as far as Dalton was concerned.

"Griff." Blaise stood and offered his hand.

Grantham shook it, taking much too long to let go in Dalton's opinion, but perhaps it was just him. Neither Blaise nor Larkinson seemed to think anything of it.

"This is research," Blaise explained with a sweep of his arm to encompass the whole room.

"Ah. I see." The furrowed brow contradicted Grantham's words. Finally he turned to Dalton, his gaze sweeping over the BDU, and then he extended a hand. "Ashbourne. Taking your duty as guard seriously I see."

Dalton shook his hand, being sure to put a little more pressure on than he'd normally use. "Absolutely."

Turning back to Blaise, Grantham said, "I just came to get the treaty update."

"Blast!" Blaise's face turned a mottled red color, and his hand immediately went to his forehead and raked back through his hair as he blew out a breath. The reaction was a bit unexpected, but not entirely out of place, given how frustrating the day had been.

Grantham's eyes widened, and he seemed genuinely surprised by Blaise's outburst. "Um, I suppose that means it isn't done?"

Shaking his head, Blaise typed something on the holo keyboard. A document showed on the monitor set into the desk. "I have about two-thirds of it done."

"No worries, there is still time. You can bring it to me later this afternoon."

"About that…. Do you suppose you could finish it up?" Blaise practically fluttered his eyelashes. The charm that oozed out of him was so overcompensating, Dalton had to bite his lip to keep from laughing.

Larkinson, ever Blaise's coconspirator, smiled too. "I can help you take the notes to your office."

Grantham never had a chance. *The poor sap.* He readily agreed and began to gather up the materials.

With a grin, Dalton shook his head and went back to work. He sat back down on the floor as Blaise and Larkinson gathered all the notes off Blaise's desk.

As Grantham made his way through the minefield of Dalton's mess with Larkinson following, Dalton quirked a brow at Blaise.

Blaise's eyes practically danced, and he lifted his arms as if to say "What?"

"You never did say, what it is you are searching for, Ashbourne?" Grantham asked.

Dalton peered up at Grantham, who was standing over him with a load of books in his arms. "The law that changed the funding for the orphanages."

With a frown, Grantham shook his head. He started to leave, then stopped at the door and turned back. "Look under the Dauber Act. I seem to remember something about pulling funds from nonprofits as a rider on that bill."

"Nonprofits?" Blaise asked. "Wouldn't the orphanages be government entities?"

"I don't think so. As far as I know, Regelence has never had any government foundling homes." With that, Grantham left.

Dalton raised his brows at Blaise.

Blaise sighed and flopped down in his chair as if his feet had just given out.

"Well, that explains why we haven't found anything. It's a rider." Dalton groaned. "Pull up the Dauber Act and see what year and month it was drafted into law."

Blaise typed something on his computer. "No government foundling homes? I'm all for less government, but that seems like a major oversight to me. I'm beginning to wonder if my focus on planetary government would be more beneficial."

Yeah, maybe Dalton needed to reconsider taking up his own seat in the Lords, because the thought of those kids being without a home.... He wasn't in the Navy, fighting for his planet, to watch innocents like Archie die on the streets because the aristocracy couldn't get off their collective arses and do something about it.

Chapter Sixteen

Apparently having a titled gentleman as a guard is becoming quite the thing. This makes three now. A viscount, a duke, and now an earl. Pray tell, where can this author get a titled guard of his own?

—From *The Classige Examiner*

Fairfax House

FEELING OLDER than his twenty-one years, Dalton let himself into Fairfax House. It was only six in the evening, but once again the foyer seemed empty and the house oddly quiet. The servants were probably all downstairs, preparing for dinner, and this wasn't a time guests typically called, but he was used to the hustle and bustle at the castle. Things at Townsend Castle didn't settle down until about one in the morning, and being in the military, there was always something going on, so the silence seemed a new experience. Normally being left to his own devices got him into trouble, but tonight he was going to use the time before dinner to see what else he could find on the Dauber Act.

He had wanted to go straight to his uncles with the information he'd learned today, but Blaise had persuaded him against it, saying they needed to investigate further and to have all their facts lined out when they approached the king and king-consort, or as Blaise planned, the House of Lords. Blaise was already drafting a new bill in his head. He even had a plan to get supporters and find someone who had already taken up their seat in the Lords to sponsor the bill, since he was underage and did not have control of his seat yet.

Grinning at the thought, Dalton headed to the library. If anyone could do it, it was Blaise. Blaise was a whirlwind when he put his mind to something. In a way, it made Dalton's career choice feel insignificant. No, not insignificant—of course his planet needed soldiers, someone to fight for their freedom—but he wasn't fighting for freedom, not Regelence's, anyway. When he finally shipped out again, he'd probably be going to

Spangloria to offer support while Regelence helped them reestablish their government. Fighting was what he knew and what he was good at, but this? Making laws was important too. Regelence needed someone to help take care of its citizens, or eventually he'd be here fighting his own people, because this had to change. It just seemed like such a daunting task. He had new respect for Blaise. He might not be a warrior in the traditional sense, but he *was* a warrior.

Dalton stepped into the library, relieved to see the updated furnishings. This new cozier library would make his research more enjoyable. If one could call pouring over books enjoyable. It would be better if he could find some liquor, but perhaps a mug of hot cocoa would do in a pinch?

Shrugging out of his coat, he laid it on the back of the new black couch and asked Stuart to light a fire in the fireplace.

His sire's desk was neat and mostly clear, but Dalton decided he was going to kick off his combat boots and work on the floor like he'd done in Blaise's office since his BDUs were probably the most comfortable clothes he owned.

Going over to the shelves, he started reading the spines of the books. The books in Blaise's office had the dates listed on them. The Dauber Act was put into law in March of 4828. As involved as his father was in Parliament, he was bound to have recent law books; he had everything else. Dalton found books on agriculture, history, art, and even some fiction as he made his way around the perimeter of the library. "Stuart, can you order me some hot cocoa from the kitchen?"

"Yes, my lord."

Dalton dragged open the heavy black velvet curtains as he walked by them. Too bad he didn't have Blaise to snuggle with. Cozy fire, snowy night, cocoa… and Blaise. He wouldn't get much work done, but it would certainly make things more enjoyable. With a sigh, he stared out at the snow drifting down and the lifts on the street for a few moments, then went back to his search.

He'd made it completely around the room without encountering a law book. He decided to check his father's study, but then a book on the bottom shelf near the door caught his attention.

An overwhelming feeling of nostalgia assailed him as he crouched down and pulled the slim book from the shelf. *The Adventures of the Blacksmith Knight*. It was just as he remembered it. The book was well-loved, with worn edges and scuffed corners. The gold leaf had rubbed off the edges in places from Dalton thumbing through it over and over again. He flipped pages just as he had when he was a child with a smile on his face. The illustrations seemed less detailed as an adult, but they brought back a myriad of memories. Why wasn't the book in the nursery?

Shaking his head, he replaced the book and stood. This wasn't getting his research done. There had to be law books here somewhere, so Dalton left the library and headed up the stairs to his father's study. He remembered seeing books in there as well, and it made sense that Ravensburg would have the law books in his study. If not, Dalton would just search on the computer for what he needed, though he preferred actual books. Wouldn't that tickle Blaise? The thought made him grin.

As he stepped onto the second-floor landing, he heard a strange sound, like someone was weeping.

Frowning, Dalton stopped and listened.

It was definitely crying. Soft, broken crying, like a child snuffling. There was also a low humdrum of talking. Crooning, really. Nonsense words to get someone to quiet down, and it was coming from Ravensburg's office. Was it one of the servants? One of their children? Dalton didn't even know if there were children in residence. Galaxy help them if Ravensburg caught them in his office.

Dalton crept closer to the crying. How was he going to search the law books with someone in there? Didn't this just figure? Dalton leaned against the wall outside the door, careful not to be seen. He'd listen, then decide the best way to approach the situation.

"Shhh…. Easy, my love. It's in the past and has no bearing on our future."

Ravensburg. Dalton flinched as though he'd been hit. He had not expected to hear his father's voice, but it was Ravensburg; he was certain of it. His father's voice was soft, soothing, and reassuring, full of love. It must be his sire crying, but why?

And why did he care? Irritation prickled Dalton along with a strange heaviness. His sire was prone to tears. The man was emotional. A sad story or a beautiful piece of music was enough to elicit tears. Dalton used to climb into his lap and hug him when he'd cry. That always worked. And then inevitably they'd end up laughing. Sire laughed as easily as he cried, but he didn't usually cry so… violently.

Easing forward, Dalton angled himself at the door, intent on peeking inside, but there was no need. If he concentrated, he could see their reflection in the picture above the fireplace. This painting had also changed. It used to be a portrait of Grandsire, but now it was a landscape. Between the weathering trees, Ravensburg's hand caressed up and down the side of Sire's head as Arthur sat in his lap with his face hidden in Ravensburg's shoulder. Ravensburg rocked him from side to side. The look on his face was as lost and forlorn as the desperate sounds leaking out of his spouse.

Dalton felt like a voyeur and knew he should leave. It was none of his business. He could use the computer to talk to Stuart and get the information he needed, but he couldn't seem to make his feet move.

Arthur snuffled some more and said something, but Dalton could not understand his words, muffled as they were by Ravensburg's shoulder.

"Shhh…," Ravensburg crooned. "You don't need the brandy. Getting foxed will not help things. We went over this last time."

"But I need it."

"You don't."

Shock rocked Dalton back on his heels. Had his sire taken to drinking excessively? Was that why there was no liquor in the house?

Arthur pulled back, holding on to Ravensburg's arms. Still crying, he brokenly said, "I want to forget. It's my fault things are like they are."

Ravensburg shook his head. "Arthur, you have to move past this. It is not your fault. You had nothing to do with his actions."

"Are you certain?"

"Yes. Unequivocally yes, my love. I'm positive. He was an evil man. If anyone is to blame, it is I. I should have been here for you. I should have known what he was capable of. I…." Ravensburg's voice grew husky, and he shook his head, looking down.

"No," Arthur declared through the tears. He tilted Ravensburg's face up. "You got Dalton out of here. If not for you—"

"Your hot chocolate, my lord."

Bloody hell! Startled, Dalton flinched, and his head hit the wall with a loud thud as he whirled around. His heart beat triple time, feeling like it had worked its way into his throat as he came face-to-face with the footman.

The man looked at him expectantly.

Shaking himself out of his surprise, Dalton glanced down and realized the man held out a steaming mug of whip-cream-topped cocoa.

Dalton took the mug. "Thank you." He stood there for several moments as the man left.

The snuffling behind him ceased.

Blast. No doubt his parents had heard. Dalton debated making a break for it but decided against it. He was too numb. What did he just overhear? His father had sent him away to protect him? From whom? A hollowness inside Dalton spread out and chilled him. He'd been lied to? Or had he? They'd never said why they'd sent him away.

"Dalton?"

Dalton turned his head and found his father standing at the door.

Ravensburg smiled at him. It was a sad, soft smile, but it was a smile nevertheless. For several seconds, he didn't say anything, he only stared, but instead of the accusation and anger Dalton expected to find, there was tenderness… love? No, that couldn't be right.

Unraveled, Dalton started shaking his head. What the fuck was going on? He opened his mouth to ask, but Ravensburg held up a hand.

"Later." He touched Dalton's cheek. Just a whisper of a caress. "We'll talk later." He turned, walked back into the study, and shut the door behind him.

His life was a lie. Why would they let him think they didn't care? Dalton felt something hot on his leg and looked down and realized he'd dropped his hand and the cocoa was running down his pant leg.

"DALTON, WE need to talk…."

Without looking up from the com-pad in his lap, Dalton sighed. Apparently he was only to have an hour's reprieve. He'd been expecting this encounter, but he wasn't at all certain he was ready for it. He should have just gone up to bed, but he knew he'd never be able to sleep after hearing his parents, so he'd gone back to the library in an effort to get some research done and occupy his mind. He hadn't gotten any more hot chocolate, but thanks to the fire he was currently sitting in front of, his pant leg was dry.

Ravensburg walked into the library like he was going to a funeral. There were bags under his eyes, and his posture wasn't quite as stiff as usual. For a moment, he just stood there with his hand on the knob as if uncertain what to say, but that couldn't be the case, because Ravensburg was nothing if not direct. Shouldn't he be lecturing Dalton about eavesdropping?

Apparently, nothing in this house was as it should be lately. Dalton skimmed his gaze down the page on the comp-pad in his lap without really reading anything. Somehow it seemed much easier viewing his parents as the enemy, but now he wasn't so sure that was the case. He wasn't happy with them for lying to him, but.... Damn it all, a flutter tried to take root in his chest. No matter how hard he tried to deny it, he had hope. He'd told himself all these years that it didn't matter if his parents cared about him, and it didn't, but what if they did? No, he wasn't going to set himself up for heartbreak. He tried again to read the page.

"About what you witnessed...."

In his peripheral vision, Dalton saw Ravensburg stop about two feet away.

"Dalton, won't you look at me?"

Dalton turned, wishing he hadn't. The sincerity on Ravensburg's face... it reminded him of when he was a boy.

His father was happy to see him. There were no airs, no holier-than-thou attitude. He was just a man, a vulnerable man. For a moment, Dalton had the insane notion to call him Papa as he had when he was a child. Instead of Father and Sire, Dalton had called his parents Papa and Daddy. He hadn't thought of Ravensburg as Papa in a long time. Papa was the man who used to sword fight with him and run through Windswept Abbey pretending to be a monster. They used to have pillow fights together. Galaxy, he'd forgotten so much. He'd shoved so many memories out of his brain to keep from being hurt, but now he was home, they kept resurfacing. It was why up until today—until he'd realized he didn't want to leave Blaise—he'd been so anxious to ship out.

After dragging the closest ottoman over beside Dalton, Ravensburg sat and grabbed Dalton's hand, holding it in his. To Dalton's surprise, Dalton's hand was unsteady and shaking.

That damned flutter increased as he stared at their hands with a sense of nostalgia, half expecting it to engulf his. The hand that used to be so much bigger than his was now the same size, as was the man. They sat facing each other. *Blast it all*, he couldn't take it any longer. "Why did you send me away?"

"To protect you, but I gather you overheard that part. It's time I explained some things to you, but first...." He clasped Dalton's hand with both of his. "I'm sorry, son."

Dalton's breath caught in his chest, and he almost forgot to breathe as a sense of the surreal washed over him. He had not been expecting an apology. He wasn't even sure what it was for, but his stupid heart decided to speed up, and that hope in his abdomen tried to spread out and really gain purchase, but then instead a swirling sick feeling took its place. Setting the com-pad on the floor beside him, Dalton crossed his legs and turned his body toward Ravensburg. "I—"

"Just let me finish. I talked to my bro—" He cleared his throat. "—your uncle at the Eversleigh ball the other night, and he opened my eyes about a lot of things, but mainly the fact that I was so caught up in my own pain, I failed to recognize yours."

Self-preservation tried to take over, and he pulled his hand away. He hated to admit any weakness, especially to someone he wasn't close to, but when the protest would have left his lips, his father shook his head.

"I didn't realize why you were acting out. I…." He looked down at his now-empty hand before making eye contact again. "What do you remember about your grandsire?"

"Not much. After Grandfather died and I went to live with Uncle Raleigh, I only saw him in passing on occasion. He was always too busy to pay me much attention, and he seemed more interested in his standing in society than family. He never visited at the castle, and I know Uncle Raleigh didn't like him much."

Ravensburg nodded and closed his eyes for a moment. He took a deep breath, then opened his eyes, looking almost relieved. "I'm glad you don't remember him. He was a monster." He took another deep breath and glanced at the ceiling. "My sire was always very high-strung, and he absolutely hated my father. Their marriage was an arranged one, and not a very well arranged one, I might add. Your uncle and I suffered for it. Me in particular, because I was my sire's favorite and he expected me to be a paragon. At an early age, I learned to be perfect or else suffer the consequences. Most of the time, I managed to be damned near flawless in his eyes until you were born. He thought your sire and I spoiled you, and he took every opportunity to tell me so. Honestly, I think it was out of spite because my father adored you."

"I miss him." His grandfather had always been there to play, even when Dalton's parents hadn't been.

"I know you do, and I know losing him was hard on you."

"It was hard on us too," a shaky voice said from the door, "but for different reasons."

Dalton and Ravensburg both craned their heads around.

Arthur slouched against the doorjamb. How long had he been there? He wore only his shirtsleeves and a pair of buckskin trousers. His hair was a mess, and he was without cravat, waistcoat, and boots. His eyes were red and puffy, and he had a five-o'clock shadow. Dalton hadn't noticed just how bad he looked through the picture glass. It was quite a shock to see him this way. The man was… well, doll-like. He always gave the appearance of being somewhat fragile, but currently that appearance was magnified by ten. One harsh word might very well send him into a swoon. "I hope you don't mind. We've hardly seen you since you've returned, and I thought I should be here to help your father explain."

"I thought you were asleep," Ravensburg said.

Arthur waved him off. "I couldn't sleep without you next to me, and besides all that, I'm fine now."

Dalton highly doubted that, and obviously his father agreed with his assessment.

Ravensburg hesitated for a moment, then said, "Come here." He extended a hand, and the smile he gave his spouse was both warm and tender.

Arthur returned the smile and glanced at Dalton before hurrying forward to take Ravensburg's hand. He got settled on Ravensburg's lap and leaned into him like it was the most natural thing in the world. His whole body seemed to relax as though he were drawing strength from Ravensburg, and perhaps he was.

Wrapping his arms around Arthur, Ravensburg seemed to relax as well. Resting his chin on his spouse's blond head, he met Dalton's gaze. "Your grandfather dying made everything—"

"Go straight to the devil," Arthur finished for him.

Nodding, Ravensburg bussed a kiss across Arthur's hair. "My sire's tenuous grasp on sanity snapped."

"But I thought you said he didn't care for Grandfather?"

"He didn't, but nevertheless, my father's demise sent him into hysterics."

Snorting, Arthur sat forward a little. "Probably because the old curmudgeon didn't have anyone to fight with."

One side of Ravensburg's lip curled up, and he pulled Arthur back against his chest. "Probably. Without your grandfather here to run what little interference he offered"—his tone changed, taking on a gravelly quality, and his eyes rolled upward—"it was a very bad situation."

Dalton frowned at the sarcasm, and the urge to jump to his grandfather's defense was strong, so when he spoke, his words came out just as sarcastic as his father's had. "What do you mean by that?"

"Settle down. I loved my father, but he was never around when I needed him. He was more interested in his own pursuits and didn't know half of the things your grandsire did to me or Raleigh. I know my father loved us, but he was not as attentive to my brother and myself as he was to you, Dalton. Maybe in some way his showering you with attention was his way of making it up to me and right that wrong, or maybe he just loved you more than he did Raleigh and me. I don't know, and it doesn't matter. I'm glad you had the relationship with him that you did."

Not sure what to say, Dalton remained quiet. This whole conversation was strange. He'd seen his parents as the enemy for so many years now, and suddenly it was like… well, it wasn't like when he was a child, but they were treating him like an adult for the first time in his life. He was afraid to trust this new direction their relationship had taken, for fear it would be ripped out from under him.

"Raleigh was never as big a target for my sire as I was. He…." Ravensburg hesitated as though bolstering himself. "I was jealous, but now…. Now, I'm glad my brother never suffered the beatings. It was bad enough he suffered the scathing remarks and constant badgering. I just wish you and your sire hadn't had to suffer."

Arthur caressed his arms and chest and anywhere he could touch, becoming more visibly agitated, as though he couldn't quite sit still. Finally he took a breath and nodded, as if coming to some conclusion, then looked right at Dalton with teary blue eyes. "He beat you for leaving your toys in the parlor. One day after your father went to the House of Lords, I had gone to get us some more pillows from the drawing room and to raid the linen closet so we could build a fort together. I was doing everything I could think of to keep your mind off your grandfather dying." His voice cracked as he continued, "You still have a scar on your lower back from him beating you with the buckle end of his belt." Tears streamed down his cheeks. "I came in, and when I saw, I flew into a rage and attacked him." His voice faded to barely a whisper. "I couldn't overpower him, but at least I made him stop hurting you. He beat me, and, and, and then he…." As if he'd retreated into himself, Arthur shook his head and wrapped his arms around his waist. "I couldn't stop him. It was all I could do to get you to run downstairs to Cook so you wouldn't see."

A chill raced through Dalton. He knew the scar his sire spoke of. It was across the upper part of his right buttocks cheek. How was it Dalton didn't remember this? Bloody hell, his sire had been beaten and raped. His sire hadn't said the words, but Dalton read between the lines. Rape was the only thing that could shake someone that badly. A wave of disgust and anger engulfed him. If his grandsire were still alive, Dalton would kill him. Damnation, his hands and feet actually felt numb. He could not stay sitting any longer. He jumped up and paced, trying to loosen the volatile energy inside him.

A hand touched his back.

Dalton froze.

"Please forgive me." His sire's voice was so soft, so full of regret?

Turning slowly, Dalton stared down into bloodshot blue eyes and swore his heart stopped beating. For several seconds, no one moved. The memory of those same blue eyes laughing flashed through his head, and Dalton wrapped his arms around his sire's small frame. "There is nothing to forgive. You were as much a victim as I was… more." Guilt tried to worm its way inside, but Dalton pushed it out. He'd been a child at the time, as helpless as his sire.

Arthur practically collapsed against him, hugging him back as hard as he could.

Dalton peered over his sire's head at his father, who now had tears in his own eyes. "Why didn't you have him arrested or…." *Kill the fucker.* Dalton would have killed him, but logically he knew that wasn't the answer. Then his father would have been punished.

"How could I?" Ravensburg asked. "Your uncle wanted to have our sire committed, but that just wasn't possible."

"Not possible?" Anger clawed its way inside of Dalton. "How was that not possible?"

Sire stiffened in his arms, then stepped back out of Dalton's embrace and clasped his hands together in front of himself.

Ravensburg frowned at him. "He was a superb actor when he needed to be. No one would have believed me. They would have thought I was only trying to ascend to the title sooner. And if somehow I had succeeded, it would have dragged the family name right down into the gutter. It would have been even more scandalous than your grandfather's whoring and flaunting his affairs with married men. Don't you think I wanted to have him sent to an asylum?"

Dalton's hands tightened into fists to keep from shaking the devil out of his father. This was the most asinine thing he'd ever heard. In consideration of his sire, he lowered his voice. "So you sent me away instead?"

"I knew Raleigh and Steven would take care of you." Ravensburg glanced at Arthur and held his hand out to him.

Arthur took his hand and allowed himself to be pulled down into his arms. "We never thought you'd think we abandoned you. Then he died, and we sent for you, and you started acting out."

"And my lowering the family name took precedence then?" Yes, his voice was harsh, but he didn't care. This whole thing could have been avoided. All of it! His father should have had the bastard committed before he ever hurt Arthur or Dalton. Reputation. It always came back to reputation.

The old Ravensburg reared his head, his voice going as steely as his spine. "Dalton, that's not fair, and it's not true."

But it was; couldn't he see that? He'd robbed Dalton of so much. His parents were practically strangers to him. His whole life had been changed by this. He'd suffered so many lonely nights, thinking he was unloved and unwanted.

Galaxy, it was all too much. He had to get out of here. He had to think.... He started toward the door, but his sire jumped up and placed a hand on his chest.

"Son, please try to understand." The frantic tone and his quivering voice cut through some of Dalton's anger, but it didn't dissipate his confusion. He nodded at his sire, then bent down and kissed his cheek. "I just have to process all of this. It's a lot to take in." He walked out with the knowledge eating at him that his life was one big lie from the time he was sent away at eight years old till now.

Chapter Seventeen

Hot chocolate! Roasted chestnuts! Spiced apples! Come enjoy the Frost Fair while it lasts. We may not have a frozen river like in ancient times, but we have a man-made skating rink, sleigh rides, ice sculptures, and much more. Get a souvenir portrait made right at the fair.

—From *The Classige Morning News*

Thompson House

BLAISE'S FINGERS danced over the piano keys, but his brain kept flirting with drafting the bill he wanted to put forth in the House of Lords. He had not enjoyed working in the political arena this much in a long time. It was almost as fun as his music. Playing a particularly difficult chord perfectly, he grinned. At the moment, he actually felt he was almost as good at politicking as he was music. He had purpose; he was a voice for the people here in his town. The idea of helping children and those less fortunate than him and getting to see the difference inspired him.

The door between his private parlor/music room and his bedroom clicked open behind him, but Blaise didn't stop playing. It was most likely Larkinson. She'd gone to the bakery down the street to get them some macaroons. They'd taken a break from Operation: Orphans half an hour ago. Well, Larkinson had; Blaise hadn't actually taken his respite till the last ten minutes, and in that time he'd come across some good information. Now he was celebrating by doing what he loved best.

"You aren't going to believe what I found." Blaise grinned but did not look up from the keys as he plucked out the sultry bridge of "Nei tuoi occhi vedo il cielo" by Lizarrago, Lizzy's namesake. "The reason there has never been a government-operated foundling home is because they were set up as nonprofits to get government assistance and encourage business growth. The government paid welfare to each foundling, and the foundling house got that money to care for the children along with a nice stipend. The Dauber Act canceled all that and routed that money into a fund for children of dead soldiers. It's all very fascinating because when one looks at the act as a whole, it does very good things, like setting up government-assisted programs to help those out of work gain employment, but the definition of orphans got muddled, and it assumes all orphans are children of soldiers killed in action. Which is a bad thing." Blaise stopped playing and frowned. "I still haven't found out exactly where that money is going, though. Did you get the biscuits?"

"I did, and I've brought tea, but… we, uh, have company."

Blaise swiveled around on the bench, expecting to see his brother—nothing got Bannon away from his art like the promise of macaroons—but their visitor was not Bannon.

Dalton stood right behind Larkinson, still in his coat, holding a pink bakery box.

"Hi." Blaise smiled, feeling warm inside, but when Dalton didn't smile back, Blaise's stomach sank to his feet. He stood. "What's wrong?"

Dalton looked… abnormal. His hair was windblown and his cheeks pink from the cold, but there was something about his eyes. They weren't full of mischief. He was tired, but he seemed haggard as well. He hadn't changed out of his BDU either, and now there was a stain on his right leg. Slowly Dalton shook his head. "Nothing, I…." He shrugged. "I took a walk and ended up here."

"I ran into him on my way back from the bakery." Larkinson, who was holding a tea tray, came forward and set it on top of Lizzy. Normally Blaise would have protested, but he was too busy trying to figure out what he saw in Dalton's eyes and why Dalton was here in the first place, and—*oh my galaxy!*

The panic on his face must have shown, because Larkinson leaned forward and settled a hand on his shoulder. "Don't worry. I brought him through the servants' entrance and up the green corridor." Larkinson peeked back at Dalton, then whispered, "He was staring up at the house like he was lost."

Yes, that was a good description of his expression. He looked lost and… lonely?

"I'll go read some more and see if I can find out where that money is going." Larkinson stood and gestured toward Blaise's bedroom. "I trust what you found is on your screen reader?"

Blaise nodded. "On my bed."

She walked over to Dalton, lifted the box lid, and took a couple of biscuits before closing it and stuffing one of the macaroons into her mouth. She patted Dalton's shoulder, then left and shut the connecting door behind her.

For several moments neither one of them moved. Dalton stood there with the pink box, taking in Blaise's sanctuary. After a few moments, he said, "I like it. It fits you."

"Thank you." Blaise glanced around at the familiar furnishings. He'd decorated the room himself. The pristine but cozy room *did* fit him. No matter how striking it would have looked, he hadn't been able to bring himself to decorate the room all in white just to show off Lizzy. He'd gone with cream and taupe, soft lighting, and a hard rosewood floor. It still made his baby grand the showpiece of the room but did not feel so clinical. The fire in the beige marble fireplace added to the warmth as did the round shag carpet beneath Lizzy. All in all, it was elegant but comfortable.

Dalton came forward, still looking a bit at odds, and handed the box to Blaise. "These are yours, I presume?"

"Yes. Macaroons. Would you like one? Larkinson and I were taking a break, and I had a craving for them."

Dalton shook his head and peered around again as if he didn't know exactly where to look, or perhaps it was embarrassment? It was an odd thing for such a self-assured man. "I should leave. I know it's not proper for me to be here, but I just…." He glanced up finally, his voice going so soft, it was barely audible. "I wanted to see you."

A strange euphoria filled Blaise, rushing from his head to his toes at the admission. Dalton had wanted to see him. The idea was as preposterous as it was exciting. Dalton had chosen to come see him when he hadn't wanted to be alone. Blaise set the box on the bench and started taking Dalton's coat off of him. "Since when do you worry about propriety?"

"Excellent point." Dalton finally grinned, a genuine show of amusement, not one of the flirtatious ones he occasionally used to disarm someone.

The relief at seeing that smile eased through Blaise and made his knees a little weak. He laid the coat across the bench as well and grabbed Dalton's hand, then led him to the chairs in front of the fireplace. "Larkinson made sure you won't be discovered, and there are no microphones or cameras in here. You can stay as long as you like." Blaise pushed him down in the chair, and Dalton surprised him by pulling Blaise down in his lap.

A featherlight kiss landed on Blaise's jaw, and then Dalton buried his face in Blaise's neck. The embrace was comforting and sent warmth all through Blaise. He was used to the arousal he felt when Dalton was near, but this was different. It made him want to hold on and never let go, so he did. He wrapped his arms around Dalton and hugged him, resting his cheek on top of Dalton's soft vanilla-scented hair while Dalton pulled him close.

"Thank you."

"My pleasure. Let me know what you need, and I will get it for you."

After a while Dalton pulled back, dropping his hands to Blaise's hips. He sat back in the chair, his head cocking to the side a bit. "I think I just needed you. I'm feeling a little less…." He shrugged. "I just learned some things that shook me up a bit. My sire…." He shook his head, his eyes suddenly looking even more haunted. "He sent me away to protect me from my grandsire." His voice rose and his brow furrowed.

Blaise had heard the story from Rexley of how Dalton's parents had sent him to live at the castle when he was a child, but Dalton had never mentioned it to him. Until now. "But that is a good thing, isn't it?"

"I don't know. I suppose." Dalton then spilled out the whole sordid story about how his grandsire was crazy and how he beat Dalton and raped the current marquess-consort.

As flabbergasted as he was, Blaise felt he should be commended for keeping a neutral expression on his face. The only thing that got him through the tale was knowing Dalton didn't need his horror; he had his own.

"I just don't understand why my father didn't have his sire arrested or committed. The man should have been punished."

"Dalton, the scandal would have been catastrophic and would have even tainted our king-consort."

"But worth it."

Not so very long ago, Blaise wouldn't have agreed, but now? "Yes, but not everyone feels that way. *I* wouldn't have seen it that way if not for you. If not for this past week. You know how hard I fought against our association. Our society is founded on our reputations; it's always been that way, and it always will be."

"But it's stupid."

"Be that as it may, had your grandsire been institutionalized, it would have cast doubts on not just his sanity, but Raleigh's, yours, your cousins', and any children all of you have. It would have undermined anything your father did in the House of Lords. Some would even question the sanity of our future king and try to oppose Rexley based on accusations of mental illness."

"It's wrong. And none of that should have mattered."

"Is it any more right to expect so many people to give up their lives because of one man's actions?"

Dalton rested his head against Blaise's chest. "I don't know. Maybe I'd have been better off not knowing any of this and continuing to dislike my parents."

"No. This could be a new beginning. Dalton, family is so important. You have to try. Promise me you will at least attempt to have some sort of relationship with your parents." Blaise couldn't help but think a reconciliation would be good for him. Help heal some of his hurt.

Dalton groaned. "I should have walked away instead of staying to listen."

"Promise me you'll try?"

"Yeah, I'll try."

"Good." Blaise smiled, knowing in his heart this was a good thing. Still, he couldn't help but tease. "Eavesdropping is effective, but not for the faint of heart. Sometimes you do learn things you wish you hadn't."

With a dramatic sigh, Dalton nodded and grinned up at him. "This is information I could have used when you were teaching me the fine art of snooping."

"I'm apparently remiss as a teacher." He cupped Dalton's face in his hands and leaned forward to buss his lips, hoping to erase the rest of the bewilderment he saw in Dalton's eyes and because he loved kissing this man. It was quite addicting. "But I'm very good at learning."

"That you are." Dalton's hands snaked up his body to his face, then threaded in his hair. He deepened the kiss, tangling his tongue with Blaise's.

The pulling sensation on his scalp had the strangest effect. Blaise's nether region decided to wake up and take notice. Then again, perhaps that was the intimacy, because being near Dalton was an intoxicating event, especially when he decided to turn on the charm, as he was doing at the moment. Blaise wanted to get closer still. He gripped Dalton's cheeks, mashing their mouths together even tighter, then dropped his hands, deciding he wanted to touch Dalton. He changed his mind again and brought them back to Dalton's neck.

A chuckle leaked into his mouth as Dalton smiled against his lips. Dalton gripped his wrists, placing them on his chest, and what a nice chest it was. He was so hard underneath the shirt. Blaise wanted to see him. Wrapping his fingers in the fabric, he started tugging it upward until they had to break their kiss.

Dalton gasped and lifted his arms. "Are you sure this is a good idea, angel?"

"No." Blaise shook his head and continued to pull until the shirt was off. He tossed it aside and leaned back to look at what he'd uncovered.

Dalton was a work of art. They might be close to the same size, but they were not made equally. Dalton had ridges where Blaise did not. Very appealing ridges. It was funny that Dalton called him angel, because Dalton was the perfect specimen, not Blaise. Being a soldier apparently did wonders for the body. Blaise simply had to touch, but he stopped short, biting his bottom lip and hovering his hands over Dalton's pectoral muscles. He'd never done anything like this and wasn't sure of the protocol. He met Dalton's eyes, feeling foolish. "Can I?" Nervousness and arousal warred for dominance within him.

"Please." Dalton gripped his wrists again and placed them on his chest.

His muscles jumped beneath Blaise's palms. He was warm and soft with no body hair. Blaise squeezed, marveling at the tone. He didn't stop there, though; he ran his hands down to Dalton's stomach, which was tight and even more rippled than his chest. There he had an intriguing trail of hair from his navel that disappeared beneath his waistband, and suddenly Blaise wanted to see where it led. He'd only caught a glimpse of Dalton the other night. He stood from Dalton's lap and held out his hand.

Dalton stared up at him with heavy-lidded eyes, and for half a second, Blaise wondered if he'd take his hand. Finally he did and stood, and a lump clogged Blaise's throat. The camouflage pants hung low on Dalton's hips, showing off even more of his lower abdomen and that intriguing trail of hair. It also showed a very impressive erection straining against that fabric.

Again, Blaise hesitated. Not knowing exactly how to voice what he wanted, he looked up at Dalton.

Dalton stared at him with a burning intensity, both patient and encouraging. He even nodded.

Swallowing down the lump in his throat, Blaise reached for the falls on his trousers. Instead of having falls, however, they split open down the center. He undid the buttons and once undone, they slipped past Dalton's hips, revealing his smallclothes. They too were like none Blaise had ever seen. Instead of the loose-fitting underthings, these were tight. So tight, Dalton's cock was clearly outlined and nearly reaching the elastic band at the top.

Blaise hesitated only a moment, but he'd gone too far to stop now. He hooked his fingers in the stretchy waistband and pulled it down. The material caught Dalton's cock, taking it too, until it sprang free, bobbing toward Blaise. He started to let go, now that he'd uncovered what he'd meant to uncover, but Dalton pushed his hands farther down, dragging the smallclothes to his midthigh.

Transfixed, Blaise reached out and touched. Was there a proper way to do this? Did he take hold as if it were his? He had no idea what was allowed and what was not. Someone needed to write an etiquette book about this. He'd always wondered what it was that parents discussed about the situation with their sons upon marriage. Maybe they passed on the proper etiquette?

"Love, you should see your face." Dalton lifted his chin with a finger and kissed his lips. With the other hand, he guided Blaise's hand to wrap around his length.

Blaise might as well have grabbed his own, given his body's response. His body tensed, going even harder. The sensation was strange. He'd had his own cock in his hands, but the warmth surprised him. When he held himself, he was too focused on the feelings in his cock and not the sensation in his hand. He glided it up and back, marveling at differences and similarities. He loved how Dalton's stomach tightened, looking even more muscled.

Dalton's cock flinched, and his breath caught. He tilted his head back on a long, ragged breath. After a few moments, he glanced back at Blaise, leaning in to kiss his lips again. "If you keep this up, I'm going to come." He started walking, guiding Blaise backward around the chair with little steps hampered by his pants around his ankles.

"Where are we going?"

"Over there." Dalton lifted his chin toward Lizzy.

"We're not doing this on my piano."

Dalton chuckled. "Beside it. Underneath it. I don't care. That's"—he pointed to the floor by Lizzy—"the only carpet in the room, and I don't want to kneel on hardwood floor."

"Kneel? Why would you kneel?"

The chuckle Dalton gave was downright evil as he proceeded to show Blaise exactly why he'd be kneeling. He got the falls on Blaise's trousers undone, then the pants and smalls off in record time. Which wasn't all that difficult since Blaise already had his shoes off. He pulled Blaise's shirt over his head next. Getting to his knees, he took Blaise's cock in his mouth in one fell swoop.

"Oh my galaxy!"

"Shhh…," Dalton pulled back long enough to whisper.

"The room is soundproof." Perhaps that was the wrong thing to say, judging by the mischievous glint in those stormy eyes.

Dalton set about making Blaise yell some more. He sucked, drawing up and back down until saliva dripped over Blaise's balls, and his toes curled in the carpet. Just as his body began reaching for climax, which wasn't very long at all, Dalton stopped. "Don't come."

"What?" Blaise tried to disguise the frustration in his voice but wasn't very successful. "You can't do something like this and say don't. I don't know how this is done, but that simply must be against proper etiquette for this type of situation."

Smiling up at him, Dalton clutched his wrists and pulled him to his level. Dalton rocked back on his arse and swung his legs around. He undid one boot and pulled it and his pant leg off. Spreading his legs, he crooked his finger at Blaise. "Come here, angel, and stop glaring at me."

"I wasn't glaring." Blaise leaned forward, catching his weight on his hands. When his cock touched Dalton's, a hiss escaped them both. Blaise pressed down, grinding his hips against Dalton's, increasing the pressure.

"You were."

As Blaise found a lovely rhythm, letting the climax build in him again, Dalton turned his head and spit into his hand.

Blaise froze, his mouth dropping open of its own accord. "That is disgusting. Why did you do that?"

"Darling, has anyone ever told you that you become very opinionated when aroused?" Dalton lifted a knee and his hand, the one now covered in saliva, disappeared, nudging between them.

"Um, no." Heat rushed up Blaise's neck and cheeks.

Again, he brought his hand up and spit into it, but before Blaise could admonish him again, the slick hand wrapped around his cock. It felt so heavenly, Blaise couldn't bring himself to care about the lack of manners. His cock butted up against Dalton, and Dalton whispered, "Push forward."

Blaise did and decided that it was perfectly acceptable for Dalton to stop doing that lovely thing with his mouth as long as he did this instead. His cock sank into the tight band of Dalton's arse, and Blaise decided the saliva was tolerable as well. His hips came to rest against Dalton's arse, and his breath caught in his throat. His testicles pulled impossibly tight, and suddenly instead of climaxing, he wanted to savor the exquisite feelings.

Dalton wrapped his arm around Blaise's neck, bringing him closer. His hot breath fanned against Blaise's cheek as he whispered, "Move, angel."

Nodding, Blaise closed his eyes and nuzzled his face against Dalton's as his hips found a steady pace. The pressure built and built. The pleasure so intense, he was barely cognizant of Dalton's hand between them, moving on his own cock. Just the thought had Blaise's passion flaring higher. He moved harder and faster, until his skin slapped against Dalton's. In no time at all, his body sped toward completion, tensing against the ecstasy. A hoarse yell was ripped from him as he exploded in a blinding fury that left him weak.

The heat of Dalton's orgasm painted his stomach as Dalton's hand grasped at Blaise's neck. They lay still, with Blaise hovering over Dalton. When his arms couldn't hold him any longer, Dalton took over, wrapping his arms around Blaise's back and holding him tight. "What is your opinion now, sweetheart?"

That it's going to kill me when you leave. "I'm not aroused anymore, but I think you are my favorite person in the entire universe."

Dalton smiled against his cheek. "That is an opinion I can live with."

The twentieth annual Frost Fair, Fifth and Waverley Street in Classige, Pruluce

"YOU WERE holding out on me." Dalton grinned as Blaise skated around him backward in a circle with a huge smile on his face. Dalton had kept them near the edge of the man-made rink in deference to Blaise, but now he realized how unnecessary that had been. The little faker.

As if to illustrate that point, Blaise shifted onto one foot, then reversed his direction with a chuckle.

He'd seen Blaise in a lot of different moods but never this playful. Apparently a night spent having sex agreed with him. Dalton hadn't even had to do as much coaxing as he'd thought he'd have to do to get Blaise to take a short break from Operation: Orphans and come to the Frost Fair with him. Now thinking about it, it could be because they were incognito again. Blaise had developed a fondness for wearing his footman's clothes, or maybe it was just being a normal person and not heir to the most powerful duke on the planet. Dalton certainly understood that. It was one of the reasons he liked being in the military.

"I never said I couldn't skate." Blaise proved that by zipping back in front of him and reaching his hands out toward Dalton. "We have a pond at Eversleigh Manor. When I was a kid, we used to skate all the time. There is an old Earth game we used to play where we'd use two nets, sticks, and a flat round piece of rubber."

Dalton took his hands, marveling at how the pink in Blaise's cheeks made his grass-green eyes even more vivid. He was glad he'd talked Blaise into coming. Honestly he wasn't sure why he'd wanted to come so badly, but when he'd woken up in Blaise's bed, with Blaise snuggled up to his side, he wanted to do something fun. He'd wanted to spend some time with Blaise outside of the House of Lords and away from their crazy adventures, though he did enjoy those. He supposed he just hadn't wanted to think.

"We didn't have the rubber puck, so we would freeze one of Cook's scones and use it." With a shrug, Blaise glided backward across the ice effortlessly, tugging him along as though they were dancing.

"You played hockey?"

Blaise grabbed his hands and nodded. "You know hockey?"

"Yes, but I'm surprised you do. We sometimes played field hockey on Lerdra in our off time." Dalton pulled Blaise close, and turned them to keep from running into a little girl who skated slowly as she pulled a sled with her dolls on it.

"Do you get to play games a lot in the Navy?"

"Yes, actually we do. I guess it's the nature of war. You have to do something to lighten things up. If we didn't have some fun, we'd go insane thinking about what we do and the danger." There was nothing quite like war to make a man thankful he was alive.

"What exactly do you do in the Navy?"

"I was a Cavalry scout, but I just finished my training for Regelence Special Regiment." Truthfully the two positions weren't all that different. Both involved Dalton getting in and out of combat zones without being seen.

Blaise's smile faltered, and his forehead wrinkled.

"What?"

"I guess I thought you had some safe job away from the action. What you do is dangerous."

Dalton shrugged. He was good at it.

"You want to go back?" Blaise cocked his head a little as though he were puzzled by the prospect.

Dalton started to answer in the affirmative, but stopped. His job was exciting, he loved the adrenaline rush, missed it when he was on leave, but it was also lonely. Did he want to go back to spending so much time alone? To lying low, observing, and praying not to get caught? Every other time when he was on leave, he was itching to return to work, but for some reason the job description didn't seem quite so appealing this time. And he hadn't really missed the excitement; there had been plenty of that here. Hell, just seeing Blaise exhilarated him. He would miss Blaise when he returned, and he wasn't sure he was ready to give Blaise up just yet. *Whoa.* That revelation made Dalton stop.

Feeling his hesitation, Blaise stopped moving his legs too. Their glide across the ice slowed, and Blaise opened his mouth to say something, but he never got the words out. Someone hit him from behind.

"Oof." Sailing forward right into Blaise, Dalton wrapped his arms around Blaise, mashing their bodies together. Somehow he managed to keep his feet from getting tangled in Blaise's skates.

"Whoa." Blaise gripped Dalton's forearms harder, wobbling a little, then stiffening. His mouth dropped open, and then as his body stabilized, his grin returned. The victory on his face was a thing of beauty.

Pressing down on Blaise's arms, Dalton caught his balance too; then out of nowhere the little girl with the sled cut in front of Blaise—or rather, behind him, since he was skating backward. Bloody hell, Blaise was going to hit that sled. Dalton's only option was to steer them hard to their left, right toward a snow bank.

"Eeeeek!" Blaise's eyes widened comically, and he adjusted his grip, grabbing Dalton's shoulders before squeezing his eyes closed.

They landed in a five-foot-high snowbank with snow poofing into the air around them like an exhausted pillow from a pillow fight. Blaise's hat flew off to the right, and Dalton's cover landed on his face. They were still almost vertical, lying at an incline, with Dalton stretched out between Blaise's outspread legs. It wasn't an uncomfortable position to be in except for the snow that had landed on Dalton's back when his BDU coat flew up.

The body beneath his began to quake and quiver, and the air around him filled with laughter.

Dalton removed his cover from Blaise's face, to reveal two shiny, squinted green eyes and bright red cheeks. Blaise laughed so hard he was barely making a sound. It was contagious, and pretty soon Dalton was laughing with him. Dalton rested his forehead on Blaise's shoulder as his shoulders shook with mirth. After several moments, he caught his breath and had the presence of mind to realize he was lying on top of Blaise in a very public place. Though things were much more relaxed for the working class, people were starting to stare. Rolling to the side, he flopped into the snow next to Blaise and grabbed his gloved hand. "Are you all right?"

Blaise nodded, still chuckling a little. "You should have seen your face."

"You should have seen yours." Dalton turned toward Blaise again and his laughter ceased.

Blaise lay beside him staring up at the sky with the most beatific smile on his face. He looked so carefree and full of life. Nothing like the stuffy, repressed man Dalton had first spotted six months ago on leave, or even a few days ago in Blaise's office. He was beautiful and everything good in the world. He made Dalton ache with longing. Made him wish he could hang on to him forever. Even with the cold Dalton's prick took notice. Before he even realized what he was doing, he leaned forward.

A cloud of fog surrounded them as their breaths mingled in between their faces. The smile melted off Blaise's lips and his eyelids grew heavy as he focused on Dalton's mouth. He licked his lips.

This was insanity. Dalton should most definitely not kiss him here in public. Especially with Blaise's hat off; someone could recognize them. It was irresponsible and reckless and… he didn't give a damn.

Dalton moved to kiss those delectable lips, but a snowball hit him square in the face.

It was cold, but not painful. Whoever had packed it had done so loosely, so no damage done. Except possibly to Blaise, who was laughing so hard he had tears streaming down his cheeks. His body convulsed, and if Dalton hadn't known better, he'd think Blaise was having a seizure. He should have looked ridiculous, but instead he was the most beautiful sight Dalton had ever seen. A contentment Dalton hadn't felt in a very long time washed over him, and he found himself leaning forward again.

"Hey, mister, ye're lying in our fort."

Stopping short, Dalton looked up.

A group of four boys stood in a half circle around them. They were a mixed group, judging from their coats. Some middle class, others the children of lower class. They all held snowballs except for one of the kids in the middle. A kid on the end stepped forward. "If you don't move so we can rebuild, they will capture our flag." He gestured to something over Blaise's and Dalton's heads.

There was a blue flag in the mound of snow above them, and on closer inspection, another group of kids stood behind Dalton. They all held snowballs too.

"Well, we can't have that." Blaise jumped up, flopped his hat back on his head, and dusted himself off. "Truth be told, I'm quite good at snowball fights. Perhaps I can be of assistance." He started mounding the snow he'd just gotten up from, then turned to Dalton with a brilliant smile still in place and a challenge in his eyes.

The kids started cheering and began helping Blaise rebuild their fort.

Shaking his head, Dalton grabbed his cover, put it on, and stood. "You will rue the day, angel."

"Ha!" Blaise turned from his architecture work with a snowball in hand and a twinkle in his eyes. The kids helping him crowed and started running about, gathering their own snow.

After that it was every man for himself. Dalton swore there was more snow on him than on the ground, but it was the most fun he'd had in ages. He had to hand it to Blaise, he gave as good as he got, but in the end Dalton and his team triumphed. They captured the blue flag and were going to go for round two when the man who'd rented them skates interrupted.

With his hands on his hips, the man stepped into the valley between the two forts. "You kids go elsewhere, and you"—he pointed at Dalton—"and you"—he pointed at Blaise—"return your skates."

The boys started a chorus of boos and someone threw a snowball at the proprietor, hitting him in the back.

Grumbling, the kids took their flags and left, as did the man. Blaise stepped up beside Dalton and grabbed his hand, still grinning. "We should get some hot cocoa."

"We can definitely do that." Dalton led them back to the shack where they'd rented their skates and left their boots. He didn't want to give up Blaise's company, but they really should head back. They had to pick up Larkinson and her sister from the milliners on Baker Street.

"Was it like this when you went as a kid?"

"What, the Frost Fair?"

Blaise nodded.

"No." It had been fun when he was a child. He'd loved coming with his grandfather, but it hadn't been… magical like today.

"Oh, I'm sorry."

Dalton stopped walking and turned to Blaise, pulling him to a stop. "Don't be. It was even better."

Blaise smiled. "I'm glad. Maybe we could come back next year?"

"I'd like that." Squeezing Blaise's hand, Dalton started walking again. If they were still together next year, if he were stationed nearby, if…. "No."

"What?" Blaise stopped walking and shook his head. "If you don't want to, then you could have just said…."

"Earlier, you asked me if I wanted to go back to the military. The answer is no." Maybe he needed to consider the offer Nate and his uncle had made him.

Chapter Eighteen

Hooligans wreaked havoc at the Frost Fair this morning, throwing snowballs. The whole affair is a bit hazy, but hearsay places a certain demon lord at the scene in a pair of stolen skates.

—From *The Classige Examiner*

EXCITEMENT WAS not always the best emotion to act on, but here Blaise was, staring up at the pink monstrosity, as Dalton called it, wondering whether he should turn around and leave.

"Are you going to knock?" Larkinson asked from behind him.

"I don't know."

With a sigh, she reached around him and rapped on the door.

Blast. "Why did you do that?" He wasn't ready. He had no idea what he'd say to Ravensburg if he was home.

"Because I'm cold. Do you want to see Ashbourne or not?" She rolled her eyes at him, and he had the insane notion to kick her in the shin again. Only knowing she'd likely kick him back stopped him. He should have left her at home, but he couldn't very well call at a gentleman's residence without an escort. Dalton was right about society's rules—they were poppycock—but he had to tell Dalton what he'd found out about Operation: Orphans. Dalton would know how to best use the info, but maybe he should have waited until tomorrow when they were back at the House of Lords.

The door opened, and the underbutler smiled at him, giving him no choice but to live with his decision. "Welcome, my lord. We've been expecting you."

"You have?" Either Ravensburg's underbutler was psychic, or they'd stepped into an alternate universe.

Above them a door opened, and Dalton appeared on the landing.

A flutter started in Blaise's belly, and despite his nerves, he found himself smiling.

"You got my message?"

"I…." Blaise shook his head. "No." But that explained why the underbutler was expecting him at least. "I came with news."

Dalton started down the stairs toward them as the underbutler pulled Blaise's coat off his shoulders. Dalton no longer wore the BDU he'd had on earlier this morning, but was now dressed casually in a white shirt, matching cravat, an emerald-green waistcoat, and beige trousers. He appeared every bit the gentleman, except he was without a morning coat and in his stockinged feet. It was not at all proper when greeting a visitor, but Blaise had given up on proper and Dalton ever going together. In fact, he'd come to count on it. It was part of Dalton's charm.

Jogging down the stairs, Dalton skipped the last step entirely. "Rutherford, why don't you show Larkinson downstairs and get her some tea? I'll take care of Lord Redding."

Rutherford gave a crisp nod, handed Dalton Blaise's coat, and escorted Larkinson to a door to their right.

Blaise started taking off his gloves, and Dalton plucked his hat off his head. "You sent me a message?" He turned and nearly bumped into Dalton. The smooth scent of chocolate and mint wrapped around Blaise, and he found himself tugged into a room. No, not a room. A closet. "What?"

A pair of warm soft lips landed on his. His last thought before Dalton licked across his lips was that this was a really bad idea. Caught up in the passion, Blaise opened up and kissed back. Wrapping his arms around Dalton's neck, he leaned in. His cock started to fill as last night came rushing back to him, and it was all he could do not to grind himself against Dalton. Dalton's hair tickled his hand. Blaise threaded his fingers into that thick blond hair and—*dust*, he still had one glove on. They were in a closet, for galaxy's sake. Dalton had made him into a wanton. Whatever was he going to do when Dalton left?

The thought jolted him right out of the pleasure, and emptiness coalesced with angst inside his stomach and chest. Blaise broke the kiss, breathing hard. He had to stop this before he was completely lost, and he wasn't sure if he meant the kiss or the affair.

Dalton leaned in, his lips brushing Blaise's again, but Blaise stopped him with a hand to the chest.

"We are going to get caught."

With a sigh, Dalton moved back and opened the door. No sooner had they stepped out than Ravensburg appeared on the second-floor landing and looked down at them.

"There you are. I was beginning to wonder if you were coming back. Hello, Redding."

Good galaxy, that was close. Blaise lifted a hand at the marquess with a silent prayer that he wasn't glowing again or blushing, for that matter. "Ravensburg."

"Come on, you can help us pick out a property. Arthur is getting us more hot chocolate." He pivoted and walked back into the room with a skip in his step. Ravensburg was always pleasant, at least to Blaise, but he was not usually jovial. And that was definitely jovial, or very close to it.

"What is wrong with him? And what property?" Blaise watched him leave as Dalton hung up Blaise's coat and put his hat on a hook in the closet.

Grabbing Blaise's hand, Dalton proceeded to take his remaining glove off. "We've made a tentative peace. I'm still not fond of his decision, and I certainly don't understand it, but he offered to help when he saw me looking through books, so I've taken him up on it."

"I'm glad."

Dalton shrugged. "They gave me back control of my accounts when I told them about Operation: Orphans."

"You did what?" Blaise's stomach clenched.

"Relax. I didn't tell him how we discovered the orphans and Foundling Town. I told him we spotted them while I was escorting you and Larkinson to the music store before you had to be at the Lords. And I told them about the orphanage."

Blaise relaxed. This could actually be a good thing. Perhaps Ravensburg would sponsor their bill?

Dalton took Blaise's other glove, stuffed both in his coat pocket, and closed the closet door.

"Dalton! Redding! Get in here." That sounded more like the Ravensburg who Blaise was familiar with.

As if to say "after you," Dalton extended a hand.

The study was very similar to Ravensburg's office at the House of Lords, with neutral colors and bold furniture. It was comfortable, sophisticated, and completely cluttered. There appeared to be a desk hidden under all the books, and there were no less than three com-pads as well. They had obviously been at this a long time.

Ravensburg stood at the edge of the desk with a com-pad in hand. His easy posture was more reminiscent of his brother, King-Consort Raleigh, until he glanced up and straightened, giving no doubt that he was the Marquess of Ravensburg. His gaze met Blaise's, and his face showed no expression at all. Blaise half expected him to start lecturing, but then he smiled. Blaise had never thought of the marquess as handsome, probably because Ravensburg had always been so uptight, but this more relaxed Ravensburg was nearly as stunning as his son. The smile made him look younger. "Dalton has told us about the orphan situation, and we want to help."

Blaise nearly sighed in relief and nodded. "I welcome the help. I was really taken in by their plight."

Dalton's hand landed on the small of his back. "As was I."

Ravensburg's brow rose, his attention going to Dalton's hand.

Blaise suppressed the urge to shrug it off.

"And myself as well. I was glad to hear that the two of you had already made efforts to help."

Heat infused Blaise's cheeks, and he wondered if that was a subtle reminder about their conversation, but then the marquess spoke and put that fear to rest.

"You've been an excellent influence on Ashbourne, and for that you have my gratitude. Now, did I hear you say you had news?"

"I've found out how Foundling Town came to exist." He made his way to the chair in front of the desk and took a seat as Dalton took the one next to him. "The textile mills have moved off planet and put hundreds out of work, and they can't provide for their families."

"Yes, I heard about that." A new voice joined them. Arthur Fairfax, the marquess-consort, came into the room with the divine scent of chocolate and a tray in his hands. He set it on the table between Dalton and Blaise and straightened, a wrinkle marring his delicate face. "It was due to a tax bill. It became much cheaper for the mills to send the work off planet."

"Yes, I seem to remember hearing something about that." Ravensburg used his free hand to scratch his chin. "We need to find out what bill that was."

The marquess-consort started pouring chocolate into cups. "It was just this past year. I remember because the haberdashery raised their prices by nearly twenty-five percent, and don't get me started on the tailor. Even the bootmaker started charging more."

They spent the next half hour going over properties for the orphanage and outlining a plan. Blaise even confiscated Ravensburg's desk and took charge of the research. They didn't find the bill they were looking for, but Blaise told them about the bill he wanted to introduce into the House of Lords to fix the problem.

Dalton looked through one of the com-pads, alternately pacing and sitting on the edge of the desk. He currently sat on the desk, beside Blaise, with his feet dangling. He seemed more at ease around his parents. It was obvious things weren't quite normal. Dalton still acted a little standoffish, he didn't trust them, but he did seem to be trying.

"Redding, I'm impressed. You have really thought this out and done your homework. I'm convinced more than ever that you will make a fine addition to the IN Councilman's Committee."

The praise should have bolstered his spirits, but for some reason it did not. It reminded him that he'd have to return to working on interplanetary issues. He'd bought himself time by having Griff do his work—which he kind of felt guilty about—but he'd have to go back to doing things for his internship. It seemed boring and pointless in comparison. This was all Dalton's fault. If he hadn't given Blaise a taste of excitement, if he hadn't made Blaise's life seem so dull…. Dalton made him want things he couldn't have. He wanted to make a difference here at home, working in the House of Lords on planetary matters, not the IN Councilman's Committee. He wanted to see the fruits of his labors with the people right here at home. He wanted Dalton…. Galaxy help him, against his better judgment he'd fallen head over heels in love with a rake. With a heavy feeling in his gut, he glanced down at his hands, realizing they were clenched on the arms of the chair. He suddenly felt as lost as Dalton had looked last night.

"You okay?" Dalton touched his hand where it rested on the arm of the chair.

No. "Yes." He glanced up and realized everyone was staring at him. "I was just thinking. Not only do we need to find the bill that raised taxes on the textile mills, we also need to locate the money that the Dauber Act has allocated to the orphans of soldiers killed in action." Blaise took the cup Arthur had just filled and sipped.

Arthur replenished Dalton's cup, then walked over to the marquess and set the pot back on the tray. He turned back to them with a furrowed brow and his lips cocked to the side. "Did you say the Dauber Act?"

"Yes," Dalton answered.

"The money is going to the IN." Arthur sat down on the sofa and took a drink of his own chocolate without saying anything else.

Blaise let go of the chair arms and leaned forward.

Dalton set his cup down and got off the desk to turn and face his sire, but it was Ravensburg who finally asked the question they all wanted to know.

"Are you certain?"

"Oh yes." Again, Arthur didn't elaborate.

They all stared at him as he delicately lifted the cup to his lips and took another sip. This time his eyes widened over his cup as he realized they were all watching him.

"Sire!" Dalton snapped. "How do you know this? We've been searching for that information for the past day."

Arthur lowered his cup and smiled. It even looked as though he puffed his chest out a little, which was comical given his diminutive size. Really, it was quite amusing that Dalton called Blaise angel, because Blaise had nothing on Arthur. Or then again, perhaps Arthur was the devil. "I heard it at a ball, which is how I hear all my gossip. I distinctly remember Lords Rushburn and Grafton discussing the Dauber Act just before Christmas. They were talking about how it would help out-of-work men find jobs. They thought that was a waste of money. And they talked about how there was a fund that was supposed to be distributed by the IN and how at least some of their tax money would benefit someone instead of being wasted." He gave them a Gallic shrug that was both elegant and proud. "What can I say, I hear things. People take one look at me and see only a pretty face."

Townsend Castle

"OOH, I think it's bigger than mine."

"No, it's not."

"I think it is."

"No, mine is definitely bigger."

"It's redder than mine."

"It's not redder than mine. But mine has a bit more purple in it."

"Can I touch it?"

Raleigh recognized all three of the voices carrying outside the study: Aiden, Colton, and Dalton. His first thought was *they are going to be the death of me*, quickly followed by *no way is it as bad as it sounds.*

Ravensburg, who had been walking beside him, pulled up short of the study door and arched a brow at Raleigh.

With a sigh and a fervent prayer that it wasn't what it sounded like, Raleigh walked into the study ahead of his brother… and considered walking right back out. He blinked and blinked again but he still saw… well, truthfully he wasn't certain what he was seeing. He started to ask, but honestly he couldn't imagine the explanation making things any better.

Wentworth stood next to the sideboard with his trousers around his knees. Aiden, Dalton, and Colton were all kneeling behind him looking at his arse. Or perhaps it wasn't quite so bad as that. Colton seemed to be holding up the leg of Wentworth's smallclothes and pointing at a mark just below his buttocks.

"What in the devil are they doing?" Ravensburg whispered from beside Raleigh in a tone somewhere between shock, amusement, and horror.

"Trust me when I tell you that we probably don't want to know."

"Does this happen often?" Ravensburg asked.

Define often. "This particular thing? No." But Raleigh was pretty sure there were still remnants of the water fight from a few days ago in the foyer. He'd found a busted balloon hanging from his father-in-law's portrait just yesterday. Crossing his arms over his chest, he cleared his throat.

Aiden turned and gave them a beatific smile as if he had not been just caught examining a half-naked man in the middle of the study. "Oh, hullo, Cony. Uncle."

Ravensburg looked at Raleigh as if asking for help on how to act after such a display.

Shrugging at his brother, Raleigh shook his head, crossed to his desk, and perched himself on top of it in his customary position. He was at a loss for once.

Lifting a hand in greeting, Ravensburg grimaced. "Raleigh, I'm not sure what bothers me more. This"—he indicated the tableau in the middle of the study—"or that you didn't bat a lash at it."

Wentworth, Colton, and Dalton turned. Just like Aiden, Colton and Dalton smiled and mumbled a "Hi, Cony" and a "Hello, Uncle," as if nothing out of the ordinary was going on.

"I've raised hellions," Raleigh whispered under his breath. He supposed he should at least be grateful Tarren and Trouble weren't involved. He turned to his brother and said, "Just ignore them."

"Why? Will they go away if I do?"

"One can only hope." He sighed. "But alas I'm not that lucky."

"We're still here, Cony," Colton grumbled. "You should tell us hello. You too, Uncle."

Now he wanted to adhere to proper etiquette?

Wentworth winced and started tugging up his trousers. He at least had the decency to blush. An unusual look for him. Until this very moment, Raleigh would have said Wentworth was incapable of embarrassment, but obviously he was no match for Raleigh's boys. Who were without a doubt one hundred percent responsible for this. "Sorry, Raleigh. They insisted. Dalton was asking about my birth—"

"Good galaxy! An orgy? Why wasn't I invited?" Rourke stepped into the study doorway and stopped short.

Groaning, Wentworth turned and set to work tucking in his shirt. "You aren't helping, Rourke."

"Obviously, because no one invited me." He made a loud sniff, as if put out by the lack of an invitation. Then the handsome rogue draped himself gracefully across the sofa with his arms on the back. As if just noticing Raleigh and Ravensburg, Rourke bounded up and bowed his head. He really did fit in the Townsend household quite well. It was a terrifying thought.

Rolling his eyes, Raleigh waved him into his seat. "Everyone get dressed and sit down."

Ravensburg met his gaze across the room, looking as though he were going to explode with laughter any moment. It was refreshing and quite promising. Raleigh decided that he would refrain from throttling his offspring. He had not seen Barclay smile that big and look so carefree since they were children. Galaxy, but he had missed his brother. It appeared as though their heart-to-heart the other night had truly helped start mending their relationship. Barclay was really doing his best to unwind a bit.

"Perhaps Dalton can stay here and I could move in with you and Arthur?"

Ravensburg chuckled. "I'm beginning to see why my son is such a heathen."

"I assure you it is entirely Steven's fault."

This time Ravensburg did laugh. "Oh come now, little brother, I know you better than that. You earned the nickname Rogue."

With a twinkle in his eyes, Dalton hopped to his feet and grinned. He started to comment, but Raleigh gave him the eye.

"Don't even think about it, Demon. Just take a seat. We'll discuss whatever it was you were all doing in a moment."

"I had nothing to do with whatever it is that is going on," Steven pronounced loudly as he strolled in.

"For once," Raleigh said under his breath.

Nate came in behind Steven, looked at Wentworth—who was now buttoning the falls on his trousers—shrugged, and said, "I don't want to know."

"Dalton started it, and it was Colton's idea. I was just an innocent bystander." Aiden crossed the room to his consort and went up on his toes to kiss Nate's cheek.

"Bullshit…," Colton said, trying to disguise the word as a sneeze.

Groaning, Raleigh tried not to smile. "Everyone, sit. We have a lot to cover. We're just waiting on—"

"I'm here. Sorry, Your Highness." Robert Jenkins came into the study, closing the door behind him. Not for the first time, Raleigh wished he could erase the sadness from Robert's eyes. He was such a good young man: responsible, smart, and hardworking. Robert had been living at the castle for the last six months. Perhaps some of the news Raleigh had tonight would cheer him up.

Steven sat down on the front of the desk next to Raleigh, resting his hand on Raleigh's thigh.

Raleigh grinned and covered the hand with his own, linking their fingers together. "As most of you know, we have finally broken the encryption on Admiral Jenkins's hard drive."

"What was on it?" Aiden asked. Egads, the boy was impatient.

Raleigh held up a hand. “I’m getting to that.” He met Robert’s gaze as the young man sat down on the sofa next to Ravensburg. “I’ve found more information on the hard drive, and I’m going to call a meeting to discuss all this with Eversleigh and the IN Councilman’s Committee, but I wanted to let you all know first. Sir Percy claims to have spotted Betty at the market here in Classige, but I now have reason to believe that Admiral Jenkins may be alive as well.”

Everyone started talking at once, but Raleigh looked only at Robert.

Robert Jenkins closed his eyes, took a deep breath, and when he opened them again, his eyes were quite shiny, but he did not smile. He had the appearance of someone who’d been told something too good to be true. Not the reaction Raleigh was hoping for, but understandable.

“Are you sure?” Robert asked.

“Not a hundred percent. I have had someone searching for Betty, since Sir Percy saw her, but we have not located her yet.”

Again more chatter from the excited group. He waited for everyone to quiet down, but he should have expected this reaction. The admiral was highly regarded. Nate and Wentworth had close relationships with him.

When everyone quieted down, Raleigh said, “We’re trying to find her before the IN does. The admiral has indicated that the IN are looking for him and Betty. He’s also left some hints to his whereabouts.”

Robert sat forward, resting his elbows on his knees. A lock of dark brown hair fell into his eyes as he peered up at Raleigh. Meeting his gaze with a puzzled frown, he said, “Why wouldn’t he and my mom stay together?”

Raleigh had wondered the same thing when he’d found the vid on the hard drive. “According to what I found, your mother went into hiding here while your father went to find something. He did not say what, but he indicated that it was of great importance and could help him prove what the IN was doing.”

More gasps and more talking.

Nate stepped forward from his place over in the corner. “So he indicated the IN is involved in a plot against us?”

Taking a deep breath, Raleigh nodded, trying to decide how much to tell them. Sadly he didn’t know much. The message had been cryptic and the information the admiral had gathered himself was nothing that they didn’t already know. But there was also information on the disk that led Raleigh to believe that the admiral might have been in on whatever the IN was up to at first. "Jenkins confirmed that the IN is trying to obtain our procreation technology, and that they are trying to build the weapon based on the schematics Payton found. I still need to delve into the disk more, but he also mentioned another planet and mercenary attacks." Which Raleigh did not want to discuss until he had more information. "Now tell me what Ravensburg and I walked in on." He gave a pointed stare at Wentworth, who raised his brows at Dalton.

Everyone else turned and looked at Dalton as well.

Dalton, the rascal, put his hands behind his head, crossed his ankle over his knee, and leaned back farther on the sofa. He opened his mouth to speak but Aiden interrupted.

"Dalton saw some weird marks on the orphans he found. They had marks but not like all of ours. He thought perhaps the orphans were like Wentworth and had one parent who was born of Regelen procreation and one who was not. So he asked to see Wentworth's birthmark."

Wait, why was he talking about orphans? Wentworth has a birthmark? Raleigh frowned. Sometimes talking to his children was an exercise in patience. He looked at Steven for help.

Steven smiled and translated. "Wentworth has a birthmark like all of ours on the back of his thigh. So it would seem he inherited it and other traits from his father."

Interesting. Raleigh had known about Wentworth's father, of course. Leith was trying to build a relationship with his son after all these years and dropped by the castle on occasion to have lunch with Wentworth and Colton. It had been a big scandal at first, given that Leith had married Wentworth's mother, which made his marriage to Leo invalid and his second son's birth illegitimate. But this was the first he'd heard about a birthmark. "So who are these orphans?"

"Blaise and I found them on an outing." Dalton dropped his hands from behind his head and looked at his father and smiled. "We've since arranged to help them by donating a new orphanage."

Ravensburg smiled back, then met Raleigh's gaze. "Arthur is sponsoring a bill to help the orphans and repeal the Dauber Act. Remember I told you about the Dauber Act?"

Right. The act that was seemingly funneling Regelence money into the IN. Raleigh grinned, not missing the fact that Dalton had called Redding by his first name, or the fact that he and Ravensburg seemed to be getting along. Ravensburg had indicated as much, but it was nice seeing it firsthand. "And what of the marks, do they match Wentworth's?"

Dalton shook his head. "No, Wentworth's birthmark is exactly like all of ours, only located in a different spot."

"I still say mine's bigger," Aiden said.

Raleigh glared at his son.

Steven chuckled beside him.

Squeezing his hand none too gently, Raleigh elbowed him. Aiden did not need encouragement. He seemed to have a knack for disrupting Raleigh's meetings.

"Ow." Steven reached over with his other hand and pinched Raleigh's thigh.

Before things deteriorated any further, Raleigh decided it was best to end things. "All right, keep me updated." He met his brother's gaze. "Tell Arthur if he needs any help on the bill to let me know. Everyone dismissed."

Dalton practically bolted up from the sofa and was out the door first.

Steven leaned close, resting his head on Raleigh's shoulder, staring at the empty doorway where Dalton had just disappeared. "Did you notice how he called Redding by his first name?" He sounded very pleased with himself.

Raleigh grinned. "I did. And I think I warned you against playing matchmaker."

Scoffing, Steven turned his head and kissed Raleigh's cheek. "You did no such thing… this time."

"Mmm…. I wonder where he is going in such a hurry," Raleigh said.

"To see Blaise?" Steven asked hopefully.

Raleigh groaned. "You had better hope not. There are no soirees this evening."

"Even better."

Chapter Nineteen

A very prominent IN Councilman's Committee intern's valet was seen sneaking a man out of the ducal town house this morning. Was the man concealed in a large frock coat, scarf, and hat the valet's lover? Or is her master not quite as pure as we've all been led to believe?

—From *Pruluce Weekly*, the Beau Monde Happenings column

NOT EVEN going into combat gave Dalton a case of the nerves like he had at the moment. This had seemed like a good idea when he'd started over here, but now he began to wonder.

"All right, give me your coat, gloves, scarf, and hat," Larkinson whispered as she opened the door at the end of the hallway.

Too late to back out now. Dalton blinked at the bright light as he entered her room and inhaled the scent of lavender. He'd sent her a message half an hour ago and asked her to meet him downstairs in the area where servants and tradesmen entered the mansion. She'd snuck him up the servants' corridor, and here they were. The same trip hadn't previously seemed as daunting as it did today.

She closed the door behind them, and he glanced around as he pulled off his outer garments. The spaciousness still amazed him. Larkinson really did have it good. Her furniture was of the finest mahogany and quite elegant. Her room colors were bold green and dark purple, and she even had a full fireplace in her room. It really was no wonder she acted more as Blaise's equal than his valet, but it was one of the things Dalton liked about her. She was not meek, and her room displayed that as well.

"I can't believe I'm doing this again." Her amused tone was louder now that they were out of the hallway.

Handing her his outerwear, Dalton leaned in and kissed her cheek. "It's for a good cause."

With a pretty blush, she snorted and laid his things over the end of her big canopy bed. "You turning my charge into a light-trouser is a good cause?"

Dalton chuckled. Definitely not the cause he was speaking of. "He is not a light-trouser, but yes, if the opportunity arises for something more"—he waggled his eyebrows—"I'm certainly not going to say no."

"You are incorrigible." She chuckled and swatted his arm, then let out a breath, and her face took on a more serious bent. "He doesn't know you are coming, does he?"

"No." Dalton turned toward the door that led into Blaise's room, ready to get on with what he came for, but she grabbed his shoulder and turned him back around.

"That's probably for the best." She started fiddling with his cravat, straightening it. Her brows drew together, and then she looked up at him as she dusted off the shoulders of his jacket. "He's been blue as a megrim since he returned from Fairfax House this afternoon, and when I ask him why, he only shrugs."

"I noticed it when we were working on Operation: Orphans." He still could not say that without the corners of his lips twitching. "I thought it was just because we hadn't found the money trail." *Could there be more to it?*

"I don't know what it is. He won't talk to me, and when I ask what's wrong, he says nothing."

"I'll talk to him."

She gave him a smile and patted his chest. "You're good for him."

"I think you have that backwards. He's good for me." And Dalton wasn't about to let that slip through his fingers. He'd done a lot of thinking in the past day—more than was probably good for him—and that was why he was here. A wave of jitters tried to take over, and his limbs felt heavier all of a sudden, but he shook it off.

"You are good for each other."

Galaxy, he hoped she was right.

She shoved his shoulder to turn him around, then pushed him in the middle of his back. "Now get in there and cheer my boy up."

"Yes, ma'am."

"Wait." Always the valet, she smoothed some of his hair down. "Okay, now go."

Blaise had it right; she was a mother hen. Dalton turned the knob and quietly pushed the door open, more than ready to see Blaise. He half expected to hear music, but it was quiet except for the crackle of a fire burning in the fireplace. The fire was also the only light on in the room, giving the wood-paneled walls an orange glow. Blaise's bedroom was a lot like his music room. It was done in lighter colors—except his walls, which were a raised paneled wood with elaborate molding—but it fit Blaise. Elegant, uncluttered, and lovely. His bed was a carved four-poster, with a beige brocade duvet, and in the middle of the pillowy cover was Blaise.

He lay on his stomach with his chin propped on his hands at the foot of his bed, staring into the fire. He'd removed everything but his trousers and his white shirt, resembling a man of leisure with his bare feet crossed. "Unless you brought some of those tarts from the kitchen, go away."

"Sorry, I'm all out of tarts." Dalton came forward and gripped the bedpost nearest Blaise's head. Perhaps he should have brought some sweets or a gift at least.

Blaise rolled to his side, looking over his shoulder. His brow wrinkled, and then he rolled back to his position on his stomach. "What are you doing here?"

Not exactly the welcome he'd have liked, but Dalton had had worse. Blaise hadn't told him to leave, so he could work with that. After making his way around the foot of the bed, he sat on the floor in front of Blaise until their heads were nearly even. He looked into those fathomless green eyes, watching the pupils enlarge. There was even a hint of a smile. "I came to see you." He traced a finger along the side of Blaise's cheek, encountering a light dusting of stubble. It was probably the most unkempt he'd ever seen Blaise, and he still looked like an angel.

Blaise closed his eyes at the caress and leaned in slightly, like a cat asking to be petted. Dalton wasn't even sure if he realized he did it. The man had such passion in him. Passion that Dalton was certain only he had seen, and he wanted to keep it that way. This man was his. Galaxy, Blaise was beautiful, the way the fire cast a glow over his skin, shading parts of his face and body.

Dalton's case of nerves evaporated, and a sense of rightness took its place. This was where he was meant to be. Whatever was wrong, it wasn't between them. Dalton crooked his finger under Blaise's chin and leaned forward to brush a light kiss across his warm lips, then his nose and his chin. His whole face was warm from the heat.

Opening his eyes, Blaise watched him but didn't say anything. Those eyes that only moments ago sparkled with pleasure were heavy-lidded and thoughtful.

"What's bothering you, angel? I thought you'd be happy with the progress we made today. My sire even offered to sponsor your bill."

Finally those full lips quirked into a grin. "Working with your sire is going to be interesting. He bounces from one thing to something entirely different but just as relevant. He's quite brilliant, but dizzying."

That was certainly true. He reminded Dalton of the quintessential mad genius. "He is at that, but that doesn't answer my question." Again, Dalton ran his finger down that stubbled cheek, because he couldn't not. They were so close. It seemed so intimate. He'd never felt this connection, the closeness, with another of his lovers.

Blaise didn't say anything for several minutes. He sat up and crossed his legs, opened his mouth once, then closed it briefly before everything came out in a rush. "I find intergalactic politics tedious and boring, and I don't want to be the next IN councilman. I don't want to only dance with political allies at balls, and I don't want to spend my evenings at the theater talking about IN policies. I don't want to watch everything I say and do and never have any fun in order to be the perfect candidate to replace my father. I don't want to play Beethoven at the family musicals. I want to play my own compositions." He finally took a breath by way of a big sigh as though he were getting this all off his chest.

Blinking at the outpouring, Dalton bit his lip to keep from smiling, sensing that Blaise would not find it amusing. He pushed himself up off the floor and took a seat on the end of Blaise's bed, next to him, and grabbed his hand out of his lap. "Then don't."

With a groan, Blaise rolled his head toward the ceiling. When he looked back at Dalton, a lock of brown hair fell into his eyes. "It's not that simple."

"Why isn't it?" Dalton brushed the hair out of his face.

Curling his fingers around Dalton's and bringing his hand into his lap, Blaise rushed on before Dalton even had a chance to say anything else. "My whole life I've been groomed to do all those things and more. It's what is expected of me. It's all I know. I wish I could be like you. You're so sure of what you want to do, you won't let anyone talk you out of it."

"Sometimes plans change."

"Yours haven't," Blaise countered.

"Actually, they have."

That perfect brow creased, and Blaise turned more fully toward him, his knees almost touching Dalton's hip. "They have?"

Dalton nodded. "I'm going to take the job my uncle and Nate offered me. I'm going to stay in Classige. So if I can change my plans, why can't y—"

"But why?" Blaise's head cocked to the side, and there was a glimmer of… was that excitement in his eyes?

And here it was, the moment of truth. It wasn't supposed to go like this. How had they gotten off the subject? They'd been talking about why Blaise had a case of the blue devils. Dalton swallowed down a knot that formed in his throat and clasped both of Blaise's hands. His were not completely steady, but thankfully Blaise didn't seem to notice. Taking a deep breath to center himself, Dalton said, "Because of you. I want to be near—"

The next thing he knew, he was flat on his back, hanging off the side of the bed, after Blaise launched himself at him. He grabbed Dalton's face, rolling on top of him and plastering their mouths together. He nearly knocked them both off the bed.

Scrambling, Dalton grabbed the bedpost with one hand and wrapped the other around Blaise's back as Blaise forced his tongue into Dalton's mouth. Their heads and shoulders hung off the bed, and it took all of Dalton's abdomen muscles to keep from collapsing over the edge. This was not the reaction he'd envisioned, but this one was so much better. His cock seemed to think so too. It went hard in record time, but they couldn't stay like this. Dalton's stomach was strong but not strong enough to stay tense for what Blaise obviously had in mind.

Breaking off the kiss, Dalton panted for breath.

Instead of stopping, Blaise moved his attention to Dalton's chin, kissing and nipping.

Somehow Dalton managed to move them sideways and onto the bed as Blaise started tugging loose his cravat. "Wait!"

Blaise stopped, looking more than a little put out about being interrupted, but Dalton had to know for sure. He needed the words.

"Are you sure this is what you want? You know my reputation isn't the best. I could impact your career. It could—"

Placing a hand over his mouth, Blaise gave him the most beatific smile. His eyes even shone. "I've never been more sure of anything in my life."

"Oh thank galaxy." Relief flooded Dalton, and he smiled so big, it hurt his face. He probably looked like a cocklehead, but he didn't care.

And Blaise didn't seem to either, he was a whirlwind, undressing Dalton systematically. First the cravat, then the jacket and shirt. When Dalton was naked from the waist up, Blaise sat back on his haunches, straddling Dalton's hips, and stared down at him. He just stayed there staring, his eyes raking in all of Dalton, and then his hands followed. "I didn't want you to go, but I was too afraid to hope."

Dalton's heart soared even higher, and he sat up, gripping Blaise's face in his hands and kissing him again. This time the kiss was gentle, slow, and leisurely, a melding of hearts as well as mouths. Dalton had had lots of lovers, but he'd never made love. This was love. A shiver racked his body at the thought. It was terrifying and exhilarating all at once. Breaking the kiss only long enough to pull Blaise's shirt over his head, he laid them down and rolled them over into the middle of the bed. This time he was the one who straddled Blaise's hips. And oh what fun that was. The ridge of Blaise's erection bit into his left buttock, proving that Blaise was just as aroused. Dalton ground himself against it. He was rewarded with a moan and a jolt as if Blaise had been shocked by electricity. His whole body stiffened, and his mouth opened wide, but no sound emerged.

Blaise skimmed his hands over Dalton's bare chest, breathing hard.

A tingle raced all throughout Dalton's back and made his balls pull tighter, begging for more. They were going to go up in flames. He could not wait any longer. Unfastening Blaise's falls, he slipped off the side of the bed. "Lift, sweetheart."

Lifting his hips off the bed, Blaise let Dalton pull his pants and smallclothes off together to reveal the elegant, pale form. His cock slapped across his belly, painting it with moisture, and Dalton had to remind himself to breathe. The man was gorgeous, long and lean and perfect from the tip of his toes to the top of his head. If there was a picture under the definition of divine, this would be it.

Blaise sucked in his stomach and his prick bobbed. So hard and red. The shine of wetness on its tip made Dalton want like he'd never yearned before. He wanted to bury himself inside this man and fuck him until neither of them knew their name. He'd had his fingers in Blaise's arse last night after they'd finally moved into the bed, but tonight? Tonight his cock was going in that tight little hole. But first….

Dalton made quick work of his boots, trousers, and smallclothes as Blaise came up on his elbows to watch. He climbed back on the bed with his prick leading the way, and straddled Blaise again, but this time he moved farther up, hovering over Blaise's chest.

"Dalton?" Those pretty eyes widened.

Gripping his cock, Dalton tapped it against Blaise's lips. "Open."

Blaise's eyes flared, and his pupils dilated more. He licked his lips and opened. His tongue came out and took a tentative taste. Then slowly he took Dalton's dick into his mouth and suckled the whole while meeting Dalton's gaze. What he lacked in finesse, he made up for in intensity. So much so that Dalton found his hands on the headboard as he rocked into Blaise's pretty mouth. He tried to remember to keep it shallow, but Blaise didn't seem to mind. His hands pulled Dalton's arse forward. The warm cavern of his mouth engulfed Dalton's cock, taking him to the very brink. With every ounce of his mental strength, Dalton pulled back, squeezing his eyes shut. He could not look at the beautiful man beneath him. He had to gain his control. Gripping the base of his cock hard, he staved off ejaculation, but it was a close thing. He panted for breath and Blaise, damn him, leaned forward and licked the tip of Dalton's cock.

Hissing out a breath, Dalton slid back. He got off the bed and walked around the room, hearing a sultry chuckle behind him. "Hush heathen."

The chuckle got heartier. "Come back, please."

With a groan, Dalton dug through his jacket pocket and pulled out the tube of lube he'd brought.

"What's that?"

"Lube, since you seemed to object to the spit."

Blaise rose up on his elbow. "Honestly, at this point, spit is fine, just get back here." His voice sounded rough with lust. His hand strayed to his cock, stroking. "Please."

Dalton groaned and practically ran back to the bed. He wasted no time getting the tube open and smearing a generous amount on Blaise's arse. When he stuck his finger in, Blaise jumped and stiffened, but it didn't last long. He started pushing toward Dalton, his eyes wide with wonder. His cock jumped in response, and a puddle formed on his stomach. His body vibrated with unspent energy, and Dalton knew the exact moment he found the right spot. Blaise gasped and began pumping his hips. It was the most erotic thing Dalton had ever seen in his life.

Wasting no time, he added another finger, then another. At first Blaise winced and his jaw tightened, but Dalton didn't stop, and Blaise didn't ask him to. He stayed there pumping in and out, stretching and giving his angel time, until he thought he'd die of desire.

"Dalton, please."

"Stroke yourself for me."

A blush spread out over those angelic cheeks and down Blaise's neck, but he did what Dalton asked. He took his cock in hand and began to stroke. Dalton grabbed the lube and squeezed more on Blaise's hole, then added a liberal amount to the tip of Blaise's dick for him to use. He took his cock in hand and pressed it against that tiny hole, torn between watching Blaise's face for signs of pain and watching his cock sink into that tight body. By the time he got all the way inside, they were both panting. "Are you okay?"

Blaise nodded. "Feels odd and a little uncomfortable, but not bad."

Dalton began to move, and Blaise gasped.

"Ahhhh." His hand stopped moving and released his cock entirely.

"Good ah or bad ah?"

"I haven't decided."

Wrapping his hand around Blaise's cock, Dalton began to stroke in time with his hips.

"Oh galaxy. Definitely a good ah."

With a chuckle, Dalton continued, taking it slow until he couldn't stand it anymore. He thrust faster and faster until his balls pulled impossibly tight. It felt as though his head was going to pop right off. His whole body tensed, waiting to throw him over the edge of the cliff into ecstasy.

A soft whimper sounded below him, followed by a roar as Blaise went as stiff as a board.

Dalton had just enough presence of mind to lean over and cover Blaise's mouth with his, effectively swallowing his sounds of pleasure, as the sticky heat of Blaise's climax painted his stomach. He followed right after, pouring himself into Blaise's body, then collapsed on top of him. Their mouths were still open on each other's.

Finally, arms wrapped around his back and a tongue flicked at his. For some reason Dalton found that hilarious and started chuckling. Soon they were both laughing, still curled together in a tangle of limbs and sweat.

"You're really staying?"

"No one could drag me away. I'll talk to your father tomorrow." Dalton propped himself up on his hands and stared down into the face he was going to spend a lifetime admiring. "I want you to do me a favor, though."

"YOUR FATHER sent word that you have a meeting at the castle in thirty minutes, so you should have just enough time to go downstairs and tell him you don't want the open position on the IN Councilman's Committee. Now lift your chin."

With a groan, Blaise raised his chin and stared at the ceiling of his dressing room. "The next time Dalton asks me for a favor, remind me to tell him no."

"Hush and be still." She scraped the razor up his throat to his chin in one smooth glide, the tip of her tongue caught between her teeth in concentration. "He's looking out for your best interest. I happen to agree with him." Tapping the shaving cream off the straight razor into the sink, she met his gaze in the mirror and smiled. "It's the right thing to do. You have never enjoyed intergalactic politics."

He started to protest, but she tilted his head up again and shaved the rest of his jaw with the same slow draw upward. He was convinced she was going slower than usual to keep him from talking. The woman was as contrary as the day was long.

"You'd be miserable. And besides, now that you are getting married, you can take up your seat in the House of Lords and you can sponsor your own bill and help the people here at home without a voice." She shook the foam off the razor again and met his eyes in the mirror. "I can't believe you are getting married. I can't wait." She'd been practically giddy about it since he told her this morning after Dalton snuck out.

"Neither can I." He'd never expected, never even hoped, that Dalton would return his feelings. He was going to have to tell Father about Dalton too—not everything of course. Father did not need to know about their looking for the box or being together—but Blaise didn't want him to be blindsided when Dalton came to speak with him. Telling Father about Dalton would be much easier than admitting to him that Blaise didn't want to be the next IN councilman. "Maybe I can just wait till after the wedding to talk to my father."

Larkinson's eyebrows hiked up, and she leveled a stare at him in the mirror as she set down the razor and picked up the hot towel lying on the vanity.

"I—"

She slapped the towel over his mouth.

Sputtering, Blaise pulled the towel off his face and glared at her.

Unfazed, she took the towel and finished wiping his face.

"This is about your stutter."

"I haven't stuttered in years." He'd had the best tutors, voice coaches, and therapist. The best money could buy, and he'd worked so hard, harder than he'd worked for anything in his life. Even now when he thought he might stutter, he didn't. Except the night the box was stolen, but those were extreme circumstances.

She applied aftershave to his face, tied his cravat, put on his waistcoat and morning coat. "No, but you still remember what it was like. You still remember those mean village boys. You know they were wrong, don't you? You are not a disgrace to the Eversleigh title."

No, but he could still remember that feeling of isolation and shame… of having disappointed his father.

"Do you hear me? That was a long time ago, Blaise. Your father is proud of you."

He knew that, but he had to wonder if he'd still be, if Blaise weren't so… perfect.

Larkinson chucked him under the chin, grabbed his arms, pulled him up from the chair, and kissed his cheek before shoving him toward the door. "You look smashing. And you have fifteen minutes before you have to leave. Off with you."

"Pushy chit," Blaise mumbled.

"I heard that."

"Of course you did. You hear everything." Blaise smiled and left the room. She was right. He needed to talk to his father before his resolve vanished.

Blaise got downstairs just in time to see what looked like Griff walking out the front door. He started to call out a hello, but Griff was gone before he could. That was odd. Why would Griff be here without waiting to see Blaise? There must be something going on with the IN Council at this upcoming meeting.

Hamilton closed the door, then looked up at Blaise. “Good morning, Lord Redding.”

“Good morning, Hamilton. Was that Viscount Grantham who just left?”

“It was indeed, my lord. He had business with the duke.” Hamilton winked at Blaise.

That was odd. Hamilton was not the conspirator sort. What could he…? Right. He was trying to warn Blaise. Blast! He’d forgotten about the treaty report. Father was probably not happy about him fobbing the job off on Griff. Oh well, he was going to have to tell Father about Operation: Orphans anyway. He might as well add that to the list. None of that was Griff’s fault, though. Blaise made a mental note to thank Griff when he saw him.

“Blaise, is that you?” The duke’s head popped out of the study. A huge smile lit his face when he spotted Blaise. He practically radiated good cheer. “Come in, come in. I was just coming to find you. I have wonderful news!”

The good cheer was not what Blaise expected. Perhaps Father was not disjointed over him giving the treaty report to Griff after all. Stepping off the last step, his bootheels echoed through the foyer, and the strange thought crossed his mind that he was walking to his doom. He rolled his eyes at himself and hurried to the door. Larkinson could be right that Bannon was not the only one who had a flair for dramatics.

Father turned and leaned against his desk as Blaise entered the study. The duke was dressed very similar to Blaise, though his colors were darker. He always wore dark colors. Partly to hide his belly, but also it made him appear more commanding, or so he said. As if he needed to be more imposing. The man was six foot two, with wide shoulders, a full head of graying-brown hair and full arched brows. Blaise looked like him, for the most part, but he’d gotten his leaner build from his sire.

May as well get on with it. Swallowing the lump in his throat and trying to ignore the butterflies in his stomach, Blaise said, “Good morning, Father. I have something I want to talk to you about.”

“Good, but I have something to tell you first. Actually, two somethings. Two very wonderful somethings.” He clapped his hands together, looking nearly as giddy as Larkinson had this morning when Blaise had told her about marrying Dalton.

Ah, Dalton. The thought grounded him some, and the butterflies dissipated a little. He hadn't thought it possible to be as close to someone as he felt with Dalton. The man seemed to know him nearly as well as he knew himself. Blaise trusted him, therefore, this was the right choice. He'd let Father speak his piece, and then he'd tell him. He walked forward and rested his hands on the back of the pale blue brocade Queen Anne chair in front of his father's desk.

"I just signed a betrothal contract in your name." Father beamed at him, rubbing his hands together.

What? Dalton had been here already? Letting out a sigh of relief, Blaise smiled. *It was done!* Not only did he not have to explain to his father about Dalton, but no way could they back out now. Not that he thought Dalton would, but it still put his mind at ease. "I didn't think you'd be this happy."

"Why wouldn't I? He's perfect for you. I know the two of you are close. He's probably the only man you dance with who is your own age. And best of all, Grantham's political savvy will be an asset to you in your career."

It was like having his cork drawn and being kicked in the testicles at the same time. His knees buckled, and he'd have fallen if not for the chair. White knuckling the top of it, he hoped against hope that he'd heard wrong. His stomach swirled, and he felt as though he might vomit. How had this happened? If Griff were there right now, Blaise would plant him a facer.

For all the mind-numbing pain in his heart, his father didn't seem to notice. He went on about how he'd made arrangements with the Earl of Greenway to announce the betrothal at the earl's ball that night during dinner and how Griff was going to put an announcement in the *Times* for tomorrow morning. Then as if that wasn't enough bad news, the duke finally took a breath and said, "We'll have to hurry the wedding so Griff can go with you on your diplomatic duties."

Blaise thought he asked, "What?" But he wasn't sure. He seemed paralyzed all over and couldn't feel his lips move. It was like having an out-of-body experience.

Eversleigh chuckled in glee. He actually chuckled, as if Blaise's entire world had not just collapsed around him. Blaise had the sudden urge to do serious damage to the chair in front of him. He wanted to pick it up and throw it against the wall. He wanted to rip the curtains off the wall and yell until he had no voice, but then the duke came forward and rested a hand on Blaise's shoulder. His chin went high and his shoulders back as he stared down at Blaise with what could only be called pride. "Today at the meeting, King-Consort Raleigh is going to offer you a job that is sure to make you a shoo-in for my replacement." He didn't wait for an answer but wrapped Blaise in a hard hug, pounding his back. After stepping back, Father held him at arm's length, studying him, then hugged him again. "I see you are speechless with joy. Come. You can tell me what it was you wanted to discuss in the lift." The duke gave him one more pat and left.

Blaise stepped around the chair and dropped into it. *This can't be happening. Please let me wake up and realize it's all a bad dream.*

Chapter Twenty

The royal youngster seems to have developed a tendre for society's darling. Could the marriage mart be losing their last prince?

—From *The Regelence Tattler*, the Royal Happenings column

Townsend Castle

HAVING BEEN asked, Dalton would have said nothing could dampen his stellar mood this morning, but after walking into the castle and spotting Percy Edmonstone flirting outrageously with his youngest cousin, he changed his assessment. He was definitely irritated. What was that jackanapes doing here?

Handing his coat, gloves, and hat to Thomas, Dalton didn't take his eyes off Percy. Why was Tarren out here alone with the man?

Percy, or rather Prissy—Blaise was right, Prissy was an apt name for the man—leaned against the banister, dripping with lilac-colored ruffles and false charm. His heavily pomaded blond hair curled over his forehead, and he held a quizzing glass in his left hand. He couldn't get any prissier if he tried. His shoes even had an inch-and-a-half to two-inch block heel on them.

Tarren stood only a foot and a half away—way too close for propriety—in rapt attention to everything the man said. Even in flat brown-topped boots, Tarren was several inches taller than Prissy. And if he leaned any closer….

Dalton strode forward. "Good morning, cousin."

Prissy took one look at the glower on Dalton's face and took a step backward. *Smart man.*

"Why are you here?"

"Dalton." Tarren gasped and gave him a wide-eyed look that said very clearly *behave*.

Dalton ignored the warning and situated himself between Prissy and Tarren.

True to form, Prissy lifted the quizzing glass to his eye and peered at Dalton as if he were some sort of insect.

Dalton had the urge to plant the man a facer right in the quizzing glass and see if it came out the other side, but he only stared back. Lifting his hand, he made a shooing motion. “Run along.”

“I’m here for a meeting that you were not invited to, Ashbourne. Last I heard, you were not a member of the IN Councilman’s Committee.” He brought his finger to his mouth and made a scoffing sound in mock surprise. “Oh, that’s right. You have to babysit Redding. How tedious.” He meant to be insulting, but Dalton didn’t take the bait.

“Bugger off.” Dalton turned from Prissy, giving his attention to his slack-jawed cousin.

There was a huff and a muttered “I never,” followed by clacking heels, and then Prissy went around them and up the stairs. It really was too bad Blaise destroyed that disk.

Dalton grinned at the show of temper. The way that peacock pranced up the stairs did a lot to lift his irritation. Too bad Blaise wasn’t here to enjoy the sight with him, or wait….

“Is Blaise here? What’s this meeting about?” And why hadn’t Blaise mentioned it? The prospect of seeing Blaise had Dalton’s day looking up again. He’d planned on seeing Blaise later when he went and asked the duke for Blaise’s hand, but he certainly wouldn’t mind seeing him now. Galaxy, he had it bad.

Planting two hands in the middle of Dalton’s chest, Tarren shoved him. “What the devil was that for?”

“That man is a complete clod.” Dalton stumbled back, righting himself and straightened his waistcoat.

Crossing his arms over his chest, Tarren frowned. “He is not. You sound like Knighton.”

Knighton was said with so much venom that Dalton arched a brow. What was Tarren’s problem with the Duke of Knighton? He was second-in-command to Wentworth in the Royal Guards and a former RSR soldier. The duke was a bang-up cove. “I always knew I liked Knighton. Edmonstone takes credit for things he doesn’t do.”

“Like what?”

“It doesn’t matter.” Dalton sighed and made a mental note to talk to Uncle Raleigh about Prissy and Tarren’s apparent fascination with him. “Is Blaise here?” Dalton couldn’t help but grin.

Tarren's eyes widened again, and he cocked his head. "Yes." A slow, hesitant smile spread across his lips. "You have a thing for Redding, don't you?"

"I plan on marrying him."

Tarren's eyes went as wide as his smile. "You?" His outrage was completely overcome by his sense of romance. Unlike the rest of his brothers, Tarren had always looked forward to leg shackling himself one day.

"Yes, me. That's why I'm here actually. Where is Uncle Raleigh? And Nate? I need to talk to them about the job they offered me." Dalton barely got the words out before Tarren launched himself at Dalton, hugging him hard.

"This is wonderful news." Letting go of him, Tarren gripped his hand and pulled him up the stairs. "Cony is about to have a meeting with the IN councilman and his committee. Hurry and you might be able to catch him."

They went to the meeting room, and Tarren practically shoved him in the door. Inside, a cacophony of voices filled the room. Men milled about, talking and standing in groups. Thankfully the meeting hadn't started.

Releasing his hand, Tarren pointed toward the room. "Looks like Nate is there, but I don't see Cony yet." Nate was indeed there talking to Wentworth.

Dalton stopped and turned back to his cousin. "Uh, Terror?"

"Yes?"

"Don't say anything about Blaise. I still have to talk to Eversleigh."

Tarren grinned, pinched his fingers together at the corner of his mouth and dragged them across to the other side. He started running toward the staircase going up to the bedrooms, no doubt to go tell Rexley, Aiden, or Colton about Dalton's impending betrothal, but they didn't count, so Dalton shook his head and grinned, but….

"Terror?"

Tarren stopped at the foot of the stairs with his hand on the banister.

"Stay away from Prissy Edmonstone."

"Uh!" Tarren threw his arms up and stomped up the stairs.

Oh yes, he was definitely going to have to talk to Uncle Raleigh about that. Shaking his head, Dalton continued into the noisy room.

The first person he spotted was Blaise, like his body felt Blaise's presence before his mind even registered it. Pleasure filled Dalton to bursting. He couldn't remember ever feeling this way just at the sight of another person.

Blaise turned and looked at him as if feeling his stare. There was something wrong. He didn't seem right. There was an ashen cast to his complexion and his eyes. Those gorgeous peepers that had been so full of laughter and joy hours before were heavy-lidded… haunted.

Dalton started in his direction when his uncle Raleigh walked to the front of the room and sat down on the front of the desk. "Everyone, take a seat. We have a lot to cover."

Well, damn! Apparently, accepting the job offer would have to wait until after the meeting. He should have mentioned it last night, but he'd been in too big of a hurry to go see Blaise.

Uncle Steven, who'd been conversing with Eversleigh, hurried around to the back of the desk and sat in the chair.

Dalton searched for a chair near Blaise but did not find one, so he sat down on the sofa between his father and Wentworth.

"As you all know, we've been looking for Betty Jenkins, and I'm happy to announce that we've found her." Raleigh glanced toward the corner of the room, giving someone a nod.

They all turned.

A lady in a pale green morning gown and with her brown hair piled into an elaborate coiffure, stood in the corner between Nate and Robert Jenkins. Robert had his arm around his mother's waist and appeared much happier than when Dalton had last seen him the prior evening, and no wonder. Betty, for her part, looked tired but happy. Her tense smile matched her son's.

Raleigh started speaking again, drawing Dalton's attention back to him. "And she is under our protection, as you can imagine, and is staying here at the castle with Robert." Again, Raleigh gave a dip of his chin in acknowledgment. "We still have no news on the admiral—it's been months since Betty has heard from him—but we are still searching for him. We're trying to find him before the IN does."

A frisson of unrest ran through Dalton. He'd heard this all last night, but something about now knowing he was staying in the IN made it all seem so much more real. It was a good thing he was taking the job to help watch Nate's back. This new job might prove to be as dangerous as being in the RSR. At least his training would not go to waste.

"Quiet down." Slapping the desk to get everyone's attention, Raleigh started again. He looked more than a little agitated, but Dalton didn't think it was from the talking. "I've called you all here today because I found something on the admiral's drive about the weapons that were stolen over a year ago. They were to be delivered to mercenaries to use against a planet called Skye in the Calluna system."

Blaise gasped and jumped to his feet. "They tried to get Skye to join."

"What?" Raleigh's brow furrowed, and he pinched his chin.

That was it! Blaise had talked about it when he'd been working on treaties.

Blaise nodded. "When I was going through treaties, I noticed that the IN has proposed membership to the planet Skye, but the planet has turned them down. Not once but twice. I thought it was really odd since most planets ask for membership into the IN, not the other way around."

"That's not good," Ravensburg whispered.

"No, it's not," Wentworth whispered back.

Apparently, his uncle agreed. "The admiral also indicated that there was something on Skye that belongs to us… to Regelence. I've decided to appoint a diplomat to go to Skye." He glanced over at Blaise, who'd taken his seat again. "Redding will head up the delegation."

Bloody hell. Dalton's breath hitched in his chest and a stab of fear lanced his gut. This was dangerous. Not only that, Blaise would hate it. "Uncle, isn't that a job more suited to a soldier, someone like Knighton or Wentworth?" Or himself, but no way was Dalton volunteering. Though if Blaise insisted on going, he was damned well going too. Dalton glanced back at Blaise.

Blaise was staring right at him. His cheeks flushed and he immediately looked away. Which told Dalton all he needed to know. He had not told his father he didn't want to work in intergalactic politics.

BLAST, DAMNATION, and dust. Not only had Blaise found himself engaged to the *wrong* man, but now he was entrenched even deeper in Regelence's intergalactic policy. *A diplomat, as if an intern wasn't bad enough.* He had to talk to King-Consort Raleigh, but first he had to talk to his father and Griff. He had a plan, and for the first time since learning of the betrothal, he didn't feel like he was going to cast up his accounts. Clutching his hands together to keep them from shaking, Blaise surveilled the room.

He should have confronted his father in the lift on the way here, but Bannon had tagged along to see Aiden, chattering the whole way and the right time had never presented itself. After thinking it through, he decided that was a good thing. He needed to talk to Griff first before Griff told anyone about the betrothal. Then he'd deal with his father.

Spotting Griff on a love seat next to Viscount Perry, Blaise willed him to look his way, but before he could catch Griff's gaze, people between them stood, blocking him from view. The meeting had ended, and everyone started mingling among themselves, breaking up into groups and sending a cacophony of noise buzzing through the room. Blaise started toward the love seat, but before he took two steps, someone slapped him on the back, offering congratulations.

He nodded and thanked them, but didn't engage in further conversation. He squeezed past another IN Councilman's Committee member and spotted Dalton. A wave of happiness and anxiousness flushed through him. His heart beat faster, and he wanted nothing more than to go to Dalton's side, but he had to fix this bumblebroth he'd landed in, first.

Fortunately, Dalton was talking to Nate and had not seen him, so Blaise hurried past. He'd made Dalton a promise, and he intended on keeping it. When he spoke to Dalton, it would be to tell him that he'd finally talked to his father not just about his future in politics but also about them. He'd tell his father that he was going to marry Dalton. Resolved, Blaise ducked his head and kept going.

He walked right up to where Griff stood talking to Viscount Perry. He gripped Griff's arm and looked over at Perry. "Please excuse us, Perry." It was rude, but Blaise found he didn't really care at the moment. He tugged Griff away, intent on having their conversation out in the hallway, but Griff stopped.

"Blaise, whatever has gotten into you?"

He turned and came face-to-face with the man who had ruined his life and found himself speechless. His hands fisted, and damned if heat didn't wash over him.

Griff grabbed both his hands in his and smiled so brightly and cheerfully that his eyes practically disappeared in his face. At one time,

Blaise had thought that was charming, but at the moment, he found it utterly disgusting how happy Griff looked. "Your father told you?" Griff asked with a guilelessness that said he had no idea how badly Blaise wanted to plant him a facer.

The urge to jerk his hands away was strong, but Blaise reminded himself he was in a crowded room and gently extracted his hands. His anger would do him no good. "Why did you go behind my back?" He congratulated himself on remembering to modulate his voice.

The good cheer slipped right off Griff's face. "I thought you'd be happy?"

"Why would you think that? We're friends, nothing more, and you didn't even give me the courtesy of speaking to me first."

"I…." His face went a bit pale. "I'm sorry." Griff sighed and looked down at his feet. The remorse came off him in waves. "I had hoped…." He glanced up at Blaise and reached for his hand again, only to stop short. "I suppose I thought you'd welcome the proposal. As you said, we are friends, and…." Griff sighed again, his shoulders sagging. "Perhaps in time…."

Blaise started shaking his head before Griff ever finished his sentence.

"Are you certain there is no chance of us making a go of things?"

"I'm sorry, Griff, but no."

With a sigh, Griff nodded reluctantly. "I don't want to lose your friendship. Let's go talk to your father and tell him everything is off."

Blaise took a big breath and blew it out, fluttering his hair. *Oh, thank the glorious stars above.* That was easier than he'd thought. A little part of him actually felt guilty, like he'd kicked a puppy, but he pushed it away. Griff should have talked to him first. "I don't want to lose you as a friend either, Griff, but we are not suited as anything else."

Griff looked away. "There is your father. Come on." Taking his hand, Griff tugged him along through the crowd. He was much politer and slower than Blaise cared for, but really it was a normal pace. He stopped about a yard from the duke and turned back to Blaise. "Just tell me one thing." He paused, but not long enough for Blaise to answer. "It's Ashbourne, isn't it?"

"No. I mean yes, but no." *Fudge.* He was making a hash of things. "We really do make better friends, Griff. We'd probably rub along well enough, but we aren't in love."

"And you are in love with Ashbourne?" His voice pitched higher with incredulousness.

"Yes." Blaise fought not to growl at the affront. He had to remind himself that just a week ago, he'd have been just as doubtful at the thought of him and Dalton together.

"Then I wish you happiness. If ever you decide that he's not right for you…." Giving him a sad little smile, Griff nodded and started him moving again.

Relief filled Blaise, but a knot still took up residence in his stomach. He hated disappointing his father.

They reached the duke as he was shaking hands with Robert Jenkins. He hugged Betty Jenkins and caught sight of Blaise over her shoulder. His bushy brows raised, and then he pulled back from Betty with a smile on his face. "Betty, you remember my son, Redding." He stepped back and held his arm out. His gaze landed on Griff and a chill raced down Blaise's spine.

Blaise knew what was coming next, and he shook his head. "Father, don't—"

"This is his fiancé, Viscount Grantham."

Betty gave him a smile and reached for his hand, pulling him into a hug. She and Robert started offering their felicitations, Robert pounding him on the back, then releasing him to do the same to Griff. It was like time stood still, like everything happened in a well. He could see their lips moving, but he didn't hear what they said exactly.

His father clapped his hands together and his raised voice boomed over the cacophony. "Attention, everyone. I'd like to add good among all the disturbing news we've heard today."

"Father, no." Panic gripped Blaise hard and he whirled around. "Father, don't." He gripped his father's arm, but the duke deftly grabbed his hand before it landed.

The duke grabbed Griff's hand in his other one and continued like he hadn't heard Blaise. "My son, Redding, and Grantham here are getting married."

Blaise wanted to die. He was certain of it and at the moment he welcomed it. His stomach tied itself in knots and his chest tightened up, refusing to let him breathe deeply. It had a stranglehold on his lungs to the point of pain.

Everyone came at him at once. There were well-wishes, backslaps, and even a lewd comment or two. Blaise barely heard any of it. He pasted a smile on his face, searching the crowd for Dalton. He had no idea what he'd say when he found him, but he had to find Dalton.

Someone grabbed his arm and propelled him forward.

Blaise turned to see who it was.

Griff was looking straight ahead with a smile on his face. Through gritted teeth he said, "Just keep walking." And Blaise couldn't find the words or will to refuse.

Together they made it to the door, and Griff let go of him. Turning his back toward Blaise, he began talking to someone.

Spotting freedom, Blaise didn't stop. He'd thank Griff later. He opened the door and slipped out, then closed it behind him. He made it to the railing of the staircase and leaned over it, trying to catch his bearings. This was not supposed to happen. Everything had just gotten a whole lot more complicated.

He was so caught up in his thoughts that he didn't hear the door open and close behind him, until his arm was snagged in a hard grip.

"What the fuck, Blaise?"

Dalton. Relief battled with angst as Blaise turned his head. Angst won out.

Dalton's jaw was as hard as granite. His stormy gaze focused like a laser on the landing below them and Dalton dragged him down the stairs.

"I can explain."

"Then by all means, please do." The words were clipped and angry. *Rightfully so.*

In hindsight, maybe he should have talked to Dalton first. "I knew nothing about it until after you left. My father sprang it on me. He signed a betrothal contract without ever talking to me."

"And you didn't tell him you refused to honor it?" His words incredulous, Dalton stopped on the stairs and gawked at him before shaking his head and continuing.

They finally made it to the ground floor, and Dalton let go of him. His hand fisted by his side and an angry tick started in his jaw, much like Blaise had seen King-Consort Raleigh's do when he was out of sorts. Even knowing that Dalton wouldn't hit him, it was frightening.

"I tried. He wouldn't let me get a word in edgewise, but I already talked to Griff and called it off."

The vexation seemed to evaporate from Dalton, but he didn't say anything for several moments.

Blaise sagged, needing something to lean on. He wanted to throw his arms around Dalton, but he couldn't, not here in the open. Instead, he caught Dalton's hand and squeezed.

Dalton squeezed back. "All right, here is what we'll do. We'll just go back in there and ask your father to come to the study. We'll tell him we're getting married. Then he can go upstairs and announce it."

"What?" Blaise shook his head, convinced he'd heard wrong. "Are you completely dicked in the nob? We can't just go announce to everyone that there was a huge mistake and now I'm marrying you instead. What will people think? We have to let some time pass." There was no way he could cry off so soon without causing a scandal. He'd have to wait a respectable amount of time. Even then, his reputation would not escape untarnished. "I'll tell my father when we get home and then…."

His hand might as well have been on fire for as fast as Dalton released it and stepped back out of reach. He smiled, but it was not a pleasant expression. "Your reputation is more important to you than I am? I can't do that again. I won't. Good bye, Blaise." He turned and walked away.

And Blaise let him, because he didn't know what to say. What could he say? He watched Dalton until the door to the servants' corridor closed behind him, and then the pain in his chest became too much. It wasn't supposed to be this way.

A sob caught in his throat, and the door blurred through his tears. He decided to take his own leave then, but a sound behind him made him turn.

As if his broken heart wasn't enough, he now had to add humiliation to the mix.

Bannon and Prince Aiden stood at the study door. Their silence and the pitying expressions on their faces said they'd witnessed the whole thing.

CHAPTER TWENTY-ONE

Hearts all over Classige are breaking. The demon lord is shipping out.
—From *The Classige Examiner.*

Fairfax House

SWIRLING THE whiskey in his glass, Dalton lifted his forearm off the balcony rail just enough to take a sip. *Ahhh….* The last of the whiskey went down with a pleasant burn. After setting it on the rail, he snagged the other tumbler and cupped it between his hands, going back to his slouch against the railing. Good thinking, grabbing two tumblers before he headed out here.

It was snowing again, but somehow instead of being magical, it seemed to mirror his mood. The clouds covered the moon, and the wind was almost nonexistent. The snow was just there, kind of like him. The chill in the air was bearable, and it was quiet out here, thanks to the blanket of white covering the treetops and the ground. A part of him hated to leave all this. He'd miss the snow, but he couldn't stay. Not now.

There was a click behind him, signaling that his solitude was at an end. Maybe if he just ignored whichever one of his parents had decided to retrieve him, they'd go away.

"Mind if I join you?"

No such luck. Dalton glanced over as his father stepped up next to him.

"Two drinks, huh?" He rested his gloved hands on the rail and stared out at the night. "I wish you weren't going. Are you sure there is nothing I can say to make you stay?" And there it was. His parents had been trying to talk him into staying since Dalton had told Nate that he'd changed his mind about being the admiral's aide and staying in the IN.

Dalton sighed. Part of him really wanted to tell his father to sod off, but he had told Blaise he'd try to make amends with his parents. Did that even count anymore since he and Blaise were no longer together? In all honesty, he supposed they'd never truly been together, not publicly anyway, and that stung. Blaise hadn't kept the promise he'd made.... Which was why Dalton had to leave. He couldn't be here in Classige and watch Blaise from afar, knowing he could never truly have him. Dalton shook his head. "I need to do this."

"I understand, but I can't help but think this is my fault. I made you feel that way about Redding, I mean."

Dalton shrugged. It wasn't entirely, but he'd be lying if he said his father's actions hadn't had some bearing on his feelings. The past couldn't be overlooked that easily, but it wasn't the main reason. He could never be what Blaise needed him to be. It just would not work. Swirling his drink some more, he watched it splash high up on the sides without going over.

His father leaned down, resting his arms on the railing, mimicking Dalton's pose, and blocked what little breeze there was on Dalton's right side, making it feel warmer. Not that it had been all that cold in the first place. It was a sight better out here than it was inside a crowded ballroom, which was on the agenda shortly. "Dalton, I'm sorry. I should have had your grandsire committed all those years ago." He was quiet for several moments, and then he turned his head, staring right at Dalton. "I was wrong, and if I could do it over, I would."

Dalton gasped. He'd never expected an apology. What's more, now he wasn't even sure he deserved it, but the fact that his father offered it.... Warmth radiated throughout his chest. "I'm not so sure you were. Wrong, I mean." He turned back to his glass, thinking this would be easier to admit without looking at his father. Did that make him a coward? "I've been contemplating something Blaise said. I dismissed it because I was still so hurt over you sending me away, but the more I think about it, the more I think he might be right. It would have hurt a lot more people if you'd had your sire put in an asylum."

"Maybe. Maybe not." He reached over and grabbed Dalton's drink out of his hand and took a swallow. The way he did it without making eye contact made Dalton think it was liquid courage, and his next words confirmed it. "It was my foolish pride. I felt guilty for not being there, and I wanted to put the whole thing behind me. Get it over with. I took the easy way out. The only people who mattered were you and your sire. The rest of us could have weathered the storm. Your uncle Raleigh is a tough, resilient man, and by the time you and your cousins made your come-out, it would have all blown over." Ravensburg started sloshing the whiskey side to side, spilling some in his agitation.

Stilling his father's hand, Dalton threw his own words back at him. "Maybe. Maybe not."

Turning his head, Ravensburg met his gaze and a slow smile slipped onto his lips.

Dalton smiled back, and just like that, they came to some sort of silent agreement. They were really going to let the past go and begin again, or maybe his parents already had, but now Dalton had a new resolve to live up to his end of the deal. "Thank you for not demanding I be home at certain hours and for giving me some freedom."

"Well, restricting you didn't work last time. I thought I'd try a new approach. I just wanted to get you back home. I hoped given time, if I could get you to come home and spend time with us, we could make you see how important you are to us."

Somehow that made everything seem so much clearer. And for the tenth time since he and Blaise had parted ways, he actually felt as though he was important to his parents.

He took the drink back from his father and finished it off. "I'll be back. It's not like I'm going to be stationed on a different planet. I won't even be on a different continent. If I ship out, it will only be for short periods."

"You'll stay at home when you come back?"

Dalton grinned and turned the empty tumbler around and around in his hand. "Yeah."

"Good." He was quiet for several moments, just staring out at the night, sharing the silence. And for once it was a companionable silence.

"Blaise lives this perfect life, and I can't be a part of it. I'm not perfect, and I don't want to be." He wasn't sure why he said it; he needed to voice aloud everything that was in his head. He needed to resolve this once and for all.

One dark brow rose in a perfect imitation of Uncle Raleigh.

"I'm not planning on running out and causing a spectacle of myself. What you've seen the past week is the real me." The whole thing was actually kind of ironic because he'd built a reputation as a dissolute to hurt his father, but in the end, he'd only hurt himself. "Blaise is so afraid of bucking the system and what society has deemed proper for him that he won't even talk to his father and tell him he doesn't want to be the next IN councilman. He's actually prepared to be miserable to please others." Everything he did was because he was supposed to. No, that wasn't exactly true. Blaise had made love to him and been with him because he wanted to, but it was all done in secret. And he'd worked hard to keep that secret, dressing in common clothes, making sure he had an alibi and his valet's help. Even running after that damned box and risking his reputation was to save his reputation. "I can't compete with his idea of perfection. I can't do that for the rest of my life." A pang hit Dalton in the chest, and damned if his eyes didn't blur.

"You love him."

Dalton didn't even try to deny it. "Very much, but it doesn't change anything."

"Are you sure? If he loves you too…."

"He does," he said with a slight hesitation, but then the truth of it hit him. Blaise did love him, but he didn't love him enough.

"Then you should talk to him."

He shook his head. "It wouldn't do any good." He couldn't change who Blaise was, and he wasn't even sure he wanted to. Part of that stuffiness was what he loved about Blaise, but he couldn't live with it. And Blaise could not live with Dalton's blasé attitude toward the world they lived in. It would drive him mad. He'd forever go around trying to correct the things Dalton did that he saw as wrong.

"You aren't going to listen to me, are you?"

Groaning, Dalton looked down at his glass again and stood up from the rail. "No," he answered, walking toward the door.

"Where are you going?"

Dalton grabbed the doorknob but turned his head to look at his father. "To get another drink. Then to say goodbye to the rest of the family."

"Do you want me to go with you?" Standing up straight, Ravensburg leaned his hip against the rail and crossed his arms over his chest.

"No."

"Dalton?"

"Yeah?"

"I love you."

Damnation, as if the breakup with Blaise wasn't enough…. Without turning around, he looked up at the ceiling of the patio and sniffed. "I love you too, Father. I'm going to miss you." Almost as much as he would miss Blaise.

Sunnyside House, the Baron of Perry's residence in Classige, Pruluce

BLAISE WALKED into the ballroom and nearly turned around and walked back out. The music was too loud, and the air was too stifling from all the bodies. To say he was slightly on edge was putting a fine point on things, but he couldn't take it anymore.

It had been only three days since he'd last seen Dalton, and it felt as though someone had ripped his heart out. He couldn't eat. He couldn't sleep, and he certainly couldn't concentrate on work. Galaxy, Blaise missed him.

At first he'd switched back and forth from wishing a pox on Dalton and desperate to see him. Sometime in the last twenty-four hours, he'd just become plain desperate. When a new guard had shown up to retrieve him this morning and take him to the House of Lords, it had been the last straw.

"Are you really sure you want to do this?"

"I have to try." Blaise glanced over at Griff and smiled. Somehow through all this, the man had become an even better friend.

"Then let's go find him." Griff extended an arm for Blaise to take. Griff felt guilty for his part in things and was trying his damnedest to make it up to Blaise. He and Larkinson had tried practically everything they could think of to take Blaise's mind of Dalton, but none of it had worked. Not even Lizzy had taken the gut-wrenching emptiness away.

Blaise placed his hand on Griff's steady arm, thankful for the strength. Larkinson had done her best with the bags under Blaise's eyes, but the lack of sleep was beginning to catch up to him.

"What is the plan?"

"I don't know… exactly." The only thing his convoluted brain had been able to come up with was talk to Dalton. It seemed as good a plan as any, but he knew what Griff was asking. He wanted to know what they were going to do when they spotted Dalton. "I suppose, I'll just ask him if we can speak, and then ask him to come with me to the library."

"And what if someone sees the two of you go in there together?"

That he had not thought about. He wasn't even sure he cared. His care for his reputation had gotten him into this mess in the first place. If he'd just agreed with Dalton and gone back and told his father the truth… well, the scandal would not have been bad. The IN Councilman's Committee was a small group of men very unlikely to gossip. Which was why they were on the committee in the first place. Father surely could have kept them quiet about the whole thing.

The music droned on with the chorus of a cotillion as they meandered their way around the people standing on the edge of the dance floor. Blaise spotted practically everyone he knew, but not Dalton. The queasiness in his stomach churned. "Are you certain he's here?"

"I heard him announced only half an hour ago."

So he'd arrived well before Blaise, which meant he must have heard Blaise announced. Was Dalton avoiding him? Blaise was beginning to think just that when he finally spotted him.

Across the room, Dalton stood talking to his cousin Prince Colton and his consort, Viscount Wentworth. Dalton wore all black, from his cravat to his boots.

A pang hit Blaise in the chest. He loved Dalton all in black. It set off his fair features and emphasized his personality. Bold, elegant, and just a little mischievous. His blond hair looked like spun gold, shiny, soft gold, and he practically glowed. He did not appear anywhere as haggard as Blaise. He actually smiled at something Wentworth said and nodded in agreement with the viscount. He was put-together and… normal… like he had most definitely not been pining. Shouldn't he seem as miserable as Blaise?

Blaise's stomach clenched, and doubt crept in. Maybe this was a mistake. What if Dalton refused to talk to him?

"Are you all right?" Griff asked.

"I just need a moment." Blaise dropped his hand from Griff's arm and backed up a few steps to get out of the way. He'd almost convinced himself this was a bad idea and then Dalton turned slightly. Not looking at Blaise but to his right. The smile had slipped off his face, and there was something in his eyes. They were… haunted. He, too, had bags under his eyes as if he hadn't gotten much sleep.

"He's leaving, you know." Prince Rexley had stepped up next to him and noticed the object of Blaise's attention.

Blaise started at the new voice. Then the words registered and a sinking feeling settled in Blaise's gut. "What do you mean?"

Rexley gave him a soft smile before gazing past him and nodding. "Grantham."

"Your Highness." Griff bowed his head.

"This is for you." Rexley handed Griff a folded piece of paper.

"What's this?" Griff asked as he opened it up and started reading.

Blaise wanted to groan. Who cared what it was. He turned back to Rexley. "What do you mean?"

"I have no idea. Winstol asked me to give it to you." Glancing back at Blaise, Rexley stared at him for several moments. "I wasn't sure if I should tell you this, but after seeing you…." He shrugged. "You look like the very devil, by the way."

Aargh! Only the fact that it would probably be considered assault and a hanging offense kept Blaise from shaking his friend. "Thank you. Now finish telling me."

"Dalton decided not to take the job that Nate offered him, after all. He's still in the Regelence Navy, and he's shipping out tonight." The tone in Rexley's voice gave nothing away, but the tick in his jaw said a lot. He was not happy about the news.

"Well, that's odd," Griff mumbled.

What was he talking about? And why was he interrupting?

Griff touched his arm. "Are you going to be okay here?"

No. "Yes," Blaise snapped and turned back to Rexley. "Why is he leaving?"

"Why do you think?"

"Because of me?" *Oh galaxy!* He was too late. Why hadn't he come to his senses yesterday?

One dark brow arched as if to say, *you think?*

Instead of pining, Dalton was running. "He wants to get away from me." His voice sounded pathetic even to his own ears. He looked back to where Dalton had stood. For a few seconds, the dancing couples concealed his view, but then parted to reveal Dalton on the same spot.

He was still talking, but now he'd been joined by the Duke of Knighton. Again his reactions seemed genial, and Blaise began to question his resolve.

"I was going to go talk to him, try to change his mind about us."

"Then do it." The sharpness in Rexley's voice got his attention. "He was hurt. I've never seen him like this, Blaise. He loves you."

"Then why did he call everything off? Why couldn't he wait?"

Rexley stared at him like it should be obvious and didn't say anything for several moments. He glanced back at Dalton. "He thinks the two of you are too different and don't suit."

Blaise looked too, focusing on those strong wide shoulders, and the truth hit him like a slap in the face. "He thinks I can't live with his past and that I want to change him."

"Do you?"

Shaking his head, Blaise stared at the man he loved. "No. I want him to be who he is. The man I fell in love with."

"Then go tell him."

As if it were that easy. "I intend to." He still didn't know what he would say, but he knew what Dalton needed to hear, and for now that was enough. He had fifteen yards to figure it all out. He started walking, but was brought up short by a whirlwind of flapping arms in the guise of a prince.

Prince Aiden came out of nowhere, like the hounds of hell were on his heels, and nearly knocked Blaise down. He panted, was out of breath, and sagged a bit as if trying to compose himself, then steadied Blaise. Unfortunately he also grabbed Blaise's arm and dragged him back toward Rexley. "Did you give Viscount Grantham a note?"

Rexley nodded. "Yes. Jeremy asked me to."

"I'm going to throttle him!" Aiden said. He thrust his fingers through his hair in a violent jab and turned to Blaise. "Bannon is about to do something very stupid."

Somehow Blaise was not surprised. His brother was always about to do something very foolish, but something in Aiden's voice said this might be worse than usual. Galaxy help him, he could not deal with another stolen snuffbox… metaphorically speaking. "I will deal with this in a moment. Right now I have to speak to Dalton." He tried to tug free of Aiden's grip, but Aiden didn't let go.

"Let me guess, Jeremy is in on this?" Rexley asked.

Biting his bottom lip, Aiden grimaced. "I'm afraid all of us are… uh, were. I tried to talk him out of it." Aiden huffed out a breath, further messing up the ebony locks he'd already tortured. "He thinks if he does this, it will pave the way for you to immediately cry off from your engagement, and then you will be able to be with Dalton sooner."

For once he and his brother were on the same page. Maybe that was exactly what he needed. No that *was* exactly what he needed.

"He's going to compromise Grantham by having him caught with a naked footman."

The music came to an end just as Rexley said, "Oh, for the love of…."

"Exactly. So, come on," Aiden replied.

Blast and damnation. Blaise was going to commit fratricide. He could not in good conscience allow Griff to be ruined because of his brother's well-meaning half-baked scheme. Glancing over his shoulder, he looked for Dalton, but he no longer stood with Wentworth, Prince Colton, and Knighton.

Panic slammed into Blaise, stealing his breath. He started walking, searching the crowd. Bannon and Griff would have to wait.

"There he is." A hand landed on his shoulder as another one pointed past him. He wasn't sure if it was Rexley or Aiden, but he didn't stop walking.

Dalton was only about five yards from the ballroom door, his long legs moving in ground-eating strides.

"I have to talk to him."

"Then go get him. We'll stop Bannon."

Again, he wasn't sure if it was Rexley or Aiden who spoke, but Blaise was already walking toward Dalton.

He picked up his pace, but the crowd was just too thick. He couldn't possibly get by them in time. The only clear path was the dance floor, and it wasn't exactly clear. Couples lined up for the next set. It was his only chance….

Fear clawed its ugly way up Blaise's insides. His father was going to be so disappointed in him, but he was now certain he could not live without Dalton. Running out onto the dance floor, Blaise ignored the stares and gasps. He focused on the exit and his love's shoulders and raised his voice as loud as he could. "Ashbourne!"

The cacophony of voices sputtered out. The room grew quieter and quieter until one could have heard a pin drop. Every eye in the room was on Blaise. Very slowly the crowd seemed to part, leaving a direct line from him to Dalton.

He felt as though he were going to faint, but he forced himself to cup his hands around his mouth and try again. "Dalton!"

At first he didn't think Dalton had heard him, but then he stopped. Those wide shoulders stiffened.

Blaise dropped his hands and started walking, aware of the stares and whispers like needles stabbing him all over. Galaxy help him, he'd never had to do anything so hard in his life. He had to enunciate very carefully to keep from stuttering. "Dalton, you can't leave." *Oh, please don't leave.... And please turn around.*

"Why not?" Dalton turned finally. His gaze took in the crowd, then settled on Blaise. He didn't appear the least bit embarrassed, but then he didn't look impressed either. His face was as hard as granite, and even from here, the arch of that blond brow was visible.

It was not what Blaise had been expecting. He'd expected a smile at least or… something. But Dalton gave no indication of his feelings. "Why not?" Blaise parroted. He felt as though he were about to cast up his accounts, and it had nothing to do with embarrassment and everything to do with his heart breaking into tiny little pieces. It was too little too late, but he'd come so far; he couldn't stop now. "Because I love you!"

"And?" Dalton had started walking back toward him.

Blaise resumed walking too. "And if you don't marry me immediately, I'll...." He swallowed hard. He had nothing to lose. "I'll tell everyone that you compromised me." He stopped two feet from Dalton, certain his heart could not pound any harder.

For several moments, they both just stood there. It was the longest moment of Blaise's life. He was on the verge of begging, when finally those perfect lips twitched and Dalton reached for him.

It was like everything stopped and Blaise breathed his first full breath in three whole days. With shaking hands, Blaise rushed into his arms.

Squeezing him so tight it was almost painful, Dalton kissed his cheek and whispered, "I love you too, angel. I love you too." He pulled back, and in true Dalton fashion, addressed the dumbfounded crowd. "For the record, it was Redding who compromised me!"

No longer caring about the crowd, Blaise blinked in surprise, then burst out laughing.

Dalton gripped his face and kissed him. His tongue swept in, caressing and leaving the lingering taste of whiskey behind. The kiss started out so hot, Blaise's toes curled inside his boots, but quickly became something else entirely. Dalton seemed to pour every ounce of sweetness into the kiss, the slow slide of his tongue and the soft breath pushing into Blaise's mouth was somehow more erotic than fast and frenzied. The kiss made him feel cherished.

Finally they parted, but not very far. Dalton still held his face, his thumbs stroking Blaise's cheeks, and their foreheads touched, giving them the illusion of privacy. The ballroom had gone utterly silent.

"I can't believe you did this," Dalton whispered.

Blaise ignored the shuffling as some lords tried to move closer. "Neither can I, but I was afraid that you wouldn't listen to me otherwise. I had to do something."

Closing his eyes, Dalton breathed deeply before opening them again. "I will always listen to you, Blaise, even if I'm mad at you." Dalton slanted his lips across Blaise's in a kiss that would leave the ton talking for years, but before Blaise could give himself up fully to the kiss, a hoarse yell rent the air, followed by a loud crash from somewhere in the hallway behind them.

"What is it?" Dalton asked, looking toward the hallway too.

"Bannon." Even as Blaise said it, he hoped it wasn't true, but he knew otherwise. "Between the two of us, the Thompson name is quite thoroughly ruined." But oh, it was so worth it.

EPILOGUE

The demon lord has finally been caught and by an angel, no less.
—From *Pruluce Weekly*, the Beau Monde Happenings column

The vestry of Regelence Cathedral, in Classige, Pruluce

"IS IT very bad of me to want the diplomat job just to keep Prissy from having it?"

Dalton shifted his gaze in the mirror from the gold cords on his shoulder—marking his new position as Nate's aide—to the door, but with his father in the way, he couldn't get a good view of Blaise.

Blaise closed it behind him with a quick snap.

Ravensburg, who'd been adjusting the collar on Dalton's IN dress whites, groaned and answered before Dalton had the chance. "Yes, it is most decidedly bad because I'm very much looking forward to not having to deal with Prissy for the next several months." It amused Dalton how his father had taken up Blaise's nickname for Percy. "If you renege and accept that job, you will no longer be my favorite future son-in-law."

"I'm your only future son-in-law," Blaise shot back.

Grinning at the byplay, Dalton gave his cords one last tug to make sure they were in the right place, turned around, and nearly swallowed his tongue.

Blaise's wedding suit made him look… angelic. *Larkinson did well.* Dalton had suggested light colors to match his dress whites, but he hadn't considered it would make his love the very image of Dalton's pet name for him. His morning coat and trousers were dove gray, his shoes glossy black, and his shirt and cravat white. His waistcoat was white with metallic silver embroidery. The only thing missing was a halo and wings. *Galaxy*, he was lovely.

Leaning against the door, Blaise scoffed, blowing hair off his forehead. "I can't believe King-Consort Raleigh gave the job to him." *Him* was said with much suffering.

"He gave him the job so you could stay here with me, now that I'm staying in Classige as Nate's aide. Well, and I think Raleigh wanted to get him out of the way. Edmonstone seems intent on sniffing after Tarren." Maybe Dalton should get another copy of that disk?

Finally, Blaise looked at Dalton and a slow, sensual smile spread across his lips. Those green eyes sparkled with interest, and he pushed off of the door. "I do believe I like dress whites more than BDUs."

And Dalton was pretty sure he liked that Blaise liked them better. He stepped past his father and met Blaise in the middle of the room. "What are you doing in here?"

The door clicked open again, and Arthur Fairfax came inside like the whirlwind he was, with the ring box in one hand and two boutonnières in the other. "Barclay, I have our—*ack*!" His gaze landed on Blaise, and he shook his head. "You aren't supposed to see each other before the wedding."

A lovely blush crept up Blaise's cheeks. "I was just…."

The door opened yet again. "Has anyone seen…. Oh, there you are." The Duke of Eversleigh closed the door behind him. He met Dalton's gaze and smiled. "You look smashing, Ashbourne." It was a genuine compliment that made Dalton smile back.

Much to Dalton's surprise, the duke had welcomed him to the family with open arms, saying if Blaise loved him, then that was enough. The fact that Blaise's proposal was seen by the ton as "the love match of the decade" probably helped, but Dalton believed the duke genuinely liked him.

"Thank you, Your Grace." Dalton became aware of Blaise's stiffening posture beside him and slipped his hand into his, offering support. Obviously Eversleigh hadn't told Blaise about his surprise yet.

The duke took one look at their linked hands and sighed. "He's here, Blaise."

"He is?" Blaise practically bounced on his toes and threw his arms around Dalton. "He's here."

Dalton chuckled, relieved.

The duke obviously was too. He smiled and winked at Dalton, then opened his mouth to speak.

Having a suspicion what it was he was going to say, Dalton gave a small head shake and disguised it as a kiss on Blaise's cheek. He'd let the duke take credit for this surprise. Dalton had another one up his sleeve.

Eversleigh gave him a brief nod in acknowledgment.

Unfortunately ships from Regelence to Englor were few and far between—the last one for six months left about two hours before the wedding was scheduled to start—so Eversleigh had officially booked Bannon passage on a craft headed to Englor immediately after Bannon's failed scandal. Though *failed* wasn't a very good description, since there had definitely been a scandal. Instead of ruining Griff, Bannon had been spotted coming out of the library. Which wouldn't have been a big deal, but there had been a very naked, and according to the rumors, very well-endowed footman in the library, waiting on Griff. Sadly, had Bannon gone on the booked flight, he would have missed the wedding, so Dalton had suggested instead that Eversleigh get Bannon and his valet on the *Lady Anna*, which was set to leave the morning after this, along with the diplomatic crew headed to Skye.

"All right, gentlemen. Shall we?" Arthur asked and immediately started directing. "Okay, Dalton, let go of Blaise and take your father's arm, and Blaise, you take your father's arm, and I'll walk behind, and…. Barclay, what are you doing?"

Ravensburg grabbed his spouse by the hand and started pulling him out of the room. Without breaking stride, Father called over his shoulder, "Why don't you boys come out together?"

What a splendid idea. Dalton made a mental note to thank his father. The more Dalton got to know him again, the more he liked him. His father and sire were going to be wonderful grandparents. Dalton's smile faded. Where had that thought come from?

Eversleigh chuckled and followed behind.

Blaise cocked his head, his brow wrinkling. "What?"

"Er… nothing. Come on. I have a surprise for you." Dalton led them out of the vestry with a sense of wonderment. He'd never thought he'd get leg shackled, and here he was. So maybe the idea of kids was something he should consider.

"Dalton, really, you don't have to get me anything…." Blaise's words trailed off, and his face lit up so brightly, Dalton had no doubt he'd seen the surprise.

In the back row of pews sat the orphans, all dressed in their finery. Finery Dalton and Blaise had purchased. And for a man who professed not to care one way or another about wanting his own children, Blaise's face sure did shine when he saw them.

Little Archie smiled and waved at them, showing off a missing tooth that had been in place the last time they saw him.

Dalton waved back and noticed Blaise doing likewise.

"You brought them?" Blaise reached up and touched his face.

"Trying to better their lives is something we've done together. I thought it was only fitting that they be here while I better mine."

For the second time in his life, Blaise made a spectacle of himself for Dalton's benefit. He kissed Dalton right there in the back of the cathedral in front of everyone. It was their last kiss… as single men.

Exclusive Excerpt

My Highland Laird

A Sci-Regency Novel: sequel to *Diplomatic Relations*

By J.L. Langley

Bannon Thompson, talented artist and youngest son of the Duke of Eversleigh, is hastily shipped off to avoid scandal after his latest indiscretion. But after crashing on a rural world, leaving him and his valet the sole survivors of Regelence's diplomatic mission, Bannon must navigate the complexities of a primitive clan society and take up a role he never wanted: helping a sexy Highlander ensure the safety of both their planets.

Laird Ciaran MacKay wants nothing more than to keep his clan safe, especially from the off-world intruders who killed his father. Suspecting complicity among his own people, he has no choice but to trust outsiders from a spaceship crash—and he can't seem to fight his attraction to the stubborn redhead.

Drawn to the ruggedly handsome laird, Bannon risks a bold affair that would ruin him in the eyes of his society. But there is more at stake than reputations as Bannon and Ciaran uncover the Intergalactic Navy's plot and find the secret of what belongs to Regelence that has been hidden on Skye.

When the rescue Bannon longed for threatens to take him away, Ciaran fears their love might not survive beyond the rugged beauty of the Highlands.

The Lady Anna, *Intergalactic Navy destroyer, under the command of Captain Brittani Kindros*

SO HELP him, if Percy Edmonstone said one more word about Blaise and Dalton, Bannon was going to plant him a facer. Or perhaps he should take it up with his father for banishing him in the first place. He'd only been trying to help his sibling and somehow he'd ended up here, on a destroyer with the ton's darling. *Stars*, didn't family loyalty count for something?

If he made it to Englor without being thrown in the stockade—or whatever the jail was called on an IN destroyer—for murder, it'd be a miracle.

Actually, destroyer jail might not be a bad idea. I wouldn't have to deal with anyone; I could just draw.

Bannon groaned at the thought and steadied the tea tray he carried. Leave it to Timothy, his sometimes annoyingly perky muse, to find a bright side. Gritting his teeth, he stormed out of the mess deck and nearly slammed into a group of sailors going in. The top of his teapot rattled, the cups fell off the saucers, and the biscuits slid off the plate.

Someone grabbed his tray to steady it. "Sorry, Lord Bannon. I didn't see you there."

Blast, he'd been so distracted with his fury, he hadn't been paying attention to where he was going. Bannon made himself relax his jaw muscles and looked up.

Lieutenant Taylor smiled at him, showing off a lovely set of dimples. The men walking with him paused too, but Taylor gave them a nod. "Go on without me." He set the cups back on the saucers and reached for the biscuits, but stopped short. "I'll, uh, let you fix the rest. Would you like me to carry this for you?"

Bannon shook his head, his anger fading somewhat. Trouble was right; Taylor was handsome with his dark good looks. A little on the short side—not that Bannon had room to talk—but he filled out a uniform superbly, and to top it off, he was really nice. Regardless what Louie thought, Bannon was certain Taylor preferred men to women. Maybe a shipboard affair would improve his mood? He'd never actually had an affair, but he was away from home, and chaperones, and.... But no, it would only make things worse. Galaxy only knew what would happen if his parents found out.

"Lord Bannon?" Taylor ducked down into his line of sight with that charming grin still in place. "Everything okay?"

"Yeah, sure. Just preoccupied."

Perhaps he'd agree to posing for me in the buff. That isn't as bad as an affair, and it's for the sake of art, Timothy whispered in his head.

Galaxy help him, he just couldn't seem to help himself. He almost voiced the request. He couldn't even imagine how far he'd be banished for that.

It would totally be worth it.

No, it would not! Great, he was arguing with himself again.

"Are you sure you don't want me to carry this to your quarters?" Taylor asked.

Oh boy, would I.

"Er, no, but thank you for the offer." He'd have to get rid of Louie, and that would raise questions. Just because he wasn't on Regelence didn't mean that everyone didn't expect him to act as a lord of the realm. Besides, it wasn't like he could brag to Trouble about his conquest, and that would take some of the fun out of it.

"Well, then I'll let you carry on." Taylor walked toward the mess deck, then stopped. "I don't know if anyone has informed you, but we're about an hour away from Skye."

Thank galaxy. "Thanks Lieutenant." Bannon continued on his way to his cabin. In one more hour, he'd be rid of Prissy, and if he spent that time painting, he wouldn't have to see the man again. At least not until he went back to Regelence. Whenever that would be.

The door, or hatch as it was called, on his cabin slid open, and once again he nearly wore the tea as Louie barreled out the door. This time one of the cups went sailing off the tray and hit the purple carpet. It rolled as everything else rattled and Bannon shifted his weight taking several steps back while bending forward to keep his tray upright. "Dust, Louie!"

"Blast, Bannon," Louie shouted at the same time.

Shaking his head, he walked past her as she retrieved the cup. "Where were you going in such a hurry?"

"To come find you."

"I told you I'd get the tea." He set the tray on the small table next to the porthole and plopped down in one of the two chairs. This seat had been a source of comfort for the last fortnight. Who knew the utter blackness of space could be so soothing? It tickled Timothy, and Bannon had already done three good paintings sitting in front of this porthole. He'd also had dozens of splendid daydreams… mostly about Lieutenant Taylor.

"You know I am your servant, right?" Setting the cup down on the tray, Louie sat opposite him.

"You're my valet and my dearest friend. Not my servant. Besides, you got the tea last time."

"A valet is a servant."

It was an old argument they'd yet to resolve. "Shut up, Louie." Bannon proceeded to pour them tea, then added three lumps of sugar to his and four to hers.

She picked up the cup and took a sip, staring at him over the top of it with one of her perfectly shaped brown brows arched. "What took so long?"

"I was contemplating whether a trip to the jail was worth it."

"It's called a brig."

Know-it-all. Bannon took a drink of his own tea and promptly added another lump of sugar. "I ran into Prissy."

With a sigh, Louie shook her head. "He will be gone from our presence in exactly one hour."

"How do you know that?" He frowned and took a sip of his tea. *Awww… much better.*

She preened, damn her, and something told him that he was not going to like her answer.

"Lieutenant Taylor stopped by to tell me. Annnd… you owe me a pound."

"Oh, you didn't…."

She preened more and touched her lips and sighed dramatically. Then she smiled, took another sip, raising her pinky high in the air, and turned her head to the right. "Oh, look, a planet. I bet that's Skye."

He wasn't falling for that. Studying her lips, he narrowed his eyes, and…. *Dust and stars!* They *did* look swollen and redder than normal. "You kissed him?"

"I'd never kiss and tell."

He grabbed a biscuit and threw it at her, then glanced out the porthole. A planet *was* out there, but it sure was cloudy. Ominous gray clouds circled it, with some shooting high up into the atmosphere around it, like smoke. It was difficult to make out the planet's round shape, but it certainly was mystical looking. He'd found the subject of his next painting and… was that lightning? *Capital!* It looked strange from that point of view, but beautiful.

She took a bite of the biscuit and singsonged, "You owe me a pound."

"Just because he kissed you, doesn't mean he isn't gay."

She gave him the most incredulous look as if to ask, *really?*

Right. It was a rather stupid statement, but she'd won their last two wagers. Drat it all, so it was his turn to win. Bannon picked up his cup and glared at her over the rim. As he set his lips to the porcelain, a loud blast sounded and shook the whole ship. The contents of his cup sloshed out onto his chin, shirt, and lap.

Bannon yowled.

Louie shrieked.

"Bloody hell! What was that?" He jumped up and brushed the tea off him. *Damn that was hot!* As he grabbed for the tea towel, the ship shook again followed by another long bang. The tea set rattled fiercely and tea sloshed out of Louie's cup. Bannon dabbed at his trousers. "*Anna*, what's going on?"

The ship did not answer. *Not good. Anna* always answered. Bannon had carried on entire conversations with her since he'd been on board. She was really nice.

"Bannon?" Louie's voice quivered, and she reached for him.

"It's all right. Probably just turbulence." Even as the words left his mouth, he didn't believe them. Did ships even get turbulence in space? He didn't know, but he suspected this was much more than a pocket of air, since space was technically a vacuum. Oh bother, this didn't bode well. His chest tightened and a quiver snaked through him. He pulled Louie up from her seat and against his chest, hugging her tight. They should probably sit back down so they didn't fall, in case it happened again, but his seat was wet.

The hatch door whisked open, and Lieutenant Taylor rushed in without so much as a by your leave. His gaze darted around until landing on them, and Bannon's unease increased tenfold.

"Quick! Come on." Taylor reached out to them.

J.L. LANGLEY said her first words at six months of age. By the time she was a year old, she was talking in complete sentences and, as most of her family and friends will tell you, she hasn't shut up since. After becoming an accomplished motormouth, J.L. set out to master other avenues of self-expression, including art, and dance.

She attended the University of Texas, where she majored in art and worked as a dance instructor on the side. Her love of artistic expression in dance landed her a career in which she taught and performed for over twenty-five years. After marriage to her junior high school sweetheart and the birth of their children, J.L. decided to try her hand at writing. To date, she has several successful novels and a handful of novellas to her credit.

She lives in Texas, where she was born and raised, with her real-life hero, their rowdy two boys, two even rowdier German shepherds, and ten goldfish, one of which is named Jaws. When she's not writing, she can usually be found with her nose in a book appreciating the communication skills of other writers.

Facebook: www.facebook.com/authorjllangley
Twitter: @jl_langley

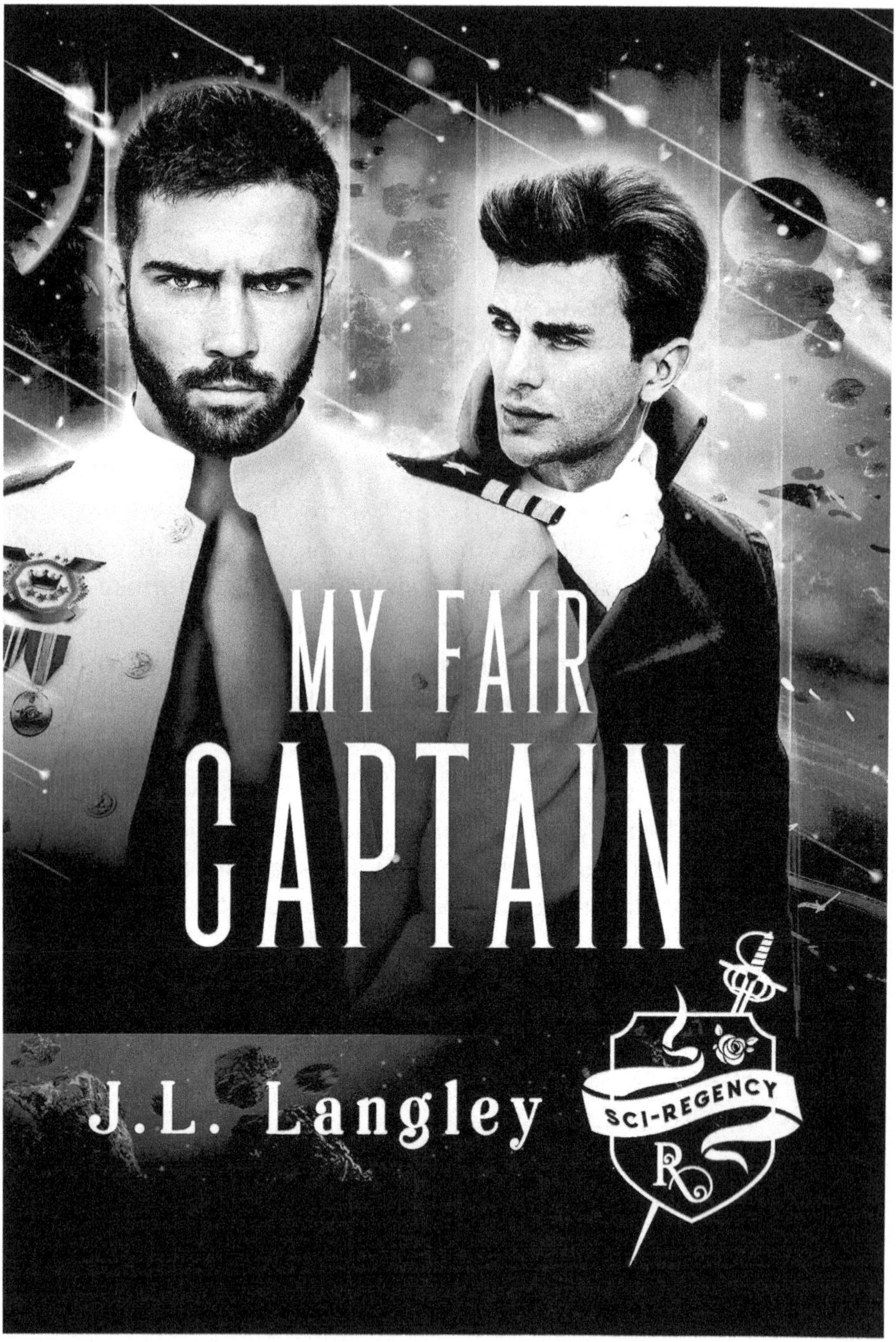
MY FAIR
CAPTAIN
J.L. Langley
SCI-REGENCY

A Sci-Regency Novel

When Intergalactic Navy Captain Nathaniel Hawkins goes undercover to investigate the theft of an IN weapons stash, the mission raises painful memories from his past. Using a title he fled nearly two decades earlier, Nate once again becomes the Earl of Deverell, heir to the Duke of Hawthorne, in order to navigate the ins and outs of a Regency world. But planet Regelence—where young lords are supposed to remain pure until marriage—has a few surprises for Nate, not least of which is his attraction to Prince Aiden.

A talented artist, Prince Aiden Townsend isn't interested in politics and the machinations of society gentlemen, and he adamantly rejects the idea of marriage and a consort. Aiden wants the freedom to pursue his art and determine his own future. But the arrival of the dashing and mysterious Deverell awakens feelings of passion and longing the young prince can't deny.

As Nate uncovers a conspiracy reaching far beyond the stolen weapons, his future is irrevocably altered by the temptations of a life he never thought he could have. Drawn into the web of intrigue, Aiden is in danger of losing his life… and his heart.

www.dreamspinnerpress.com

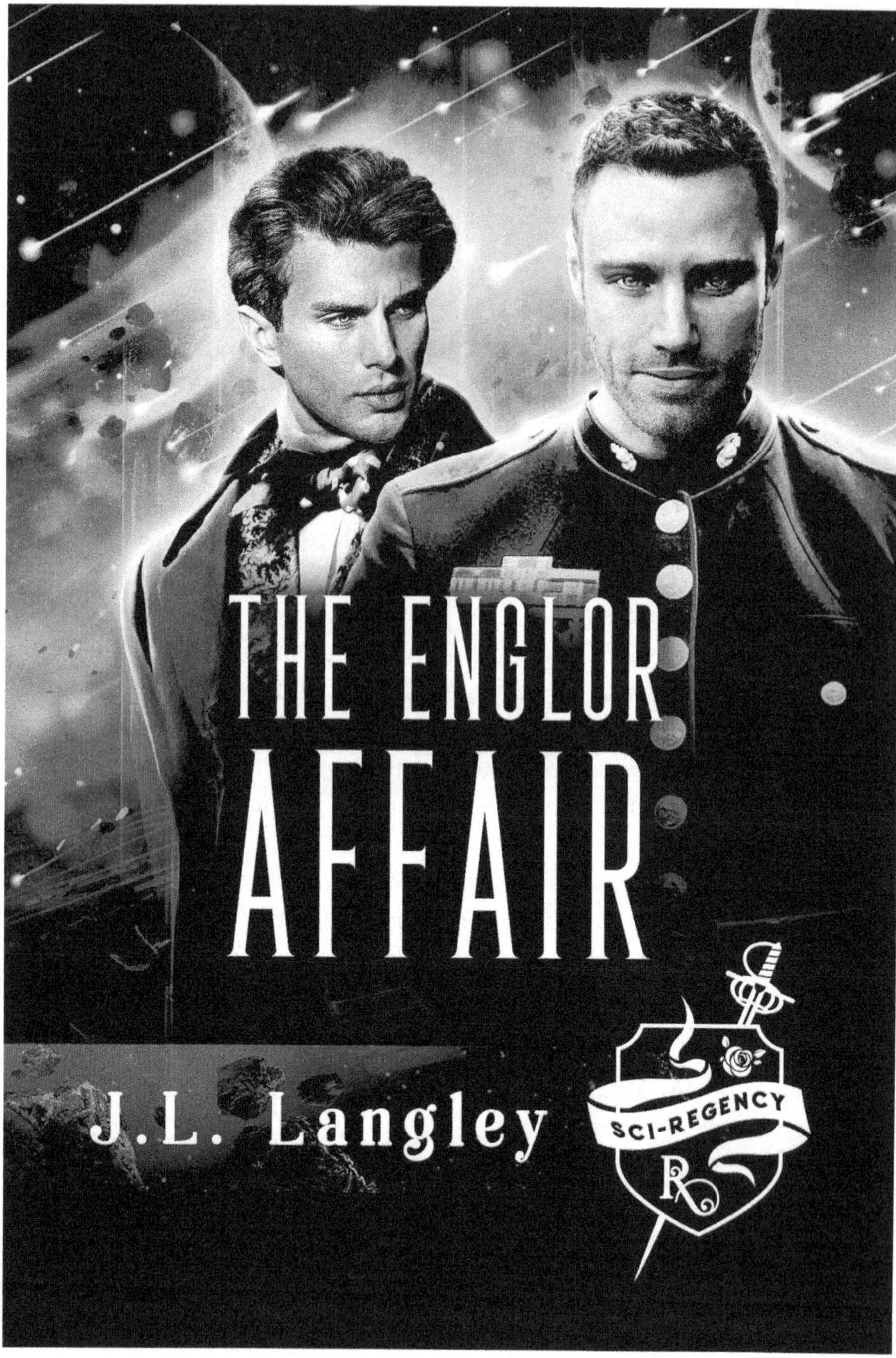
THE ENGLOR
AFFAIR
J.L. Langley
SCI-REGENCY

A Sci-Regency Novel: sequel to *My Fair Captain*

Anxious to escape the confines of Regelence society, if only for a little while, Prince Payton Townsend poses as an admiral's aide to further investigate a dangerous conspiracy. Payton plans only to use his computer skills to help navigate the tangled web of mystery and deceit on planet Englor, then return home, but he finds himself drawn to the charismatic Colonel Simon Hollister.

Simon, however, is no mere soldier—he is heir to the throne of Englor, and his life is meticulously planned to include a bride and heir. Unlike Regelence, the Regency society on Englor disapproves of same-sex relationships, and Payton and Simon's attraction plays out in a daring secret affair, one Simon never expected would grow into love.

Risking scandal and certain ruin if they are discovered, Payton and Simon uncover more about a common enemy and a deadly plot that imperils both their worlds. But in this game of interplanetary intrigue, love might be the ultimate casualty….

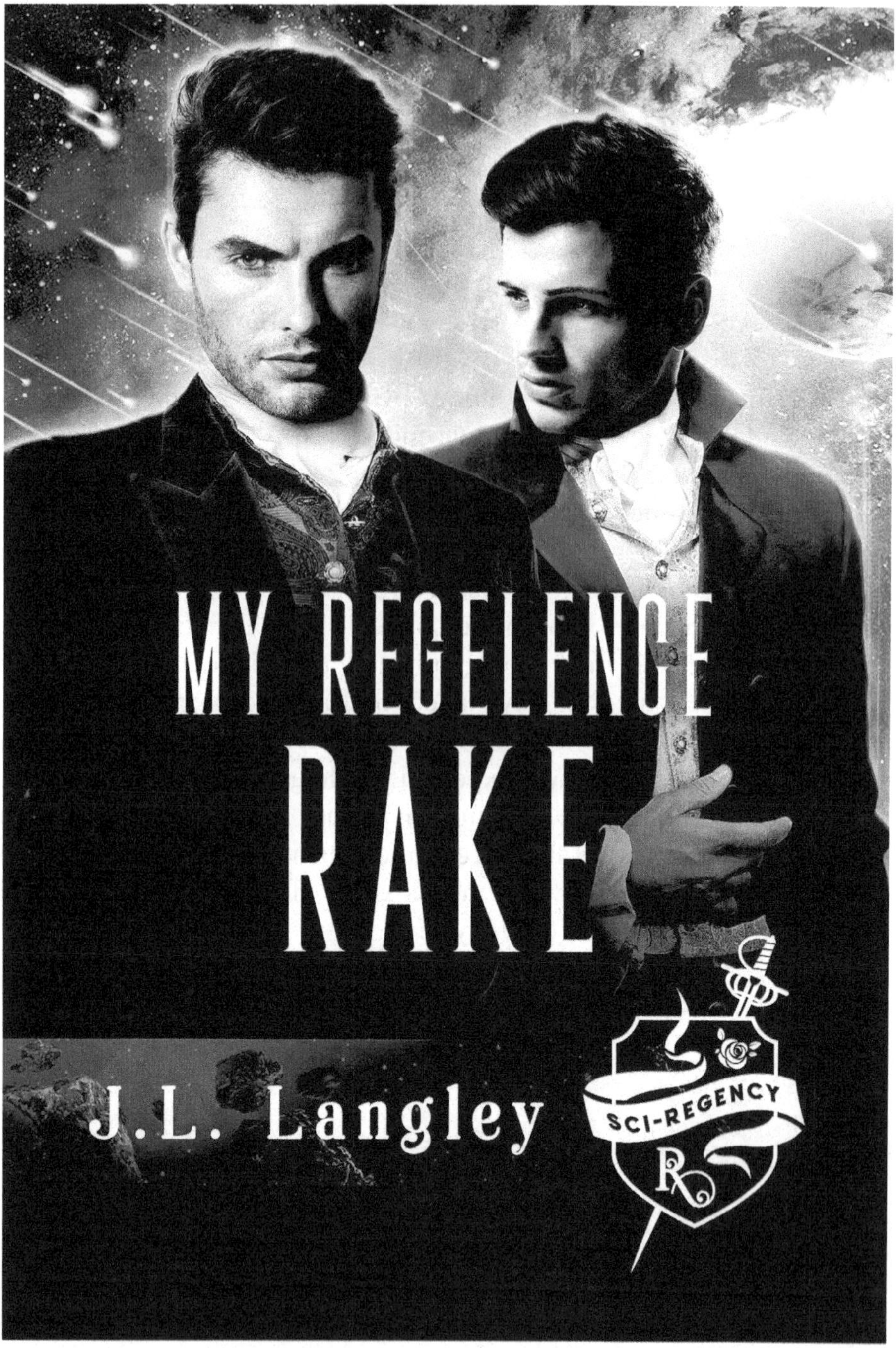
MY REGELENCE
RAKE
J.L. Langley
SCI-REGENCY

A Sci-Regency Novel: sequel to *The Englor Affair*

Sebastian Hastings, Viscount Wentworth, is captain of the Royal Guard by day and scandalous rake by night. To protect the royal family of Regelence from the plots of the Intergalactic Navy, Sebastian makes it his priority to personally oversee their safety.

Prince Colton Townsend is done pining after the roguish viscount and focuses his attention on his second love—horses. Following his dream of owning a racehorse breeding farm distracts Colton from his heartache… until Sebastian begins shadowing him.

When a good deed at a horse auction sparks public rumors, Colton just might get the man and the marriage he's longed for. But Sebastian's duties and secrets keep him walled off from those who would get close.

To reach Sebastian, Colton takes one last risk that might break his heart….

www.dreamspinnerpress.com

Also from Dreamspinner Press

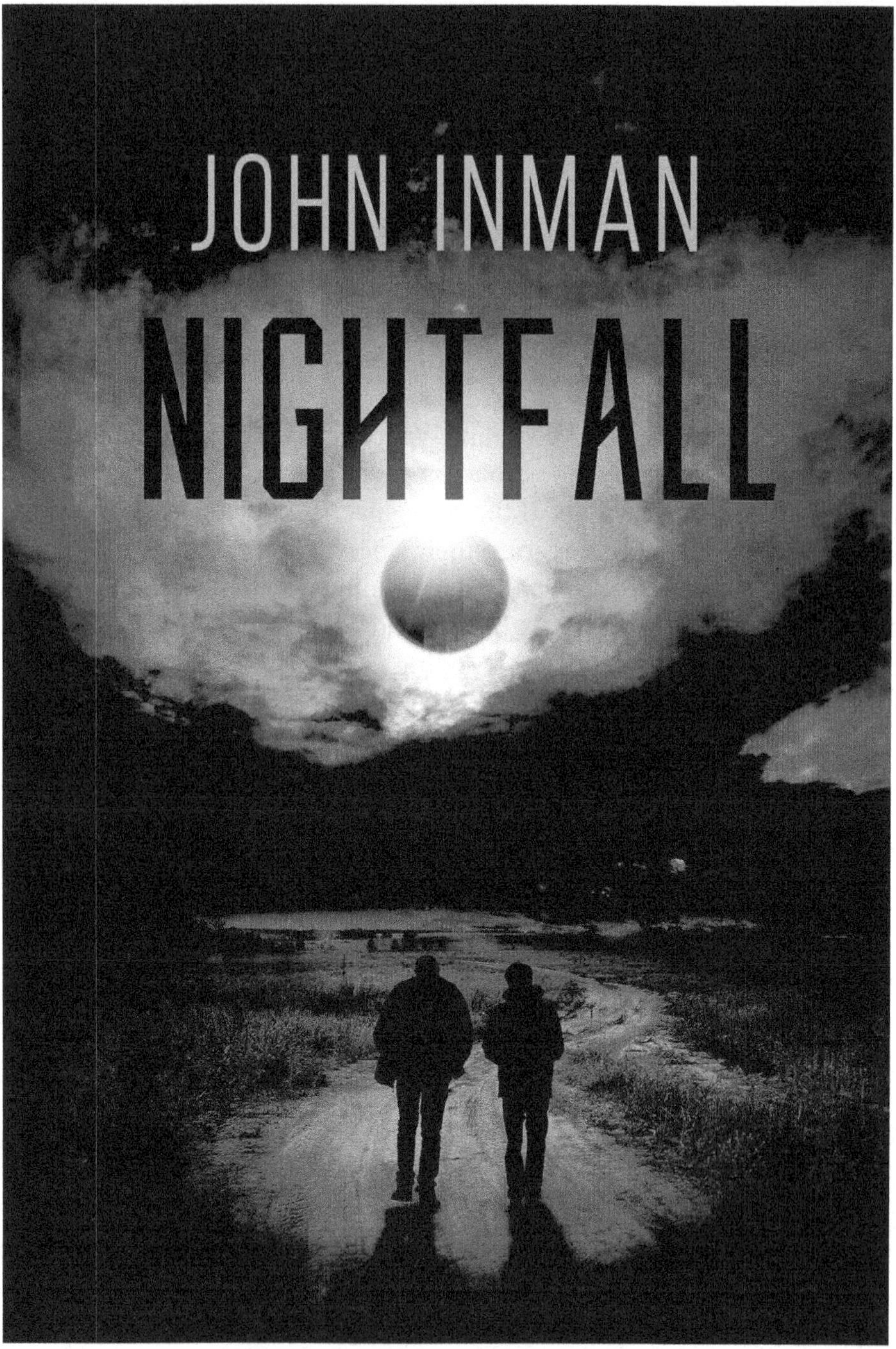

www.dreamspinnerpress.com

Also from Dreamspinner Press

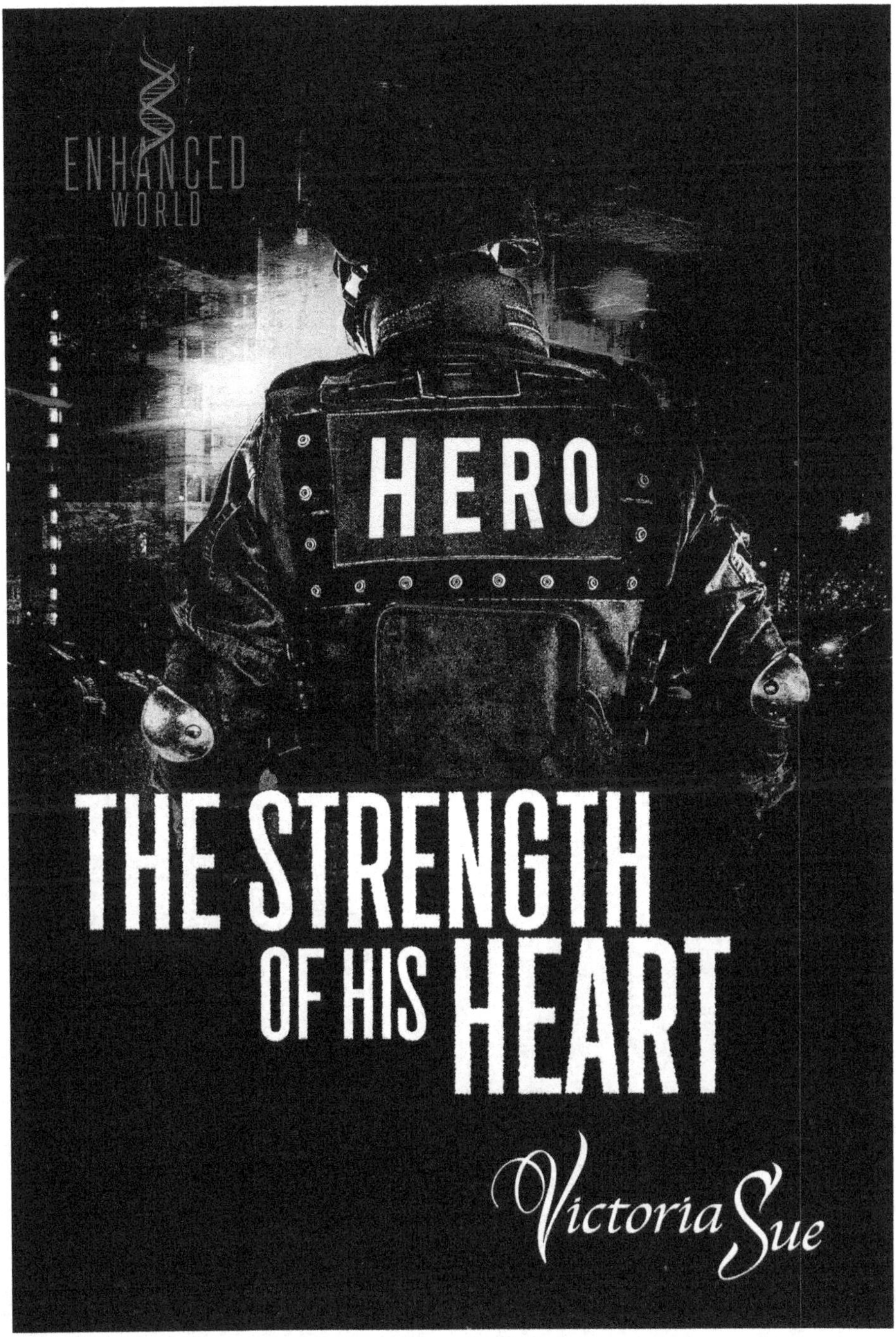

www.dreamspinnerpress.com

51374266R00163

Made in the USA
Columbia, SC
16 February 2019